the peer and the puppet

B.B. REID

WHEN RIVALS PLAY SERIES

Chief Editor: Rogena Mitchell-Jones of RMJ Manuscript Service LLC
Co-editor: Colleen Snibson of Colleen Snibson Editing
Both of Two Red Pens Editing www.tworedpens.com

Cover Design by Amanda Simpson of Pixel Mischief Design
Interior Design/Formatting by Champagne Book Design

dedication

Mama, is this weird?

also by
B.B. REID

note

The Peer and the Puppet is an interconnected standalone. The plot introduced continues in the following novels.

prologue

The Puppet

THE HARD BODY BETWEEN MY THIGHS CAME TO LIFE, AND I REVELED in the feeling. The vibration from the purring engine could rock me to sleep better than any lullaby. Closing my eyes, the peeling walls of the repair shop fell away, and I was on the circuit surrounded by stands filled with spectators screaming my name as I raced for the finish line.

"How's she holding, girl?"

Snatched from my fantasy by the sound of my boss' gravelly voice, I cooed, "Like a newborn baby."

Gruff grunted and chuckled, making the sixty-year-old's impressive beer gut jiggle, and his sharp blue eyes lighten as he stroked his gray, bushy beard. He was also the only person I knew who possibly loved bikes more than I did. He definitely knew more—I'd give him that.

"Think she needs another run?"

I nodded while concealing my growing excitement. Even though I was confident the owner wouldn't have any problems, I never risked sloppy work. If bikes were plants, I'd have a green thumb.

Gruff took me under his wing seven years ago once he got tired of chasing me away. When all the other kids were forging friendships, I was sneaking into Russell's Repairs. Sometimes, I'd simply watch the guys work, but on the more daring days, I'd give in to my urge to run my fingers over cold, hard metal. The first time Gruff caught me, he threw me out onto the pavement. He said the shop was no place for a kid.

Having no sense of self-preservation, I snuck back inside the next afternoon and almost every one after that until one rainy afternoon, I found a new sign banning profanity. No one ran me off that day. Tim, one of the workers, had even brought out a chair from the office, which was much more comfortable than crouching behind metal shelves filled with used parts. It wasn't long before Jasper—Gruff's only other employee—taught my first lesson. Gruff, whose real name was Robert Russell, had offered me nothing but an occasional grunt or grimace. His rough demeanor was actually how he got the nickname. Weeks later, when Rosalyn discovered where I was spending my free time, I learned the grump was really a big ole sweetheart. I was a latch-key kid without a sibling or friend, so Gruff had offered to keep me out of trouble during the hours she worked as a hotel maid. Her reluctance was embarrassingly obvious, but to my delight, she agreed. It would have sucked to sneak around again.

Gruff quickly became sort of an understudy to the father I would never know. Jasper and Tim also undertook brotherly roles until a swanky new automotive shop opened up a few towns over, and they moved on to greener pastures. Cherry's three thousand souls was a mere drop in the bucket. Most of the locals had to travel to Rochford, a small city thirty minutes away, for business and work—Rosalyn included.

"Well, hop to it, kid. I'll make the call."

Gruff ambled into his office, and I grinned as I swung my leg over the bike and retrieved my gloves and helmet. I got my license a few months after I turned sixteen, but I didn't have a bike of my own yet, so I relished any opportunity to ride. I was eleven when I finally convinced Gruff to teach me how to ride—off the record, of course. Widowed, and with his only son living a couple hours away, it was hard prying him away from his shop. It was a good thing I made him promise when I became his employee that he'd teach me. I thought it was a fair bargain—he needed the help, and I needed the lessons. He still even paid me a small wage that I saved for a bike and used to enter bidding wars for unique and sometimes rare helmets. So far, I'd collected twelve, a couple signed by professional racers, and others signed and sold by legendary undergrounds.

I quickly shoved on my worn leather gloves and pulled on one of my newer additions—Number Ten, a black, old-school, full face with a yellow outline and detachable eye shield and visor.

"I'm off, old man."

My boot was poised to kick back the stand of the Ducati 1199 Panigale when Gruff stuck his head from his office. He had the cordless plastered to his ear with a stern expression.

"No joyriding, Four." My smile was challenging, making the wrinkles on his forehead deepen. "I mean it."

"Up one way and back again, Gruff. I promise."

I passed through town, lazily eyeing the people spilling in and out of our few shops. Cherry was a frictionless place. The small Virginian town offered little, so anyone in residence was either a native or running away from something. Rosalyn rarely spoke of her past, but I learned a long time ago which party we fell in.

I reached the edge of town and noticed the local soap maker vigorously scrubbing her shop window. She whipped her plump frame around as I parked at the curb in front of her shop. Her distress was palpable as she clutched the soaked sponge to her ample chest.

Her fear didn't wane until I lifted my helmet to take a closer look at what had upset the sweet woman. Spray painted on the glass was three-quarters of a red X with writing underneath.

I am not led.

My mind raced as I read it a second and third time. "Who did this?"

The vandalism couldn't have been personal. Patty was a

kind, middle-aged widower, who made the best scented soaps and spoke only in soft tones, even when angry. We met in the frozen food section of the town's only grocer when she scolded me for speeding through the parking lot. She quickly departed before I could apologize, so when I saw her watering the plants in her shop window, I paid a visit. She'd graciously accepted my apology by offering me one of her soaps: coconut water mixed with açaí berry, melon, jasmine petals, and vanilla. Now it's the only soap I'll use.

"Some out-of-towners rode through here last night causing trouble. The sheriff's had his hands full tracking them down."

This was the part where I would say something consoling, but I was pretty creeped out myself. I am not led? It sounded like some cult bullshit. "I'm sure they're gone by now," I assured her, though it sounded more like a question.

"I hope so." She pointed her soapy sponge at me. "You be careful, hear?"

"I will." I brought the Ducati back to life, shoved my helmet on, and headed for the open road. Late that night, I was scrubbing my dinner dishes clean after another night of 'grilled cheese for one' when my phone chimed. Anticipation didn't allow me to dry my hands before I hurriedly flipped open my phone.

It's a go. Curtis Pond Rd. Usual time.

The crowd parted, and I coasted through on the back of the orange, black, and white Ducati. No one ever asked questions, so I never had to explain why I showed up on a different bike every race. Borrowing bikes I helped to fix in Gruff's shop without his knowledge was risky business, but so far, my luck held.

Spotting Mickey's brown tattooed skin and shoulder-length dreads as he talked to another rider on the sideline, I stopped at the marked line and lifted my helmet. The smell of decay from the swamp on the other side of the trees hit me instantly. A tense Mickey swaggered over as fast as his sagging jeans would allow.

"I should have given your spot away. You know," he said with sarcasm dripping from every syllable, "to someone who actually bids to race and can show up on time."

I just barely kept from rolling my eyes. Mickey had a violent track record, but he didn't scare me. I was too valuable. I pretended not to notice him checking me out as I laughed and leaned forward. Worn black and yellow leather creaked as I rested my forearms on the handlebars. "I had algebra homework, and we both know you'd lose way more than you'd make if you cut me out." I could always count on Mickey's bet in my favor because he could always count on me to win.

Fourteen races and I was still undefeated.

Riders spend thousands of dollars on an advantage only to be showed up by a sixteen-year-old girl who proved more than once that it's the rider who wins races.

Mickey didn't crack a smile like he usually did when I sassed him. Instead, he glanced to my left, averting my attention. My competition waited astride a silver Ninja ZX-10R. It was faster, so I'd have to be clever.

As I admired the bike, I peeped at the bold black X painted on the side. Unlike the one vandalizing Patty's window, this one had a fox and crow's head inside the top and bottom angle, a nineteen and eighty-seven inside the left and right, and a ribbon that read, *I am not led* across the middle. The very same was tattooed on the rider's hair-dusted hand. A short, stocky body covered in black leather was all I could make out since he'd kept his helmet on. He didn't bother to return the favor of checking out his competition, but the small crowd standing on the left side of the clearing had no such reservations. My palms began to sweat under their scrutiny. I was used to animosity, but this felt different. There was promise in their eyes if I won—a threat not to show up their friend. Despite my unease, I smirked at the lot earning a few bared teeth.

"As much as I love your fire, Four, be careful with this one, alright? He and those fools he's with don't sit right with me. My crew feels the same way." It was then I noticed most of the usual crowd waited on the right shoulder of the back road *away* from the riffraff.

"Then why let him race?"

He shrugged powerful shoulders. "Because his money's green either way."

My thighs tensed around the Ducati, and my stomach rolled as I studied Mickey. "Who'd you bet on?"

Light brown eyes laughed, and it was his turn to smirk. "You."

I felt myself relax knowing I'd still have a friend if I crossed the finish line first. Mickey was always the one left defusing the uproar when money was lost. I felt bad for putting him in the position, but he was also the reason it was still safe for me to return.

"Alright, snowflake, you know the rules. No bullshit."

"Told you not to call me that!" I shouted at his back. "Racial slurs go both ways. You wouldn't like it if I called you chocolate thunder!"

He laughed, flashing his gold grill, and waved me off as he joined his boys on the sideline. They began to yell encouragement as they rubbed their hands together in anticipation of the money I'd make them if I won.

Some redhead strutted by in heels and shorts so far up her crack that her firm ass hung from the hem. She lifted two red flags in the air once she stood centered between us.

There wasn't much left to say or do now that bets had been placed. No one wanted to risk someone coming along and calling the cops. I shoved my helmet on and said a silent prayer. I usually pictured myself crossing the finishing line to get my head in the game, but instead, I was drawn back to the small crowd of thirty or so. Behind them were a couple of bikes and a few cars and trucks lined up on the shoulder. Just as I was ready to flip my visor down, a man dressed in faded blue jeans and an even more faded gray T-shirt stepped into my line of vision. He had the same X tattooed on the side of his neck. Once he had my attention, he lifted his shirt just enough for my heart to skip a beat as I locked eyes on the gun tucked into his waist. While I wasn't sure if cult members carried guns, I was pretty certain these guys weren't religious zealots. My next breath shuddered out of me at the clear warning.

Don't win.

I could feel the wind whipping against the sliver of exposed skin on my nape and the rider on my right closing in as we approached the first turn. I wasn't worried about losing any more than I was worried about winning. What the man wielding the gun didn't know was I didn't race for the money. I raced for the addiction. He should have known better. Someone daring enough to chase a high at one hundred and eight miles per hour wouldn't be too concerned with self-preservation. I wouldn't be sticking around to collect my cut of the winnings anyway. After my third win, Mickey and I agreed it was best if I kept riding once I crossed the finish line. It also didn't give anyone a chance to follow me home. I didn't worry about Mickey cheating me, either. He may have been a thug, but he wasn't stupid enough to double-cross the person fattening his pockets.

We took the first turn neck and neck after I slowed just enough not to lose control. Once we'd straightened, I retook the lead, though I didn't have as much gain on him as before. His bike was faster, but it seemed the lion had no courage. The world blurred as I accelerated until he was no longer on my tail, but desperation had him accelerating too, and we began to battle for the lead. I played it cool, already thinking about the second turn, which was narrow and twice as sharp. Taking the corner on the inside at high speed would be tantamount to suicide. The rider would be forced to take up the rear in order to safely execute the turn without losing enough speed to cost him the race. The advantage wouldn't be much, but it was the only chance I had.

With only a couple hundred feet left between the turn and us, the rider finally pulled back. Smiling hard and already feeling the victory in my veins, I prepared to corner the bike. No sooner had I adjusted my weight than a man stepped from a grove of black willow, and the flash of stainless steel in the moonlight caught my eye. The leering face of the gunman didn't belong to the man at the starting line. This one was sent to make certain I didn't win...or finish at all. My euphoria vanished as I jerked the bike across the invisible centerline and into the right lane just as we took the turn.

I was airborne only for a moment.

The cry that ravaged my throat as I crashed and tumbled down the unpaved road, the crunch of metal as the bike skidded off the road, and my opponent accelerating down the straight-away was mostly drowned by my earplugs and helmet.

Somehow, the silence made me feel all the more helpless.

Finally, I lost momentum as the edge of the road met grass but not before the bone in my leg gave with a sickening crack against a rock the size of my head, ripping one last scream from me. I was aware of each breath I took, fearing the one that would be my last. I didn't think anyone could survive that turn.

I ripped off my helmet just as a rock was kicked toward me, and dirt clouded the air. Edging away, I screamed in frustration and pain when the broken bone in my leg protested.

Maybe my death would be quick.

Sorrow crept inside and mingled amongst pain and fear. I never thought I'd go out in a blaze of glory—I was just another fish trapped in a small pond—but I never expected to be killed over a lousy three grand. The only fight I had left was to scream and hope someone heard. I took a deep breath, readying my vocal chords, only to cough and choke when dust found its way into my throat.

Scuffed brown boots stopped near my head. Not wanting his face to be the last I saw, I stared at the stars. "Lose or die. I thought we made it clear?"

"Couldn't lose to a pussy," I croaked. Begging was pointless, and consciousness was a tide drifting further and further away. *Fuck it.* Maybe Rosalyn would finally have peace.

With two clicks of his tongue, he lifted the gun, but the last thing I heard wasn't his voice or the bullet leaving the chamber. It was a racing engine.

Hmm...much better.

chapter one

The Puppet

"THE GOOD NEWS IS YOU'LL CERTAINLY WALK AGAIN." The tall, bubbly redhead discarded her gloves and smiled.

"And the bad?"

"I'm afraid you won't be taking midnight rides for quite some time."

I sunk back against the reclined hospital bed and sighed. I should be happy just to be alive, but all I could think about was how I would explain all of this to Gruff. I'd lose my job for sure and rightly so, but would he forgive me? Would *I* forgive me?

I was mindlessly flipping through channels after the doctor promised to return with my discharge papers when the door opened, and Rosalyn rushed to my bedside.

"I thought I'd never see you again!" she said with a sob.

Confusion and guilt kept me from responding. Had it been unfair to think she might be happy if I died? She definitely would have been better off. I looked away before her tears undid me, and that was when the large hands holding Rosalyn's petite shoulders and the man they belonged to captured my attention.

He wasn't dressed in a lab coat or nurse's scrubs. Even if he had, his touch was too familiar to be that of a polite stranger. He wore a white dress shirt that would have stretched tight over his broad chest if it weren't slightly gaped and wrinkled. I could see a light splattering of tawny-colored hair that matched his full head. The charcoal slacks he wore were also wrinkled, but the matching dress shoes were still perfectly polished and scuff free. Even with the neatly lined scruff on his lower face, this man looked expensive and exactly the kind of man Rosalyn usually courted. My eyes rolled, which didn't go unnoticed if the amused smile toying at the man's lips was any clue.

"How did you—" I paused to clear my throat, but it only made my throat burn.

Rosalyn's latest flame guessed what I needed and quickly poured a glass of water from a pink pitcher. Cobalt eyes assessed me as he handed over the glass.

"Thanks," I said after I emptied the cup. "How did you find out?"

"I'm your mother," Rosalyn reminded as she plumped my pillow. "Of course, they called me." I hid my shock at hearing her admit her motherhood. Without a doubt, she was pretending for the handsome man offering her comfort.

Never for me.

Rosalyn laid a trembling hand on her chest as her eyes welled up again. "Oh, Four, I was so worried."

Not as good of an actress, I said, "I'm sorry I ruined your weekend." She had left yesterday morning for yet another get-away with the man scrutinizing me over her shoulder.

"Don't trouble yourself with that. We're just so happy you're okay."

I stole another glance at the other half of her 'we.' Rosalyn Archer was the *love 'em and lose 'em* type. She was never without male companionship, but they never lasted long, either. Maybe that was why she'd stopped bringing them around and stayed away instead. I'd lost my desire for a father long before she'd lost the hope of providing me with one. It wasn't as if I were completely without. Gruff filled the role as only a loner who'd earned his name could.

"You must be Thomas." Even though I no longer met Rosalyn's lovers, she still talked about them. Thomas McNamara was the name she often spoke with a sigh and the man who currently fed her notions of happily-ever-after.

"Silly me," Rosalyn chirped. "Where is my head?"

"You're emotional," he murmured. "It's to be expected."

She leaned into him, and it seemed too natural. As if she'd done it a thousand times before. Panic speared my chest. The average lifespan of Rosalyn's relationships was three months. My own father had disappeared before she even knew of my conception.

I quickly counted the months to when I first heard this man's name.

Eight months.

I'd been too busy with the shop and racing and the consuming fear that I wouldn't be good enough to go legit once I graduated to realize she had sunken her claws deep this time.

Oh, God. Maybe I *had* died, and this was hell.

Rosalyn worked full-time as a maid at NaMara, an international five-star hotel chain inherited by Thomas McNamara himself. His business trip had turned into pleasure when he'd laid eyes on Rosalyn Archer. Her beauty had been something that skipped a generation. Most women, including her own daughter, paled in comparison. Dark blonde hair that I inherited flowed in waves almost reaching her tiny waist. Slim hips seemed to dance when she moved on legs that went on and on. Wide brown eyes flecked with gold—also inherited by me—captivated men everywhere. Skin deep, she was the perfect woman. Beyond it, however, lurked something that sent men fleeing as fast as they'd appear.

But Thomas had done what no other man could, and with the realization came another—he was either a fool or trouble. As he stared back, unperturbed, I had a sinking feeling it was the latter.

"Rose." His deep voice commanded attention without needing to raise a single octave. I tore my gaze away to search for this Rose, but there was no one else in the room. When Rosalyn looked over her shoulder at him, I realized *she* was his Rose.

"Yes, Thomas?"

"Why don't you see what's keeping the good doctor?" Without waiting for her agreement, Thomas gently steered her toward the door.

Rosalyn paused to look me over, and her lips, without their usual vibrant red, trembled as she nodded. "Yes, of course." And then she was gone, leaving Thomas and me alone.

"It's nice to finally meet you. Your mother has been quite adamant about keeping you a mystery."

I wanted to tell him that he was just another one of many, but flaunting her reputation to fend off her latest beau would only hurt her. I've caused her enough grief.

"Your mother's a chatterbox," he said when the awkward silence stretched. "I guess it skipped a generation."

"Among other things."

He studied me for a long moment. "Interesting...I see much of her in you."

A little embarrassed that he'd known what I meant, I shrugged off the compliment, and then awkwardness filled the silence once again until he sighed.

"I'm sorry we had to meet under these circumstances."

I was sorry we met at all. It would only make their inevitable breakup harder on Rosalyn. Thankfully, I was saved from replying when she returned with Dr. Day. They got the same run down that I had. The bruises would fade, and my leg would heal, but I couldn't erase the last twelve hours. One sleepless summer later, I learned just how true that was.

chapter two

the Puppet

BLACKWOOD KEEP SOUNDED LIKE A PLACE WHERE THE SUN NEVER shined, life couldn't grow, and hope didn't exist. That morning, Gruff found me straddling his red 1975 Honda CB400F Cafe Racer, crying a river with a pocket full of cash because I couldn't work up the courage to run. I ran into his arms, begged him to tell me what I should do, and as always, Gruff had been a man of few words.

"You mind your mother, and don't go chasin' trouble, kid. Hear?"

Even though Gruff couldn't hide his own sadness, he sent me on my way, and just as the sun was setting, I arrived in Blackwood Keep, Connecticut.

My hope that this new start would end soon died at each peek of the beautiful homes beyond the curtain of green.

I was forced down this highway to hell a week after the race. Gruff had shown up on our doorstep, not to fire me but to warn that the Feds were poking around. Two Special Agents arrived later that day to question my involvement with the Exiled—a violent gang polluting the east coast. It didn't take much for me to connect the dots after that. These *Exiled* had been the ones marked with the X.

Apparently, Mickey's humble gambling ring landed on the FBI's radar after he'd gotten mixed up with them. One harrowing interrogation later, the agents lost interest in me, but after planting the seed that a vicious gang was after me, Rosalyn was spooked.

To make matters worse the client whose bike I totaled threatened to sue. I had been ready to forfeit every penny I'd won, but Thomas swooped in with his gold-plated fountain pen and leather-bound checkbook and saved the day.

And it didn't end there.

I'd probably still be slumming it if it had. The billionaire's fast-talking lawyer then saved me from losing my license. I still had to pay a fine for speeding, but Thomas had taken care of that, too.

Summer passed, Gruff forgave me, Rosalyn kept her sanity, and once my leg healed, I naively believed it was all behind me.

But then Rosalyn announced that we were leaving Cherry.

We stayed long enough to pack, but as it turned out, there wasn't much Rosalyn had been unwilling to part with. For a week, I sat back as she bestowed our things on the neighbors. The day Thomas arrived in a pearl white Lincoln Navigator, she left with little more than the clothes on her back.

"…and then there's Robin Point. It used to be a private beach for locals, but some guy sued, and now it's open to tourists." Thomas had been giving us a history lesson of Blackwood Keep as he drove us to his home, but I couldn't muster the interest. It wasn't until I noticed Rosalyn frowning at me from the front seat and Thomas stealing glances in the rearview mirror that I realized some response was expected.

"Sounds good."

"Your mother tells me you've never learned to swim. I'm sure Ever can teach you if you're up for it."

"I'm sorry…" I couldn't decide who to focus on as I recited the name in my head. At last, I forced myself to ask the burning question. "Who's Ever?"

Thomas and Rosalyn had some silent conversation that ended with her biting her lip and Thomas letting out an aggravated sigh.

"He's my son." I couldn't hide my flinch, which might have

prompted him to say, "It wasn't my intention to corner you. I thought your mother would have told you by now."

Well, I was already uprooted from my home, why not get one more blow in while I was down? Out loud, I said, "It's fine."

"You'll be fortunate to know someone at your new school," Rosalyn added.

"Yes," Thomas confirmed. "Maybe you'll have a few classes together."

Great.

I ignored their attempts to soften the blow and resumed staring out the window.

So Thomas had a son.

I wonder how *he* felt about our new living arrangements.

I trailed behind the couple as Thomas gave us a tour. Home seemed too inadequate a word to describe the monstrosity sitting on five acres of the greenest grass and the tallest trees I'd ever seen. I didn't know much about the rich other than their piles of money, but I never would have painted an accurate picture of just how glamorous they lived. I pictured the two-bedroom single-wide we left behind...it probably would have fit inside the two-story foyer.

After meeting the housekeeper, a jolly woman with graying blonde hair and red glasses, Thomas led us through heavy wooden sliding doors and into a living room three times the size of ours back home. There was a fireplace at each end, adjacent sofas made of bronze and gold fabric with ornate carvings and rolled arms, and a coffee table made of ivory, marble, and dark oak. Three sets of bronze French doors decorated with gold billowing curtains opened onto a terrace spanning the rear of the house.

A rectangular pool sat perpendicular to a two-bedroom pool

house. Thomas then explained that we could find the theater, gym, indoor pool, massage, and the steam and sauna rooms on the lower level. Rosalyn openly expressed her awe as he showed us the library, billiard, family, kitchen, dining, and breakfast rooms.

I'm surprised he doesn't have an elevator to get around this place.

"And you can find the elevator on the east wing if the stairs become tedious." Unwillingly, my jaw dropped, causing Thomas to chuckle. "I know it's a little much."

He seemed ready to say more, but with lips pressed tight, he averted his eyes, and for the third time that day, I was stumped. I peeked at Rosalyn, but she was too focused on the grandeur to notice his pain. I sighed, knowing this romance wouldn't last long, and once more, I'd be the one to piece Rosalyn back together. With a forced smile, Thomas promised to show us the *rest* of his home when we were better rested. I shouldn't have expected less since I'd googled his name the moment I was released from the hospital.

The McNamara family was worth more than the goddamn Hiltons.

Upstairs, he quickly pointed out the master suite before leading us past two more bedrooms, down six steps, and past a second set of stairs at the end of the hall. This second hallway seemed longer as we passed the elevator, a laundry room, powder room, and his son's room before finally stopping at the very next door.

"This will be your room." I was careful not to give my thoughts away as he turned the elegantly carved bronze knobs and pushed open the door. "Decorate it however you wish. This is your home now."

The sincerity in his eyes made me realize why he'd lasted longer than the others had. Rosalyn wasn't the only one with stars in her eyes. As I crossed the threshold, I wondered who would be the first to shake free of the illusion.

The room was twice the size of my old bedroom, and the bed in the center could easily sleep three or four. A plush yellow comforter and pristine white sheets stretched tight over the mattress with a mountain of pillows resting against a cream tufted headboard. "Your mother told me yellow was your favorite color, so I had Christina order some items I thought you might like."

"Is she your daughter?" I questioned, barely managing to keep the sarcasm from my voice.

"No," Thomas answered tightly. "Christina's my assistant." He walked past and pushed open another door. "This is your closet." I managed a quick look inside and barely glimpsed shelves, drawers, and racks before he moved on to another door. "And this is where you'll find the bathroom."

I walked inside and couldn't help but gape at the elegance as I spotted a small crystal chandelier hanging above. It was a *bathroom*, for fuck's sake. The marble floors were black and white, and the walls of the bathroom were midnight blue casting the room in mostly shadow until Thomas flicked on the lights.

The opulence wasn't something I'd get used to in this lifetime.

A massive walk-in shower with glass walls stood on one side of the room. At least, I'd never have to worry about elbow-room whenever I washed my hair. I held back a snort when my gaze passed over a toilet surprisingly *not* lined with gold. An oval bathtub with a deep drop sat in the corner, and my bones quaked at the invitation. I caught a glimpse of my astonishment in the mirror spanning the double vanity and quickly looked away.

That was when I noticed the door facing my own.

I hoped it wasn't another closet. I barely had enough clothes to fill a corner of the first closet. "What's through there?"

Thomas seemed surprised since it was the first bit of interest I'd shown since arriving, but then he chuckled almost nervously.

"I hope you don't mind…you'll be sharing this space with Ever. On the occasions I entertain, I prefer to keep the other bedrooms with more private baths available for guests. On the other side of that door"—he pointed—"is Ever's room."

When we first arrived, Thomas said his home had six bedrooms, seven baths, and six half bathrooms, not including the two-bedroom guesthouse. Just how hospitable was he?

"You must throw quite a party," I answered dryly. Rosalyn had her lip between her teeth again. Still, I waited for her to voice how inappropriate it was to have her sixteen-year-old daughter share a private bathroom with a sixteen-year-old boy—one who was very much a stranger. Instead, she shot me an apologetic look and laid a hand on Thomas's arm.

"Thomas, honey, where is Ever? I'd love to have Four finally meet him."

Me.

Not us.

Because she'd already made the prince's acquaintance.

I wasn't sure why I felt betrayed, but Thomas's frown as he looked at his watch was enough to distract me from the emotion. "I'm not sure. He should have been here." He pulled out his phone and quickly punched a couple of buttons before lifting the phone to his ear and strolling for the door.

The door closed with a soft click, but then I could hear him bellow, "Get home now," in his thick northern accent. Rosalyn faced me with a hand on her chest and eyes wide.

"I hope you'll be comfortable here, Four." Because why be happy when you can settle for wealth?

"You don't need to talk to me like I'm a guest, Rosalyn. This is my home now, remember?" Thomas's words thrown back at her caused her to drop the Stepford act.

"I've had enough of your attitude. You made the choices, young lady, and now Thomas just wants to help."

My lip curled slightly. "I'm sure." I threw myself down on

the bed and sighed when my body sunk into the plush mattress. Eternal resentment aside, this bed was *the shit*.

I swept the room with a careful eye—sheer curtains that welcomed twilight, a cream cushioned bench at the foot of my bed, white writing desk complete with a matching chair, and an oval floor-length mirror with LED lighting.

All the appropriate trappings for the newly found princess.

I snorted.

Rosalyn lingered, likely wondering how long before I messed this up for her.

"You don't need to worry," I said while staring at the twinkling chandelier, "I know what's at stake."

Moments later, I was blissfully alone.

I hadn't realized I'd fallen asleep until a knock on my door woke me. I checked my phone and saw that only an hour had passed.

"Four?"

I smirked at the hesitant note in Rosalyn's voice. As usual, she wanted to avoid me as much as I did her. I rolled until my dirty, worn chucks hit the floor, then strolled over to open the door. Rosalyn Archer could turn heads in sweatpants and a ratty T-shirt—not that she'd ever be caught dead—but she was absolutely breathtaking when set to stun.

Shoulders and arms left bare in the slender white dress, her natural makeup applied with precision, and her dark golden mane was swept into a simple bun. Around her elegant neck, she wore a string of pearls I'd never seen before while matching earrings adorned her ears. Her forced smile died quickly when I simply stared back at her. "I just wanted to see how you were getting on. You haven't left your room."

"It's been a long day."

She nodded while fidgeting with her pearls. "Thomas arranged for us to have dinner on his boat, but Ever still hasn't come home."

I held in my laugh when her cheeks colored. Of course, he wouldn't bother showing his face. Thomas and Rosalyn were the only two living under the delusion that we'd all be one big happy family.

"I just wanted to say goodnight and tell you the cook set aside some dinner for you if you get hungry." She started to walk away when I reached out to take her hand.

"Where is he taking you?" Even with a grudge, I couldn't help feeling protective of her. She was just so goddamn fragile.

Her answering smile was soft and indulgent. "To meet some of his friends."

"And you'll be back tonight?"

With a nod, she waved delicate fingers in goodbye. "See you in the morning."

Only if I don't decide to hot-wire one of Thomas's cars.

I watched her strut away on white pumps with red bottoms before I ducked back into my new room.

Fuck my life.

My stomach's growls and the curiosity I had for my new home amplified until I could no longer ignore them. Free from scrutiny, I decided to put off food a little while longer and explore.

Questions about the fugitive prince had been the hardest to ignore. Maybe that's why I didn't keep going like I should have when I reached his door. Hand hovering over the knob, my teeth sunk into my bottom lip—a telling habit I inherited from Rosalyn.

What if he was on the other side?

Pressing my ear to the door, I heard nothing.

For some reason, I wanted on the other side of that door. But how would I explain my obvious snooping if I were caught?

Maybe it won't be unlocked.

With the promise of only a peek, I took a deep breath and tried the knob.

Of course, it turned.

Taking that as a sign, I pushed open the door far enough for me to…slip inside.

I really should have known better than to trust myself to have control.

Lost in shadows, I dared not move. My only light came from the moonlit sky. As soon as my eyes adjusted, I moved deeper inside. The nightstands on each side of the bed held lamps with metal shades, so I tiptoed to the right and switched on the lamp. The dim glow allowed me to see just enough.

And what a disappointment it was.

Empty and passionless.

The walls were a dark gray, matching the sleek headboard, which had a black shelf built into the wall above it. There wasn't much occupying the space. A glass jar filled with coins, a full pencil cup, a trophy, and a picture frame. I picked up the trophy to study it closer. It was a football trophy with a guy poised to run. Dated a year ago, the inscription read, *Ever "Speed" McNamara* and was awarded for the fastest running time in Brynwood history.

I guess we both lived in the fast lane.

Smiling, I set the trophy down. Finding nothing interesting in the pencil cup or jar of coins, I leaned forward to view the picture.

"Shit!" I yelled in a loud whisper. I'd lifted my knee onto the bed without thinking and disturbed the neatly made bed. The dark gray comforter and matching sheets underneath were stretched tight on the other side, an obvious contrast to the wrinkle under my knee. *Maybe he won't notice.* Not wanting to disturb the bedding any more than I already had, I stretched until my body strained and peeked at the woman in the photo. Short dark hair curled stylishly around delicate ears, and olive skin glistened under the sun, but somehow, honey golden eyes outshone the sun. The picture was faded and marked with lines where it was once folded, but even then, her beauty was unmistakable. She couldn't have been much older than her late twenties. Thomas had claimed to not have a daughter… So could this have been his wife?

Feeling as if I were disturbing something sacred, I stood and fixed the sheets as best I could before looking around. I'd never been inside a teenage boy's room, but shouldn't there have been smelly socks, Penthouse magazines, and video games lying around or something? There were no posters of busty women adorning the walls. Ever's room was simply sleek gray lines and cool, crisp smells. I was tempted to peek under the mattress for porn magazines and dirty pictures, but it seemed a little desperate. I wasn't even sure why I cared so much.

A sleek, silver laptop rested on a desk that blended well with the decor, but other than a few journals and pads, and a tin cup full of pencils, nothing was exciting there, either.

I tiptoed over to his closet and flipped the light switch. Predictably, clean, pressed, and starched, and clothing filled the space. I was, however, surprised to find a pair of dirty cleats sitting in a corner. Blazers, vests, and sweaters of red and navy, each bearing the gold insignia of *Brynwood Academy*, hung neatly in one section while in the next were black, tan and navy slacks. The shelves had built-in lighting, casting a glow over polished black dress shoes. Pulling out one of the drawers, I found navy and red ties with gold lines crisscrossing the length and matching cuff links.

Such pompous bullshit.

Just as a laugh trickled out, I remembered I would soon be suffering the same fate as this kid.

Stomach twisting, I rushed from the closet and quickly slipped from Ever's room. My heart thundered as if I'd just run ten miles. I couldn't believe I'd gotten away with that.

I was feeling a bit light-headed when I sat down with a plate of roast beef, carrots, and potatoes, so I ravenously tore off the saran wrap, but then my phone vibrated in my back pocket. I considered ignoring it, but I had a pretty good guess who was calling. Ignoring my hunger pains, I quickly flipped open the receiver, hopped from the stool, and ran for the stairs.

chapter three

the Puppet

ONE SHORT CONVERSATION WITH GRUFF MADE IT CLEAR THAT I'd left home, but home hadn't left me. As I skipped down the stairs, I decided nothing could bring me down.

But then I rounded the corner into the kitchen.

And the smile I wore died.

The steaming plate of food I'd left behind had been scraped clean until nothing remained but a single drop of carrot juice. It was the only evidence there had even been food at all. It was as if the perp had *licked* it clean after devouring the food.

Thinking I was mistaken, I searched the countertop for a second plate of food, but instead, I found a jar of peanut butter that hadn't been there before.

Someone had eaten my food.

And I was no longer alone.

I tore my gaze away from my emptied plate and noticed a large hand with tanned skin gripping the handle of the refrigerator door, and clean forest-green high-top sneakers and gray jeans peeking from underneath. The only sound was of him moving things around inside, completely oblivious to my presence.

Before I could consider a more polite greeting, I cleared my throat and watched as more of him appeared until his head was completely visible over the top of the door.

Jesus, fuck, he was tall. The thief easily topped my five foot six with nine or ten inches.

With dark roots and dusty ends, he wore his hair slicked back. His eyes were a dark gold just like the woman in the picture, but rather than warmth, they held the same glacial intensity as his father's blues.

A dark eyebrow quirked, and I realized I was gawking. "Is there something you need?" he prompted flatly. It didn't help that his voice was like velvet.

"Hi." I awkwardly waved. "I—I'm Four." No response. "You must be Ever?" More silence. "Um…" I glanced longingly at the exit, but then my gaze fell on the empty plate, and I remembered why I even opened my mouth. Sticking my hip out, I threw a thumb over my shoulder. "Did you eat that?"

"I was hungry."

"But it was *my* dinner."

"Thought it was for me." He stepped back with a shrug and allowed the refrigerator door to close.

I couldn't think beyond the wide shoulders encased in a very *open* short-sleeved, button-up of the same forest green as his shoes. The subtle cut of his abs and chest had definitely earned the right for him to show them off so confidently. Still…I couldn't figure out why I was feeling tongue-tied and flushed. I *never* noticed boys. Not even when puberty hit and Della Grady, my sole and now former friend, got into boys while I got into bikes.

Ever moved to the island with a bag of celery and orange Gatorade and deftly unscrewed the jar of peanut butter before making quick work of peanut-butter-coated celery. Thankfully, his casual demeanor as I stood by with an empty stomach allowed me to forget how goddamn *smoldering* he was.

"Do you always go around eating random plates of food?"

He paused from dipping another piece of celery into the jar of peanut butter.

"Since I was the only *resident* home at the time," he shot back casually, "it didn't seem so random to me."

My fingers curled into fists. The prick had only made it more obvious that he'd known who the food had been meant for.

"What's the matter, Ever? New kid on the block made you feel less special?"

He went utterly still.

A second later, he was in my face.

"Except you aren't," he sneered. "Your mother's little house-keeping salary couldn't afford for you to live within fifty miles of here." I stood frozen as he slowly looked me over and quickly discarded what he saw. "Think of your time here as a temporary upgrade in your mother's benefits package." His smile was predatory. "You know…for all the overtime."

Did he really just call Rosalyn a whore?

I felt tears sting the back of my eyes even as I gripped muscular shoulders and shoved my knee between his legs. I didn't wait to see if he went down, but his grunt of pain followed me out of the kitchen, so I ran like hell for the front door.

I was once again at the mercy of my emotions. I thought I'd just walk out of Blackwood Keep and never look back. No big deal. Two or three hours later, however, I realized I was as far from the exit as I could get when I wandered onto the beach.

Exhaustion had me accepting defeat quicker than I'd like, but I'd deal with that in the morning, too. My legs felt like twigs, and each step was more painful than the last. I had only begun to consider sleeping on the beach when I smelled the smoke.

It was the sound of Maroon 5's "Animals" that had me limping across the sand, and when I cleared the dunes, I spotted a group partying around a bonfire. Solo cups littered the ground around them, and I didn't bother questioning if those coolers contained alcohol.

All but one seemed to be having a good time. He sat far

enough from the flame that I couldn't see much of his face, but I could tell he was brooding as he stared at the water. A girlish scream tore my attention away, and I watched as a guy holding a cup with liquor pouring over the rim gave chase to a leggy blonde.

"Fresh meat!" Heads turned, and I realized I'd been spotted. The guys began to hoot and holler while the girls sized me up. I was still mostly in the shadows, but it wouldn't matter how I looked. The guys were drunk and horny, and to the girls, that alone made me competition. I backed away when a bare-chested blond in red board shorts and his darker, lankier cohort eased closer. "Don't be shy," board shorts cooed. "We don't bite." Their wolfish grins said otherwise.

"Yeah, come party with us."

I snorted. "You two sound like you belong in a bad vamp movie." I ignored the snickers and focused on keeping space between us. My pursuers didn't seem offended, but that was likely because they were completely stoned.

"I'm starting to think you're the one who bites," board shorts said with twinkling blues. "For future reference, I'm single."

"Thanks for the invitation, but I'm just passing through."

"Not without a beer, you're not." He was close enough now to grab my hand, and against my better judgment, I let him pull me toward the bonfire. When I stood amongst their circle, someone handed him a beer, which he then shoved in my hand.

"Got a name?"

"Four."

He barked a laugh and then cocked his head. "That's not a name, girl. That's a number."

I was careful not to look him in the eye as I shrugged. "Well, I'm Four," I repeated. He wasn't the first to find my name strange. No one knew why Rosalyn named me Four, and for her sake, I kept it that way.

"It's cool. I'm Drake, and this"—he pointed to his friend with the mop of dark curls—"is Ben."

I nodded and looked around at the rest of the group who had lost interest and returned to partying. There were maybe fifteen people, mostly male and my age.

"You're not from around here." Drake hadn't bothered posing it as a question.

"What makes you so sure?"

"Your lack of entitlement." I lifted my unopened beer can in salute. "And no offense, new friend, but those are the shittiest pair of chucks I've ever seen." The stoners peered down at my dirty green and white sneakers, but there wasn't even a hint of malice.

Feeling self-conscious, my feet shifted in the sand as I muttered, "I think they have character."

The two of them chortled, and then Drake smoothly wrapped his arm around my neck and drew me even closer to him and the fire. The flames licking at my face, arms, and legs kept me from pushing away. It felt good against the chill at my back.

"So is everyone in Blackwood Keep rich?"

"No, but people who come to this portion of the beach usually are. Everyone thinks we're snobs."

"Aren't you?"

He snorted and squeezed me against his side. "Not all of us. Beach is a beach." His smile grew as he gazed down at me. "And some of those girls whose daddies make shit money are *really* hot."

Deciding I didn't feel like being hit on all night, I pushed away and chucked my beer in the sand. "Thanks, but no thanks. I'll be going now."

"Aw, don't go," he whined. "I'll be good. I promise."

"If you mean that, let me use your phone."

His eyebrows bunched. "Why?"

"I need a ride home."

He quickly downed the rest of his drink and crushed the cup before tossing it in the sand. "Phone's dead, but I'll drive you."

I started to turn down his offer when I heard, "You're shit-faced, Cromwell. You won't be driving her anywhere."

I turned my head at the new voice. At some point, the brooder had abandoned his seat to stand closer to the flames. Green eyes stared back at me over the fire while the ocean's breeze ruffled light brown hair.

"What do you mean, Rees?" Drake spread his arms wide and grinned. "I feel like flying."

"Yeah, into a ditch." He cut off Drake's response with a sharp shake of his head and said, "She can find her own way home." This Rees guy then dismissed me with a flick of his eyes.

Drake looked as disappointed as a stoned person could. "Sorry, Four." He shrugged though I could see his frustration. "The Prince of Blackwood Keep has spoken."

I didn't care about losing a ride from Drake. Rees, otherwise known as asshole, had made a valid point, but it was clear this *prince* didn't speak up out of concern. He'd merely used Drake's intoxication as an excuse to alienate me.

I walked away but not without a backward glance. Rees's back was turned, but I could just make out the phone plastered to his ear. I had already been forgotten.

Ten or fifteen minutes later, I reached the main road with goose bumps crawling up my bare arms. I couldn't see more than a foot in front of me, and just as I hoped that nothing lurked in the dark, blue and red flashing lights lit up the night. Despite my relief, I kept walking until my name was called over the loudspeaker.

There was only one way he could know my name.

I turned and waited as the cruiser stopped, and a muscled officer with a bushy brown mustache and bald head exited.

"Four Archer?" he asked again.

"Yeah?"

"I'm Officer Trip. I'll be escorting you home."

It didn't really sound like I had a choice, but I still found myself saying, "I'll be fine." I turned away only to stop dead at the stern turn in his tone.

"It wasn't a request, and I don't want to have to place you in cuffs, miss."

I considered my options—haul ass or face the music. If I ran, and he caught me, I'd still have to face the music while feeling like the biggest idiot. Not to mention, Rosalyn would freak. She was only one fuckup away from locking me in the tallest tower she could find.

"How do you know my name?" I questioned as Officer Trip led me to the cruiser.

"The name Thomas McNamara mean anything to you?"

I sighed as he opened the back door. "Yeah."

"He reported you missing an hour ago. Young lady, there are things out here that bite that you wouldn't see coming in the dark. I don't recommend you try this again." He shut the door, and I laid my head back with my eyes closed. Maybe it was hunger and exhaustion, but the world began to spin when he hopped in and reported that I'd been found.

It was another minute before he began to pull away from the shoulder and another when his curse had my eyes popping open in time to see a white Lamborghini Aventador flying past. Officer Trip cursed again before speeding after the car. He quickly activated the loudspeaker when he managed to catch up.

"This is your only warning. Slow down!"

My heart beat faster as the driver seemed to ignore the cop's orders and sped down the unlit road. Just as Officer Trip was ready to turn on the siren, the brake lights flashed.

The irritated officer muttered to himself as he followed behind the car until it turned off in another direction.

"I'm going to offer more unsolicited advice, although it might not be worth much considering the person you're living with."

"And that is?"

"Stay away from Vaughn Rees. Ever too…if you can manage."

I met Officer Trip's gaze in the rearview mirror. "You don't have to worry about that."

"Do you have any idea how worried I've been?" Thomas and Rosalyn were waiting on the front steps when Officer Trip pulled into the circular drive.

Ignoring Rosalyn's puffy eyes and Thomas's tight jaw, I slipped inside while Officer Trip had them distracted.

I only made it halfway up the stairs before Ever appeared at the landing, wearing the same clothes from earlier but with his shirt mercifully buttoned. For a moment, he didn't move, and neither did I, but then he blinked, and the threat was there. He descended the stairs, and I had a hunch he wanted to push me down them. I carefully backed down, but he kept coming, his eyes only for me. A single step was all that separated us when his father appeared and ordered us into the family room. Ever simply shifted and kept going as if nothing had happened.

"Why did you leave this house?" Thomas questioned when everyone except Ever was seated.

"I didn't know I was a prisoner."

"You're free to come and go, but you should be reachable at all times, and curfew is midnight during the summer and weekends."

I nodded and hoped that would be the end of his interrogation. I wouldn't give that prick leaning against the wall the satisfaction of admitting he'd been the reason I ran.

"Why did you leave?" Rosalyn demanded.

"I just needed some air." Behind the couple, a mocking smirk appeared.

"Ever says you ran out of here crying," Thomas pointed out.

"I..." I dug my fingers into the cushion to keep from

scratching Ever's eyes out. There was no way I could correct them without admitting that I attacked his precious prince. "I'm still adjusting." *Saddle up, McNamara. I'm staying.* And because I couldn't keep my eyes off him, I saw Ever's smile spread as if he'd read my mind and was hungry for the challenge.

Thomas cleared his throat, stealing back my attention. "Yes, well, we take responsibility for tonight. We shouldn't have left you alone your first night in a new home. I didn't consider your point of view."

"And what exactly is my point of view, Thomas?"

His gaze narrowed thoughtfully. "That you'd give any-thing—absolutely anything—to be back in Cherry." He leaned forward, resting his forearms on his hard thighs. "I know it's hard leaving home, but understand this...running away will not be tolerated."

I felt my lip curl. "Is that a threat?"

Rosalyn extended her hand, but I moved away before she could touch me. She was clearly on his side.

"It's a very serious warning, Four. Your mother and I are trying to do what's best. Try with us."

Rosalyn was back to gnawing her lip again, a wordless plea for me to heed Thomas's warning—for her sake, not mine. Never mine. I could already feel myself capitulating.

"May I be excused?"

They gave their nod of approval, but I faltered when I real-ized I'd have to pass Ever. It wasn't like he'd pounce in front of his father, so with my head held high, I left the family room. It wasn't until he spoke that I realized he'd followed me. I whirled around on the stairs to face him. With our parents out of the way, nothing was keeping either of us on our leashes.

"What did you say?"

"Your smell has a habit of lingering after you're gone."

Mortification had me hurrying up the stairs again. Sure, I'd worked up a sweat, but I didn't think it had been offensive.

Drake definitely didn't seem to mind, although he *had* been high out of his mind. I could feel him on my heels as I rushed down the hall. He didn't speak again until I reached my door.

"I thought maybe Mrs. Greene was trying out a new air freshener."

I'd turned to face him when the epiphany came swift and hard. *He knows I was in his room.* "I—I don't know what you're talking about."

He crowded me until he trapped me against the door and only a finger of space remained between us. I could hardly draw my next breath as his own breezed over my skin.

"Yes, you do."

I watched as he leaned forward just the tiniest bit and...inhaled. The sudden hum between my thighs and stirring in my stomach alarmed me. I looked away to hide my reaction and didn't move until I heard the soft snick of his bedroom door closing. Not wasting time, I threw open my own door and rushed inside. It felt good to breathe again.

I stood frozen as I listened to him move around the bathroom. Moments later, the shower was running. I was still rummaging through the boxes Thomas must have had brought up when the shower shut off. I pretended I wasn't listening to every sound coming from within that bathroom, but ten minutes later, when the hair dryer shut off, I realized I hadn't moved the entire time. With a self-loathing curse, I toed off my sneakers and grabbed my toiletries before padding across the room.

When I turned the knob, however, I found the door locked.

He must have flipped the lock for privacy but forgot to unlock it. My fist slammed into the door when I realized I'd have to get him to unlock it, which completely ruined my plan of never speaking to him again.

Not that he'd care.

I wanted to scream and rage when I reached his door, but I'd catch more flies with honey, so I used my knuckles to knock lightly. Maybe I'd hate myself less after I washed away the sand and sweat sticking to my skin.

"Ever?" I called when a few seconds passed. I knocked again but was met with the same silence. "I know you're awake. I need you to unlock my door." I knocked harder this time and for a minute straight to no avail. Growling, I prowled back to my room and tried the door again, but it was still locked. "Asshole," I muttered before grabbing my clothes and toiletries and heading to one of the guest rooms.

I bet he wanted me to run and cry to our parents about how he was being a big, bad bully.

Fuck him.

As long as he didn't want me here, I'd pretend to play for keeps. After all, you don't grow up in Cherry without learning how to milk a cow. Smiling to myself, I entered the first guest room I could find and locked the door for good measure. Locking me out of our bathroom was the last battle he'd win tonight.

After a steaming hot shower, I was much more levelheaded when I returned to my room, but just to settle my curiosity, I checked my bathroom door.

It was unlocked.

chapter four

The Peer

THE SOFT KNOCK ON MY DOOR HAD ME LOOKING UP FROM THE TEXT Vaughn sent in response to me quitting the team. It was a dick move considering the season was about to start, and Vaughn and I had just made varsity, but we've also been best friends since the day we ate a fistful of sand together on the playground. While he couldn't know what I'd do with the vital information he shared, he knew me well enough to know I'd do *something*.

"Ever," the southern voice called followed by another knock when I refused to say shit. It was amusing the way she attempted to conceal her anger. I was willing to bet there was not a damn thing sweet about Four Archer. "I know you're awake. I need you to unlock my door."

I smiled at her whining as I texted Vaughn my plan. My father had naively expected me to be hospitable and share a bathroom with some swamp girl who probably never even received all of her vaccinations. I had never cared much about being the bigger person. I only cared about getting my way, and Archer would learn that soon enough.

There was a chance she'd run and tell my father, but my gut told me she was the type to fight her own battles and even if she weren't it wouldn't stop a thing. I'd only make her life hell another day.

My father was still very much a married man when he moved his whore and her wild daughter into the home he once shared with my mother. The day he broke the news I had half a mind to walk out just as she did. I had still been considering it up until the moment I laid eyes on Four Archer. I couldn't explain why but at that moment I knew I wasn't going anywhere.

I couldn't say the same for her.

My phone beeped just as I heard Archer mutter something that sounded like "asshole" before walking away.

#17: Are you out of your mind???

I rubbed my temple and considered the possibility that I might be before texting my reply.

What did you expect, V? He can't keep her. No fucking way.

I threw my phone down not caring about what he had to say. My mind was made up, and nothing was going to change it. It's been three years, and since then I've lost hope until my best friend unknowingly gave it back.

Except for this time I was no longer willing to sit back and pray.

Hope was for the weak and the foolish.

I looked around my room seeing only change and nothing of the past. Stepping into my room had once been like looking inside a kaleidoscope. Typical of any teenager, after forging through puberty, I went through phases faster than I could change my underwear. My parents had encouraged me to embrace my ever-changing curiosities, assuring me that it was perfectly normal…until I took it too far. Because of one night that I could never take back, I made a point to surround myself with only what was necessary so that there was no risk of temptation.

Because once I found trouble, it was impossible to stay away. I lived for it and would have probably died for it.

I could recall with vivid clarity the time I came closest to death. It was the summer before my last year of junior high— before everything went to shit. Jamie and Bee—my cousin from Boston and my other best friend—had ditched us to be alone so it was just Vaughn and me—along with some kids from school—watching football tryouts when I boasted that I'd make first cut when the time came. I was a runner and a fast one too. The fastest Brynwood had ever seen. I had considered joining the track and field team, but Vaughn had convinced me to focus my talent elsewhere when he pointed out that the football players got more pussy.

At thirteen it seemed like a pretty fair argument.

Of course, my classmates had their doubts and challenged me to prove my speed. And of all the ways I could have, I chose the most daring. In front of six witnesses, I had claimed I could outrun a train. When I look back, it wasn't my proudest moment, but it was the memory that always made me feel alive.

My phone chimed bringing me back to the present:

BEE: Meet your new stepsister yet? ;-)

I heard my teeth grinding as I typed.

The hick and I will never share a last name.

The fact that it felt like a lie pissed me off even more. There was no way my father would actually marry the gold digger. Not when my mother was still out there. My parents had been in love, and I knew if I could just get them in the same room together, we could turn back time. Four Archer would be back in the swamp where she belonged, and I'd have my family again.

BEE: She must be pretty...

Knowing Bee was fishing, I closed my eyes to pray for patience. Instead, I pictured big brown eyes, pink lips forever pursed in a defiant pout, golden hair wrangled into a disheveled ponytail, and the most exquisite ass I'd ever come to behold.

NOPE, I texted back.

I tossed my phone on the bed and ignored the answering chime as I headed for the bathroom. After taking a leak and washing my hands, I flipped the lock on Four's door. I thought I'd just walk away. I really wanted to. But then I realized I wanted to be on the other side even more.

Not giving a shit if she was in her room or not, I yanked open the door and stepped inside. As I looked around, it became clear that whoever had decorated this room didn't know Four Archer at all. Hell, I've only known her for less than a day, but even I knew frills and pastels were not her style. She was bolder without intending to be, and it was because she didn't give a shit. This room had been decorated for someone who wanted to be handled with kid gloves.

There was a small pile of boxes in the corner that one of the help must have brought up sometime while Four was out looking for the nearest exit. The fact that she was willing to do it on foot told me just how much I'd pissed her off.

I still felt a slight ache in my balls for my trouble. When she fled, I had every intention of running after her and showing her the proper way to handle the family jewels, but that had been out of the question. It took me over five minutes just to pick myself up from the goddamn floor. By then the little troublemaker was long gone.

You better believe I looked while picturing my hands wrapped around her pretty throat.

After too much time passed and she didn't come back I told myself I was only worried about what story I'd tell my father. Under no circumstances was I concerned about what might have happened to her.

Unfortunately, my father and his whore made it back first but seeing an opportunity to get my pound of flesh, I told them without being asked that Four had run away in a fit of tears. I had no idea if she was crying or not, but I knew my saying so would piss her off either way.

Vaughn had called shortly after my father and Four's mother lost their shit to say he'd found something of mine lost on the beach. I didn't need to ask what he'd meant. Once I informed my father of Four's whereabouts he wasted no time calling in one of the many favors owed by the Sheriff's department. I covertly cashed in a favor of my own and told Vaughn to stay on her ass in case she spotted one of the Sheriff's boys first and bolted.

There was no way in hell she was getting off that easy. Four's presence in Blackwood Keep had awakened something within me, and I wanted more of it.

Tipping over to the only open box, I peered inside. Navy blue coveralls stained with oil was the first to catch my eye. Lifting it, I smiled as I studied Four's name written on the white patch belonging to Russell's Repairs.

So my little troublemaker liked to get her hands dirty.

Good.

So did I.

chapter five

The Puppet

OUR DAYS OF PLAYING THE DOCILE PRISONER FOR THE MCNAMARA
men left me exhausted. Who knew being pleasant twenty-
four seven packed could be so…unpleasant? And it all seemed
to backfire because, after that first day, I saw little to nothing of
Ever McNamara. Thomas didn't even bat an eyelash at his son's
constant absence.

Today was now the morning of my fifth day in Blackwood
Keep and my first day at Brynwood Academy. A couple of days
ago, I was given the same red and navy uniforms I'd found in
Ever's closet along with a credit card for my 'needs.' Thomas
then forced me to sit through a lecture on financial responsibility before informing me that Ever would be driving me to and
from school until other arrangements could be made. He didn't
explain what he'd meant, but I wondered if the man had actually
been implying he'd buy me a *car*.

Eyes at half-mast as my toes sunk into the plush carpet, I
stretched and listened for signs of bathroom occupancy. Hearing
nothing but the birds chirping, I quickly grabbed the caddy I
picked up when Rosalyn had driven us to town in the Navigator
for supplies. Along with everything else, she'd ditched the Taurus
before leaving Cherry. Rosalyn had questioned why I needed a
caddy, but I'd refrained from telling her that I didn't trust Ever not
to dip my toothbrush in toilet water. Not that *I* had considered it
or anything…

I made sure to lock both doors before eagerly stepping into the shower. I'd spent thirty minutes under the spray the first time. The water jetting from all sides had felt like a full body massage, one that I desperately needed this morning but didn't have the time to spare. After blow-drying, my hair fell in shiny waves around my shoulders before I threw it into a ponytail. Rosalyn loathed them. She thought it was 'shameful to hide such beautiful hair.' I thought it was a goddamn nuisance, which was why I'd had Patty free me of the long tresses. Rosalyn had mourned for months.

Once I collected everything, I unlocked his door. I'd only taken a few steps when a wicked smile spread across my lips, and I hurried back to his door. I was reaching for the knob when the door was pushed open. I just barely saved my face from being clobbered.

"What are you doing in here?" I hissed as I clutched my towel to me. Black boxers were all Ever wore.

"Door wasn't locked." His head cocked slightly. "What were *you* doing if the door was already unlocked?"

"I—I didn't know I'd forgotten to lock it," I lied.

He grunted and moved around me. I couldn't help stealing another peek at his body even though he hadn't bothered looking anywhere beyond my face. One day, I'd question why I found that insulting. I watched as his gaze landed on my yellow caddy. Without permission, he reached out, lifted my bar of soap, and brought it up to his nose.

Fuck.

A lump lodged in my throat as he wordlessly returned the bar and handed over the caddy.

"Get out."

I grabbed the caddy and fled.

Downstairs, after donning the navy blazer, white blouse, and khaki skirt, and opting for scuffed Vans instead of the shiny black oxfords, I found Rosalyn in the breakfast room, robed in turquoise silk, sipping her coffee as she stared out the window. The terrace doors were thrown open, inviting the morning breeze inside.

"Morning." She faced me with a smile that became genuine when she took in my uniform.

"You look lovely."

I smiled as I slid onto the bench across from her. "Thanks. Is this for me?" My mouth watered as I stared down at the scrambled eggs, bacon, toast, and fresh fruit.

"Yes. Ever had some orange drink, and Thomas already left for the office."

I nodded as I chewed on a piece of bacon. It was the right ratio of crispy and chewy just as I liked it. "Did you make this?" I already knew the answer. Why else would Ever pass up a hot meal for Gatorade? Eating something else would have been too obvious, and his father didn't seem like he messed around.

She beamed as I devoured another strip of bacon. "I wanted to make sure you had a good breakfast." She resumed staring out the window when I didn't respond. I was too busy hoping that I hadn't completely lost her to the McNamaras.

I finished eating and kissed Rosalyn's warm cheek before running upstairs to grab my backpack. I didn't know the protocol for being forced to accept a ride from a person who hated you, so after checking the time, I decided to just wait outside. I'd seen Ever come and go in a blacked-out Range Rover, so when I emerged and saw his ride waiting in the driveway, I awkwardly stood by it. Ten minutes passed before Ever emerged in a long-sleeve navy sweater, with the collar of his white dress shirt popping from the neckline, and black pants. He'd dutifully worn the red tie and shiny black oxfords that I had wrinkled my nose at before stuffing mine in the darkest corner of my closet. He had his two-toned hair brushed back and controlled with gel that made his thick hair shine.

If there ever were a preppy God, Ever would have been him.

"If I'd known you were such a diva, I would have slept an extra five minutes," I quipped as he approached.

He took his time looking me over before speaking. "The option to walk is always available to you." His tone remained perfectly flat, and I began to wonder if he even had a personality. He was always so refined and in control. Nothing seemed to ruffle his royal feathers.

I hopped in after he unlocked the Range Rover and waited while he tossed his backpack in the back. I didn't realize I was tapping my foot until I caught him eyeing my bare legs. He seemed unimpressed, however, when he met my gaze again.

"Problem?" he questioned.

"We're going to be late."

He smirked as he turned the ignition and put the car in gear. "And?"

"And I'm in enough trouble thanks to you," I reminded.

"Me?" He couldn't have sounded more disinterested.

"Yeah. You."

His lip curled as he drove us down the tree-lined driveway. "I'm not the dumb hick who thought she could be the next Patsy Quick in a fucking swamp."

"Fuck you."

Ever's condescending snort had me flushing with humiliation even before he said, "Not even with a paper bag and a thousand condoms."

Self-preservation flew out the window when my fist collided with his temple. *Too far.* He swerved into the next lane and cursed as he quickly regained control of the Range before slamming on the brakes. By the time I unfastened my seatbelt to fight or flee, he was already yanking open my door and pulling me out by my arm. My warning growls went unheeded as he slammed the passenger door shut and pushed me up against it.

"The first two were free. You hit me again, I hit back. Are we clear on that, Archer?"

I stared into the angry depth of his eyes, and the only thing I could do was smile, knowing I'd finally gotten to him. "Go to hell."

"I am hell, so you'd better wise up."

Feeling as if he'd carved the warning into my skin, I didn't respond, and he finally let me go. I debated getting back in with him until he threatened to run me over if I didn't. Guilt didn't rear its ugly head until the red bruise appeared on his temple. I sighed, knowing it was wrong for me to hit him, but I still couldn't bring myself to apologize. Ever didn't speak another word as he drove, and ten minutes later, he was pulling onto a huge campus with brick and glass buildings and fields of green. I was still gawking when he parked, grabbed his bag, and hopped out. Ever's name could be heard from every direction when I slid from the car. He ignored them all. The moment the door closed, he engaged the lock.

There would be no hiding.

I became all too aware of the stares and whispers.

Just apologize.

My lips parted to speak, but then the words died in my throat when the asshole from the beach suddenly appeared next to Ever. They stood of equal height and build, but their features were noticeably different…and fucking remarkable. Where Ever was regal, Vaughn was boyish, and that had to be where the trap lay because under the aristocracy and allure brewed a storm. Vaughn had chosen to wear a red sweater vest over his white button-up with the sleeves rolled up with a navy tie and navy pants.

"Glad to see you made it home in one piece," he smugly observed.

"No thanks to you."

He simply smiled as if he knew something I didn't.

I crossed my arms, forgetting my nervousness. "It's a good thing you weren't too busy wrapped around a tree to notice."

His lips twitched as he leaned against his car. "Wouldn't that be the pot calling the kettle black?"

My gaze switched to Ever, who glared at his friend as he shouldered his pack. "It seems I've become a hot topic."

Ever snorted as he stepped onto the concrete and into my space. We now stood so close that his every exhale blew a strand of hair that had escaped my messy ponytail. "Don't flatter yourself."

He walked away without another word and the ball of nerves inside my stomach finally unraveled. Vaughn's gaze flickered back and forth between Ever and me before he pushed away from his car and followed.

The parking lot and manicured lawn quickly emptied.

What the hell?

I rushed for the arched entrance.

Jefferson High looked nothing like this with its simple white structure and a ceiling that occasionally leaked when it rained. No one ever bothered to complain, knowing there would never be money in the budget to fix it.

Luckily, the headmaster's office wasn't hard to find. I picked up my schedule along with a new student slip, but when I tried to leave for my first class, the secretary informed me that I was to see the headmaster.

I stifled my groan and took a seat like a dutiful Brynwood academic. Almost immediately, the door to the headmaster's office opened, and a stout man with a receding hairline of gray and a kind smile appeared.

"Miss Archer?" I stood and shook the headmaster's offered hand. "I'm Headmaster Burns. Brynwood Academy is pleased to have you, young lady."

He then showed me into his office where another student with mocha skin, whiskey eyes, and brown hair pulled into a neat bun waited. The lower her gaze swept over me, the higher her eyebrows rose.

"This is Tyra Bradley. She's one of our finest students. I've assigned her to be your guide for the next couple of weeks to help with your transition. If there is anyone who can get you settled in, it's her."

"Hey, I'm Four."

She nodded politely but didn't lose that wary look.

All right then.

"Miss Archer, if you have any questions, I have an open-door policy. Brynwood also enforces strict but necessary rules that we would like to see *all* students follow."

I noticed him studying my uniform with a deep frown, so I glanced at Tyra for help. We looked the same minus the tie and pompous shoes, of course.

"Is something wrong with my uniform?"

"The tie and oxfords aren't an option, Miss Archer. I also advise that you do not pass through those doors again with your shirttails untucked from your skirt."

Heat bloomed on the back of my neck as I shifted from one foot to the other. "Sorry, I didn't know." He nodded but continued to stare curiously. "Is there something else?"

"I'm just surprised that Mr. McNamara didn't educate you on uniform policy. As Brynwood's president, it's one of his duties to ensure it's being enforced."

And the aristocratic ass must have known I'd have to see the headmaster before class.

Motherfucker.

I was saved from offering an explanation by Tyra. "First period will be over soon. I think we should get going so I can show Four around in time for second."

"Good idea, Miss Bradley. And Four…" I shook the hand he held out as he flashed a warm smile. "Welcome to Brynwood."

"Why do I have the feeling we got off on the wrong foot?" I questioned after I caught Tyra stealing her third glance. We'd been walking and speaking only on a need-to basis since leaving the headmaster's office.

With a sigh, Tyra stopped in the middle of the empty hall. "We didn't…not really," she fumbled to explain. "It's just that when I heard you were living with Ever McNamara, I expected the worst."

"A rich bitch?"

"Exactly."

"Well, as it turns out, I'm just some rich man's charity case… and I assumed the same about you."

"Then we have something in common. I'm also some rich man's charity case."

"Oh?"

"I'm here on scholarship. You?"

"That's not exactly how I'd define my situation. Rosalyn is dating Ever's dad."

"Rosalyn?"

I often forgot that normal was not calling your mother by her first name. "My mother."

"She lets you call her by her first name? How cool."

"Sure." I cracked a smile to hide the truth, and she did the same. "So I barely said two words in there. What made you change your mind?"

Her eyebrows rose as she looked me over. "Honestly?"

Catching her drift, I chuckled. "Yeah, okay." I started walking again.

"Sorry!" she rushed to say as she followed. "It's just that none of the girls here would ever be caught dead not giving a shit."

"I get it," I murmured. "I don't belong here."

"It's refreshing."

"Why's that?" I questioned as I spotted the bathroom and headed for it.

She followed me inside and took a look around to make sure we were alone before she answered.

"Because I don't, either."

I eyed her curiously. She definitely looked the part of a Brynwood elite. "But you're wearing the tie and the shoes."

"Yeah, because they cost my dad a fortune." She blew out a breath and squared her shoulders as if readying for a brutal blow. "I'm only here because my dad coaches the football team. They gave me a scholarship that I can only keep if I maintain a perfect average. I can't even afford to get a B."

I shrugged as I tucked in my shirt. It didn't matter to me how much money her dad didn't make. "It seems like you're holding up your end of the deal pretty well."

"I don't date. None of the guys here would date beneath them anyway. And the only students who would be seen with me are scholarship students, too. All they do is study. All *I* do is study. That and work at the coffee shop."

It seems I'd found another loner.

I couldn't wait to tell Gruff.

I tapped my finger against my chin and studied her. "How do you feel about spending your Sunday nights watching sword fights, dragons breathing fire, and people doing it?"

Dimples appeared on both cheeks as her smile spread. "It sounds awesome."

"Well, Tyra…" I linked my arm through hers and walked us to the door. "I guess this makes us friends."

She began opening the door just as a group of guys approached. Recognizing the tallest one, my hand quickly curled around the door to keep her from opening it further.

"What is it?" she whispered.

I didn't answer her. I couldn't. The group had stopped mere feet away from the bathroom door. Tyra stood on her toes to peek over my left shoulder.

Ever stood in the middle of the hall with Vaughn and three others—a real bruiser with dark hair, a Korean kid with a mohawk, and a Dave Franco look-alike—as they tossed a football back and forth between them.

"You should reconsider quitting the team," the bruiser said to my darling 'stepbrother.' "The only players I know that are as fast as you are playing for the pros."

"Yeah," the Franco clone agreed. "We really need you as our running back. Stephens is good, but he's not quick enough to catch Turner's girly throws."

The bruiser, who was obviously Turner, shoved him into the wall and threatened to use him for target practice.

"Besides," the mohawk spoke as he tossed the football to Ever, "if you and Vaughn get drafted for the same team, you won't have to end the bromance."

Ever flipped him off and tossed the ball to Vaughn.

"Is your dad still pushing for you to work for him?" Turner prodded Vaughn, whose jaw tightened as he nodded.

"I can't believe he tried to bribe you with a Lamborghini," the Franco clone tittered. "What does he do again?"

"He dabbles in a few trades. None that I'm interested in."

The mohawk clapped Ever on his shoulder. "That settles it. What do you say?"

Ever gave a sharp shake of his head. "Too busy."

The guys' shoulders dropped.

"Is it because of that chick you rode in with this morning? What's her name again?"

"It was a number or something," the mohawk pondered. "Six or Seven, I think." Only when they continued to list and argue numbers did Ever deign to correct them.

"It's Four," he enlightened with zero emotion.

"Wait, her name is *Four*?" The Franco clone doubled over. "Four...Ever...*forever*." Thinking himself clever, he laughed even harder. "The universe is really screwing with you, huh?"

Ever didn't respond.

"Dude, she looked like Dorothy in Wonderland when she climbed from your ride," Turner chortled. "Who is she, anyway?"

"She's nobody."

"Asshole," Tyra whispered.

My only reaction was to clutch the door tighter.

"A nobody wouldn't make you tense like that," Turner observed. Maybe he wasn't as dumb as he looked, after all.

"I'm probably going to inherit the mansion, and she's bringing down the property value."

"That's cold," the mohawk murmured.

Ever shrugged, and only Vaughn remained silent as the rest of them laughed at my expense.

"A few more weeks and my dad will be done playing house with the gold digger."

"A few weeks, huh?" The Franco clone rubbed his chin. "I bet I can smash in one."

Turner sucked his teeth and eyed him skeptically. "Why would she waste good pussy on you when the King of Brynwood sleeps in the next room? If anyone fucks her first, I bet it's him."

Ever leaned against the wall and shoved his hands in his pockets. "I don't want her."

"What?" his three lackeys hollered.

"I know she's a little less sophisticated than what you're used to, but she's sort of cute," Turner argued. "Definitely fuckable."

"Yeah, she's a little plain, but did you see her ass?" The Franco clone whistled.

"Maybe if she ditched those homeless man sneakers…" the mohawk suggested.

"Who cares about what she's wearing?" the Franco clone argued. "It's what's underneath that counts."

"Yeah, but nicer wrapping wouldn't hurt."

Turner turned to Vaughn for judgment. "What do you think, Rees? Would you fuck?"

Vaughn tossed the ball rapidly between his palms, but the smirk he tossed at Ever made me wish I was anywhere else. "She gives too much lip. Pass."

"Damn," the mohawk muttered. "I guess that settles it. Four's an undesirable."

The guys didn't look completely convinced, however, and Ever definitely took notice. "I'll tell you who I'd fuck," he said slowly.

The way they leaned in, you'd think Ever was about to tell them who killed Tupac.

"Who," the Franco clone eagerly prodded.

"Marianne Little."

The lackeys moaned appreciatively, and I was good as forgotten as they listed her best assets and what they'd like to do to her. I barely felt the comforting hand Tyra laid on my arm. I was ready to fling open the door and rip into them, but the bell chose that moment to ring, prompting Ever and Vaughn to finally walk away with their lackeys trailing behind.

I didn't have an appetite when the lunch bell rang, so I sat in a corner stewing while Tyra talked my ear off.

"Four?" I looked up from staring at the green beans in the corner of my lunch tray to find Tyra staring back at me. "Are you okay?"

I groaned and pushed away my tray. "I'm not very good company, am I?"

She shook her head and stabbed at her meatloaf. "After what those assholes said about you, I'd be upset, too."

It wasn't just those cronies' words that upset me. Ever had just *let* them say those things. In just one day, I'd learned who held power in this school, and it wasn't Headmaster Burns. Ever could have shut them up if he had wanted.

"If you don't want to go to Ever's party tomorrow night, you can come over and watch *Outlander*…" She had been ready to say more, but her voice trailed off at the look on my face.

"What party?"

"The back-to-school bash. Well…it's also a party for Ever's seventeenth birthday."

I swallowed down the lump in my throat. "Where is it?"

"His house. I mean…it's your house, too."

I shrugged. "You were right the first time."

"So are you going? Barbie has been handing out invitations all day. Of course, *I* didn't get one. Not that I'd want to go." Her button nose wrinkled as she stabbed her meatloaf again. I was beginning to think she was picturing someone's face.

"Who's Barbie?" I'd question who would name their kid Barbie, but considering my own name, judgment was off the table.

"Ever's girlfriend," she answered matter-of-factly.

The cafeteria, the other students—it all faded away.

Since the moment he'd stepped around that refrigerator door, I hadn't been able to break free of his spell. Not even when he was being an utter dick. How had I never considered that he belonged to someone?

The reality felt like a heart-stopping blow, and I had no idea why.

"They've been a thing since the eighth grade," Tyra chattered obliviously. "Barbie is a total bitch, but if you ask me, I think she can do better."

"Why do you say that?"

Tyra took a look around before whispering, "Because everyone knows Ever sleeps around. He lost his virginity three years ago, and people say it wasn't to her. They say Olivia Portland was his first love." Her voice dropped even lower when she added, "After he fucked her, she wanted him to break it off with Barbie, but he refused. She stalked him, it became a shitstorm, but then her family left town, and everyone moved on."

I took a deep breath and chose my next words carefully. "This *Barbie* didn't break up with him?"

"That's the weirdest part. I don't think she really cared. They're a weird couple if you ask me. Don't think I've even seen them kiss before."

My mouth became as dry as a desert. "Maybe he isn't big on PDA." I opened my carton of milk and took a sip when I wanted to chug it.

"Could be…except I caught him fingering a girl once."

Some of the milk I spat out landed on Tyra, and she squealed, drawing attention, before quickly grabbing some napkins.

"Sorry," I forced through my choking.

"I guess I deserved that." At my look, she fell over laughing, drawing even more attention. "I totally got you."

"What?" I took an angry swipe at my mouth.

"I kid. No one ever sees Ever do his dirt."

"So how do you know all of this?"

"Because girls talk and because fucking Ever McNamara is like climbing Mount Everest or winning the lottery." I rolled my eyes at that. "I know you hate him, but it's true. He's incredibly selective. Vaughn Rees, too." She rolled her eyes at the mention of his name. "You aren't hot unless they say you are."

"God forbid a girl thinks more of herself."

"You don't understand. They aren't just a meal ticket. They're *the* ticket."

I couldn't deny that my interest was piqued. "I know the McNamara's are rich, but what makes Vaughn so special?"

She shrugged. "His mother's family founded Blackwood Keep. They're pretty loaded, too."

"Is that why they call him the Prince of Blackwood Keep?"

"Yeah, but there's a rumor that his father is into some real heavy shit."

"What kind of shit?"

"Don't know," she answered nonchalantly. "His father might as well be Voldemort. We don't speak his name."

I snorted. "And I thought only the folks in Cherry were heavy on superstition and rumors."

Her expression turned serious, and she grabbed my hand. "I'm serious, Four. I agree that Ever deserves a good kick in the dick, but if you go looking for trouble, they'll bring it to you. Ever and Vaughn are not to be fucked with."

I smirked. "Been there, done that."

"What do you mean you *did that*?"

It was my turn for nonchalance. "I kneed him in his special place my first night here." When she stared back at me as if I'd just told her I once kicked a puppy, I shrugged and added, "He deserved it."

Her gaze narrowed. "Did you also give him that bruise everyone's been talking about?"

I fought a smile. "Maybe."

"Everyone's been wondering who was crazy enough to fight Ever, but he's been tight-lipped, as usual."

"Maybe he doesn't want anyone to know it was a girl."

She giggled and let go of my hand. "You're crazy, and I must be insane for daring to be your friend."

This time I did smile albeit hesitantly. I'd been a loner for so long that I wasn't sure I even wanted a friend. When she smiled back, bright and honest, I decided the idea wasn't entirely loathsome. "You only live once."

Her reply was cut off by the sudden appearance of three girls. Two of them—both brunette—wore navy blazers, but not the blue-eyed blonde leading them. Red painted lips stretched wide as she eyeballed me. "You must be Flower."

"Four," I corrected.

"Oh." She giggled, and on cue, the two behind her echoed. "How silly of me. I'm Amanda."

"Okay."

Without invitation, she sat down next to Tyra, who didn't bother to be subtle when she scooted her chair over. If Amanda noticed, she pretended otherwise as she beamed at me. Her friends chose to remain standing, which gave me hope that whatever this was wouldn't last long.

"I'm sorry for the intrusion. I just had to know if the rumors were true."

"What rumors?" Tyra barked. I was taken aback by her sudden hostility, though Amanda's phony charm never faltered.

"Oh, just that Ever McNamara has a new stepsister."

"I wouldn't count that as newsworthy, and I'm not his stepsister."

Her perfectly arched brows pulled in at my statement. "So, you're just living together?"

"Pretty much." I had no intention of discussing Rosalyn's love life with strangers.

"Interesting." She suddenly looked a little less friendly as she sized me up. "I hope you don't mind me saying, but you're really pretty."

I could see where this was going. This scene felt like a *Mean Girls* reenactment, but instead of Africa, I was the new kid from the swamps. "I'm not interested in Ever."

She feigned being startled as her claws sheathed. "No one would blame you if you were. I mean, even you can admit that he's insanely hot."

A light bulb suddenly flickered on. "Well, between you and me…" She leaned forward, and I ignored Tyra's bulging eyes. "I think his looks are just God's way of compensating for… you know…*other*…inadequacies."

Amanda lifted manicured nails to cover her surprised gasp as her mouth formed a perfect O.

"Do tell, Four."

So I leaned in and told them a story.

It started as a little white lie. Some well-deserved payback. A distorted secret that no one else was supposed to hear. By fifth period, it had become a rumor doused in gasoline. Tyra had stared at me in horror from across the table after Amanda and her crew of gossips left the scene.

"What?"

"That was a bad idea, Four." I could swear her shoulders shook as she whispered, "A really bad idea."

I'd waved her off and ignored the turning of my stomach, but now, as the stares, whispers, and looks of pity followed me, I knew it was only a matter of time before he uncovered the source.

Fingers curled angrily around my bicep as I was switching books, and then I was turned and pushed against my open locker. I could feel the cold chill from inside my locker breeze past the bare skin of my neck, but it was nothing compared to the glacial bite of Ever's eyes boring into me. It seemed the aristocratic ass had more bite than I gave him credit.

"What the fuck, McNamara? Hands off the merchandise." I tried to shrug off his hold, but he only tightened his fingers.

"You find humor in spreading lies, Archer?"

"I don't know what you're talking about."

He stepped closer, forcing me to accept the bite of the metal to avoid the press of his hips against mine. "You don't?"

"Nope." My lips made an audible pop, drawing his attention.

His thumb gently brushed my bottom lip as if he had the right. "I think you do."

I could hear the whispers and feel the stares, but Ever didn't seem to care. He continued to brush my lip and gaze at me thoughtfully as if he were deciding what to do with me. He wasn't fooling me, though. His gentle touch was a trap. His power was in his restraint. As if he'd take his time with me…

Our gaping classmates abruptly parted like the Red Sea, and my silent prayer was answered when Headmaster Burns appeared. He looked uncertain, however, when he saw who was causing the commotion. Thankfully, he recovered and cleared his throat with a stern look.

"Mr. McNamara. Ms. Archer. You need to put about two feet of space between you and get to class."

Ever seemed unperturbed as he calmly focused on Burns, but then my little sigh of relief drew him like a moth to a flame, and in his eyes, I saw his promise of retribution.

"We'll settle up soon, Four. Welcome to Blackwood Keep." Ever speaking my name for the first time felt forbidden, and the lingering threat he'd whispered in my ear before walking away felt very real. Suddenly, Tyra and Officer Trip's warning that Ever was trouble didn't seem so empty.

Not only did I tell the biggest gossip at Brynwood that Ever McNamara had much to compensate, I may have also told her that I'd innocently walked in on Ever as he was leaving the shower and that he had a shrimp dick—a dick so small it curled into itself for love because no one else would.

I may have screwed up.

Tyra offered to drive me home when I found Ever's Range Rover missing from the parking lot after school. I guess I should have expected that. By the last bell, the rumor that spread like wildfire was completely extinguished. That didn't mean it was over for me, though. Ever would come for his pound of flesh, and I'd be waiting.

I think it was safe to say we were no longer dancing around each other. Ever and I had locked horns.

"Do you think you'll be okay?" Tyra said as she parked next to Ever's Range Rover in the driveway.

I nodded, but she was too busy ogling McNamara manor to notice.

"I'll be fine. What's he going to do, kill me?" I'd meant to lighten the mood and ease her worry, but Tyra's frown only deepened.

"Just be careful, okay?"

I assured her I would because she seemed to need it. I damn sure wasn't afraid of that pompous prick. We had exchanged numbers hours before, so I promised to call her later before I headed inside.

"Oh, there you are," Rosalyn greeted. "Ever said you made a friend and caught a ride with her instead." I was getting sick of that cunning bastard's web of lies. "I'm so happy for you." Most mothers would hug their daughter at hearing the news, but Rosalyn and I weren't most mothers and daughters. Rather than a warm hug she offered a wavering smile. "I suppose I don't need to ask how your first day went."

"Uneventful," I lied. "Headmaster Burns said I have to wear the tie."

"Honey, I have to be honest. I was shocked that you even wore the skirt."

"Yeah, well, it was the lesser of two evils." There was no way in hell I'd wear the dress. The dorky pants were even worse. I used the excuse of homework to escape upstairs before she could ask more questions. Homework assigned on the first day was a tradition I was unfamiliar with, but I wasn't surprised. Brynwood's sole mission was to prepare their pupils for the finest universities.

And with Ever declaring war, I welcomed the distraction.

My room would be my safe haven until I figured out how to deal with him.

A couple of hours later, I closed my textbook. The work had been challenging but not too grueling. I stood, stretched, and considered a shower before dinner. Thomas had come up an hour ago and announced that we'd all be having dinner together.

I could hardly wait.

After my shower, I threw on a pair of cotton shorts and a tank and then followed the flavorful smells into the dining room. Thomas and Rosalyn were already seated, as was Ever, who slouched in his seat, his attention completely fixed on his phone.

"There you are," Rosalyn greeted, drawing Ever's gaze. "I was just about to send someone up for you."

I found it hard for some reason to focus on anything but Ever. He looked rather smug about it as he slid his phone into his pocket and sat up. He'd taken off the sweater but kept on the rest of his uniform.

Thomas sat at the head of the table with his hands steepled, and Rosalyn sat at the other end clutching her glass of water. My place was set in the middle…directly across from Ever. Moments after I took my seat, someone appeared with my plate and a glass of water. I was eagerly slicing my steak when Thomas turned to me.

"So how was your first day at Brynwood?"

I paused and thought my answer over. "It was…interesting."

"Interesting? How so?"

"The atmosphere was different." Brynwood had privilege written all over it, making my old high school seem like a jungle in comparison. The teachers were far more innovative, and even the student's engagement exceeded the norm. Thomas was waiting for me to explain, but I didn't want to admit that it had been intimidating, especially with his son as a witness, so I said, "It was nice not having to share a textbook."

"Everything you'll need was taken care of in your tuition. I saw your transcripts. You're a smart girl. Money shouldn't impede your education."

I wasn't moved by his attempt to win my affection with fine things, but I was also playing a game with his son that I had every intention of winning, so I flashed a darling smile and thanked Thomas for his generosity. Rosalyn beamed proudly from her end of the table while Ever watched me through narrowed eyes.

"I also learned something interesting about Ever."

"Oh?" Thomas' gaze flitted to his son, but Ever's mask had already slipped into place.

"Yes." I took a sip of my water for suspense. "He has quite a few admirers. Everyone seems to look to him at Brynwood. They care about what he thinks and does."

"Ah." Thomas's nervous chuckle made me wonder if he knew all along that his son was an asshole. "Well, he did make the winning touchdown at the junior varsity championship last year and Ever has always had a leading personality. It doesn't surprise me that the other kids look up to him."

Thomas was beaming with pride for his son, and if I wanted, I could disgrace his little prince. *Maybe he'd back off if I showed him I could fight just as dirty.* I'd never survive here if I didn't. Even now, I was the one playing defense.

"Ever, I can't imagine what it's like to be you." I bat my eyes for good measure, but to his credit, he didn't react. *What a robot.* "I just hope you don't abuse it. A lesser person in your position could make it easy for someone to feel isolated and... undesirable."

Ever played his part with a charming smile, but the storm in his eyes warned me to turn back now. "If you ever feel unwanted, I'm sure there are ways I can fix that."

I didn't miss the veiled threat even though it went completely over our parents' head. "I'm a big girl. I'll manage."

Thick lips twitched with humor.

"We'll see."

chapter six

the Puppet

Ever's party was the hot topic at Brynwood the next day, and everyone seemed to have forgotten about the rumor I'd started. Since I lived with the host, I couldn't exactly be uninvited, but when I learned that Thomas and Rosalyn would be spending the night on his boat, I called Tyra.

"Sorry, Four. I can't hang out tonight. One of the girls called in sick, so it looks like I'm stuck here until midnight."

After hanging up with Tyra, I growled and ran my fingers through my hair. Ever had brought home the entire football team, and they were currently downstairs pregaming and setting up. If I couldn't get out of the house, I would be stuck hiding in my room all night.

Wincing, I began to consider attending his stupid party. Hiding like a social pariah was exactly what Ever would want. But what if I showed that rich prick that he wasn't getting to me?

Feeling wicked, I threw on the oil-stained overalls I wore when working at Gruff's shop and my most threadbare pair of Converse.

He wants a hick? I'll show him a hick.

Deciding I'd be fashionably late also gave me time to work up the courage to crash his party. I passed the time by studying, and when the music became deafening, I closed my textbook and finally made my way downstairs.

I was put off by the number of people crowding the house

and was tempted to turn and run, but my getup had already earned a few stares, so I made my way to the booze. They had turned the formal dining table, which could easily sit ten, into a bar with bottles, discarded solo cups, and shot glasses filling almost every inch of the surface. Ever was nowhere to be found when I grabbed a bottle of Jameson and forced my way into the overflowing living room. The furniture was pushed against the wall, turning the formal space into a dance floor.

It wasn't my scene, so I pushed my way into the less crowded yet smoke-filled billiards room. I found the room mostly occupied by guys, and I considered moving on until I spotted two familiar faces playing pool. Stacked on the wooden rail closest to Ben was a wad of cash, and Drake wore a sour expression as he lined up the balls. I stood back to watch them play, and five minutes in, I realized that Drake was stunningly poor at pool. Lucky for him, I wasn't so bad. I waited until the round was over before tapping him on his shoulder. He paused from hurling insults at his friend to look over his shoulder. I waited for him to recognize me, which, thanks to all the weed, took longer than normal.

He whooped and pulled me into a bear hug without warning. "Was wondering when I'd see you again!" He then twirled me around once before setting me on my feet.

"Almost thought you didn't remember me."

"Nah," he said with a wave of his hand. "I always remember the hot ones." He lazily scanned my oil-stained coveralls. "And you look damn hot in this get up. Got to love a dirty girl."

This guy. I rolled my eyes but couldn't hold back my grin. I was quickly learning that Drake had no shame.

He noticed the bottle in my hand and quirked a brow. "What are you going to do with that, girl?"

I simply smirked and said, *"Sine Metu,"* before downing two shots worth in one swallow.

Drake whooped and hollered again and patted my back when I coughed. I'd been drinking since Gruff caught me in his stash when I was twelve, so I recovered quickly and offered the bottle to Drake, who downed two shots worth and handed it to Ben.

"So," I said as I nodded toward the pool table. "You suck."

"Nah, Ben's just a cheating shit."

Ben flipped Drake off as he downed a shot worth of Jameson and plunked the bottle onto the rail.

"How about I win some of your cash back?"

Both of their brows rose at my offer. "You any good?" Drake asked skeptically. I was beginning to wonder about the girls they bred in Blackwood Keep since I was pretty sure some of them responded to this chauvinistic crap with open legs.

"Better than you," I sassed.

Drake wore a shit-eating grin as he rubbed his hands together. "All right then. Saddle up, Four!"

I glanced at Ben, who still didn't look convinced. With a shrug, he began racking the balls, so I walked over to the rack of cue sticks. I was contemplating my choices when the doors to the billiards room slid open.

I felt the air in the room shift, and a tingle work its way down my spine. My back was to the room, so I couldn't see who had entered, but given the way heat bloomed in my belly, I didn't have to.

"Well, if it isn't Brynwood's most wanted," Drake greeted. I heard the guys slapping hands and the door shutting behind them. "You're just in time. My future girlfriend is about to kick Ben's cheating ass at pool."

"Girlfriend?" Vaughn scoffed. "Who the hell would be desperate enough to go out with your junkie ass?"

Please don't say me. Please don't say me.

"Aw, man, you just wish you had my charisma, and she's right there."

Feeling all eyes on me, I sucked in air before blindly selecting one of the pool sticks and turning to face the room.

Vaughn's eyebrows rose while Ever lazily looked me over.

When he found the pool stick in my hand, however, the bored look fled, and he was suddenly very alert. I pretended the change didn't intrigue me and walked over to the bottle of Jameson, saluted the pair, and took a swig. There was no way in hell I'd get through this now without the liquid courage.

After swiping chalk on the tip of the pool stick, I tested it, earning a whistle at my bent position. I ignored the feeling of their eyes on my ass as I practiced my stroke. The cue stick was all wrong, but it would have to do. My legs felt too weak to do more than stand.

When it came time to break the balls, Ben said, "Ladies first," with unchecked smugness.

I didn't waste time lining up and breaking the balls before quickly sinking a solid. I didn't bother to watch Ben's face as I sunk a second. After sinking a third, however, Ever moved into my peripheral, and when I realized my only possible shot meant getting close to him, my palms turned sweaty as I moved around the table. He didn't give an inch when I positioned to line up the shot. I could feel him standing close, and if I shifted my leg back even an inch, he would be pressed against me. I chanced a look over my shoulder and saw that I didn't have his attention after all. He had his head turned, so I followed his gaze until I landed on Drake.

Even more surprising was Drake's obvious displeasure as he stared back at Ever. After another tense moment, however, his shoulders slumped, and he nodded.

What the hell was that about? Confused, I peeked over my shoulder again and found Ever watching me—*challenging* me. Someone cleared their throat, and I turned to refocus on the game. Ever didn't move away, and I missed the next shot. As I moved around the table to get away from Ever's heat, Ben eagerly took up position before sinking the next three shots, tying the game. I didn't look Ever's way as I plotted my next shot and lined up, but I could feel him watching me. Vaughn suddenly appeared next to me and plucked the bottle of Jameson from the table. He handed it to me.

"You look like you need it."

"I'm fine."

"Your hand is shaking," he pointed out with amusement. "Take a drink."

It wasn't a request.

My hand obediently wrapped around the bottle, and I took a short sip. I didn't want to get anymore tipsy than I already was. The whiskey did the trick, and I was back in position. I heard Vaughn guzzling down some of the whiskey before walking away with it. I watched out of the corner of my eye as he handed it off to someone. He spoke a few words, and the kid nodded before leaving with my bottle.

Well, fuck.

After the game, I had been planning to get trashed enough to fall asleep safely behind the locked door of my bedroom, blissfully unaware of his lordship. Now that plan was shot to shit.

I sunk the next two shots before missing the next. Ben missed his next shot and brooded as I sunk my last ball. There was only the eight-ball left, and it was a tricky one. The angle I needed brought me back to Ever's side of the table, but thankfully, I didn't need to be as close. A few unknowns voiced encouragement, but I ignored them all as I lined up my cue stick. In the next breath, I sunk the fucking eight ball.

Drake, seemingly forgetting his disappointment, shouted before picking me up and twirling me around until I was ready to puke. I warned him, and he immediately set me back on my feet. When I kissed his cheek, he shot Ever a glance before quickly walking away to collect his cash. Just as quickly, Drake was back with his arm wrapped around my shoulder. Unable to tear my gaze away from Ever, the wad of cash Drake offered me went ignored. Vaughn was now speaking low to Ever, but all of his attention seemed focused on me as he scowled. It made me wonder where his girlfriend might be and why he wasn't ruining her night with his foul mood.

"You up for another game, Four? Ben thinks he can win back his cash." I forced myself to look away and pocketed my half of the cash.

"I'm out. I have a date with a bottle of Jameson and a good night's sleep."

He groaned and tried harder to convince me, but I pried myself away and got out of dodge.

The house was even more crowded than before, and most of the party had shed their inhibitions. I passed more than one topless guest on my way to the dining room. After reuniting with the whiskey, I headed for the main stairs, but then the music cut and multiple cell phones started going off. Suddenly everyone seemed to move at once, and I was being pushed and herded in the opposite direction. When we reached the stairs that led below ground, I had no choice but to follow or be trampled.

We ended up in the theater room, which couldn't accommodate everyone, so some of them lingered in the hall or went back to the party. The large screen was blue, and I was wondering whose bright idea it was to play a movie at a house party when I recognized the guy bent over his laptop as the mohawk—one of Ever's lackeys.

"Good evening, ladies and gentlemen. If you haven't heard, this is an auction, so take your wallets out and get ready to bid."

"An auction for what," a guy from the crowd shouted.

"I'm glad you asked, cupcake." The mohawk tapped a few buttons, and my heart plummeted to my stomach as a racy picture of Rosalyn appeared on the screen. My fists balled at my sides as I listened to the increasingly vulgar comments from a few guys. I pushed through the crowd until I was standing in front of the mohawk.

"What the hell do you think you're doing?" *How did they even get this?*

He seemed even more amused when he noticed me standing there. "Well, if it isn't the lady of the night! Good people of Brynwood, if you didn't know, Ever McNamara has a new sister, and she's been feeling pretty undesirable, so this auction is just for her. Found in the swamps of Virginia, her fuck-hot mother went for the low price of nineteen thousand a year to one of the *richest* men in America!" That bit of news earned a few snickers from the crowd. "This model before you, ladies and gentlemen, is newer and my guess is she doesn't have as many miles, so I'll start the bidding at nineteen thousand and one."

"I'll take her," someone shouted.

My breaths came hard and fast as bid after bid was shouted. The room became a blur. My ears rang. The blood in my veins boiled. I hadn't realized I was moving until the mohawk was falling and the last of the broken bottle of Jameson fell from my hand.

No, no, no! What did I do?

The pounding of my heart drowned out the sound of their gasps and curses, but I could feel their gaping stares. And worst of all my tears didn't fall until I turned and saw Ever standing there.

"Jesus, fuck," Vaughn whispered as he stared wide-eyed at his friend passed out on the floor. Ever, however, only had eyes for me. I could only cry harder when I saw the regret on his face. *He did this.* A whimper escaped my throat before I pushed past him and ran from the room.

I furiously dumped my backpack before stuffing some clothes and all the cash I had inside. Fuck the game and fuck Ever. If Rosalyn wanted these people, she could have them. I was *done.* All I needed was a car.

I rushed through the bathroom and found my first fortune of the night. The door leading to Ever's room was unlocked. I used the light from the bathroom to search his room and found what I needed on his nightstand. I didn't stop to consider if the grand theft of a ninety-thousand-dollar car would only make matters worse. Snagging the keys, I rushed back through the bathroom and didn't bother looking back. The only thing I'd regret leaving behind were my helmets I'd worked so hard to collect, but they were just things, and at least I'd be leaving a part of me behind for Rosalyn. *If she even wanted it.*

The hush as I descended the stairs unnerved me. People talked and whispered amongst themselves as they poured from the house. No one noticed me slip into the garage. I hopped in the Range, and with a pocket full of cash, I left Blackwood Keep and swore to never look back.

chapter seven

the Puppet

FOUND THAT I MISSED THE SMELL MOST OF ALL. IT SMELLED LIKE HOME. I caught the rag Gruff threw me, and I wiped the oil from my hands.

"You ready to tell me why you're back in Cherry?"

"I told you. I was homesick."

"Showing up on my doorstep first thing in a fancy truck that ain't yours and a sad little backpack tells me you left in a hurry. Then there's the river I heard you crying in my spare this morning."

I sighed, knowing he wouldn't let it go until I gave him answers. "Blackwood Keep chewed me up and spat me out. I can't go back."

Gruff shook his head in disappointment. "You know you can't face your problems running away."

"I don't want to face them. I want to forget them."

"That's coward's talk," he spat.

Little did he know that I was okay with being a coward if it meant not having to face Ever again.

The next morning, I arrived at the shop and found Thomas having coffee with Gruff.

He took one look at me and said, "It's time to come home, Four."

"I am home," I retorted with my arms crossed.

"You don't think you're being a little selfish? Your mother is worried sick."

"Then why isn't she here?"

"She's been ordered to stay in bed. My doctor had to *sedate* her when I told her you ran away."

"I—I didn't mean to—to…" I let the words die and sighed. It didn't matter. I wasn't going back.

"Why did you run?"

"You should ask your son." I tried to keep my voice level and failed when the vision of his friend bleeding from his skull flashed in my head.

"He's had his hands full. Apparently, Daniel Kim slipped and hit his head at the party." Thomas took a deep breath and exhaled. "What did Ever do?"

I didn't know how to answer that since Ever hadn't ratted me out to our parents. It didn't mean I owed him a damn thing, but if he decided to talk, I wouldn't just have Thomas and Rosalyn to deal with.

"Nothing. I just saw an opportunity and took it."

"You're saying that kid needing a few stitches isn't the reason you ran away?"

"Yes."

His eyes bore into me, searching for proof that I was lying. When I couldn't take his scrutiny any longer, I turned to Gruff for help, but there was only disappointment.

"Can you please tell him I'm okay here?"

Gruff closed his eyes tight as if in pain before shaking his head slowly. My arms fell to my side.

"Your mother needs you, girl, and if you got demons waiting for you, it's time you faced them."

I wanted to rail and scream at him for his betrayal but hadn't I done much worse? Besides, Gruff could get into heaps of trouble if I stayed, so I considered my options. If I became a runaway, my life would suck, and Ever would win. If I went back and faced him, the next two years could get *very* interesting.

I said goodbye to Gruff and returned to Blackwood Keep with Thomas, ready to do battle, but there was one thing I hadn't considered…

chapter eight

the Puppet

One Year Later

"OH LUCIFER. I'M GOING TO PUKE."

I glanced at my roommate's pale face. Becca had begged me to take her when she caught me sneaking out of bed, and it had been fun to have a wingman, but with less than five minutes until we'd be caught, I was beginning to regret it. Becca's stepmother had her sent here so she could jet set all over the globe, spending her dead husband's fortune.

"We just need to hop the fence." It didn't seem wise to mention the second-floor window we still had to climb through—we'd cross that bridge when we got there. We made it to the chain-linked fence, and I quickly climbed up twenty feet before scaling down and jumping the last few feet. The blue-eyed Texan was still slowly making her way up the other side when I glanced nervously at my watch.

Three minutes.

"Becca, not to be insensitive but light a fire, yeah?"

She groaned as she swung her leg over the fence. "Why did I let you talk me into this?"

"That's not quite how this happened," I said once she dropped down. I ran the last couple hundred feet to the rope of sheet dangling from the window, and she groaned some more as she followed me. "We just have to get through the window, and we're home free." I ignored the burning muscle in my arms as I climbed. It was nothing compared to the fear of another year here if I was caught.

At the top, I slid open the window and flung my leg over the sill just as I heard the sound of Becca's retching and footsteps approaching our door.

"Becca, someone's coming," I yelled down to her bent form. "Stay there." She didn't answer as another bout of retching rendered her speechless. I hastily pulled up the rope of sheets and shut the window before stuffing the sheets under Becca's blanket. I barely had enough time to make the shape look human and get into bed before one of the attendings stuck her head inside. I'd pulled my own blanket up to my chin and shut my eyes, but I could feel the light she shone on my face. The light quickly passed, and I chanced opening an eye to see her flashlight now lingering on the lump. A few seconds later, the door creaked shut, and I waited until her footsteps faded before rushing to the window.

"Are you okay?"

"I think so," she croaked.

I tied one end of the sheet around my bedpost before tossing it down.

"Fucking-A, Four! That was close." She was panting as she sprawled on the floor.

I didn't respond as I shed my leather jacket and peeled off black jeans before climbing back into bed.

Becca eventually picked herself up from the floor and mumbled something about never drinking again before dressing in her nightclothes and slipping into bed. "Thanks for tonight, Four, but if you don't mind, I think tonight will be the last of my adventures."

I chuckled, completely unsurprised that my prudent friend got her fill in one night. "I told you to slow down on the drinks."

"Yeah, but that cutie with the glasses kept giving them to me so he could see my panties."

"For sure," I mumbled.

It wasn't long before her drunken snores filled the silence. Sleep didn't come as easily for me. Instead, I stared at the ceiling and wondered if I could survive another year in exile. I never believed in a million years that she'd go through with it—not when she took me to apply for a passport and not even when she had my things packed, but just days before my seventeenth birthday, Rosalyn sent me away.

Every phone call from home had gone ignored, and her letters remained unopened. When Thomas and Rosalyn showed up for Christmas, I refused to see them, and they hadn't forced me. Up until a month ago, Rosalyn never gave up trying to get through to me, and in return, I mourned the daughter she deserved. A tear slipped from my eye as I wondered what the other three would have been like.

Obedient

Beautiful.

Kind.

Fate had dealt Rosalyn a cruel hand when it chose me.

I had a hell of a time dragging myself out of bed the next morning. Becca, suffering her first hangover, was even worse off. We were making our way to the computer lab to print off the materials we needed for class since we weren't allowed personal laptops or cell phones. Even our social media and email accounts were suspended, not that I ever had one. We were completely cut off from the world as part of our 'rehabilitation.'

"Miss Archer." I turned to see Ms. Wendell, the head attending, quickly approaching until her thin frame towered over us. "Come," she ordered, her German accent thick. I held in my groan. Because of her fire-red hair that she always wore in a French bun and her ferocious disposition, everyone called her the dragon.

"Why?"

Thin lips pinched together at my violation, and Becca attempted and failed to hold in her giggle. Rule One: We are *never* to question or argue with an attending. The attending was an all-female staff who made up the teachers, the counselors, the cooks, and the nurses at Natasha Madison's School of Ladies.

"Mind your manners," she hissed. She then shifted her focus to Becca. "I suggest you move along, Miss Wilson, or that's five demerits."

Becca squeaked, fearing her pristine record would be smudged, and skirted off without a word. I wordlessly followed behind the attending. My palms became sweaty when I saw where we were headed—Madame Madison's office. No one ever saw the Madame unless they were in serious trouble.

"Wait here," Ms. Wendell ordered before disappearing into Madame Madison's office. Surprisingly, I had yet to see the inside of her office, but I imagined the walls were covered in blood, the floor with the skulls of her former students who couldn't be reformed, and if you listened hard enough, you would still hear the screams of her victims. "She will see you now."

I wondered if Madame Madison could smell fear.

The first thing I noticed when I trudged into her office was the floral wallpaper. A pristine white area rug covered most of the wooden floor. Music played softly from a speaker I couldn't see, and along one wall was a board filled with pictures of countless girls in the burgundy and gray uniform.

"Good morning, Miss Archer."

I looked at the woman behind the desk for the first time. The Madame had short blonde hair, warm blue eyes, and—I swallowed my laugh—a frilly pink shirt. She didn't look at all like a woman in the business of stealing souls. "Morning."

She stood from her desk, and I took in the black pencil skirt and high *high* heels. I imagined holding a wheelie for ten miles would be easier than walking ten feet in those things.

"I apologize for the disruption in your day, but I have news from home."

My amusement fled. If Thomas and Rosalyn were reaching out through Madame Madison, then it couldn't have been good news.

"Did something happen?" I braced myself for the news that Rosalyn had ran off yet another beau. Just when I began to think Thomas was different after all…

"No, dear. Your mother and father are fine." I started to tell her that Thomas wasn't my father when she dropped the bomb. "You're going home."

I straightened at the news. "I'm what?"

"It appears that your parents are no longer in need of my services and have made arrangements for your return."

"When?" I choked out.

"Tomorrow." She leaned against her desk and linked her fingers together. "It was strongly recommended that you stay with us as none of your direct supervisors believe that you have been reformed." She assessed me with kind eyes. "Do you feel you are truly ready to return home, Miss Archer?"

My eyebrow arched. "Does it matter what I think?"

"I'm sure if your parents knew you weren't ready to return, they would reconsider. I could petition for you to stay, but I need to know you want to change."

I bit my lip before giving a sharp shake of my head. "I can't give you that, Madame Madison."

"And why is that?"

"I have a score to settle."

chapter nine

the Puppet

T HE FOLLOWING EVENING, I WAS GREETED WITH A KIND SMILE AND A kiss on the cheek from Mrs. Greene. I stood in the empty foyer, waiting for the click of Rosalyn's heels, but the hush over the home was telling.

"Where is she?"

"Oh, your mother is very sorry she couldn't be here." She rubbed the back of my hand consolingly. "Their flight from California was delayed because of the storm." One of the maids called for her, so she patted my hand and said, "I'll just be a moment, and then I'll show you to your room." She hurried off before I could assure her that I remembered where it was.

Shrugging, I moved to the stairs. From the looks of it, absolutely nothing had changed. And when I passed by Ever's door, I kept my gaze straight ahead and lightened my steps. I pushed open my bedroom door, and rather than yellow that was too pale and white that was too pure, there was chaos.

Rumpled black bedding was hanging partway off the bed. One of the pillows had been tossed onto the floor while the other was crushed against the wall where a headboard should be. Hanging on the wall over the bed was the American flag and two others—a green, white, and orange vertically striped flag, and a white X-shaped cross on a field of blue. I tried to remember which country the flags belonged to, but geography wasn't my forte.

From the posters to the video games to the crumbled pile

of dirty clothes by the bed, my room had been taken over. On one wall were four guitars—two Stratocasters, a Firebird, and a Fender Jaguar. Surrounding them hung records, some in the album slips and some bare. I wanted to run my fingers over the polished wood and found myself taking a step when a deep voice stopped me.

"Curiosity will get you in trouble, kitten."

It was the unusual accent that had me spinning on my heel. I was tongue-tied as I drank in the sight of a bare chest, abs, and arms that had been used as a canvas stretching all the way up his neck. I couldn't tell how far the tattoos dipped below the waistband of his jeans, but his bare feet were free of ink. Mahogany hair dripped water onto his chest as dark eyes flecked with gold studied me.

"Does it speak?" he taunted when I remained silent.

"You sound funny."

His head tilted, and the light caught the diamond piercing his right nostril. "I could say the same."

I shrugged and said, "I'm from Virginia."

"You sound like you're from Alabama."

"And you keep forgetting the r."

"That's Beantown, baby."

"Go Red Sox."

He chuckled, breaking the ice, as he unwrapped his towel from his neck and tossed it on the messy bed.

"So, is your mom dating Thomas, too?"

"Not really." His smile, if possible, made him even more gorgeous. "She's his sister."

I took my foot out of my mouth to apologize and got a wink for my trouble. I felt the blush creeping down my cheeks and changed the subject. "How old are you?"

"Maybe you should start with my name," he mocked as he pulled a black T-shirt from his dresser and slipped it on.

"Right...what's your name?"

"Jameson," he supplied as he swiped a pair of black socks from the floor and sniffed them before tugging them on. "Call me Jamie, though."

"All right, Jamie. I'm Four." I offered my fist for him to bump. It was a test. Ever would never bump my fist. His eyes darted from me to my fist, and with a shake of his head—as if he guessed my motives—he bumped his much larger fist against mine. "You sure you're a McNamara?"

"It's Buchanan, actually—Dad was a Scot." There was a flicker of pain in his eyes, but before I could offer my condolences, he said, "You're not at all what I expected."

I wasn't sure I wanted to know what that pompous prick said about me, but I asked anyway. "What were you expecting?"

"Some snaggletooth inbred who could barely put a sentence together."

I'm going to kill him.

"Come now, don't be subtle. I'm sure your cousin had a lot more to say about me."

"Actually, he barely mentioned you."

I felt like I'd been kicked. "You don't need to lie for him. He's done a lot worse." It was unfair that while I'd been pining for revenge, he'd barely thought of me at all.

Jamie eyed me. "Don't take offense, lass. That's just who Ever is."

"And who might I be?"

A chill swept my skin leaving goose bumps in its wake, and I desperately tried to recall the pep talk I gave myself on the plane.

This time would be different.

I'd be smarter and quicker than I was a year ago.

I wouldn't cower in his presence.

Taking a deep breath, I faced the tall, athletic frame filling the doorway.

"A cold bastard," Jamie answered with a grin.

"I wondered what was keeping you," Ever mused with his eyes on me. "Now I see." The bite in his tone was unmistakable. All that was missing was his sneer, but Ever McNamara was much too poised for that.

"Unwad your knickers, cousin. I found Four here snooping around. Thought I'd have a little chat."

Slowly, Ever's gaze drifted lower.

My breasts were fuller now, and his lingering scrutiny made it clear he noticed. Reluctantly, he moved on to peruse my taut stomach and the subtle curve of my hips and thighs.

It was impossible not to notice his own changes. He stood at least an inch taller, and there were dips, bulges, and hard planes beneath the white button-up and blue jeans that hadn't been there a year ago. I didn't think it was possible for Ever McNamara to be...more.

"It seems *some* things haven't changed," he said as he leaned a shoulder on the jamb.

"Sorry to disappoint you," I muttered even though I wasn't in the least.

"I'd have to care." His attention shifted to Jamie. "Let's go."

I'd been dismissed.

Jamie started for the door, but then he stopped with a mischievous grin. "A buddy is throwing a thing before school starts. You riding?"

Ever took the liberty of turning down his offer before I could. "She stays."

"Four?" Jamie pushed, completely ignoring his cousin. It was refreshing to know at least one person in Blackwood Keep wasn't afraid of Ever.

"Thanks, but no thanks. I think I'm just going to crash."

Jamie looked disappointed, but he didn't bother arguing.

I followed them from the room just as Mrs. Greene appeared.

"There you are! I meant to tell you that Mr. McNamara had

you moved into another bedroom. I hope those boys didn't give you any trouble."

The boys in question peeked over their shoulder.

"They were perfect gentlemen," I lied and caught Jamie's grin just before they rounded the corner.

"Oh, good! Let's get you settled."

chapter ten

The Peer

"**M**AKE WAY FOR YOUR KING!" SOMEONE SHOUTED OVER THE music. The horde of sycophants parted, and I hid my cringe as I moved through the swaying figures. I suppose I deserved the position. I definitely earned it.

Translation: *I've been a supreme dick.*

"King, huh?" Jamie questioned with a lift of his brow. "You've been busy." Girls called Jamie's name and grabbed at his shirt while he bumped fists with a few guys from the basketball team. I took advantage of his sudden distraction and ditched him in the crowd. Jamie would pry, and I didn't care to explain myself. I never do.

Vaughn, my right hand and enabler, descended the stairs and clapped my shoulder. "Thought you weren't coming."

"I wasn't, but my father is full of surprises." Vaughn sipped from his cup and waited for me to elaborate. "Archer's back."

"Shit, man. Thought we got rid of her for good."

"So did I, but she's like a fucking cockroach." Getting rid of the grease monkey had been more than just amusing. It had been necessary. Four Archer was a constant reminder of a past that needed to stay buried, and if I wasn't careful she'd be the chink in my chain.

"Only because you were holding back." Vaughn eyed me knowingly.

I shrugged as if Archer didn't plague my every waking thought. "She wasn't worth the effort."

"And now?"

"I've got other priorities." He knew that as well as I did, but the fucker was baiting me. "I'm done with her as long as she remembers her place."

"And when the wedding bells ring?"

My nostrils flared at the thought of Thomas marrying the social climber. While she hadn't turned out to be an evil bitch—my father would have seen through her two years ago if she were—I knew something about Rosalyn Archer was off. So I did some digging.

"That will never happen." After the dirt I had found, I'd make sure it never got that far, but my father could have his fun for now.

Amusement lightened his eyes. "Your father marrying may be something even *you* can't stop."

My lip curled at the challenge. "Wanna bet?"

"Her mom may be a docile thing, but Four is a different breed. She'll go down fighting."

I pretended my heart wasn't racing at the promise of Four's challenge. She'd only end up the spoils of the war she waged and damn if that didn't get my cock hard. "She gets in my way again, I won't hold back. Her year in reform school will feel like a day at the spa."

"What are you girls whispering about?" Jamie was sweating, no doubt from dancing with the endless line of willing girls.

"Your mother," Vaughn retorted.

Jamie shoved him before cracking a smile. "She's too much woman for you."

"I'll be the judge of that," Vaughn retorted smoothly. "So, you've met the new stepsister?"

"She's not my stepsister," I barked and then gritted my teeth for playing into his hands.

They simply smirked at each other while ignoring me. "I did." Jamie snickered. "That chip she's carrying around is even bigger than his."

Vaughn nodded with a gleam in his eye. "This should be fun."

The crowd parted, and there was only one person besides us who could part this sea of drunks. Vaughn immediately refocused on drinking, and Jamie stiffened beside me.

Fuck, not now.

But it was too late. The strawberry blonde stood in front of me. She wore a pink miniskirt with a sheer floor-length wrap, black crisscrossed strappy heels, tight white T-shirt, and a black bomber jacket. She wrapped her toned arms around my neck, and I dutifully slipped mine around her small waist.

"What are you doing here?" I whispered in her ear.

"Same as you, I suppose." She pulled away and avoided my gaze.

"Bee." I spoke her childhood nickname as a warning. She hated Barbie even more than she did her given name, Barbette.

"It's fine." Her button nose scrunched. "*I'm* fine," she corrected.

I sighed and let it drop because she was even more stubborn than I was. Jamie stole her attention anyway when she noticed him *conveniently* flirting with a pair of blondes. I pinched the bridge of my nose, knowing what would occur next.

"No need, girls. That one's already infected." Her glossy lips spread into a smile as Vaughn draped his arm over Barbette's shoulder.

"You're a cold bitch, you know that?"

She planted her hands on slender hips. "Just doing my civic duty."

Jamie patted the blondes on the butt and sent them on their way. They'd find him later if he didn't run into something better before then. When he smoothly stepped into Barbette's personal space, Vaughn stepped away, and I swore. Of course, Barbette didn't back down. In those heels, she matched Jamie's six feet two while standing so close their lips almost touched.

"For all the shamming you do, you suck at pretending it's

not my dick you really want. Tighten your shit up, Bee…or is it Barbie now?"

"Do you really believe I'd lie with filth?"

"Why not?" Bitter eyes trailed her body. "You used to love it."

"You're an animal."

Jamie's smile was lascivious. "In every way, baby."

I'd heard enough.

"Jamie, go get yourself a drink." From his profile, I had a clear view of his jaw clenching.

"You don't order me."

"I can make you, but that would be embarrassing for you."

He didn't flee like most. Jamie shifted and spread his arms as if to say I was welcome to try. I knew from all the fights we'd had when we were kids that it would be a long and bloody one.

"No, that's okay," Barbette stammered while stepping back. "I was just leaving."

"Yeah, you do that." Jamie's gaze followed her as she fled.

"Man," Vaughn drawled, "you should just fuck her and get it out of your system."

"Nah…" Jamie threw me a withering look. "I don't want his leftovers."

I started to point out that he'd had plenty of my leftovers since returning from Scotland, but he shoved past me and disappeared into the crowd.

Vaughn ran his fingers through his brown locks. "Remind me again why dating Bee is worth all that? You and I both know you don't want her."

I snatched a half-empty bottle of vodka from the hand of a passing classmate and sent him running with a look when he started to protest. It's been a while since I've indulged but with Four back in town and the constant refereeing between Bee and Jamie, I had every intention of getting hammered until nothing mattered.

"Because it pisses him off."

chapter eleven

∞

The Puppet

'VE HEARD THAT ABSENCE MAKES THE HEART GROW FONDER, BUT WHAT did those guys know? Thomas seemed relieved when he thanked me—actually *thanked* me—for coming back while Rosalyn acted as if I'd been returning from vacation.

"How was your time in Europe, dear?"

"Rehabilitating."

It was now the morning of my senior year. My uniform was freshly pressed, and the black patent leather slippers were shined. It wouldn't be enough for me to blend in, not after what I did to Daniel Kim, but it would have to do. I was pulling my hair into a ponytail when a knock on my door interrupted me. I stood motionless in the middle of my bedroom, contemplating the presence on the other side. After yesterday, I wasn't expecting Rosalyn to see me off to school, and Thomas was usually at the office before breakfast.

That left me with two possibilities, neither of them desirable.

Maybe I could sneak out the window…

"I know you're in there," a masculine voice called out. "I can hear you plotting."

Jamie.

The lesser of two evils.

I snatched open the door and found him with his arms crossed over his chest as his lean frame rested against the doorjamb. I waited for him to speak, but he was too busy staring at my bare legs.

"Can I help you?"

Picking up on my chilly reception, he said, "Not a morning person, eh?"

"It's not the hour that bothers me," I hinted.

"Relax, kitten." He held out long arms, clad in a crisp white dress shirt, in surrender. "I come in peace."

The red vest he'd chosen paired well with his mahogany hair while the black slacks hugged his toned legs even better. I would have told him he looked nice, but his ego was bigger than Kanye West. Besides, he may not be a snob like his cousin, but he'd probably still have his back when it counted.

"Let me guess…you're the good guy?"

He answered with a sharp shake of his head. "Never," he added with a grin. "But I did come to offer you a ride to school."

Thomas didn't bother dictating the arrangements as he did a year ago. Had he expected us to pick up where we'd left off?

"Why would you help me?"

"Why not? You do something to me?"

"You're Ever's cousin." Was I the only one aware of the line drawn between us?

"And?"

I let down my guard enough to smile. Someone who didn't fall over themselves to please Ever McNamara was exactly what I needed. I held up my finger so he'd wait and ducked back inside to grab my backpack.

"Good girl," he praised.

"You do know that I'm not a dog, right?"

He laughed as he practically leapt down the stairs, leaving me behind. When I passed through the doors leading outside, the first thing I noticed was Ever leaning casually against the Range. He was busy texting on a phone years ahead of mine, which still flipped.

My heart skipped a beat. It was a warning that I'd admired him for too long. Ever's allure was rare, eclipsing everything around him. The temptation was blinding. Common sense withered in his presence.

The wind blew, tousling his hair, and my heart skipped again.

Freeing myself from his snare, I surveyed the large circular drive. Ever's was the only vehicle in sight, and Jamie was heading straight for it.

I hovered over the first step unsure of what to do.

Ever had yet to notice me.

I still had time to slip back inside the house.

But my chance to pretend I was never there was taken when Jamie obnoxiously yelled from the passenger window, "You coming or what? Those fine legs won't get you to school on time!"

I gritted my teeth just as Ever's head popped up.

His eyes flashed with surprise, but then his mask was back in place before I could reach the last step. Standing up straight, he stuck his phone in his pocket and smoothly slid into the driver's seat. Realizing Jamie had trapped us both, I sighed and hopped inside the car.

"Told you she'd come," Jamie gloated.

They actually discussed this?

Ever simply turned up the volume, and Seether drowned out most of Jamie's yammering. I'd chosen to sit behind Jamie and couldn't keep from stealing glances at His Majesty.

His neck was strong without being bulky, his jaw angular, lips full above a cleft chin, and a nose that was perfectly straight.

Maybe that's why he keeps it so high in the air.

Admiring the stylish cut of his two-toned hair, I failed to notice we'd stopped at a sign until his head turned just enough for him to catch me staring. It was too late to look away and pretend. His eyes were completely hidden by the dark tinted sunglasses, but somehow, I knew they raked me as I'd done him...*his* exploration felt much more invasive.

Only when he had his fill did he turn back without a word and let off the brake. Ten minutes later, I was out of the Range and practically running for the entrance before he could cut the engine.

I could feel the cousins' attention the entire way.

With my head down, I headed straight for the headmaster's office and almost made it undetected when I felt fingers gently curl around my bicep. Feminine squeals filled my ear as I was pulled into a hug.

"I can't believe it's really you!"

I quickly returned Tyra's hug before she could rupture my eardrum. Other than the bangs that now covered her forehead, she hadn't changed much.

"How's it going?" I kept it casual even though I was excited to see her. After what I had done to one of their own, it didn't seem wise to bring attention to myself. I was a little surprised there hadn't been a mob waiting at the gates.

"I should be asking you. You're the one who disappeared for an entire year without a word."

God, I didn't want to talk about that. "I'd fill you in," I lied, "but I have an appointment with Burns."

"Are you sticking around this time? I'm almost afraid to let you out of my sight. One minute you were here and"—she snaps her fingers—"the next you were gone."

"I can promise I won't disappear before lunch." I promised to meet up later before racing to the headmaster's office with eyes firmly cast on the freshly waxed floors. The halls were filling quickly, and I couldn't chance anyone else recognizing me. Since I was a former student, I was hoping to skip the counseling and just pick up my class schedule, but that wasn't meant to be. Burns wasn't nearly as welcoming as he'd been the year before. After a stern warning that violence against fellow students wouldn't be tolerated, he relinquished my class schedule, and I was on my way.

My schedule was mostly electives since I completed most of the required courses for graduating and had no plans of attending college. It would be straight to the pros for me. I could have been competing legitimately years ago, but Rosalyn had withheld her consent. I could feel the resentment seeping from my pores, so I took a deep breath. In a month, I'd be eighteen, and then only my consent would matter.

When I walked into my third class of the day, 20th Century American Women's History, it wasn't surprising that the entire class was female. I was the last to arrive, so I sunk into the only empty chair, and the teacher, a petite redhead with pale skin, began handing out the syllabus and questionnaire.

Mrs. Roberts had her back turned, so I took the opportunity to look around. Everyone seemed to be engrossed in the forms or each other, but that nagging feeling of being in someone's crosshairs remained.

No longer covert, I twisted my body, and that was when I saw her. Even if it hadn't been for her drilling a hole in my forehead, I would have noticed the strawberry blonde with ivory skin, blue eyes, and pouty lips. She was breathtaking.

Until now, I hadn't suffered any lingering scrutiny. This chick looked as if I spit in her cornflakes.

Don't be silly, Four. She doesn't eat carbs.

The girl finally broke her stare when the teacher asked us to pass up our questionnaire. I quickly scribbled in the rest of my answers and forced my focus on the teacher for the rest of the hour. I was sure I'd learn who the bombshell was eventually.

"How is your first day back?" Tyra cheerily greeted as I grabbed an apple and stuck it on my tray. I'd forgotten to text her like I promised, but she didn't seem to mind as she grabbed food and followed me to an empty table.

"Better than I expected. No one seems to care I exist." *It was perfect.*

Her lips parted. "You haven't heard?"

My laugh was dry as I shook my head. "You're the only one here who talks to me. Why would I hear anything?"

She leaned forward and for all my claims of not caring, I leaned forward, too. "You weren't the only one to return to Blackwood Keep. Jason's back."

"Okay…who's Jason?"

"He was Ever's archenemy before you came along." Her lips pursed as she looked me up and down. "Although I don't know how much of an enemy you could be if he's giving you rides to school…"

I waved her off even though my belly did cartwheels at the memory of how he'd looked at me. "I'm sure he didn't have a choice." Before she could pry, I changed the subject. "Why do they hate each other?"

"Remember the girl I told you who took Ever's virginity and then became totally obsessed with him—Olivia Portland?"

How could I forget? "Sure."

"Well, she's Jason's sister."

"So, Jason hates Ever for screwing his sister? Were they friends or something?"

"I may have given you the watered-down version. It was your first day, and I didn't want my first real friend running for the hills."

I was definitely a flight risk, but it had nothing to do with who Ever screwed in the past. "What *really* happened?"

"No one knew how bad she had it until she walked into the boy's locker room and tried to slit her wrist in front of him."

The carton of milk I had in my hand slipped and spilled all over the table. Tyra cursed and hurriedly grabbed napkins. For once, I didn't care about the stares.

"Shit! I'm sorry."

"See? This is why I didn't want to tell you." She huffed as she threw more napkins over the spill.

"I'm fine. It's cool." *It was so not fucking cool.* I helped her clean up my mess and took a deep breath. "What happened to her?"

Tyra's skeptical look turned resigned when I squeezed her hand. "All I know is that she lived, but her family was too embarrassed to stay in Blackwood Keep."

"Why do you think they came back?"

"A diploma from Brynwood opens ivy league doors and pretty much any door you want. If I had to guess, I'd say that was the reason."

"And Olivia?"

"Probably in psychiatric care."

That poor girl. I scoffed and shook my head. "Hard to believe he's who everyone chose to idolize."

"High school is a mind fuck for us all," Tyra muttered. "Although it's not like he asked for her to go all fatal attraction on him. She knew he had a girlfriend."

My skin heated, and I looked away. Knowing he had a girlfriend and hearing about Olivia's undoing didn't stop me from wondering what it would be like in Ever's bed.

The admission nearly knocked me off my feet.

I've never denied that Ever was hot—beautiful really—but now I also knew why there was a burning ache in my belly every time he was near.

Was I the next Olivia Portland?

"Doesn't change the fact that he's a dick."

"Ever's running things because he makes it possible for people to be accepted. The kids whose parents aren't doctors, lawyers, or millionaires walk these halls with their heads high because of him. And no one gets stuffed in their lockers for being gay or captain of the chess club."

"And the undesirable?"

"Your first day was the first time anyone's said it since he took over."

"I guess I just bring out the best in him," I mocked.

"He's not so bad. Stay out of his way, and he won't even notice you're here."

Yeah…easier said than done.

I forgot to respond when the girl from Women's History walked by. My gaze followed her until she stopped at the crowded table in the center of the room. It was filled to the brim with bruisers in letterman jackets and girls with easy smiles. And reigning over them all was Ever.

Tyra peeked over her shoulder to see what had stolen my attention and then whispered, "That's her."

"Who?"

"Ever's girlfriend. Her name is actually Barbette, but everyone except for their inner circle calls her Barbie."

I watched her sink gracefully into the chair next to him, but then Jamie said something that made her stiffen. Ever gave him a look, but Jamie was already bored. He looked around the cafeteria, and when he caught me watching their exchange, he flashed his teeth and headed for the door.

Well, that was weird.

My attention shifted back to the middle of the room. Ever was taking a sip from his orange Gatorade and staring dead at me. Barbie touched his hand fisted on the table, and I was forgotten.

Typical privileged kid and his pretty things.

"Why?"

"Well, you've seen her," Tyra answered with an eye roll.

"I mean, why don't *they* call her Barbie?"

She shrugged as she frowned at her broccoli. "Ever and Vaughn call her Bee. I don't really know why, and if you ask me, I think Jamie has a thing for his cousin's girlfriend. He calls her Bette, and whenever he does, she either gets all gooey-eyed or she bares her claws. Everyone pretends not to notice."

This was starting to sound like an episode straight out of *The Young and the Restless.* "And Ever's okay with that?"

"I doubt he notices. He hasn't cared about much since his mother skipped town."

Finally.

The one missing piece to the puzzle.

"No one really knows if she's alive or dead," Tyra added while frowning at the middle table. "Ever hasn't been the same since." Her pensive tone suggested she was just now putting together the pieces herself.

Still, it was hard for me to imagine Ever as anything but severe. "How was he before?"

"A lot more fun to be around, that's for sure," a deeper voice answered. Jamie folded his long frame into the chair next to me and snagged my apple from my tray.

"What is it with you McNamaras and stealing food?" I tried to snatch it back, but he quickly bit into it.

"I'm not a McNamara," he retorted with a mouth full, making his Boston accent sound even weirder. "I'm a Buchanan."

"McNamara...Buchanan...shouldn't you be with the other snobs?" He was too busy making eyes at Tyra to answer. She tried to conceal the effect his staring had on her by rolling her eyes. "And can you stop eye-fucking my friend, please? She's not interested."

"I think we should let the pretty girl speak for herself."

"She's not interested," Tyra confirmed.

Jamie grunted. "Damn shame. I have a sweet tooth."

Tyra crossed her arms, which only drew his attention to her breasts. "Are you referring to my coloring?"

"Yup," he boldly answered without moving his eyes away from her chest.

Tyra looked ready to slap him, so I gripped his chin and turned his face toward mine.

"Her eyes aren't down there, douchebag."

He clicked his tongue and sang, "You shouldn't touch me. We have an audience."

My hand quickly fell into my lap. I knew who he meant. "So what?"

Jamie waggled his eyebrows. "Well, I'm game if you are."

"Never gonna happen."

He snorted. "Especially if my cousin has anything to say about it."

I glanced at Tyra, who seemed equally confused. "Why would he care?"

Deep dimples appeared as he smiled around a mouth full of Granny Smith. "You're not that naïve."

"Humor me."

Rather than do so, he changed the subject. "Did I hear you two discussing him?"

"And if we were?"

"I'd be careful with rumors." He cast an indignant glance at Tyra, who lifted her chin in return.

"So enlighten me."

"Hell no! I'm not getting in the middle of his shit with you."

The bell rang so I stood, refusing to beg. If Jamie wouldn't spill, I'd just have to get the beans elsewhere. I started to walk away when he swiftly grabbed my arm.

"You're playing a dangerous game, Four." For the first time since meeting him, the playful twinkle in his eyes was gone. "Cross him an inch, and he'll go a mile to ruin you."

"No need to worry," I lied. "I'm just making small talk." I pulled my arm from his grip and dumped my tray. I only made it a few feet before I heard the classic tune and then the first verse of Lynyrd Skynyrd's 'Sweet Home Alabama' playing through the school's speakers. Since I seemed to be the only one eager to get to class, I was the only one standing when a couple of guys burst through the doors and began to do-si-do around me. They weren't even in rhythm, but the cafeteria erupted into laughter anyway.

My fists balled.

I wanted to pummel the guys until they were bloody pulps.

But I couldn't get revenge behind a cell.

Ever was slouched with his arm thrown over the back of his chair. There was no trace of humor or satisfaction or even the regret I witnessed when he humiliated me the last time. He simply watched his lackeys perform, and only when they slapped hands and took off did I have his undivided attention. Was he expecting me to run away in tears like last time?

Not gonna happen.

"That was pathetic!" I shouted.

His subjects fell silent, waiting to see what their king would do. I didn't stick around to find out. I was breathing fire by the time I was far enough for the laughter to fade.

Ever had made it clear he didn't want peace.

Good.

Neither do I.

I hadn't realized I was being followed until a hand on my shoulder stopped my charge. Thinking it was another prank, I turned with my balled fist raised.

"Whoa!" The fight left my body when I realized it was just Tyra. "You do realize if you had hit me, I would have to hit you back?" she sassed with her hand on her hip.

I muttered an apology before starting down the hall again with her at my side.

"So…what did you do?"

"What do you mean?" We reached my locker, and I quickly grabbed the materials for my next class.

"How did you get under his skin? Ever McNamara has never stooped that low before."

I sighed, getting sick of everyone believing Ever was some god to be revered. "I didn't do anything. He hates me because I don't belong here, and he's right."

"Have you seen the way he looks at you? I totally believe he can't stand you, but I think he—" She suddenly looked unsure.

"What?"

"I think he wants you just as much."

The bell saved me from responding, and we parted ways, but a minute later, I received a text from Tyra.

TYRA: Think about it.

I wanted to tell her that all I did was think about it, but never in a million years would I admit to desiring a boy who treated me so horribly. I stepped over the threshold of my English class and found that very boy sitting in the back.

Vaughn was seated on his right with some blushing bombshell parked in front of him. He had a hand planted on the back of her chair, and the other twirled the end of a long brown lock between his fingers as he whispered in her ear. Like a magnet, my gaze returned to Ever who was sketching something inside a small notebook. He didn't even notice the avid admirer sitting next to him.

"Ms. Archer, glad to have you back," the rotund teacher greeted with a clipped tone. Ever's head jerked up as if he'd just had a bucket of cold water thrown on him. "Please...have a seat."

I headed for the only empty seat available at the front of the class, but Mr. Driscoll had other plans.

"Actually, I'd like you to switch seats with Ms. Brooks. I'd rather she be able to concentrate on the lecture."

When I realized he meant the brunette whose drool probably puddled the floor and maybe her seat too, I grew annoyed. Vaughn was just whispering sweet nothings to the girl in front of him but *that* he noticed?

The pretty brunette stood in a huff and bumped my shoulder when she passed. I wanted to rip her eyes out. Maybe then I wouldn't have to sit next to *him*.

Mr. Driscoll, noticing that I still stood, glowered over the rim of his glasses. "Ms. Archer, I'd like to begin."

Ever's lips twitched as he sat back slowly, never taking his eyes from me as I moved down the aisle and slid into the desk. The teacher immediately began going over the syllabus. Vaughn, with his hand now groping his conquest's ass, leaned forward to wink at me.

They were two peas in a pod, and I hated them both.

I tried to follow along with the teacher's ramblings, but I

couldn't stop watching Ever from the corner of my eye. He twirled a pencil between long, tanned fingers, drawing my attention to his bruised knuckles. They hadn't been that way during lunch.

I hadn't realized I was openly staring until the pencil suddenly stopped twirling.

"See something you like?"

The space between my thighs warmed when I envisioned him touching me with those fingers. *Oh, no. Don't go there.* "Fighting?" I nodded toward his knuckles. "Are you sure the peerage would approve?"

"The what?" His confused frown was almost adorable.

"The peers and peeresses." His blank stare held, so I added, "The other rich assholes."

Understanding dawned and he smiled. "Peer…" His finger caressed his cleft chin. "Is that my pet name when you're whispering about me with Tyra Bradley?"

I snorted at the same time my face heated. *He's obviously been paying attention.* "What makes you think we've been talking about you?"

His eyebrow perked as if the answer was obvious, and then he turned his head toward the front of the class.

I'd been dismissed.

I straightened in my seat.

Fuck him and what he thinks.

But what if he thinks I have a crush on him like every other girl in this school?

Before I could consider my dignity, I was facing him again. "Just so you know," I whispered heatedly, "I *was* talking about you, but it wasn't about what you think. It will *never* be what you think. Got it?"

"What do I think?" he retorted while focusing on his syllabus. I hated how easy it was for him to ignore me.

"Coy doesn't suit you."

A whisper of a smile graced his lips. "*Lying* doesn't suit you."

chapter twelve

The Peer

FOUR ARCHER WAS A PUZZLE PIECE I COULDN'T FIT INTO PLACE. SHE was equally infuriating and fascinating, and I could never let her know. It would give her the power I enjoyed dangling just out of her reach.

Sometimes, I wondered if *she* was getting to *me* instead of the other way around. All I could think about was her. A plain Jane with no money and no class had proved the most tempting of all. Go fucking figure.

If I were truly honest, I'd say it was only natural that I was drawn to Four. She was the trouble I'd once craved.

I slid my shades into place the minute I stepped into the sunny September afternoon. The parking lot was full, and no one seemed to be in a rush to get home since it was the first day. Most of us spend our summers out of town or abroad, so everyone was busy getting reacquainted. I bypassed the cliques and headed straight for my car that was a little too fucking crowded. Barbette stood next to the driver's door with her arms crossed, pretending to ignore Jamie tonguing down some chick against the passenger door. *Why the hell would she stick around?*

Our little triangle irritated the shit out of me, but Barbette needed the illusion. It was complicated as hell, and one day, Jamie might forgive us.

But if he didn't…fuck it.

I did what I had to do for my friend.

"Take your bullshit somewhere else," I hissed in my cousin's ear.

He flipped me off and continued to dry-hump the shit out of his playmate for all to see. I guess he was still pissed about earlier, but he fucking deserved it. I rounded the hood and swore. Barbette was on the verge of tears. She noticed me, and just like that, her mask was in place.

I took her in my arms and kissed her cheek because it was expected. One peek over Barbette's shoulder revealed Jamie looking two seconds from ripping my head off. He'd forgotten all about the girl he was practically fucking. I put some distance between us but kept my hands on her slender hips to keep up appearances. "You okay?"

"Can you come over for dinner tomorrow night?" She'd completely blown off my concern. "My parents are wondering why you haven't been around."

I'd rather swallow nails than have dinner with her creepy fucking parents, but I made a vow to her four years ago. "I'll be there."

Relief flooded her eyes. "Thank you."

I wanted to ask her if anything happened, but Barbette was a vault. The only people who could crack her perfect exterior were her parents...and my douchebag cousin.

For a moment, I searched for the girl she'd once been—for Bee. When only Barbette stared back at me, I kissed her forehead and sent her on her way. Across the parking lot, Jamie was hopping in a car with the girl he'd been making out with, and together, they sped away. The rest of the school followed suit, and minutes later, I was alone in the empty parking lot.

Where the fuck is she?

Thinking she'd caught a ride with her friend, I started to text the number my father made me program. I didn't feel like getting shit from him if I left her ass stranded here. Four didn't know that when my father warned me of her return, he also threatened to send us *both* away if there was a repeat of last year. Under no circumstances could I allow that to happen. Four would learn her place even if I had to teach her myself.

I was still typing out a text when I heard a familiar chime. My mind had already shifted gears by the time I pulled the burner phone from the locked glove compartment.

"This is Boyd."

If someone were to search 'Ever McNamara,' they'd find one person with that name—one of Conall McNamara's four heirs.

So when I was initiated, I became Daniel Boyd.

To the world, I was no one.

But to Exiled, I'd be so much more.

"You've been MIA," Shane, Exiled's head enforcer, greeted. "That makes me nervous, Danny Boy."

"I had personal shit to deal with." It was a struggle to keep my voice level when I despised the man.

You're no better than him. Not anymore.

"Don't give a shit about your personal life," he barked. "You pull this shit again, and I'll find ways to keep you motivated. Are we clear?"

"We're clear."

"Good. I'm calling a meeting. Make sure you show up, or I'll start with someone you love."

Just then, Four came into view, her steps hesitant and brown eyes wide from seeing me still hanging around. An image of Shane with his hands around her pretty little neck flashed through my mind, and I heard myself saying, "I'll be there," before ending the call.

What. The. Fuck?

This girl was more than just trouble.

She was dangerous.

chapter thirteen

∞

The Puppet

WAS SURPRISED TO LEARN THAT THE PRESTIGIOUS BRYNWOOD OFFERED auto mechanics as an elective until I arrived and found that the entire class roster consisted of five students including myself. Still. I could walk through those doors every day knowing I'd have something to look forward to doing. The instructor seemed to know his stuff, and his grumpiness was nostalgic. It was like being in the shop again, although no one could replace Gruff. Dave—he'd insisted Mister was his father—had taken notice of my way around car parts. I told him all about Gruff and his shop back home, and he seemed excited to finally have someone with a real interest in mechanics in his shop.

My next surprise came during Track and Field, my final period. I'd been obsessed with bikes and racing since I was ten years old, so I never bothered learning what else was out there. When Coach Lloyd put us on the track, the world faded away, and it was like being on the back of a bike again. I ran until my lungs burned and my legs turned to jelly.

School had ended thirty minutes ago, and I wouldn't put it past Ever to leave me stranded, which was why I couldn't conceal my surprise when I spotted the Range in the deserted parking lot. Ever stood with his foot propped on the bumper as he talked on one of those cheap throwaway phones. From his scowl, I guessed the conversation was unpleasant. I was more than a little curious about the phone call when he ended it seconds after noticing my approach.

He didn't move, and I pretended disinterest, but as I reached for the door, he issued a clipped, "No."

Oh, I'm so not in the mood, McNamara. "Is there a problem?"

He shoved his hand into his pants' pocket, and it was a struggle to keep my jaw from dropping when he handed me his keys. "Take my car home."

"Without you?" I glanced at the empty parking lot. "How will you get home?"

"Don't worry about me." He was his usual surly self, yet somehow this felt different. Something was up.

"And Jamie?"

"He caught a ride."

"Oh...so you were waiting for me?" A raised eyebrow was my answer. "Thanks, I guess." I finally took the keys and ignored the heat blooming in my lower tummy when our fingers touched.

Ever walked away without looking back, and I couldn't help but watch him go. He moved with such masculine grace and— *was going into the woods?*

I told myself not to follow him.

Begged myself not to follow him.

I tossed his keys into my backpack and followed him.

Fortunately, I was born and raised around nothing but trees, so it was easy for me to move through them without being heard. It was a short walk to the edge of a clearing where he stopped. I ducked behind a tree, and it was a good thing I did since Ever glanced over his shoulder before stepping into the opening. I peeked around the tree and watched him head for an open-planned shed that had seen better days. Parked underneath it was a green Crown Victoria that had also seen better days. I held my breath as I watched him open the trunk and lift a duffle from its depths. I jumped when he slammed the trunk closed, then felt foolish. Still, my reaction was the least silly thing I'd done all day. Following him in the first place was definitely at the top of that list.

He threw the duffle on the trunk and began stripping out of his uniform. My fingers dug into the bark.

I should turn away.

I knew I should.

But...I couldn't.

With his back to me, piece by piece he bared his body: shoes, jacket, tie. I couldn't see as he released the buttons on his dress shirt, but my breathing quickened anyway, and when he slipped the shirt from his body, my breathing shuddered to a stop.

The bold marking between Ever's shoulder blades mocked me. It couldn't be a coincidence. It was too bizarre. Too real. Tattooed on Ever's back was an X, and underneath it an inscription I couldn't make out but had a pretty good idea of what it read. *I am not led.*

Ever was Exiled.

I ran back to the parking lot after Ever drove off in the Crown Victoria. Nothing in the last five minutes made sense. Why would Ever, a boy who had everything, join a gang of murderers?

Inside the Range Rover, I turned the AC up as high as it would go, closed my eyes, and imagined it was the wind whipping at my face as I defied death. Suddenly, my heart was racing in a good way. My skin tingled as I chased the high. It felt better than ever before.

Because I'd finally found revenge.

A quarter mile from the school, on my way back to the palace, I spotted the Crown Vic. The tint shielded the driver, but I knew it was him. That left me with two choices. I could go home and tell Thomas what I knew or follow him and see what he was up to.

An hour later, I was trailing Ever through seedy New York neighborhoods until he turned down a street with an abandoned building at the end. There was no way I could go unseen, so I parked on the main road. It was a good thing this part of the city seemed deserted. A Range Rover wouldn't be easy to miss. I hopped out and prayed his truck would still be there when I returned.

Jogging down the path, I spotted the Crown Vic parked among a sixties model Impala with gleaming black paint and chrome grilling, a red Porsche Cayman, and a black Camaro with white stripes. It was probably stupid—no, *definitely* stupid—but I inched closer until I reached the shadows hugging the condemned building.

With my back pressed against the side of the building, I sifted through the voices spilling over the moss and vine-covered threshold until I recognized one. There was a window above me, and if I stood on my tiptoes, I could see inside. I didn't have to question if they'd kill me if I were caught.

My life had become one big irony. Rosalyn uprooted us from our home to protect me from these monsters only to have one of them living across the hall.

I'd laugh if I didn't want to live.

I glanced up at the window again and realized I was much too curious for my own good. Standing on my tiptoes, I rested my fingers on the brick windowpane to keep myself balanced. I took in the intimate group of menacing men. I could hardly believe Ever was one of them, but there he was in all black with a skully cloaking his gorgeous hair. He had his mask in place as a man who looked like he ate babies raged. The tattoo on the back of his shaved skull marked him as Exiled.

There were three others. The one closest to me had brown hair swept back from his forehead with the sides shaved close. His back was to the window, so I couldn't see his face, but I could see the mark at his nape. The other two stood in the shadows of the building, making it impossible to see their faces, but I was willing to bet they were Exiled.

My attention returned to Ever, and my heart stopped when I saw him staring straight at me. I ducked and considered what to do. It was too late to run. I could already hear them moving. I had no chance of making it to the car and even less of fighting them off, but I searched for a weapon anyway. There were bits of broken glass lying around, so I picked up the biggest one and ignored the pain when it bit into my hand.

Moments later, instead of fighting for my life, I listened as the cars started and drove away. I dropped the glass but waited an extra minute before peeking around the corner.

Ever was a mere foot away with his shoulder propped against the wall looking seconds away from strangling me. I screamed and landed on my ass.

"What the *fuck* are you doing here?" he demanded as he stalked me.

I crawled backward on my hands until I realized I couldn't fight from this position. As soon as I hopped up, he gripped my biceps and turned our bodies, pressing my back against the wall.

"I asked you a question."

"Let go of me!"

His fingers tightened, but when I grimaced, he immediately loosened them. Maybe he wouldn't kill me after all.

"Why did you follow me?"

"Isn't it obvious? You were up to something, and I wanted to know what."

His hands fell from my arms, and I was grateful. The rage in his eyes shook me to my core. "How much did you hear?"

Not a damn thing. "Enough," I lied, satisfaction lacing each syllable. I had a death wish.

"Fuck!" he exploded. The curse sounded foreign passing through his lips. It seemed beneath him, yet it intimidated me as nothing ever had.

"I saw their tattoos. I know they're Exiled." I purposely left out that I'd also seen his mark because it meant admitting to watching him undress in the woods. Whenever I closed my eyes, I could still see the muscles that hadn't been there a year ago.

"How exactly would you know that?"

"Had a run in with them last year. It's how I ended up in Stepford." He glowered at my reference. "I'm guessing your father didn't give you the whole story?"

"Doesn't matter. You don't know what you're talking about." He took a step back and started to walk away until my next words stopped him.

"Maybe your father can figure it out."

Before I could say more or take a fighting stance, my back was against the brick again, and this time, he had my wrists locked above my head while honey brown eyes blazed.

"Rethink your next move, Archer, or I promise to make you regret it."

"The only thing I regret is the day you were born."

He leaned close, head bent, until his lips almost brushed mine. "Back at you, baby."

The endearment had me shivering. Afraid he might feel my reaction, I bucked against him. "I never said you could touch me!"

Chuckling, he swept his lips across mine. "I never asked."

Desperate now, I moved to knee him, but he quickly shoved his thigh between mine. My breath caught as I watched his Adam's apple bob. Why must everything he does be so goddamn enticing?

"Let me go."

Thick lips brushed mine again, and his voice was smoother when he spoke. "Promise not to tell?"

No, no, no. I hated the whimper that escaped me, and even more, I hated the boy who drew it out of me. I needed his kiss as much as I needed his downfall. When Ever's hips pressed against mine, and his mouth skimmed my neck, I feared I'd be burned alive.

"Promise me," he demanded softly.

"I promise—" Words eluded me when Ever softly bit into my

neck, and his cock pressed against my fluttering stomach. I was grappling to keep my wits. "I promise you're gonna regret knowing me, McNamara." Slowly, he freed my skin from his teeth, and then our eyes met as I lifted my head from the wall and growled, "Now let me go."

I expected his wrath. Instead, he shrugged and stepped away, ending the pretense of seduction. I was left a ball of flame while he became a shard of ice. "You want revenge for the humiliation?"

"*Yes*," I hissed.

"What about your time in Europe?"

Logic was screaming to turn back now, but I couldn't. I had to know. "What are you talking about?"

"Did you think it was my father's idea to send you to reform school?" His tone suggested I'd been naïve. "I practically put the brochure in his hand, Archer."

Confidence gave way to disbelief after he shoved the truth down my throat. "So what? You'll set me up again and send me back?"

A derisive snort and then, "I can do better than Natasha Madison's School of Ladies." He cocked his head to the side. "How important is your mother's happiness to you?"

I became a statue. "Leave Rosalyn out of this."

"Keep your mouth shut, and I'll keep mine."

My heart raced, and my palms turned sweaty. "I don't know what you're talking about."

"Then, if I were you, I'd figure it out quickly. I feel like singing."

"I have nothing to hide!"

"I didn't say *you* did." The silence that followed was almost telling.

No. "What do you know?" I demanded with my fists clenched and my voice grave. All pretense of innocence had slipped away.

"I know that your mother is batshit crazy and that her pussy must be lined in gold for my father to have missed the signs. It's a good thing *I'm* not fucking her."

I exhaled and with the release came the realization that I'd been outsmarted. Ever had me backed into a corner with no escape.

How did he know?

However he found out, there was no going back. "So I keep my mouth shut and you keep yours?" I held out my hand to seal the deal, and already, my skin tingled. *Bastard.*

He sighed as if disappointed and ignored my hand. "If only it were that simple, but I can't trust what I don't control."

My hand fell to my side when the flesh covering my entire body burned. "What does that mean?"

His eyes flashed with anticipation. "It means, puppet, I finally have a pet name for *you.*"

Dinner that night had been yet another stilted affair.

Jamie joined us halfway through with a bruise covering most of his left cheek. Thomas questioned him relentlessly, but Jamie avoided answering. Ever casually sipped his water while Rosalyn stared into her own glass. It didn't seem to bother her or Ever at all when the yelling began. Thomas eventually ordered Jamie into his office, and together, they disappeared, leaving Rosalyn, Ever, and me to finish dinner together. I was mulling over Ever's bruised knuckles, which Thomas never seemed to notice, when Rosalyn finally spoke.

"How was your first day back, dear?"

"It was like I'd never left." But I did, and I still couldn't find it in me to forgive her for sending me away. Now that I knew Ever had talked them into it, I wasn't sure I ever would.

An awkward silence fell over the table as Rosalyn stewed in her guilt. I was content to keep it that way, but of course, Ever had other plans.

"You should tell her about our arrangement," he casually

suggested. He never even bothered lifting his gaze from his plate. As if toying with me was as natural to him as breathing.

I could kill him.

"Your...arrangement?" I could hear the alarm in Rosalyn's voice and wondered if I'd have to shove pills down her throat in the morning. With wide eyes, she waited for an explanation, and I wracked my brain for one.

"We have English together," Ever offered when the silence became telling.

"Oh, how nice," she rushed out with obvious relief.

I glared at Ever across the table when Rosalyn busied herself studying her nails. If the table weren't so damn wide, I'd kick him and wipe that dazzling smile off his face. What it did to me frightened me more than his veiled threats did.

"If you ladies will excuse me," Ever announced as he rose from the table. "I have shit to do."

Rosalyn flinched at his swearing, but he pretended not to notice. Despite our agreement, I couldn't resist returning the favor and toying with him since I had a good idea what he was going to do and who he was doing it for.

"Should I tell your father where you're going?"

He simply winked, and I pretended a certain part of me didn't weep as he walked away.

"What an odd boy," Rosalyn remarked when he was out of earshot.

"I wouldn't exactly call him odd."

"He's much too intense for his age." She then eyed me curiously. "And don't think I didn't see him wink at you." Her gaze sharpened when I froze. "What was that about?"

I dug my nails into my thigh, a reaction she couldn't see. I'd stupidly fallen into his trap once again.

Oh, Ever...you're going to pay.

And I wouldn't just rip him from his throne. I'd crush him under my heel like the worm he was.

"A boy too into his looks?" She seemed to accept my answer and went back to sipping her water. "Aren't you going to eat?" She'd barely touched her plate.

"I'm full."

"You've hardly eaten anything."

"I had a big lunch," she replied in a tone that warned me away from the subject.

My appetite was suddenly gone, but I forced the rest of my food down so I wouldn't look like a hypocrite and excused myself. I had the feeling my room would be my sanctuary until I graduated. Brynwood was relentless in its pursuit of educating, and so, at the end of the first day, I found myself with homework. I headed for the simple ivory desk and felt my heart race when I came across a folded slip of paper. There were no lines, but the jagged edges showed it had been torn from its binding.

Someone knocked on my door, but I ignored them and flipped open the paper.

Once upon a puppet, she spun a tale to the mad king.
- The Peer

"What does that even mean?" I didn't have to question who the note was from.

Haughty bastard.

Another knock, this one more demanding, had me tossing the note on my desk.

Thomas, with his tie undone and his shirt rumpled, stood at the threshold with a grimace.

"Have you seen my son?" he demanded. My stomach knotted when his gaze swept the room.

Did Thomas think Ever was with me? The words *Your prig of a son hangs with gang bangers* teased my tongue, but suddenly, the note made sense.

It wasn't a riddle.

It was an order.

He'd known Thomas would look for him, and he wanted me to cover for him.

How did I go from plotting to ruin this guy to saving his ass? Thomas looked ready to explode.

"I haven't seen him since dinner."

"Your mother says he mentioned an errand and that you might know where he went." My tit for tat had placed me in Thomas's crosshairs and Ever seized the perfect opportunity to use me.

Ever - 1

Four - 0

"Yeah, he, uh…went to the store."

"The store?" His frown pulled even deeper. Was it so unusual for the prince to do his own shopping? How freaking privileged of him.

"Yes, the store. He said he needed…deodorant."

"Deodorant?"

"Got to have deodorant." It wasn't that I was a terrible liar, but he never said that I'd need to lie well for him.

"I figured he might have gone down to the school to watch his old teammates practice."

Well shit. "Yeah, I think he mentioned something about stopping by."

"All right…thanks, Four." He walked away, and I shut my door with a shrug. I don't think my story sold, but it wasn't really my problem, was it?

Ten minutes later, my door flew open. A shirtless Jamie stood on the other side of the threshold with his hand covering his eyes.

"Are you decent?"

"Yes, but you could have knocked."

"That's a shame." He sighed. "I was peeking."

"What do you want?"

He flopped onto my bed and rolled onto his side before resting his head in his hand. "What's the deal with you and my cousin? You boning or what?"

I sighed and slammed my textbook shut. "Not that it's any of your business, no. I'm not screwing your cousin."

He snorted. "Not yet anyway."

My body heated with anticipation. *God, I hated these narcissistic—*

"You're blushing," he teased.

"Trust me, it's never happening. Your cousin made it clear to his friends that I'm an undesirable." I think I hated that word even more.

"He said that?" Jamie cackled. While I could only nod, his grin only grew. "That sneaky motherfucker!" Despite his words, there was admiration and delight in Jamie's eyes.

"Want to fill me in?"

"Marking you undesirable ensures no one will pursue you."

"Yeah, I got that. What I *don't* get is why it matters to him."

Jamie looked at me like I was dense. "My cousin doesn't want anyone touching what's his."

"Give it a rest." I groaned as I spoke. "We're not hooking up. It's too weird given that our parents sleep in the same bedroom."

"So you're saying, if they broke up, you'd be game?"

"Absolutely not. He and I are from two different worlds, and Ever has no problem making sure I remember that. Or weren't you there this afternoon?"

"You're talking about your welcome present?" I nodded, and he shook his head with a smile. "Ever didn't arrange that. I did."

What? My arms folded as my gaze narrowed. "I thought you said you weren't getting involved?"

"I'm not, but that doesn't mean I won't have a little fun."

"Either way, I'm sure he appreciated it." I guess that

answered the question about whether I could trust Jamie. He wasn't my friend although I wasn't entirely sure he was Ever's either.

"I didn't do that for Ever." He then pointed to the bruise on his right cheek. "I did it to piss him off."

"Why?"

Jamie's voice flattened when he replied, "It's complicated."

"Complicated like you having a thing for his girlfriend?"

He stiffened before slowly rising from the bed. I couldn't take back my words, and after what he did to me, I didn't care to, so I stared after him as he headed for the door. He stood on the threshold, back stiff, fingers strangling the knob.

Damn it. An apology was poised on my lips because I wasn't a vicious bitch, but then he spoke.

"She was mine first."

chapter fourteen

The Peer

PRESSED IGNORE ON MY DAD'S FIFTH CALL AND SLID FROM THE CROWN
Vic I'd paid for with cash from a man who didn't care who I
was or what I needed it for. The Exiled had seized Queens from
Thirteen, the rival gang who cast out Nathaniel Fox twenty-eight
years ago. Despite the kill order, if he was ever caught within
Thirteen territory, which nearly encompassed the entire east
coast, he founded Exiled with his late partner Crow and had made
a point to be a thorn in Thirteen's side ever since.

Tonight's mission was to commandeer another piece of
Thirteen's operation—a house in Long Island with half a million
dollars' worth of cocaine stashed inside. The only problem was
the elderly couple currently occupying the residence.

Four men were seated around the table when I entered the
room, and all but one greeted me.

Wren Harlan, one of Fox's most trusted lieutenants and
Shane's protégé, didn't trust me, and he never bothered to hide it.
He wasn't much older than I was—two years, maybe three—and
because he'd been born into Exiled, it was all he knew. At the
meeting this afternoon, he'd been itching for a fight, and I had
been all too ready to oblige when I caught Four's wide eyes staring at me through that window.

Always so troublesome.

I took the only empty seat left, and Shane began speaking
from his perch at the head of the table. "Now that Danny Boy's

graced us with his presence, let's go over the plan." He nodded to Wren to take over.

"It's simple," Wren began. "Our scout says they're already down for the night, but it's impossible to do the job quietly, so we subdue them." With his eyes trained on me, he added, "I don't like surprises or amateurs with happy trigger fingers." He then met the gaze of each person around the table. "No one. Kill. The elderly."

"You know Sonny Franzese is a senior citizen," Siko pointed out. Not only did he look like Joseph Sikora, but he also had a few screws loose hence his street name. "And *he* wouldn't hesitate to shoot us if we tried to rob him."

Eddie, a Hispanic cat from Harlem, sucked his teeth. "Isn't he dead, puto?"

"Nah, I think he's still alive."

"Damn, he's got to be old as fuck. Like a hundred, right? You think he can still get it up?"

"Enough," Wren snapped.

Siko and Eddie immediately fell silent. Since Wren had likely earned his stripes in unimaginable ways, the respect came naturally.

"If it's kill or be killed, I expect you to use your head."

Shane, Siko, and Eddie nodded their agreement. I didn't react, and it didn't escape Wren's notice.

"But if I find out they died for any other reason, you'll feel their pain tenfold."

I met Wren's stare head-on. I had no intentions of killing anyone, though I made one convincing monster. The disguise, after all, was the only thing keeping him leashed. He may be hardened, but even Wren knew that someday everyone met their match.

There wasn't anything left to say once Wren finished laying down the law, so Wren, Siko, Eddie, and I made our way to Long Island in Wren's '66 Impala while Shane stayed back. I had to admit

Wren had taste. The polished interior of the Impala looked as if it had been completely restored while keeping its classic appeal.

The only sound as we made our way to Long Island was Siko and Eddie squabbling in the back while Wren brooded behind the wheel, and I was left with my thoughts.

The ruthless persona I adopted as Danny Boy didn't come easy this time. I didn't even need to question why. I've peddled drugs, kicked in doors, and roughed up people who probably didn't deserve it, and until Four, I haven't felt shame. She blew into town thinking she was a storm. She had no fucking idea. When I was initiated, I decided a soul was optional, and no brown-eyed girl was going to change that.

"Having second thoughts, Boyd?" Wren hadn't taken his eyes off the road, so either he had a gift or he was taunting me as usual. "It's not too late to pussy out."

I chuckled even though the last thing I felt was humor. "You looking for a bigger cut?"

"I don't like the idea of getting my head blown off if you hesitate."

Siko would be the lookout while Eddie dealt with the residents. Wren had chosen me to help him extract the dope, most likely to keep an eye on me. It meant I was expected to have his back while he had mine. The only problem was neither of us trusted the other to do so.

"I won't hesitate."

He glanced away from the road, and we locked gazes. Forced to concentrate on driving, he broke the staring contest first, but I could see the muscle in his jaw ticking. He couldn't figure me out, and it frustrated him.

It was the same feeling I had about Four Archer.

Case in point: I was on a mission that would likely end with my head getting blown off, and instead of focusing, I was obsessing over some wild girl who tempted me like no other but was too naïve to know that I'd dare to do something about it.

This afternoon's episode had me discreetly checking the side-view mirror. I'd found my car keys on my desk when I made it home, so I knew she had no way of following me, but Four had proven herself more than capable of surprising me at every turn. My mother warned me that one day I'd meet a girl who wasn't afraid of a challenge. I'd laughed her off, but now more than ever, I wished she were here to tell me what to do with her little prophecy.

I forced myself to swallow the bitter pill when Wren barked, "We're here."

Siko and Eddie abandoned their bickering and sat up straighter. The brand-new two-story home had vinyl siding, burgundy shutters, and a freshly cut lawn. The small neighborhood was slumbering in the wee hours, but Wren cut the lights anyway and parked at the end of the street. We covered the lower half of our faces with black bandanas before jogging to our target. The cold press of the pistol in my grip was a reminder of just how wrong this could go. I just hoped Vaughn had come through because I had a plan of my own.

Siko slid into the shadows while Wren worked on the door. Within seconds, Eddie and I were following him into the darkened home, guns drawn, with only the moonlight shining through the curtains to help us see.

Wren nodded to Eddie, a silent order to take care of the slumbering couple upstairs. I was forced to stay in character as he moved quickly and silently up the stairs. Wren led us to the basement where our informant told us the coke would be stored. He tried the door, and finding it locked, tucked his gun into his waistband and set to work on the lock.

He was still working when I heard it.

The faint thump came from above. Wren didn't seem to notice as he continued working. I figured the coast was clear until the second thump came, and his head tilted the barest amount.

I considered slamming my pistol against his skull, but I didn't want to play my hand too soon. Wren shot up from his crouch and was headed for the stairs when a single gunshot—muffled by a silencer none of us had—filtered down from above. Heavy footsteps traveled across the upper floor at the same time we heard a second gunshot. This time, it came from outside.

The stairs creaked under heavy footfalls at the same time someone entered the house. Trapped, we only had a second, maybe two, to make a decision.

Grabbing Wren, who shook with rage, I forced him through the back door. We hopped the fences separating the yards until we reached the end of the street. The coast was clear, so we made for the car. Wren wasted no time speeding off while pounding and swearing at the steering wheel. His friends were either dead or we'd just left them to die. My money was on the former.

The trip back to Queens was silent. Most notable was the absence of Siko and Eddie's banter.

It wasn't supposed to go down like that. I only wanted the couple out of harm's way, but staring down at my hands, I saw the blood on them anyway. It belonged to Siko and Eddie.

Wren seemed calm by the time we reached the compound, but I quickly learned he had merely been lying in wait. I didn't see the blow coming, but goddamn, I felt it. Growing up, Vaughn, Jamie, and I would beat the shit out of each other as well as a few others, so I knew how to take a hit, but Wren packed a pretty powerful punch. I'd never been hit that hard. I was both pissed and in awe.

I spat out the blood while glaring back at him. He hadn't said a word, hadn't voiced the question, but I knew why he'd attacked. I would have done the same. "You're still breathing because of me," I warned. "Don't force me to rectify that."

"If you wanted to be a coward, that's on you, but you should have left me."

"To die?" I questioned incredulously.

"To help my brothers!" he roared.

"They were already *dead*, Harlan."

His gaze narrowed, and I realized I'd said the wrong thing. "Why are you so sure of that?"

"None of us had silencers, so trust me...it wasn't Siko and Eddie doing the shooting." It was the only truth I could give him. Anything more could expose my hand in their deaths.

He was silent for a long while before turning away. The crumbling house where we'd met only a couple hours before loomed ahead in the shadows, and just when I thought I was in the clear, he threw over his shoulder, "I will *never* trust you...*Danny Boy*."

chapter fifteen

the Puppet

WAS HAVING A DREAM. A VERY GOOD DREAM. A DREAM I'D NEVER IN A million years admit to having under *any* circumstances. Not even torture.

Sadly, my dream ended, and I was jarred awake drenched in sweat. The T-shirt I'd worn to bed was bunched around my waist, showing off my cotton panties. I blushed when I recalled in vivid detail what caused such disarray.

And then I froze when I realized I wasn't alone.

A quick glance at the foot of my bed showed a figure in dark clothing leaning forward with his forearms casually resting on his knees. The scream that tore from my lips was silenced when the figure leaned over and calmly rested his palm over my mouth.

"My father is a light sleeper," Ever calmly warned. "And I'm sure you don't want to explain to your mom why I'm in your bedroom at three in the morning." My heart continued to race even after he lifted his hand, but I didn't scream. "Good girl."

"Why are you here?" I hissed while scrambling to pull down the T-shirt still bunched around my waist. I lifted the comforter I must have kicked away in my sleep and covered my lower half.

Oh, God, he'd seen everything. I felt like I had been caught red-handed considering he'd been the one I'd—

Fuck my life.

"You told my father I went to the store for deodorant."

"And?" I sounded as exasperated as I felt.

"He didn't buy your story."

I could imagine considering he was sitting in my room fully dressed at three in the morning. It didn't take seven hours to buy deodorant.

"Not. My. Problem."

"But it is. We made this deal together, and we'll honor it... together."

I sighed. "So, what did he do to your highness? Take a spoon?" I mocked.

"Grounded," he grunted.

"Poor you."

I didn't expect his smile. It was soft. Indulging. My overly large T-shirt had slipped from my shoulder, so he trailed his finger over my skin. "I'll have to punish you, Four."

"Punish me?" That was laughable. "I'm not your child."

"No, swamp girl. You're a puppet. *My* puppet." He stood from my bed and headed for the door. "If I'm grounded, so are you."

I told myself I was still dreaming and that he wasn't actually saying these words. "What does that even mean?"

"It means I'll have fun anyway."

Too exhausted to argue, I sighed and met his gaze. "Get out of my room, McNamara." I thought there was nothing else he could say or do until his parting words.

"You sound lovely when you come, Archer."

I knew the moment he had entered the kitchen the next morning. He didn't speak and hardly made a sound. I simply felt him. I ate breakfast at the island and was already dressed in my uniform when he sauntered in with a T-shirt in his hand and long gray pajama bottoms hanging loosely around his hips. He didn't acknowledge me as he filled his plate with the food Mr. Hunt, the cook, had made. After last night, I expected more.

I'd lain awake for at least an hour after he left my room, thinking about what would happen come morning. And when I finally slept, he'd invaded my dreams once again, but this time, the hands that roamed my flesh had been covered in blood. It was obvious Ever had been out doing Exiled's bidding, and it was surprising just how much it bothered me. What evil deed had they demanded from him, and more importantly, what price would he eventually pay for those deeds? The boy who invaded my dreams had brought warmth, and light, and love, but the boy who caused my nightmares… I shuddered.

After filling his plate high, instead of keeping the table between us, he sat next to me, giving me a whiff of his shampoo.

Or maybe it was his body wash.

Whatever it was, the intoxicating scent had me forgetting all about the ruthless gangbanger. No way could anyone other than Ever McNamara make me blush. I could feel him everywhere without even touching him. It was distracting.

"Why are you sitting so close to me?"

"Because I make you nervous."

I could feel my lip curl. "Gets your rocks off, does it?"

He licked his lips and grinned. I felt kicked in the stomach.

"No, but I like how my nearness takes your breath away."

"It does not." *It so does.*

He put his arm on the back of my chair and leaned in to whisper, "I can even hear the need behind your lies."

"Stop it." He was driving me crazy, and he didn't even need to touch me to do it.

"I don't think I can." His lips skimmed my ear, and I barely bit back a moan.

"Ever, please." Common sense told me that he was only getting back at me for getting him grounded, but my body didn't care as it responded to his touch. I clearly needed to take notes on vengeance. What method was more clever than making your victim beg for it? "We're enemies," I said more firmly.

"Says who?" When I felt him nip my ear, then lick the abused flesh, I wanted to give in to whatever this was, but then I remembered a year of isolation that had been all his doing.

"You did," I answered through gritted teeth. "When you told your father to send me away." Before he could get inside my head and succeed in making a fool out of me, I hopped from the stool and almost knocked Jamie over when I tried to flee.

"Whoa," he cautioned. His hands on my arms halted my escape. "Where ya headed, Speedy?"

"Let me go."

"What's the password?" he teased. Either he was completely oblivious to the tension in the room or he just didn't care. Perhaps he was using me again to get under Ever's skin. Whatever his reason, I was ready to knee him when Ever's growl froze us both.

"Take your hands off her."

I looked over my shoulder and saw that he'd abandoned his breakfast and now stood with his fists clenched.

"Why would I do that, cousin? You seem to enjoy having your hands all over what's mine."

"I'm not going to ask again," Ever shot back. I didn't miss that he'd completely ignored his cousin's accusation, and apparently, neither had Jamie.

Without warning, Jamie gently pushed me behind him and was ready to charge his cousin when Thomas suddenly appeared between his son and nephew. I never even noticed him enter the kitchen. A minute more and Ever and I would have been caught.

"What the hell is going on here?"

"Ask your son," Jamie sneered.

Thomas wasted no time regarding his son, who looked positively murderous. My heart skipped a beat. Knowing Ever was Exiled, I wasn't so sure I shouldn't heed his current mood.

"Well?" Thomas demanded.

Ever's gaze had fallen on me while he blatantly ignored his father.

I stopped breathing.

Why must I anticipate his every move with bated breath?

It was all for nothing anyway. He rolled his eyes, shoved on his shirt, and calmly strolled from the kitchen, leaving his father without an explanation and me feeling more empty than ever.

chapter sixteen

∞

The Peer

PROMISES WERE SOMETHING I FOUND IMPOSSIBLE TO BREAK, WHICH was why I rang the doorbell ready to play the gentleman. I was surprised when Bee, dressed in a white cocktail dress, appeared on the other side of the door. Her parents were the type who felt it was beneath them to answer their own doors because of their wealth.

The panicked look on Bee's face cleared the moment she saw me.

"You came."

I sighed and handed her the bouquet of roses. Elliot and Melissa would have expected nothing less for their daughter. "I said I would."

She scanned my gray wool blazer, white dress shirt, black tie, and chinos before nodding her approval and waving me inside. Her parents, dressed in their dinner finery, waited for us in the sitting room.

"Mr. and Mrs. Montgomery," I greeted with excitement I didn't feel. I played my role well, shaking her father's hand and kissing her mother's cheek.

"Son, I told you before. Call me Elliot."

"Habit, sir." I fought an eye roll.

"I can't find fault with a good upbringing, can I, son?" He clapped me on my back and offered me a drink even though I was underage.

I shook my head, knowing it was a test.

One of the help came to announce that dinner was served. Bee was standing dutifully by my side, probably as rehearsed, when her mother beamed at the bouquet she held. "What lovely flowers, young man." To her daughter, she said, "Shouldn't you put those in water?"

"Excuse me." My girlfriend wasted little time fleeing the room and leaving me with her parents.

"Shall we?" Melissa announced.

I followed them to the grand dining room. The feast was a little much for a casual Friday dinner, but over the top was the Montgomery way. *And how I got into this mess.*

Bee returned just as we were seated.

"Son, I'm glad you could find time in your schedule to join us for dinner. Barbette tells me that you are no longer playing football."

"That's right. I had to make room for more important endeavors."

"I see. Care to share?"

Not a chance. "It's mostly extracurricular. I'm hoping it will improve my chances of being accepted into a good architecture program. I figured it was time I was serious about my future." *Just keep feeding them bullshit.*

"Yes, the future is exactly what we wanted to discuss."

Bee was damn near catatonic when I glanced across the table. We both knew what was coming, had prepared for this moment, but it didn't stop my skin from crawling. I just wish Bee had given me a fucking heads up. The look on her face told me she knew what would happen tonight and even after everything she still hadn't trusted me to keep my promise. I felt my jaw clench as I recalled just how much I lost and how far I'd gone to help my friend. *Too fucking far.*

"And that would be?" I questioned with a hint of hostility. Fuck pleasantries. He was just lucky I was still seated and not headed for the door.

"You and my daughter have been an item for years now. Long before I can say I cared for Barbette to start dating," he lied through his teeth.

"We have."

"So I assume that her best interests are your priority." His words felt like shackles slamming shut, and it was all I could do not to chew off my own leg and get the hell out of here.

But Elliot Montgomery wasn't wrong. Bee was one of my best friends, and I cared about her. I definitely wouldn't be here if I didn't.

"I'd do anything for your daughter."

I should have been able to lie with practiced ease and profess that I was in love with his daughter, but a vision of brown eyes and a messy ponytail kept the words locked away.

I gritted my teeth.

Four's been nothing but trouble since she kneed me in the balls. It was like she'd been holding me by them ever since. I needed to get over this infatuation I had with the troublemaker like I needed my next breath. If I took her to my bed, it would never stop there. She'd want more, and I would take everything she had to give before destroying her. Just like Olivia Portland.

And even if Four turned out to be unbreakable, I already knew that I wasn't. Four will unleash me if I let her. I couldn't allow that to happen.

"And her honor?" Elliot probed. "What would you do to protect that?"

Tired of this dance, I met Elliot's stare dead on. "What is this about?" All pretenses abandoned, I needed him to get to the fucking point.

Elliot steepled his fingers as his demeanor shifted from gracious to stern. "We'd like to know if you plan to marry our daughter."

I was turning eighteen in a couple of days, and Bee was barely seventeen fucking years old, but that didn't seem to bother

Elliot as he sat at the head of the table expecting a proposal for his daughter's hand in marriage as if I'd knocked her up. My fists balled on my thighs. If I turned him down, Elliot Montgomery would have someone else seated at his dinner table the very next day, ready to offer his daughter on a platter to a man who didn't care about her honor or her interests.

I stared into the eyes of the girl who taught me how to climb a tree and who lit a candle for my mother every Sunday. This was the moment Bee and I had been anticipating since that night four years ago. I promised to protect her no matter what it took, but at fourteen, I had no idea how much that promise would one day cost me.

"Yes," I answered, feeling Bee's relief as if it were my own. "There's nothing and no one I want more."

Those words burned.

Like someone had just poured acid down my throat.

chapter seventeen

the Puppet

I FOLLOWED TYRA INTO A BLUE TWO-STORY HOME SITTING ON STILTS with two stacked balconies facing the beach. She was teeming with excitement next to me, which was no surprise since she had begged and begged and *begged* until falling dramatically onto the floor and crying that she'd be a virgin forever.

"Whose place is this?" I shouted over 'My House' by Flo Rida.

"It belongs to the Rees', but Vaughn's the only one who ever puts it to use, which doesn't surprise me. They live in this grand castle, and the guest list is so exclusive that hardly anyone other than family has ever stepped foot inside. I heard that their security is tighter than a virgin's ass."

My brows rose at her bitter tone, but I decided it was best not to peek behind that curtain right now.

"Really? That's not suspicious at all," I responded sarcastically. It made me wonder why someone who wasn't a celebrity or the President needed that much security.

Tyra shrugged while looking around the party. "I told you. There's a rumor that Franklin Rees wears suits, but it isn't to punch a clock." With all the wealth and prestige surrounding this town like a bubble, I wouldn't have thought it possible, but that was before Ever McNamara made the impossible ordinary.

I looked around too and spotted Jamie deejaying near the speakers with a gang of girls surrounding him. He seemed in his element as they swayed their hips in low-cut tops and skintight bottoms.

Things had been staler than usual since his almost fight with Ever yesterday morning, but the tension quickly fizzled when Vaughn announced he was throwing an eighteenth birthday bash for Ever. Apparently, Thomas had banned parties at the palace after last year. I just hoped there wouldn't be a need to crack open another skull this year. I never did get to apologize to Daniel Kim, whose parents had been furious. Even though Ever hadn't ratted me out, fingers were still pointed. Thomas sending me away had kept the Kims from pressing charges, but the bad blood remained. I could practically feel the target on my back whenever I crossed paths with Daniel Kim.

Ever's actual birthday wasn't until tomorrow, but partying on a Saturday night ensured everyone would be well and sober come Monday morning. Not to mention, he was still technically grounded, but Thomas had temporarily lifted the ban because well...you only turned eighteen once. As for me...I didn't consider myself his to punish.

I hadn't made it far inside the party when I felt an arm over my shoulder. "You have on too many clothes," Jamie shouted over the music. "I can barely see your skin!"

I'd worn black jeans with a white and black Evil Dead T-shirt and Vans that had seen better days. Tyra had begged for me to wear my hair down, but I refused. The natural bounce and volume of my wavy tresses made me feel too...feminine.

"That's the point!" I yelled back.

Jamie had apologized yesterday, and it was hard not to forgive him since he'd chosen to do it in the most embarrassing way. In the hallway, as the entire school was changing classes, he literally threw himself at my feet. Ever, on the other hand, went back to pretending I didn't exist. He also didn't show up for dinner last night. I guess everything had returned back to normal. Maybe. When I told Tyra about this morning, while leaving out the parts that had made my panties damp, she gave me a strange look but said nothing.

"I've been instructed to give this to you."

My stomach did that fluttering thing again when Jamie handed me a folded note. The paper was all too familiar as I recalled the note I'd received two nights ago.

Ever obviously knew I was here, but how did he know I'd come?

I searched the crowd and every dark corner and almost gave up looking when I saw him. Above the dance floor, with his hands resting on the balcony railing, Ever lorded over his subjects with his trusty sidekick, Vaughn, by his side. He wore a white button-up with the sleeves shoved to his elbows, a tie the color of blood, black jeans, and kicks. Vaughn wore only a destroyed denim vest, showing off his abs and chest, with black jeans and kicks. The two of them together look like trouble. Like a conqueror and corruptor.

I'd caught the conqueror staring, but he didn't bother to look away. He jerked his head toward the note in my hand. The order was clear.

Looking around, I assured myself that everyone was busy chatting or dancing. Jamie was occupied fixing Tyra a drink, and I wondered with a small smile if he knew getting under her blue mini skirt would never happen or if he simply appreciated the challenge.

While the coast was clear, I quickly flipped open the note.

Once upon a puppet, she remembered her limits and stayed away from Jameson.
-The Peer

I wondered if he'd meant whiskey or his cousin. Either way, the translation was the same: Don't get drunk, and don't cause trouble. My face heated as I inhaled and exhaled at a faster tempo. He hadn't spoken a word to me since yesterday morning, and when he finally did, it was to order me around? My gaze returned to the balcony, and when I held his, I tore the paper to bits and let it rain onto the dance floor. Later, I'd feel bad about trashing someone's home, but right now, the only thing I cared about was teaching the King of Brynwood a lesson.

Vaughn had an actual bar that one of our classmates was tending like a real bartender, so I made that my first stop.

"What will you have?"

"Something strong!" I shouted over the music.

He nodded and set about fixing me a drink. What he handed back looked like water with a lime. I gave him a suspicious look before taking a sip. It was definitely strong…and disgusting.

Taste didn't matter as long as it got me wasted.

Before I could disappear into the crowd, my gaze was drawn back to Ever. Barbie now stood by his side, looking cover-ready in a long-sleeve mini sequined dress. With a snort, I realized the color matched Ever's tie.

She was tall and prim.

Stainless.

In her gold heels, she almost stood shoulder to shoulder with Ever. Together, they looked like the perfect power couple. Ken and Barbie.

I drank and danced until that fact didn't bother me.

I drank and danced until nothing bothered me.

I drank and danced until I couldn't drink and dance.

Or so I thought.

Two girls carrying a two-tiered cake surrounded by sparklers approached the birthday boy, and Vaughn called for everyone to sing. When the candles died, Barbie did the honor of feeding him his first bite, and no amount of alcohol would ever help me unsee it.

Tyra placed a hand on my shoulder, drawing my attention away from the lovebirds. *I think I'm going to be sick.* "We can bail if you want."

I didn't dwell on if Tyra was observant or I was just being obvious as we made for the front door. Tyra had stayed sober, and it was a really good thing because I was having trouble walking on my own.

"Jesus!" she fussed when I stumbled.

"Sowy," I slurred as sincerely as I could.

"I suppose you needed the fun," she grumbled.

Watching Ever be fed birthday cake by his pretty, polished Barbie doll was not *fun*. I wanted to scrub my eyeballs with bleach and a Brillo pad.

I was slurring some version of another apology when I stumbled again. This time, it looked as if I was going down and taking poor Tyra with me. *Oh, man, this is gonna suck.* The ground started to get closer. I braced myself for the humiliation and hoped I was too drunk to care, but then I felt strong hands holding me up. I was turned and held against a hard chest as even stronger arms wrapped around my waist. Ever became a furnace, protecting me against the chilly night.

"I'm going to spank your ass," he growled into my ear.

I shivered despite his body heat, and when I peeked up, his regal features were twisted. I burst into a fit of giggles. *Maybe I shouldn't have drunk so much.* He growled some more, and then my feet were no longer on the ground.

"Put me down, Mc-Na-ma." He winced when I butchered his name, but then his jaw hardened when I said, "You'll get your hands dirty."

"Shut up," he barked.

I did shut up but only because of what caught my eye as he carried me away. It seemed Vaughn had saved a wide-eyed Tyra from falling. He still held her in his arms while she stared at him as if he'd grown a second head. Behind them, Barbie stood in the doorway watching us leave together.

I shook Ever's shoulder, and he bent his head slightly so I could whisper in his ear. "Your girlfriend's looking," I warned and then choked on my laugh.

He shook his head and didn't speak another word as he buckled me into the Range Rover. I fell asleep during the short drive home and woke up to him carrying me up the stairs. Lifting my head, I studied him. Even through my blurred vision I could tell that he was pissed.

"You're mad at me." I pouted. *Oh, God, was I still drunk?*

He kept his gaze straight ahead as he headed for my room. "What was your first clue?"

Tonight was as much his fault as it was mine. He pushed, so I pushed back. Round and round we went. "You shouldn't order me around."

He did look at me then, his voice soft when he spoke. "I can't help it."

Feeling sleepy and strangely content, I sighed and rested my head against his shoulder. "Try."

"No." He didn't even attempt to consider it.

"Why not?"

"Because I like it too much." Inside my room, he laid me on my back and knelt to peel my sneakers off my feet. When he moved to the button on my jeans, I panicked and grabbed his hands.

"Relax." His tone was gentle, but I knew better than to think that it was anything but an order.

Too curious and drunk to fight him, I did as I was told and let him work my jeans over my butt and down my legs. It was impossible not to blush when his eyes fell on my simple, gray cotton panties, and he fingered the material.

"I like this color on you," he purred.

"Is it your favorite?" Ever and gray had much in common: cool, balanced, sophisticated…emotionless.

"No, actually. It's green."

He pulled me up by a fist full of my shirt. Recalling what he was wearing the day I met him, I slurred, "Like the forest?"

He smiled faintly as if he didn't want to. "Like the forest," he confirmed.

"Mine's yellow," I offered. I doubted he cared.

"I noticed." The ball in my stomach ignited, and before I could recover, he slipped my shirt over my head.

"I'll be cold." Wordlessly, he peeled back my covers and waited for me to climb inside. It took a while since I was dizzy as fuck, but I felt his warm hand on my skin guiding me. "Was babysitting part of the deal?" I questioned once I settled.

"My father would have skinned me alive if I left you to fend for yourself." Of course, Ever wouldn't care otherwise.

"So only blackmailing me is allowed?"

He shoved his fingers through his hair and frowned. "I could have hurt you," he quietly admitted, referring to the night I followed him. "I wanted to hurt you."

"What stopped you?"

"Does it matter now?" he countered.

"I bet your mother would be proud." I caught the doubt in his eyes before he looked away. "Tell me something about her."

He chuckled dryly, and I didn't understand why until he said, "She would have loved you. You are the karma I deserve."

I stretched and buried deeper under the covers to hide what his words did to me. "This doesn't change anything. I'll still hate you in the morning."

Standing, he said, "You don't hate me, Four, but you will."

"Oh yeah? What makes you so sure?" I challenged with a yawn. My eyes were already drifting shut.

"Because for the first time, you're going to do what you're told."

I had a foul taste in my mouth, and my dry lips felt like they'd been sealed shut when my tongue tried to break free to wet them. Sunlight poured in through the open blinds, and I cursed its presence when I opened my eyes. Judging from the way I felt, last night had not gone well. I sat up and took inventory. The clothes I'd worn were folded neatly at the foot of my bed, and another note waited for me on my nightstand.

Once upon a puppet, the peer awaited her in his chambers.

I dug the heels of my hands into my eyes and groaned as details from last night came flooding back. I'd gotten shitfaced to spite Ever, but I never imagined he'd be the one babysitting me. I knew I couldn't risk defying him again, but there was no way I could face him without toothpaste, a hot shower, and a brush.

The house was quiet when I emerged from my room and tiptoed to Ever's half an hour later. I debated if I should knock, and after a second of deliberation, I grabbed the knob and pushed open the door. My hope that I would invade his space as thoroughly as he had my mind died when I looked around the empty room.

It was the same as before: clean, gray, and meticulous. The picture of his mother was the only proof that a boy with a beating heart lived within these walls. I was debating if I should leave or wait for him when the door to the bathroom opened and he stepped through.

I knew I was staring, possibly drooling, but it was impossible to look away. He wore nothing but a towel, and water dripped from the ends of his silky brown hair and down his chest before disappearing under the towel.

He didn't seem surprised or at all bothered by my ill-timed presence. With a nod toward his desk, he said, "Have a seat."

"Most people say good morning."

Ever didn't react other than to stare at me until I obeyed. From his desk chair, I watched him disappear into his closet and listened as he opened and closed drawers. When he came back, he was still bare-chested, but now wore navy blue track pants with three white stripes down the sides, and in his hand was one of his red uniform ties.

"After last night, I suppose the least I can do is wish you a happy birthday." I smiled, but he didn't smile back. *Okay, getting weird.* "Ever?"

He tossed the tie on the bed and came to stand behind the chair. "I gave you an order, and you disobeyed me. Again."

"You don't speak to me unless it's to order me around." I shrugged. "I was pissed."

"Being a brat isn't part of our deal."

"Well, maybe I want to renegotiate."

"It was never a negotiation."

"Then our deal is off. Tell your dad that Rosalyn has a past. I have news of my own." I stood to leave but his hands on my shoulders, shoving me down, ensured that I didn't.

"A little advice?" His fierce whisper sent a chill down my spine. "How I make you feel is irrelevant. What I'll do if you piss *me* off should be your only focus. You need to fear it…for your own good." A sheet of paper and a pen appeared in front of me. "Now write this down: I will not drink to excess. Fill the page, front and back."

I peeked over my shoulder and just as I feared, Ever was *dead* serious.

"You're out of your mind." I tried leaving again, but he planted his hands on the desk, caging me in.

"And you're out of your league, little troublemaker. So, write the fucking words."

"And if I don't?"

"Then I'll have some fun."

The room and everything outside it faded as we glared back at one another, silently trying to break the other's will. His minty fresh breath was a cool but inept balm against the heat radiating from his bare chest, and suddenly, I realized just how close he was and how much it was affecting me. With a sneer that made him smile, I picked up the pen.

Anything to get him to move to the other side of that room before…nothing.

Absolutely fucking nothing.

Ever retreated to his bed, and I watched as he grabbed a sketchbook from the nightstand and plucked a pencil from the cup shelved above his bed. He seemed engrossed as he stared at the pad for a few seconds, but then he suddenly looked up and caught me staring. I felt my teeth bite into my bottom lip, and almost like a reflex, his gaze dropped, and he licked his own.

Yeah, nothing's going to happen like pigs are going to fly.

I turned away and put pen to paper while trying to ignore the fact that we were alone in his room with the door shut and our parents oblivious. When both sides of the page were full, I smiled down at my handy work.

"Oh, teach?"

I listened as he stopped mid-pencil stroke and stood from the bed. I worked hard not to give myself away when he lifted my atonement from the desk.

A moment later he sighed.

"I bet you don't know just how predictable you are."

The smile I didn't know I wore dropped.

Predictable?

What the hell did he mean *predictable?*

I schooled my features so I wouldn't let on that I was bothered by yet another one of his unsolicited opinions of me. In lieu of writing what he wanted, I'd listed the components and specifications of a 1999 Suzuki Hayabusa. Gruff certainly would have been proud.

"If you'll excuse me, I think I'll get some breakfast." I pushed away from the desk, forcing him back. This time, Ever let me stand, but with one quick move, he was sitting at the foot of his bed with me on his lap.

"I'm going to give you *one* chance to apologize." My lips parted so I could tell him I wouldn't be doing that now or ever. "But, Four"—his arms wrapped tighter around my middle while his lips brushed my ear—"only one."

"Why should I when you never do?"

"I don't regret what I've done."

"Neither do I."

He sighed, and seconds later, my shorts were around my ankles, and he had me bent over his lap.

"What are you doing?" I squealed. I might as well have been wrestling a tree. My panty-clad bottom was exposed, and I was sure my face resembled a tomato.

"My father believed sparing the rod spoiled the child. Now he thinks mistakes can be a necessary evil...I'm not my father, Four. Putting yourself at risk, tarnishing my family's name, and pissing me the fuck off? *Huge* mistake."

It could have been anger or fear that made my body tremble in his lap. I couldn't tell. I was experiencing them both in equal volume. "So, what? You hurt me a little, and I'll be brought to heel?" I scoffed. "Imagine that."

"Oh, I do. More than you know."

"I didn't take you for the kinky type." I pushed and pulled but couldn't get free.

He snorted, not at all bothered by my struggles. "I'm not... but I like seeing you like this."

The fight left my body as I peeked over my shoulder. For once, his eyes weren't cold or taunting. "Like what?" I sounded much too eager for the answer.

"Pliant." He ran a hand over my butt. "I like you tame, and I like you wild. Maybe I'll keep you both."

"You don't get a say."

His eyebrow rose in response. "Is this your first day?"

"So, spank me," I huffed and wiggled to get free. "I can take it."

"You think so?"

"Or maybe I'll just scream." Seriously, *why* hadn't that occurred to me before?

"And when our parents find you bent over my lap with your ass cherry red, I want you to tell them *exactly* why I made it so."

Oh...right.

Seeing no other way out of this, I sunk my teeth into his calf.

He grunted, and I had only a second when he released me to escape. I rolled off his lap, but when I made for the door, I tripped over the shorts at my ankles. *Damn it!* Ever was hauling me up before I could untangle myself. Somehow, our struggle ensued without either of us making much sound beyond a grunt or growl. I wasn't sure how long we'd been wrestling before Ever lost his footing, dodging the elbow aimed for his nose, and sent us both crashing onto his bed. There, we both seemed to surrender, our heavy breathing the only sound. With my head resting on his chest, I closed my eyes, and his out-of-control heartbeat became my anchor. It occurred to me, however, that one of us would need to claim victory, so I angled my head and found him watching me.

"Still like me wild?" I winked.

If his control was a tightrope, it just snapped.

Suddenly, flat on my back, thick lips crashed into mine. If ever I were to think back to this moment, it would be for one thing. Bliss. Not even with Michelangelo's imagination could I have painted it better. My first kiss.

My arms wrapped around his neck. Hard and demanding became soft and giving. Ever groaned, and I opened up to devour the sound. He didn't hesitate to sweep his tongue inside while the hand he would have used to bring me to heel massaged my lower belly. Sometime later, when we both needed air, he lifted his head and stared down at me with lust-filled eyes.

"Jesus, Four." His chest heaved as he fought to catch his breath. "Can I touch you?"

My brow lifted because he'd never asked for permission before, but then understanding dawned when the tips of his fingers dipped underneath the band of my cotton panties.

I was suspended between lust and common sense when a knock on Ever's door had us jumping apart.

"I hate to interrupt, but you're needed downstairs," Jamie called.

"Fuck," Ever growled. He seemed unhinged as he jammed his fingers in his hair.

I wanted to laugh, but I was done making mistakes today. Or so I hoped. I still couldn't believe what happened, and I just *let* it.

"Let Four know her mother is waiting for her downstairs, too." Jamie snickered, and we listened as he walked away.

"I need to go," I announced after shaking off the euphoria.

"We need to talk."

"Can't imagine what for." I avoided his gaze as I lifted my shorts from the floor. They must have fallen completely off sometime while we fought. I couldn't believe I actually wrestled him in nothing but my panties and a tank top. I felt myself blushing again and angrily shoved my legs into my shorts.

He blew out air, and I smiled to myself. I guess the prince had a temper after all. "Come to my room later."

I barked out a laugh. "More orders."

"Yes," he hissed. "Come, or I'll find you, and I won't care who's around."

"Whatever." My shorts were back around my hips, and I quickly buttoned them so that I could get the hell out of there, but then he turned me around to face him and hauled me back into his lap. My body seemed to have a mind of its own. With my knees framing his waist, forearms resting on his shoulders, and his hands cupping my ass, I let him kiss me again. Somehow, his lips jump-started my hips, and soon, I was grinding down on him as we both fought for dominance.

"Goddamn it, Four." The need in Ever's voice tempted me, but it was the warning in his eyes to steer clear that held me back. "I'm going to be inside you soon enough."

"Don't bet on it."

His chuckle was sexy and masculine as his hands massaged my ass. "I don't need to. I'm starting to believe you being in

Blackwood Keep wasn't God or some deity's sick sense of humor. It's fate, baby."

"Fate or not…" I moaned around his tongue when he fed it to me. "…this isn't happening again." I dodged his lips and hopped off his lap while I still had the chance. I wasn't about to be tamed by him or anyone else. Deal or no deal. Ever sat on the foot of his bed looking hungry and predatory as I backed away to the door. Slowly, he was becoming a contrast to the cold and emotionless boy I met a year ago. It was as if I were the flap of the butterfly's wings that started his storm. I couldn't look away. I couldn't turn and run. Completely enchanted, I watched this tempest brew.

The sounds outside his room were beginning to unnerve me. What if we had been caught? How would we have explained my swollen lips and Ever's hard-on? This had to end right here and now. "Stay away from me, McNamara."

Amusement softened his features. "Not going to happen, Archer."

chapter eighteen

The Peer

TWENTY MINUTES AGO, I'D HAD FOUR'S SHORTS AROUND HER ANKLES and my tongue down her throat, and now I sat across from her eating fucking birthday cake with her mom and my dad like our situation was normal. I had taken my time coming down after Four ran from my room because a family breakfast with a raging hard-on wasn't an option.

I forked another piece of coconut cake, my mother's favorite, into my mouth, but I didn't taste it. I didn't exactly care for my father continuing a tradition of birthday cake for breakfast with his plaything and her daughter, but I kept my mouth shut. My father and I have barely spoken since he brought them to live in the home he once shared with my mother. The supposed love of his life. Getting your rocks off was one thing. Replacing the memories my mother created here with us was a new low of fucked up. He didn't seem too concerned with repairing our relationship any more than I did. Maybe it was because he knew that the only way he could was to send them away. Yeah, I told Four that fate had brought her here, but my dick had been hard at the time. I was thinking clearly now, and I realized Four was right. What happened in the bedroom couldn't happen again. The next time she broke the rules, our deal was off. Getting rid of them would be a piece of cake, which brought the question of why I hadn't done it already.

"Son," my father called from the head of the table.

Everyone's attention had shifted from cake to me.

"Sir?"

He dropped his linen napkin on the table and stood. "Take a walk with me."

I followed him out of the kitchen and through the front door, stopping short when I saw what awaited me.

"Happy birthday, son."

My surprise was genuine as I admired my father's gift to me. The Range was only a couple years old, and my father was at the top of the list of people I'd been a dick toward, so a car wasn't what I'd been expecting. And not just any car.

A freaking G Wagon.

The matte army green paint job had to be custom. It paired well with the dark tint and black rims, making it clear he knew me better than I would have given him credit.

I didn't know what to say or do, so I lamely offered my father my hand to shake. He stared at it for a moment, and I could tell he was disappointed, maybe even sad, but then he took my hand and shook it.

"What do you think of me turning the keys to the Range Rover over to Four? You wouldn't have to drive her to school, and she'd have more freedom."

Freedom?

No, freedom was the last thing the troublemaker needed.

"I think the last time she got behind a wheel, she made it four hundred miles before you caught her. If she runs again, she won't make finding her easy this time."

"Ah…you might be right." He handed me the keys and patted my back. "Try to keep it under a hundred, huh?"

I was aware of him watching me while I got a closer look. I was grinning ear to ear by the time I sunk into the black leather seat and admired the interior. My father had set me up with the Range Rover after I got my license because he said it was safer than anything I might wrap around a tree. I guess he still wasn't taking chances, but the hefty price tag on the G Wagon told me he trusted me more than he had two years ago. I wanted to take it for a spin, so I hopped out to tell my father.

He simply waved me off and headed back inside. Something made me glance up before I could duck back inside. Four stood at one of the windows upstairs staring down at me with her arms crossed and a curious expression. I considered kidnapping her—I had a hunch she wouldn't come willingly— and taking her for a drive so we could have that talk. Just as I was ready to give in to the urge, Jamie burst through the front door tugging a shirt on.

"Don't even think about taking that beast for a spin without me."

Jamie became a tornado once he climbed inside and started fiddling with buttons, and when I looked up again, she was gone. With a sigh, I dropped back into my new ride and tried not to burn rubber when I took off.

I guess some things just aren't meant to be.

I was sitting across from Franklin Rees two days later while Vaughn was at football practice. I hadn't told him I was meeting with his father because he'd insist on coming when his focus needed to stay on football. Getting drafted and being star quarterback was his dream, but Franklin fully expected his son to one day become his successor.

"I understand my son told you about your mother." Being the leader of Thirteen who only knew him as Father had visibly aged Franklin. The fine lines spreading from temple to temple and thinning salt-and-pepper hair were evidence of that.

"As you should have...sir."

Vaughn had discovered the truth behind my mother's disappearance and hadn't thought twice about incurring his father's wrath when he shared it with me. We'd managed to keep my dealings with Exiled a secret until a few nights ago.

"Given this suicidal plan you have to get close to Fox, I'd say I made the right call."

"I've been Exiled for eight months and hunting him for twelve. I'm obviously still breathing and even closer to Fox than you've ever been."

"I didn't say you weren't smart—resourceful even—but what will you do if you're caught, and there's a gun to your head? I've witnessed the coldest of men unable to look death in the eye."

"I won't get caught."

"You may be smart, but Fox is worse than ruthless. He doesn't need a reason for his sins. He just needs the power to commit them."

"Is this why you called me here? To talk me out of going after him? Excuse me if I have a hard time believing you actually care."

"No, son. I called you here to offer my assistance, but I need you to look me in my eye and tell me that I can trust you."

I frowned at a man whose own son didn't trust him and he expected me to? "Why would I do that? I didn't ask for your help."

Franklin remained stoic as he made a quick phone call, requesting someone's presence. Not even a minute later, the door behind me opened.

"You don't want my help, kid, but you're going to get it." Before I could shove to my feet, I felt the cold muzzle of a gun pushed against the back of my skull. "Or I'll make you disappear."

I only had one card to play, so I played it. "Vaughn would never forgive you, and then he'll *never* be Father."

"He'll never know. You and my son have been friends since before either of you even knew how to tie your shoes. I've gotten to know you very well without your or my son's knowledge, so I'm willing to bet you didn't tell him about our meeting."

Fuck.

I knew Franklin would carry out his threat if pushed—you

don't earn the throne he sat on by making empty threats—but I wasn't about to beg for my life like a fucking chump, so I sat very still and considered my only option.

"Who?"

Franklin nodded behind me to the gunman I'd yet to see, so I twisted in my seat and found myself staring into the smiling face of a ghost.

"Hello, Danny Boy."

"Siko?"

"Thought I was dead, huh? Nah…Eddie and I set the whole thing up," he boasted.

My mind raced until one question pushed through the chaos. "Why?"

"We were trying to take out Shane and Wren, make it look like a job gone wrong, but there was a last minute change of plans, and Shane sent you in instead."

"And you helped Harlan escape," Franklin accused. "Why?"

"I told you I didn't want to be responsible for anyone dying. Vaughn thought he could trust you," I lied. "Clearly, he was wrong."

Vaughn had actually been against telling his father anything, warned me not to trust him, but like a fool I had insisted.

Rage deepened the lines marring Franklin's face as he leaned over his desk with his fists planted against the wood. "Don't lecture me about my son. His loyalty should be to me and me only. I couldn't give a shit what you wanted."

"Then find someone else to be your mole."

"Kid…I'll have your brains splattered on the wall before you can take your next breath."

"Then do it. If I were afraid of dying, I wouldn't be Exiled. I wouldn't be hunting Fox, and I wouldn't be telling you to go fuck yourself as I am right now. You came to me because you obviously need me. Siko and Eddie are dead as far as Fox is concerned and getting someone else that close to him will take too long. So here's the thing—I don't work for you, so I don't take orders from you. You want my help, then convince me to spare the fucking time or else, in two seconds, I'm gone."

The room fell so silent that you could have heard a pin drop down the hall. Any second now, I expected Siko to send a bullet through my skull and end it all. Franklin seemed to stare right through me as if he'd been transported to another place.

Just as some of my bravado started to slip, and I begin to think I really was going to die, Franklin sighed as he sat back down. He nodded to Siko, and I felt the pressure from the gun lift. "I'm not going to kill you." He waited for a reaction. I didn't give him one. "Because you're right. I do need you, but you also need me. You're in over your head."

I shrugged, neither agreeing nor disagreeing.

"If you agree to be my eyes and ears, I'll do everything in my power to make sure you stay alive. It's the least I can do for my son."

"Don't pretend you're doing it for him. Thirteen comes first, and it always has. Just ask him."

"Enough, kid. You've made your point." He waved me off, making it clear he had no intention of changing. "We're finished here."

I didn't waste time making for the door just in case he changed his mind and decided to kill me.

"Son." My hand fell from the knob, but his leaden tone warned me not to turn around. "If you succeed, you're going to find a lot more than what you were looking for."

"I told you I'm not afraid of dying."

When he didn't respond, I ripped open the door, ready to bolt, but then he sighed and said, "You're going to wish it was that simple."

chapter nineteen

∞

the Puppet

One Month Later

I T WAS HOMECOMING, AND TYRA HAD SUCCEEDED IN DRAGGING ME TO
my first Brynwood football game. I didn't understand where
her sudden fascination came from, but anywhere was better
than another evening in the palace. It had been a month since
Ever tried to spank me and when he failed, kissed me instead.
We'd pretty much gone back to pretending the other didn't exist,
but there had been a lingering look or two.

The band and the cheerleaders were working hard to get everyone pumped. Jefferson High certainly couldn't compete with
Brynwood's morale and talent. It was a packed house, so I didn't
think we'd get seats, but I followed Tyra to the bleachers anyway.
She was scanning the front row, and I started to tell her it was a
pipe dream until two guys I usually saw following Ever, Vaughn,
and Jamie around rose from their seats behind the team bench.
I thought it was just luck until they nodded and took off. Tyra
didn't seem surprised as she sank into one of the seats and started
texting. Perks of being the coach's daughter I guess.

A deafening roar came from the crowd, and Tyra's head shot
up from her phone when the team ran out to meet their oppo-
nents on the field. Vaughn suited in a jersey numbered seventeen
was the last to emerge with his arm casually thrown over Ever's
shoulders as he laughed at something Ever said.

Tyra's sharp inhale drew my attention, but she was back to rapidly texting on her phone, so I shrugged and watched the most wanted boys in school separate. Ever went to stand on the sidelines with the coach while Vaughn jogged to join the huddle. The game began soon after that, and I was happy to have something to focus on. Keeping my eyes off Ever, however, became impossible as the game went on. He wore blue jeans and a plain white T-shirt with his red and navy letterman jacket. Because his back was to the stands, I couldn't see his face, but I noticed his shoulders tensed when a play went south or one of our players was tackled. Thanks to a smooth pass off from Vaughn, our team made the first touchdown of the game, and Tyra, along with the rest of the homestand, stood to cheer. I shrugged and stood as well to clap and cheer.

Big mistake.

Ever turned, and his determined gaze searched the stands. It wasn't me he was looking for. No way could he have picked my voice out of the crowd.

But then he caught me watching him, and my fingers dug into my jean-clad thighs when he said something to the coach and headed toward the stands. He didn't bother to take the stairs, though. He hoisted himself onto the platform and climbed through the rails.

"You could have just taken the stairs," I griped when he towered over me.

"The look on your face was too priceless to pass up."

"Well, if you don't mind, I'm trying to watch the game."

"Didn't look like it."

I felt my heart skip a beat. "Excuse me?"

"You heard me." He sat in the empty seat next to me, leaned forward to rest his elbows on his thighs, and went back to watching the game, pointedly ignoring me.

I huffed and tried to concentrate on the game, but all I could think about was his arousing scent and his hard thigh pressed against my own. I peeked at him from the corner of my eye to see if he noticed, but he was completely zoned in on the field.

Take a walk, and get your shit together, Archer.

"I'm going to the concession stand," I announced to no one in particular.

Ever tore his attention away from the field, and I could feel his irritated gaze following me as I made my way down the bleachers. The crowd was thick, so it took me a while to make my way through it. When I finally made it to the concession stand, I purchased a bottle of water so I didn't return empty-handed. I wouldn't put it past Ever's arrogance to notice that he had been the reason for my abrupt departure.

"Four?"

Recognizing the voice, I was already grinning when I turned. "Well, look who crawled out from under their rock."

Drake opened his arms, and I stepped into them. I was so happy to see him, I didn't even mind that he reeked of weed.

"Girl, it's been way too long since I've seen you," he said when I stepped out of his embrace.

"Ditto."

"So, how's life been?"

"Complicated."

He nodded and, thankfully, didn't pry. I stood back and listened as he ordered enough snacks to feed ten.

"Where are you sitting?" He then nodded to his friends hanging in an unlit area. "Want to hang with us?"

"Thanks, but I need to get back to my friend." We hugged again and exchanged numbers before parting ways. I was almost halfway back to the stands when I ran into Ever. He didn't look happy, but that wasn't really my problem. I tried walking past when he grabbed my hand and pulled me into his body.

"Are you okay?"

"Why wouldn't I be?"

"Because you're running from me."

"Isn't avoiding each other what we do?"

His gaze narrowed. "So, you're mad at me?"

"Mad would imply that I cared, which I don't." I tried to tug my hand from his, but he gripped me harder and started the walk back to the stands. We returned just as another touchdown was made, so no one noticed us holding hands as we made our way to our seats. Some kid who had freshman written all over him now sat where Ever was sitting before, leaving only one seat left next to Tyra. When he noticed Ever, his eyes bucked, and he started to rise, but then Ever surprised us both when he motioned for the kid to stay and sat in the vacant seat behind me.

I glanced at Tyra to see if she noticed any of the exchange, but she was still fixated on the field. I never knew she was such a huge football fan, but I suppose it made sense given that her father coached the team.

Because of my dad, I had found racing.

I didn't discover who he was until I was ten years old. Rosalyn had kept the only clue to his identity in her jewelry box. Like all young girls do, I'd been playing with her jewelry and makeup when I found the ring. It was heavy, made of platinum with a green gem setting, and dangled carelessly from my finger when I'd tried it on. Even so, I couldn't bear to part with it so I hid it under my pillow. I thought it would be safe there until I came home from school one day to find the house and Rosalyn in shambles.

She'd found the ring and actually accused me of conspiring with a man I didn't know. Only when I'd nursed her back to sanity did I convince her to give me his name with the promise that I'd never ask about him again.

I didn't need to.

It had only taken a single web search to find all the information I needed about Benjamin West—more commonly known to the world as Benny West, a retired NASCAR driver. He was currently living in Charlotte, North Carolina with his wife of *twenty-two* years and his seventeen-year-old son. It didn't take a mathematician to know why it hadn't worked out between Benny and Rosalyn. Not only did I have a famous father, but I was someone's big sister, and he could never know about me. Rosalyn didn't know that I'd discovered who my father was beyond his name. Before he retired, I tuned in for every one of his races. My fascination hadn't been a slow burn. It inflamed me the moment I first watched my father win by a hair. Until a year and a half ago, Rosalyn always assumed my fascination with bikes and racing was a phase even though it lasted seven years and never waned.

I could hardly believe it had been over a year since I last straddled a bike. Of course, Gruff and I still kept in contact, even after I was sent away. I'd occasionally write him letters, and he'd respond in a few short sentences, making them more notes than letters. Reading his 'letters' always made me feel like I was home.

The wind blew, and I shivered. Not used to fall in the north, I'd chosen to go without a jacket and opted for a red printed thermal instead, but it wasn't doing a good job protecting me from the elements. I wrapped my arms around myself to ward off the chill and refocused on the game, but then the heavy feel of something cloaking my shoulders stole my attention. I glanced down and saw it was navy leather with red sleeves swallowing most of my body.

Ever had given me his jacket.

I debated declining his offer, but his scent beckoned me into its warmth. I wanted to roll around in it until it lingered on my skin. I was still considering giving it back when he leaned over to wrap me tighter in his jacket.

"Don't take it off."

A second gust blew through the stands, and his order was suddenly one I didn't mind obeying. I slipped my arms through the sleeves and sighed when his heat and scent surrounded me. His jacket was huge on me and a bit heavy, but man, was I warm. Tyra glanced back at Ever and then shot me an inquisitive look. Knowing how it must have looked, I shrugged, feeling guilt clawing at my skin. After one last suspicious look, she went back to watching the game.

I bet Ever was proud of himself.

We won the game by a landslide. Everyone in the stands was still going wild when Ever took off without a word and without his jacket. It wasn't until the crowd began dispersing that I felt the stares. People were beginning to notice the McNamara name boldly flaunted across my back.

Tyra had been going on and on about some celebration at the Point tonight, but eventually, even she noticed the attention.

"People are staring," she huffed.

The wind was blowing steadily now, and the air was chillier, but it didn't compare to the discomfort of people staring, so I shed the jacket. Shivering, I looked around for Ever. The team was busy shaking hands with the opposing team when I caught a glimpse of him on the other side of the gate standing with Vaughn and the coach.

"Come on." I started to pull Tyra with me onto the field but stopped when she resisted.

"Um…I think I'll just wait for you here."

I faced her with my hands on my hips. "Wasn't it you who only recently proclaimed herself my best friend through thick and thin?"

"Yes," she answered slowly.

"This is the thick, my friend." I grabbed her hand again, and this time, she didn't fight me.

Vaughn was the first to notice our approach. His gaze passed over me and lingered on something over my shoulder before he nudged Ever. They were standing in the middle of the field, and I hadn't even covered half the distance, but I could still tell that Ever wasn't happy with me yet again. The coach stopped mid-sentence when Ever walked away to meet me across the field.

"I know you're cold," he said with a growl. "Put the coat back on."

"I'll be fine." I held out his jacket, but he didn't even look at it.

"Put. It. On."

My arm dropped to my side, and neither of us cared that his jacket was practically lying on the field now. "Why do you care so much?"

"You're no use to me sick."

"Please. You got bored toying with me weeks ago."

Tyra's wide eyes shot back and forth between us, but I was too pissed to care how our argument might look.

"Four, so help me..." He took a step toward me, but Coach Bradley clapped a hand on Ever's shoulder, keeping him at bay.

"Son"—the coach chuckled good-naturedly—"everyone knows you catch more flies with honey than vinegar."

Ever rudely shrugged off the coach's hold and grabbed my hand before stalking off. His G Wagon, which was totally boss, was parked at the dark end of the football field, and we were headed straight for it. I resisted a little harder, so he threw me over his shoulders and slapped my ass. I was blushing hard as I looked around but the field and the stands were mostly cleared. When we reached his car, he trapped me between him and the hood after setting me on my feet.

"You really need to learn some manners."

"Put the jacket on." I was getting ready to deny him again when he added, "Please."

"If you had only listened, I would have told you it wasn't necessary for me to wear this anymore because I'm going home."

He shook his head. "Tyra's going to the campfire."

"And?"

"She would have talked you into going."

"You don't know that." I had no intentions of being around Ever and his people for an entire night.

"I do know." His hand cupped my hip, and I could feel his fingers splayed over my ass as he tugged me closer. "I know that the last thing you want is to be stuck at home with our parents."

I sighed, exasperated even as my toes tingled. "You're not seriously starting this up again, are you?"

His nose grazed the side of my neck. "So what if I am?"

"The last time you touched me like this, you turned to ice after you had your fun. I'm not a toy, Ever."

"Yes, you are, puppet. My father is a rich man, so I've never wanted for anything." He fingered the end of my ponytail and stepped back. "But then you proved to me that the best things in life really are free." I watched from the corner of my eye as he walked around to the driver's side. "I don't care if you come to the bonfire or crawl under a rock, but I care if you're no use to me. Put on the fucking jacket."

Ever's prediction came true. Tyra had convinced me to go to the celebration bonfire after the game. The beach was already full when we arrived. There were also a few fires burning with our classmates drinking, dancing, and making out around them. Brynwood's finest, the football players, partied hardest amongst the crowd while music poured from the red Jeep Wrangler Sahara Jamie bought a couple weeks ago. I'd been bumming rides to school from him ever since. The back hatch was open, and I didn't notice Jamie sitting in the back until he called my name.

"A party ain't a party unless Four Archer's in the house!"

I couldn't help admiring how tempting he looked in the red beanie that only covered the crown of his head, hoodless Red Sox sweatshirt, and blue jeans. "You don't mean that one bit."

"No, I don't. You need to loosen up, girl. I get enough of my cousin's stuffiness."

"What? I'm loose," I defended.

His expression turned stale as he looked me over. "You look constipated."

Tyra tried to be a friend and hold her laugh in, but it burst out, and I found myself joining her. "Jamie, I can't decide if you're the best or worst kind of frenemy."

"Frenemy?" He had the nerve to look genuinely confused. "We aren't cool, Four?"

"Not when you use me to mess with your cousin."

Tyra's ears practically pricked at my comment. Despite us being close, I hadn't told her what had occurred between Ever and me when no one was looking. Tyra loved to gossip like no other. Sure, I trusted her, but I trusted only me with my dirty secrets.

And Ever McNamara was most definitely my dirty little secret. And I was his.

"Aw." Jamie clutched his chest. "I thought you forgave me."

"I have, but I won't ever forget, so maybe think twice before you put me in the middle of your feud again."

"You were a necessary evil, Archer." He tugged on the sleeve of Ever's jacket as if my wearing it made his point. *Maybe it did.*

"I was not amused, Buchanan."

"Fine." He groaned and pulled me into a tight hug. Unable to resist, I hugged him back. Jamie could be quite charming when he kept his mouth closed. I had only just relaxed when Tyra's phone pinged.

"Uh, I'm going to catch up with you later, Four."

My head lifted quickly from Jamie's chest. Was she seriously ditching me after begging me to come? "What?"

She was already backing away with a sheepish look. "You're good with Jamie, right?"

"Tyra…"

"I'll be right back. Promise!"

I was left gaping after her as she hurried down the beach.

"This will be the last time I let her drag me anywhere."

"Aw, don't be too hard on her," Jamie advised. "It's not her fault, after all."

My nose wrinkled as I looked up at Jamie. "What do you mean?"

His eyebrows lifted. "You really don't know?"

"Know what?"

"Vaughn and your friend...they're hooking up."

"No, they're not."

"Yeah, Four. Have been since Ever's birthday bash."

"She would have said something to me."

"Would she? Have you even told her about you and my cousin?"

"Why would I when there's nothing to tell?"

"Tell that to someone who doesn't see the way you two look at each other when you think no one is paying attention."

"Have you ever considered telling stories for a living? You have quite the imagination."

"You must be driving my cousin's head wild," he said as if I hadn't spoken. "He's never been rejected before."

"I don't know why. His personality sucks."

"Yeah, but they don't want *him*, they want our money."

I sometimes forget that Jamie was just as privileged as Ever. Maybe because he was down to earth while Ever kept his nose in the air. "No amount of money could make me suffer through life with that spoiled prick."

Jamie playfully brushed his thumb down my cheek while gazing at me lovingly. "And that's why you're his one, lass."

I batted his hand away and grumbled, "You won't be saying that when I knock him off his pedestal."

"Ever's need to protect and avenge gave him one hell of a mean streak. You shouldn't push him."

"Why should I listen to you? You push him all the time."

He shrugged, but I could see the torment in his eyes. "I've got nothing Ever hasn't already taken."

"Why don't you get even? No one can be *that* forgiving."

His eyebrows rose as a lascivious smile brightened his features. "Is that an invitation?"

"I'm just curious why you hang out with him even though you claim he betrayed you. The two of you fight all the time, but you're hardly ever apart."

"We're at each other's throats, but that doesn't mean I don't have his back and he doesn't have mine. No one's allowed to fuck with him but me."

"But *why* are you still loyal to him?"

"We're family," he answered with exasperation. "And no girl will ever change that."

"Even if she's *your one*?"

His nostrils flared. "She showed me years ago that she wasn't." He took a sip of his beer and looked off into the distance.

"If that were true, then seeing her with him wouldn't torture you so much." His gaze met mine. "Anyone can see that it does."

"Maybe I just don't want her to be happy."

"I'm having a hard time believing you're that selfish."

"You don't know me well."

"But I have good instincts." It was the only thing keeping me from crossing the line with his cousin. If I strayed too close, Ever would find his way into a part of me that was forbidden to him.

He smirked. "Instincts won't be enough to save you from falling for my cousin."

Laughter burst from my stomach, though my heart sobbed with despair. "First, I'm making eyes at him, and now I'm falling in love?" I was bent over, wiping tears from my cheeks when Ever spoke from behind me.

"Who's the lucky guy?"

I straightened up immediately and caught the satisfied look on Jamie's face. He must have seen Ever coming and set me up. With a look, I promised retribution and turned to face Ever.

"Where's your girlfriend?"

Jamie stiffened beside me, and Ever's jaw hardened. *I can play, too, boys.*

"Four," Ever warned.

"Shouldn't you be more concerned about her and less with me?" You could cut the tension with a knife. Jamie's jealousy was palpable, but it was the emotion in Ever's eyes that sent a chill down my spine. I knew antagonizing them was a little more than petty, but I was getting sick of them playing me like a fiddle.

"Barbette knows how to behave."

Jamie's low growl raised the hairs on the back of my neck.

"Wow, McNamara. She's your girlfriend, not your pet," I instigated. I could practically hear the steam blowing from Jamie's ears.

Ever's eyes narrowed, and then he was reaching for me, but Jamie's next words stopped him cold.

"I don't know what she fucking sees in you."

In the blink of an eye, Ever's demeanor shifted from mildly annoyed to ruthless. "No...you don't, which is why she's no longer yours."

I didn't expect my heart to plummet or bile to rise at seeing Ever so possessive of another. Jamie looked ready to rip Ever apart, yet he shoved his cousin, which was less than he deserved, and stalked away down the beach.

I'd forgotten Ever was standing there as I watched Jamie go until he growled, "Happy with yourself?"

Not really, no. "I'm not the one dating your cousin's ex."

Ever fell into step beside me as I walked away.

"Barbette and Jamie chasing each other's tails for a couple of summers doesn't make me a traitor."

I whirled on him, but he was already a few paces away.

Jogging, I caught up and swiftly cut him off. "What the hell are you talking about, McNamara?"

"Their so-called *relationship* happened when we were *kids*. It was over quicker than it started." With a bored look, he moved around me, but I quickly fell into step beside him. I'd worry that someone might mistake this for a romantic stroll on the beach later. It was time I got some answers.

"Why did it end?"

"I don't know, Four." He sounded annoyed while avoiding my gaze, which told me he wasn't being entirely truthful. "They don't talk about it, and I don't ask. When those summers ended and Jamie returned home to Boston, they would write to each other, but one day, the letters just stopped."

"Why did he stop writing her?"

Ever shot me a look and said, "She stopped writing *him*."

"Oh."

"Jamie didn't waste time hopping on a train to Blackwood Keep to find out why." He smiled faintly at the memory. "My aunt and uncle were furious when they discovered their fourteen-year-old had snuck away to travel two-hundred miles alone."

"So what happened?"

"Jamie got his answer, and Barbette went home with a bruised knee and scraped hands. The next day, her parents showed up at our house and demanded that Jamie stay away from her."

"And did he?"

"He didn't have a choice. A few months later, Jamie's father moved his career and his family to Scotland. Jamie visited before he left. Probably to make up with her but..."

"By then, you and Barbie were an item."

He looked at me quizzically.

"Tyra told me."

"You shouldn't believe everything someone tells you."

"It's not as if I could ask *you*." I clutched his jacket a little tighter when the wind blew. "So, why are you going steady with your cousin's ex?"

He stopped short and tapped the side of his forehead as if the question was trivial. "Has it ever occurred to you that I might just be into her?"

"No...and that's the problem, my dear prince. You don't touch her, you don't kiss her, you don't look at her like..."

"Like what?" he snapped.

Like you look at me. I shoved the truth down and locked it away as he shifted closer with cruel eyes.

"Why do you care anyway? I'm blackmailing you to keep your mouth shut, yet you're worried about my love life?"

Yeah, my priorities were really screwed, but I had my reason, and it followed me into my dreams. I cleared my throat, erasing the vulnerability from my voice. Now if only I could do the same for my heart. "I care because of those kisses you stole a month ago. I never imagined my first kiss would be with a boy who belonged to someone else."

He closed his eyes while I held my breath.

Too much. I said too much.

When he opened them again, there was a gleam that suspiciously resembled satisfaction. "If you're feeling guilty, don't."

"That's not good enough."

He sounded resigned to a fate he didn't want when he said, "It will have to be."

I tried to cross my arms, but the weight of his jacket made them heavy, so I settled for balling my fists even though they'd been completely swallowed by the sleeves. "Or maybe I'll tell her what a cheating asshole you are."

I was completely thrown when he shrugged and smoothly lowered his body until he sat in the sand.

Did he care so little for his girlfriend's feelings?

Disgust rolled through me and on its heels...elation. I had to be the worst human being on the planet.

He suddenly reached up and tugged me down next to him. I frantically looked around, scared of who might see, but the bonfire was only streams of smoke in the distance.

"It's all right," he said with a secret curve of his lips. "You're safe with me."

Alone in the dark on the beach?

I'd be safer in the sea with hungry sharks.

As we listened to the waves crash, I wondered what his mother would have to say about her son, the rake. "Tell me about your mom."

He looked away, letting me see his tight jaw and nothing else. "What about her?"

"I was told she disappeared. That she might have even…left?"

He shrugged as if it didn't matter. "She did leave."

My head was spinning from all the questions that seemed too insensitive to ask. With a lump in my throat, I could only choke out, "I'm sorry, Ever." They were the only words that seemed right. Fisting my hands in the sand to keep from pulling him close, I watched his nostrils flare as he stared out at the water.

When he spoke again, each syllable was laced with shame and regret.

"My father and I didn't really give her much reason to stick around. He was always working, and I was always causing trouble."

"You were growing up."

"I was making her *sick*."

"I don't understand."

"The morning she left, she was going to visit her sister in New York. She hated the city, and I never knew why. I only knew that I made her desperate enough to go back." In a much quieter voice, he added, "She was only supposed to be gone for the weekend."

"What did you mean by you were making her sick?"

"She had anxiety. Before she left for her sister's, she had an attack. Her blood pressure had gotten so high her doctor recommended she get away from whatever was causing her so much stress."

"What happened?"

"My mother found out a girl tried to kill herself…because of me. I was too stupid to know she was suffering before I—"

"Before you slept with her?"

Ever simply stared back at me through sad eyes. My heart felt strangled in my chest as I recalled Jamie's claim that Ever had changed. Maybe guilt had been the reason. Ever still went to parties, but I'd never actually seen him *enjoy* them. He didn't dance, drink, or hookup with girls even though there was always a line of them waiting to be chosen.

"Was her name Olivia Portland?"

Adam's apple bobbing, he looked away.

"I shouldn't be surprised that you know," he said after a while.

"You didn't think the most popular boy at school would be excluded from gossip, did you?" My teasing was meant to lighten the mood, but his expression only became more solemn.

"I'd rather you get your facts from me. At least then I could be sure you believed only the truth."

I was startled by his admission but smart enough not to let it show. "Why should I trust you not to lie to me?"

"There are worse things I could do to you. Lying should be the least of your concerns."

"I see Exiled is training you well," I remarked snippily.

"Good." His smile was faint but dripped with deadly intent. "I'll need them to."

Ignoring the phantom feel of icy fingers trailing down my spine, I hastily tried to dissect his meaning. It was the first indication he'd given that he was Exiled for a reason other than simply seeking a thrill.

"Why join a gang? You have everything you could ever want."

Eyes shooting flames, he said, "You don't know shit about what I want."

"Then enlighten me. You seem to know all of my secrets. Level the playing field."

He bared his teeth and smirked. "I know your secrets because I'm clever." Amber eyes that reminded me of autumn dropped to my lips where a sneer was forming. "And you're reckless," he whispered.

"I'm reckless because I have to be. It seems to me like you joined a gang because spending Daddy's money got boring, and you needed a thrill."

Only a millisecond passed before I was shoved onto my back. I had to quickly close my eyes to keep the sand from getting in my eyes. Ever didn't move or make a sound, but he didn't have to.

I could feel him.

When I opened my eyes, he was crouched low over me with his elbows resting on his thighs.

"You constantly bring up my family's money as if it's what truly separates us. Would you like to know the difference between you and I, little troublemaker? You run from your demons. I chase mine."

Heart pumping and skin flushed with shame because maybe he was right, I could only muster through gritted teeth, "Get off me."

"You're free to go," he replied matter-of-factly.

Still, he didn't move an inch.

And because he wasn't actually restraining me or even touching me for that matter, I realized he expected me to crawl if I wanted to leave.

Feeling murderous by the time I stood, I furiously brushed the sand caked on my skin and clothes, then started the short trek back to the bonfire without looking back.

Maybe Ever was right about being the clever one. I couldn't help but feel as if I had drawn the short stick. We lived in the same house, rode to school together, shared meals, and have even kissed, but while he seemed to know my every thought, desires, and fear, I realized that I was not even close to discovering his.

Once I reached the bonfire, I headed straight for one of the large blue coolers. Before I could reach for the white lid, however, some guy shoved a fresh beer in my hands.

Returning his smile, I lifted the can. "Cheers."

I had only just popped the top when the beer was plucked from my hand by Ever. I was too shocked to do anything but watch as he took a healthy gulp of *my* beer and gave who I assumed was our classmate a threatening look that sent him running to the other side of the party.

"Why did you do that?"

Rather than respond, he began rummaging through the cooler until he pulled out a beer, popped the top, and handed it to me.

Clutching the cold can to my chest, I repeated my question.

"Don't take a drink from anyone else except Vaughn or Jamie," he ordered.

"Afraid I'll smear the McNamara name?"

"Nothing you do will be worse than what I'll do if some-one—" His eyes seemed to glow while heat bloomed in my belly, and desperation for him to finish that sentence filled me. Instead, he looked me up and down and said, "I still haven't decided if you're worth the trouble yet."

I was still sneering at his retreating back when Tyra appeared out of nowhere and grabbed my shoulders.

"I've been looking for you everywhere!" she yelled.

"Are you okay?" Even while she shook me, it was hard to miss her flustered appearance.

"Where were you?" she demanded.

"In the corner feeling abandoned," I deadpanned.

She managed to look guilty and satisfied all at once.

"Weren't you just talking to Ever?"

"Are you really hooking up with Vaughn?" I shot back.

Her mouth fell open, and she resembled a fish as she stared back at me. "Where did you hear that?"

"Does it matter?"

She shifted from one foot to the other and studied the sand. "I guess not."

"Why didn't you tell me?" *Hypocrite. Aren't you keeping secrets of your own?*

"Thought you'd be upset. You hate Ever, and Vaughn's his best friend. I felt like I was betraying you."

I almost corrected her about my feelings for Ever until I reminded myself that I *did* hate him. Or at least, I should. I came back to this town with the sole purpose of getting back at Ever McNamara, and instead, I found myself wanting to get close to him for entirely different reasons.

"I'm a big girl, Ty. You should do what makes you happy."

It sounded like the truth, but it felt like a lie. I wanted to lash out and tell her that I did think hooking up with Vaughn was a betrayal. That she'd chosen *their* side. I couldn't help but be wary and afraid. I'd lived my life having a mother who chose men over me every single day. Why would Tyra be any different?

"Really?" she squealed with her eyes wide and her hands clasped.

Just then, I felt her excitement and hope, and I realized these feelings she had weren't a fleeting or sudden thing. Tyra had wanted this—wanted him—for a while. Likely before she ever knew I existed.

When I nodded, and she pulled me into a hug, I vowed that Tyra's heart wouldn't be a casualty of my war with Ever. Not by his hand or mine.

"Good!" She gave me one last squeeze of gratitude before letting go. "Because I have *soooo* much to tell you like what an amazing kisser he is."

I groaned, now realizing the trap I'd fallen into. Gossiping about boys was so not my thing.

"I didn't expect a guy like him to be so...*attentive*."

My eyebrows rose at the direction this conversation was going. I also couldn't help but wonder how far they'd gone. "Have you..."

"Slept with him? God, no. I've been holding him off because—" She nervously chewed on her lip, and I filled in the blanks.

"Because you're afraid he'll lose interest once you do?"

She nodded and looked bashful as she said, "I really like him, Four, and sometimes, I believe he's truly interested in me."

"Vaughn is probably used to having pussy served to him on a platter, so if he's sticking around, I'm sure it's because he likes you." *Or saw her as a challenge.* I couldn't voice my fear and risk erasing the happiness etched all over her face. Tyra was practically glowing. "Does your father know about you and him?"

The glow was instantly shrouded by panic. "No, and I plan to keep it that way. He'd never approve of me dating one of his players. *Especially* his quarterback."

"You can't keep it a secret for long, Ty. People will talk."

"We're keeping things low key."

"And whose idea was that?"

"Both of ours."

I could sense she was becoming defensive, so I dropped the subject, chugged some of my beer, and tossed what was left into one of the blue barrels.

"I'm surprised you're drinking after Ever's party."

If she only knew how I had to battle more than a hangover the next morning. "Uh, yeah. Have I apologized for that yet?"

"You did," she called over her shoulder as she searched the cooler, "but I doubt you were sober enough to remember."

Oh, but I remembered so many other things about that night. Ever driving me home, carrying me to my room, undressing me...

"Damn. There's no more beer. Only the hard stuff."

"Hey, I've got you covered, ladies." Some guy with shaggy

brown hair dug into the cooler next to him and produced two beers. He handed one to Ty and the other to me.

I shook my head and told myself I was just avoiding another hangover. He shrugged and introduced himself as Ryan, and then Tyra and I introduced ourselves. The guy mistook that as an invitation to hang around. Tyra started to take a sip when Vaughn appeared over her shoulder. I watched with wide eyes as he snatched the drink from her hand and shoved it into Ryan's chest. Some of the beer spilled on his yellow and white striped shirt.

"Hey, man. What's your problem?"

"You. Now leave my fucking party."

"It's a beach. It's public property."

"You're either stupid or you don't know who I am." No one anticipated Vaughn fisting the guy's shirt in his hand and lifting him as if he weighed nothing. "This *all* belongs to me, jackass. *Including* her."

"Vaughn!" Tyra screeched in horror. "Put him down *right* now."

His eyes flashed with irritation when he regarded my friend. She folded her arms and cocked her hip.

"I'm not kidding. I'll leave," she threatened.

Wordlessly, he tossed Ryan into the sand and stepped into Tyra's space. Since she was bite-sized, she had to lean her head back pretty far to return his glare.

"Don't take drinks from anyone," he ordered and then stalked off. Vaughn's scene hadn't gone unnoticed, and I knew Tyra wouldn't be able to keep him a secret for long.

chapter twenty

The Peer

WATCHED THE WHOLE THING GO DOWN FROM THE MOMENT THAT eager fool approached the girls to the moment Vaughn returned looking like he'd swallowed piss.

For once, she hadn't disobeyed me.

I was a little disappointed. I'd been looking forward to a second chance at spanking her ass, but knowing Four had finally learned her lesson got me just as hard. Go figure.

I had a hard time keeping my laughter in check when Vaughn stood in our circle again. "Everything okay?"

"Eat a dick."

"Tyra really got under your skin, huh?"

Vaughn blew air through his nose. "That broad's impossible. I've used all my best moves, and she's turned me down every time."

"So move on."

"Can't," he said with a grunt. "She's too interesting."

"Yeah, but blue balls make you crabby," Jamie instigated. "Besides, there are plenty of interesting girls who aren't stingy. Donna Hill? She gives an interesting blowjob. Vicky Clark? Her handjobs are *mind*-blowing."

"One of these days, you're going to catch something you can't get rid of," Vaughn warned. "You've only been back for a few months, yet you've slept with more of the girls in this town than Ever and me combined."

"That's because they can't get enough. I have a fresh and… exotic…perspective on things."

"Bullshit," Vaughn spat. "You're no more Irish than Ever. Just because you've lived in Ireland doesn't mean you aren't an American shit like the rest of us."

I lost my composure then. Jamie pretended to be offended for all of three seconds before he split his sides.

"True, but I can fake the accent and chicks dig it."

After Jamie's father died two years ago, my aunt had left Scotland to live closer to my grandparents in Ireland. It hadn't been enough to keep Jamie out of trouble. When he was expelled, Aunt Dilwen washed her hands of him and shipped her eldest son off, thinking my father could set him straight. *Lot of good he's doing.*

"Just sounds like you're gargling mouthwash to me, but whatever gets you laid, man."

"McNamara!" Turner called. He struggled to keep his hulking frame upright as the drink from his cup sloshed over the rim.

Vaughn scowled seeing Turner violate one of his rules: No getting hammered during the season. And for a guy Turner's size to barely keep from face-planting in the sand, he'd probably have to drink half a fucking keg.

"We have a prop-sit-ion for you."

Cooper and Kim weren't far behind, and luckily, they seemed sober enough as they grinned my way. "Yeah, what he said…or tried to," Cooper guffawed.

"Why is Turner shitfaced?" Vaughn was seething.

"We told him to quit," Kim answered with a shrug, "but he kept saying he was fine. I guess the drinks snuck up on him."

Vaughn didn't respond, so the three blind idiots, too stupid to know better, visibly relaxed. I knew he would wait until they were each sober to dole out punishment, so I turned to Turner. "What do you want?"

"You. Back on the team."

Before I could turn them down for the fifteenth time, Cooper rushed to add, "And we've got a way to convince you."

"And how are you going to do that?" Vaughn questioned with mild interest.

"Barnes," Kim answered. "We want Ever to race him."

"He's our new running back, and he's *fast!*" Cooper gloated. "Could even be faster than you one day."

I looked to Vaughn for confirmation, but he simply shrugged.

"So what? He beats me and…" By now, we've drawn a considerable crowd, including Four, who appeared way too invested for my liking.

A curious Four was a dangerous thing.

"If Barnes wins," Kim dictated, "you have to come back to the team."

Vaughn sucked his teeth. "If Barnes beats Ever, we won't *need* him back on the team, jackass."

"Oh."

The crowd roared at my former teammates' expense.

"Who's got the fastest run time?" Everyone turned to the person who voiced the question.

Of course, it had to be her.

There was a pause, and I couldn't help but notice Kim staring Four down with unmasked hatred.

I wanted to pluck his eyes from his head and feed them to him.

Cooper was the one to finally answer. "McNamara. By two hundred milliseconds."

She smiled and chuckled at some secret joke. "Well, boys, you could do this one of two ways." She made eye contact with each of us, even Kim, and only when she was assured that she had our attention did she continue. "If Barnes beats Ever's run time, he gets to keep his spot on the team."

"And if he doesn't?" Cooper questioned.

"Then Ever will still hold his title, and the Knights get their fastest runner."

"What's the second option?" The nervous voice that rose above the rippling of the crowd sounded like it belonged to Barnes, but I was too busy picturing my hands around Four's pretty throat to verify.

"Ever has to beat his own time. If he doesn't, he's still the fastest runner and will rejoin the team. If he succeeds…he does whatever the hell he wants." Discreetly, she rolled her eyes, and I might have been the only one to hear her unspoken *as usual*.

The guys, including my treacherous best friend, didn't waste time huddling to discuss their options. If they were smart, they knew which option to pick. Shaving more than a couple hundred milliseconds at a moment's notice would seem improbable even if you've kept up your training. But shaving even ten milliseconds when you haven't…impossible.

I couldn't tear my eyes from Four while she was doing her best to avoid meeting mine. Her leg began to bounce impatiently as we all waited for my former teammates to make a fucking decision. I could have simply walked away and refused to compete, but this was no longer about the team. This had become yet another battle between Four and me.

My puppet was tugging at her strings again.

From my peripheral, I saw Jamie push through the crowd and join the huddle even though he wasn't on the team. Vaughn ignored him, and no one else dared to say shit. The sound of Jamie's snort finally drew my attention away from Four. I watched Vaughn shake his head and then his lips moved.

The guys started to argue, and then Jamie loudly said, "You should listen to him, Einsteins. He's captain for a reason."

They argued for a few seconds more and then appeared to make a decision. Based on Jamie's smug expression and Vaughn's exasperation, I already knew what they'd decided.

Cooper was the one to deliver the judgment. "We choose Ever."

I turned my head in time to catch the small smile on Four's face.

"To Brynwood!" Turner roared and they all cheered.

"No." A hush fell over the crowd as everyone's attention turned to me. Mine solely belonged to Four who still wore a satisfied smirk. "To the tracks." Confusion was painted on her face as I knew it would be on each face in the crowd except for Vaughn and Cooper who had been there the last time I pulled such a stupid stunt.

"You can't be serious," Cooper objected. "You were just lucky the last time! Not to mention there were cameras. You almost went to juvie." Out of the corner of my eye, I saw Four's eyebrows kiss her hairline.

"We'll do it in a blind spot. All I'll need is forty yards."

"And some Windex and a Squeegee for when we have to scrape your demented ass off the Red Line," Jamie voiced with a scowl. Four eased closer and tugged on his arm, redirecting his focus. I watched as he bent so she could whisper something in his ear. I knew what she must have asked judging by the way her lips parted and her skin paled when he answered her.

Her reaction was exactly the one I had hoped for. Maybe next time she'd think twice before opening her pretty mouth to challenge me. I couldn't pretend to be pissed though. Already, my senses were heightened, and the world no longer seemed so gray. I felt lighter on my feet.

"The Line will be here soon," Vaughn informed. "You sure you want to do this?" I couldn't tell what he was thinking, but that was just Vaughn's M.O. You wouldn't know unless he wanted you to thanks to a father who raised him by using any weakness Vaughn showed against him.

Everyone, including Four, seemed to be holding their breath waiting for my answer. "I'm sure."

No one wasted time heading for their vehicles once they had my answer. The ride to the tracks seemed shorter and a little grave. One would think I was headed to the gallows. Ironically, I was probably the only one not worried about me dying. No, my fears were focused elsewhere. There was a chance that Four would finally see past my glamour—the silver-spooned pomp with no balls and a big bank account. I wasn't sure I was ready for that.

Too late to turn back now.

Twenty minutes later, suited up in some of the gear Vaughn kept in his car and with my muscles properly stretched, I did a couple of lunges. There was more I should have done, but I was ready to get the shit over with so I could figure out how I could possibly balance football and Exiled.

After I wrung Four's neck of course.

Vaughn appeared by my side and clapped my back. "You ready?"

I eyed him for a moment and said, "You wanted to choose Barnes."

He grunted and then smiled. "Still don't know anyone who's faster than you."

"I haven't trained in over a year."

Vaughn shook his head. "You're a natural."

I couldn't hide my surprise. "You want me to win?"

His expression turned grave. "I know how important it is that you find Fox. I want you back on the team, but I wouldn't jeopardize that."

I felt my shoulders sag. "Thanks, man."

Vaughn suddenly looked uncomfortable. "We're not going to, like, hug or anything, are we?"

"Get the fuck out of here," I ordered while snickering.

"Fuck no! I want a front row seat to this."

I shook my head at his eagerness. "I still think you chose wrong. Barnes had better odds."

He rolled his eyes. "Barnes is lazy. He doesn't push himself."

I snorted. "He probably only joined the team to get laid."

"Didn't we all?" Vaughn countered.

Our laughter died when I caught sight of Four standing on the sideline. She was gripping the rail barring the dirt path parallel to the tracks as if her life depended on it. What she didn't know was that after my nearly fatal attempt to outrun a train, I came back a few times that summer and ran the very path she stood on until I knew down to the last second how much time and distance I needed to not become windshield wiper fluid. When I smiled and winked at her, she turned her head away.

Vaughn noticed where my attention was directed and said, "What are you going to do about Archer challenging you?"

I paused as if considering my options, but I already knew what I was going to do from the moment she opened her sweet mouth. "I'm going to make her weep."

"Excellent choice. I bet her tears taste like candy."

I got into position. "Wasn't the kind of weeping I was referring to."

Vaughn backed onto the sideline with a lascivious smile. "I know."

The Red Line sounded it's horn as it passed a crossing a quarter-mile away, so one of the guys shouted the distance I would run and the time I needed to do it in. Then he warned me to get ready.

When the train was about two-hundred and fifty yards away, I blocked out everything after that and concentrated on breathing. Pretty soon, I had tunnel vision, and at the end of that tunnel was Four.

Like a rocket, I took off.

"That was insane!" Jamie praised.

I had beaten my time by twenty milliseconds with a heart-stopping fifteen yards separating me and the Red Line. That had only been five minutes ago, yet it seemed like an eternity as I waited for someone to tell me it was all a joke.

But no one did.

Vaughn had simply crossed his arms, looking smug, while Jamie gave me a play-by-play as if I weren't the one to do it all.

Cooper, Kim, and Turner had simply left without a word or a handshake. So much for being a team player. They were just lucky I didn't give a shit.

Four and her little friend had moved on, and it was taking every ounce of control I possessed not to follow her around town like a fucking stalker. I was pretty sure she had been the sole reason I'd gone to the damn bonfire in the first place. Vaughn and Jamie kept trying for my attention, but I couldn't stop searching the damn tracks.

I should have told her to stay put. As tempting as it always was to push her limits, I could only do so much under the constant scrutiny of our classmates.

"Four left with Tyra...to bake a fucking cake." Vaughn's statement caused my head to snap in his direction, but he was staring down at his phone as he texted.

"Why the hell would they want to bake a cake at this time?" Jamie questioned.

Vaughn's gaze lifted from his phone screen to meet mine. "Did you know that Four's birthday is tomorrow?"

"What?"

"Bet that makes your dick hard, eh, cousin? Definitely got me pitching a tent."

Jamie grinned, and I shoved him back. "Shut the fuck up." To Vaughn, I said, "Where did they go?"

Tyra lived just outside of Blackwood Keep with her father where the cost of living was astronomically lower.

Jamie had ditched us to hook up with one of the cheerleaders while Vaughn and I found ourselves outside of Coach Bradley's home.

"You don't think this is a little much?" I questioned.

He shrugged and moved onto the porch. "We're already here."

As soon as we reached the front door, it opened to show a pissed-off Tyra. She was tiny as shit, barely looked more than a hundred pounds, and the bangs she wore made her look twelve instead of seventeen, but she glared at Vaughn as if she were twice his size and height. He stared back down at her with unchecked cockiness. I had to admit she was beautiful with her smooth dark skin, large brown eyes, and sable hair. Vaughn, along with every red-blooded male at Brynwood, was still kicking himself for letting her escape his notice this long. Knowing the sharks were circling, waiting for his scraps, he definitely wouldn't be tossing her back into the water anytime soon.

"You can't just show up here," she fussed. "My dad is upstairs sleeping."

"I gave him an expensive bottle of scotch from my dad's cellar. He drink it?" Coach always celebrated a win by drinking heavily after, and it seemed Vaughn had exploited that fact. I would have laughed except I knew it wouldn't be appreciated by Four's little friend.

"There was half a bottle left on the kitchen counter."

"Then he isn't waking up anytime soon." Without another word or permission, he pushed past her and disappeared into the house.

I stood there feeling awkward as shit until she sighed and said, "I guess you can come in, too."

"Thanks."

She stepped aside and quietly shut the door once I was inside. I looked around, but when I didn't spot Four, I glanced over my shoulder.

"She's in the kitchen," she offered.

I didn't hesitate once she pointed me in the right direction. I found my new obsession half-heartedly mixing cake batter in a large glass bowl with my jacket discarded on the stool next to her. Vaughn was sitting at the island dipping his finger into a smaller bowl filled with frosting.

Tyra marched into the kitchen and snatched the bowl away, but Vaughn simply pulled her into his lap. He spread the frosting on her neck and proceeded to suck it off right there in front of us.

"Vaughn Franklin Rees, you're embarrassing me!"

"I knew I shouldn't have told you my middle name," he said with a low growl before licking the last of the frosting from her skin. "This is good buttercream, Ty-ty."

Four was mixing the batter faster now to likely drown out the sound of my friend molesting hers.

I cleared my throat. "Is there somewhere you can take that?"

Tyra glared at me while Vaughn stood with a grin. "Absolutely."

"I need to help Four finish the cake," Tyra protested.

"Ever can help her." Vaughn glanced between Four and me. "We wouldn't want to make his birthday girl uncomfortable."

"Vaughn," I warned.

He shrugged and stood with Tyra in his arms before carrying her out of the kitchen.

A moment later, we heard Tyra screech, "No, not upstairs. My dad!"

The sound of Vaughn's heavy footsteps running up the stairs followed, and then a door slammed.

Four sighed, the first peep she had made since I walked through the door, and turned to me. "You do know that what you did was idiotic, right?"

I shrugged. I wouldn't brag because it was pretty fucking stupid, and I no longer had the excuse of being only thirteen anymore.

"Ever heard of Greg Plitt?"

"No."

"He was a celebrity fitness trainer who died earlier this year. Want to know how?"

"No."

She ignored me and said, "Plitt was killed trying to outrun a train for some stupid energy drink commercial."

"Yeah, well I had something he didn't."

"Oh yeah? What's that, hot shot?"

"You."

We both noticed her blush but neither of us spoke on it.

"Can you take me home?" she requested timidly.

"What about your cake?"

"I don't know what I'm doing, and I don't think she'll be done up there anytime soon," she grumbled.

I had the feeling it was more than just the unfinished cake that upset her. "You don't approve." When she shot me a quizzical look, I gestured upstairs. "Vaughn and your little friend."

"Her name is Tyra, and I don't trust him."

"You don't know him."

"Which is obviously why I don't trust him," she countered.

"Doesn't matter if you do or don't. They're having fun, and it's not any of your business."

"It will be when she's crying on my shoulder."

"You assume she'll be the one hurt. Why?"

She shifted her weight onto her hands planted on the countertop. "Last week, two girls were suspended for fighting because they thought they had a claim on him."

"Vaughn never promised them anything."

"Like he never promised my friend?"

"If she makes assumptions, that's on her."

"Well, maybe he should be upfront with her. Don Lemon once said, 'There's a degree of deception in silence.'"

"So you're taking relationship advice from a news anchor?"

"It's not about love, moron. It's about honor."

"She'd think he was an asshole if he told her not to expect anything."

"You don't know that."

My head fell back onto my shoulders. Four was the most fearless girl I'd ever met, but she was also the most naïve. "I do know that, Archer."

I knew all too fucking well. Taking advantage of what I thought was a harmless crush and sleeping with Olivia haunted me every fucking day. I knew what everyone assumed, and I didn't bother to correct the rumors. The truth was *she* had come to *me*. I didn't stop to consider who she was or why she offered herself to me. I was fourteen and only concerned about winning a stupid bet. Jamie, Vaughn, and I had been competing to see who could ditch their virginity first and I had won. Surprisingly, Jamie had been the most reluctant even after his fallout with Bee while Vaughn had been too chicken shit. Not to mention, I was technically in a relationship with my cousin's ex-girlfriend but sleeping with Bee was the one line I couldn't cross. I will never know why Olivia chose me to sleep with and why she chose me to watch her die. I only know her family will never let me anywhere near her to ask. I don't blame them. I had once been a plague on this town and everyone in it.

"Because you're such an expert on women?"

I stepped behind her, leaving no space between us. Her round ass pressing against me had my dick rising from slumber. "Would you let me inside you if you knew there would never be anything else?"

"If it's what I wanted." Her rigid body told a different story.

Not in a million years would Four let me have her without owning a piece of me in return. She wasn't that kind of girl, but I'd play along anyway.

"Is it what you want?" My hands curved her hips as my lips brushed her nape. "Me inside you?"

"You're twisting my words."

"What if I told you," I said as I slipped the button on her jeans free, "that it's all I can think about?" It was the most honest thing I've said to her since her return. While she's been plotting to ruin me, I've been imagining ways to get her on her back. To start.

"I would tell you it will never happen..." She drew a sharp breath when my fingers slipped inside her panties. "...with or without the commitment."

"Is that why you're so wet?" Her whimpers as I circled her clit sounded so sweet. "Because of all the sex we're not going to have?"

I told Vaughn this was how I'd make her pay for trying to humiliate me and foil my plans, but as I toyed with her pussy, I found myself wanting to make her come for entirely different reasons.

"Absolutely," she said, panting. "Ever McNamara not getting what he wants for once is my favorite fantasy."

I dipped my fingers lower, drawing another gasp from her lips. "I hear you, Four, but it's five minutes to midnight. Do you know what that means?"

"No," she whined.

Cupping her pussy, I kept at her clit with my thumb. I didn't want to miss a fucking thing when she came. "It's time to blow your candle out."

Her body shuddered, and then she pressed her ass against me when my finger pushed inside her. *Fuck, she's tight.* I wrapped my arm around her waist to keep her still. I didn't want the first time I took her to be in the middle of Coach's goddamn kitchen.

"What if someone comes?" She was too busy riding my hand to see me bite my lip and close my eyes in relief. If she had denied me, I probably would have thrown away pride and begged at her feet.

"Then they'll see how sexy you are when you come." Because nothing short of 'no' from her lips would stop me from debasing this girl. I gently filled her with a second finger to drive her wild in my arms, and it nearly crippled me to stop there. I knew just by how snug and eagerly she gripped me that she was untouched. A virgin. All mine. And if I hadn't already sold my soul, I knew I'd do it right then to keep her that way.

Tragically, it didn't even matter.

By the time my father tossed them back in the slums, I will have carved my name into her heart, soul, and pussy.

Four suddenly flooded and clamped down on my fingers as if she read my thoughts, and despite my claims, I clapped my hand over her mouth. I decided not only would her sweet cries be for my ears only, but I'd make sure to hear them as often as I liked.

"We're not through," I warned. She was already slumped in my arms and fighting to catch her breath. Holding her up with one hand, I pulled her jeans down with the other until they pooled around her sneakers. Her panties were next, and then I was plopping her on the counter.

"It's cold!" she squealed.

"Shut up." I nudged her thighs apart, and she let me. My throat bobbed as I became captivated by her. I wanted nothing more than to have her bare and spread like a feast for a king, but we *were* in someone else's home and uninvited at that. Casting a glance toward the doorway, I made sure we were still alone.

And then the frosting caught my eye.

"Stop bossing me around."

I grabbed the bowl and dipped the fingers sticky with Four's juices inside. "Stop being a brat." I ran cream-coated fingers over her sex "Or I won't make you come again."

"I can't anyway." She sounded so sure.

I sat on one of the barstools and tugged her closer to the edge of the island. "Say you want me to go down on you."

"Is that an order?"

"If that gets you wetter." She could pretend my taking charge didn't turn her on, but I'd proven her wrong once, and I was about to do it again. For a while, there was nothing but the sound of my fingers unhurriedly gliding through her wetness. She seemed content to let me play with her, another orgasm on the horizon, but then she wailed in frustration.

"I'm just not sure what we're doing here!"

"I told you not to think. Thinking comes later."

"I think they call that regret."

"And what did I say about thinking?"

"Yes, master."

I gently bit the inside of her thigh. "Smartass."

Her fingers dug into my shoulders with brown eyes wide and vulnerable. "Ever, I don't want to be toyed with."

"I promise you I'm *very* serious about tasting you."

"I mean after. I don't want to regret this. Don't make me a—" She inhaled when I swept my tongue up her slit. "Fool," she finished with a moan.

I chose not to respond. Instead, I devoured her. I may have wanted her more than my next breath, but I didn't trust her any more than she did me.

Was it deception?

Probably.

But she tasted too exquisite—like cool spring water after a lifetime in the desert—for me to care.

Her shoes, jeans, and panties ended up on the floor, the reason why they'd still been on forgotten. Her legs were spread wide, leaving her pussy on vulgar display, so I seized her writhing hips, and when I felt her fingers tighten their grip on my hair, I pushed my tongue into her pussy. She came apart an instant later. I sucked her clit once more to prolong her orgasm, and this time, she clapped her hands over her own mouth as she came.

Fuck yeah.

When I lifted my head from between her thighs and stood, I had a tent in my pants the size of Mt. Everest. Pressing my hips into the counter to chase away the need to fill her, I licked my lips, tasting buttercream and…her. "Best cream I've ever tasted. The frosting's good, too."

She shivered on the counter and stared up at me through lowered lids. "I never expected crass from you."

"That's because you don't know me well."

It seemed to be the wrong thing to say when her face fell. *Shit. Fuck. Shit.*

"And yet I let you do…that."

And just like that, the euphoria from tasting her was gone. How could she treat what she shared with me like some horrible thing? Anger rose too fast for me to push it back down. I heard myself saying, "I ate your pussy, Four. Don't make it a big fucking deal."

"Oh, God." Horror clouded her features, and she pushed my hands from her and scrambled off the counter. Hurriedly grabbing her jeans and shoes, she didn't look at me as she stepped into them. She didn't even bother fastening them before exiting from the kitchen and leaving me behind with her discarded panties and that goddamn buttercream.

chapter twenty-one

the Puppet

I WAS THE WORLD'S BIGGEST IDIOT. HOW COULD SOMETHING THAT HAD felt so right end so horribly wrong?

That was an easy one.

Ever had opened his mouth and ruined everything.

He had been the first boy to ever touch me, and I thought the gift I'd given him—my first orgasm—would have meant more to him.

He had been right the night of his party. I didn't hate him—not like I did right now.

Regret washed over me like a wave until I was drowning. If only I hadn't suggested that stupid race. There was no way I could deny his touch after witnessing such agility. His race against the clock had only lasted a few seconds, but it was forever carved vividly into my memory. It also made me wonder...

If I ran and he chased, would I even stand a chance?

I didn't realize I was crying until I stumbled on the last step thanks to my blurred vision. Tyra and a shirtless Vaughn emerged from her room to witness the spectacle I was making of myself.

Tyra immediately rushed to my side while Vaughn stayed glued on the landing. "What's wrong?"

"Can you make him leave?" I couldn't look anywhere but at the carpet.

"What did he say to you?" Vaughn questioned with a sigh.

His concern was probably genuine. He certainly didn't seem the type to be fake for anyone.

Still, I didn't respond or even look at him. His loyalty was to Ever.

"It's okay," Tyra consoled with a hand on my back. "They were just leaving."

"Seriously?" Vaughn spat. His concern had quickly given way to irritation.

"She's upset, Rees."

I looked up in time to see him roll his eyes at her last naming him and yank his shirt down his muscled torso.

"Fuck it. Fine." He stomped down the stairs, clearly not giving a shit if he woke her father from his drunken sleep.

"So you're going to leave with an attitude?" she yelled after him.

I was certain we'd all be caught soon.

"Pretty much," he snarled from downstairs. A second later, the front door slammed, and an engine roared as Vaughn and Ever sped away.

"Spoiled rich brat," she muttered. "God, sometimes I swear he isn't worth the trouble." Turning to me, her eyes bucked and her jaw dropped. "Son of a—you're shaking! What did Ever do to you in there?"

I debated telling her what went on in that kitchen, but embarrassment wouldn't let the words free. "Nothing that should have surprised me." Except he was full of them. Like when he had his hands down my pants and used his mouth to drive me crazy.

"Let's go finish your cake and talk about it."

I paused at her mention of the cake.

So much for keeping what happened a secret. "Um…I'm really sorry, but it's not a good idea to use the frosting."

Her frown deepened. "What happened to the frosting?" At my blush, understanding dawned, and suddenly, Tyra had trouble keeping eye contact. "Okay," she squeaked, "no cake then." After an awkward silence, she said, "I'm sorry your birthday had such a shitty start."

"It wasn't all bad." Everything that came before had been so very good.

"Well, I'm just going to go grab the sanitizer. Meet you in the kitchen?" She took off without a response.

The peer begged her forgiveness.

I found the note waiting for me on my pillow later in the morning. Since facing Ever made me want to throw myself off the nearest cliff, I'd slept over at Tyra's. The palace had been empty, so I was able to escape to my room without incident. Deciding a shower was in order, I tossed the card in my trash bin and shed last night's clothes minus panties. When Tyra and I had returned to the kitchen, I'd discreetly searched for them, but the purple cotton had disappeared. I didn't dare allow myself to think about them being in Ever's possession or why he took them.

The hot water cleansed my body, but it did nothing to erase last night. I never expected him to apologize, so forgiving him had never entered my mind. Frankly, it was the last thing I wanted to do. The first was forgetting what happened between us. A knock sounded at my door the moment I finished dressing, and I opened it to find Jamie, also dressed in his uniform, on the other side.

"Birthday girl!" He snatched me up in a bear hug before I could say anything. "Happy birthday."

"Thanks," I choked out.

His arms immediately loosened, and he set me on my feet. He then stepped back but not before placing something on my head.

"Uhh…" I touched the plastic object with curiosity and started to remove it.

"Leave it. It looks good on you."

"What is it?"

"A tiara for a princess."

I snorted. "I'm no princess."

"Couldn't agree more. Let's go!"

He clasped my hand in his and held it until we reached the kitchen where Rosalyn, Thomas, and Ever waited.

"Happy birthday!"

Thomas and Jamie wore bright smiles while Ever was watchful, and Rosalyn was like a statue carved from despair. Of course, she hadn't given Thomas the memo. We *never* celebrated my birthday.

"Sit, be merry, eat cake with us," Thomas offered cheerfully. It was then I noticed the buttercream cake sitting in the middle of the island. I finally met Ever's gaze.

"I wasn't expecting cake." I had eyes only for Ever but not in the romantic, all-consuming-love way. I wanted to plunge the knife meant for cutting the cake into his black heart.

"Of course, there would be cake. I didn't expect my son to bake one himself, though."

Ever baked me a birthday cake?

It was then I noticed the bit of flour on his cheek. Thomas's expression turned thoughtful as he gazed at his son, but he quickly shook it away and beamed at me. "Hope you like buttercream."

"Love it."

Jamie launched into song, and Thomas and Ever followed. On the last note, I made the same wish I did every year, and then I blew out the candles. I stared into Rosalyn's empty eyes over the rising smoke, but like every year, there was no genie to erase her pain. An oblivious Thomas picked up the knife and extended it to Ever. "Why don't you do the honors?"

Ever took the knife from his father and cut five perfect slices before placing them on the expensive china. We all dug in while Rosalyn ignored her slice of cake and excused herself. Too bad my sorrow couldn't leave with her. I hoped her rejection would escape their notice until all three men frowned after her. When their questioning gazes turned to me, I smiled and pretended all was fine.

She's heartbroken.

She doesn't hate you.

She's just sad.

The mantra was an old friend, chasing away tears and self-hatred.

"Do you have exciting plans after school?" Thomas questioned. I could tell he was trying to lighten the mood and distract me from Rosalyn's absence.

"Tyra and I were thinking about hanging out at the beach."

"That sounds like fun," he replied absently as he checked his phone. He excused himself, leaving me alone with Ever and Jamie.

"My uncle's full of shit. That's a lame way to spend your birthday," Jamie said as soon as Thomas was out of earshot. Ever didn't say anything, but I could tell he agreed.

"Well, I don't exactly have popular friends to throw me birthday parties."

They smirked at my snappy comment. They may have thought my plans were lame, but it was more than I ever expected.

"You have us," Jamie corrected with waggling brows, "and we can give you better than a party."

"Oh?"

"Yeah...skip school with us."

"Not going to happen." I wasn't exactly giddy to spend the day at school, but I wasn't giving Ever another chance to set me up. No way was I spending another year at Natasha Madison's School of Ladies.

"Have you ever been to New York?"

I met Ever's gaze, but his expression remained perfectly blank as if he weren't the least bit worried I'd expose him. Maybe Jamie already knew. Despite their feud over Barbie, they were thick as thieves.

"No," I lied. Well, it was more like a half-truth. I technically have been, but there had to be more to the Big Apple than crumbling buildings in seedy neighborhoods. "But I don't think I need to risk suspension to visit. We've got that campus tour at NYU in a couple of weeks."

"You really think those stuffed shirts at Brynwood care about showing you a good time?" Jamie clucked his tongue. "Wake up, pretty girl. Their only concern is offering up prestigious young souls to those ivy league sharks."

I paused taking a bite of my cake. "So this is how you get girls to sleep with you? You convince them they'll lose their soul if they don't?

He grinned. "There's nothing wrong with leading a few lost girls to salvation."

Rolling my eyes, I shoved down more cake.

"Skip school," Jamie begged some more. "We'll take you."

"Won't they call our parents?"

Jamie snorted. "So?"

"You didn't come home last night, and your mother didn't bother to question where you were," Ever absently pointed out as he watched me lick buttercream from my thumb. "I think you'll survive skipping a day."

I felt my cheeks flame. Was it so obvious that Rosalyn was oblivious to me? And why was Mr. Discipline even agreeing to this when he's worked overtime to keep me in line? "I guess we'll never know because I'm not going anywhere with you."

He stared at me for a long, *long* moment.

"Did you get my note?"

"That crummy apology? Yeah, it's currently at the bottom of my trash can where it belongs."

Jamie's head had been whipping back and forth between us. "Something happen with you two?"

"No," we answered at the same time.

"Wait…Ever actually apologized for something he did?" Jamie stared at me as if I held the cure for cancer in the palm of my hand. "What are you doing to my cousin?"

"You've got it all wrong, Jamie. All the cards are in his hand. I'm just the one getting dealt."

"So you're a victim now?" Ever spat. "As I recall, you got off twice, and I was the one left with blue balls."

"Whoa…what?"

Neither of us acknowledged Jamie.

"I didn't ask you to do that!"

"But you loved it," he countered calmly.

"I only loved it because you lost." At his frown I got smug. "Yeah, you thought you'd bring me to heel, but it was you on your knees and *me* calling the shots."

I wanted to punch him when he smiled so beautifully. "If that's how you take charge, then I gladly offer you my surrender."

Exasperated, I gave up before I could give in. "I'm done talking to you. Have fun in New York." I flipped him off for good measure and moved to the sink to rinse my plate. I should have known he wasn't done with me.

Spinning me around, he gripped my neck. "Another taste and I'm yours."

Ever seized my lips before I could turn him down. Countless tender kisses later, his gaze clouded with regret.

"I'm sorry I was an asshole, okay?"

It was pathetic how badly I wanted to forgive him. "No. It's not okay. You're always an asshole, but what you did was despicable… even for you."

"I know." He exhaled and rested his forehead against mine. "Just come to New York with us. Give me a chance to make it up to you."

"Why should I?"

"Because I can't stay away from you. I'm trying, Four, believe me. I try so fucking hard, but you keep pulling me in."

I prided myself on the firmness in my tone when I spoke. "Rest assured it's not on purpose. I pull you in, you push me away. I never wanted this war, Ever. You did. Why should I be the only one with scars?"

His throat bobbed as he swallowed hard. "I push you away because you don't know what you do to me and I'm not sure I want you to know."

A peck on the lips led to another and more still until our kiss deepened, and we were making out. Ever wasn't the only one confused by his emotions. One minute I wanted to spill his guts and the next I wanted to mount him. Forgetting where we were, my arms locked around his neck while his hands found their way under my skirt so he could cup my butt.

Jamie cleared his throat, causing Ever to break the kiss with a groan. "We need to leave soon so my father doesn't ask questions." I was mesmerized by the lust thickening his voice until he said, "Go pack a change of clothes in your bag and meet us outside."

"I didn't say I'd go with you."

His grin was sly. "But you're gonna." He then patted my ass, sending me on my way.

Upstairs, I ranted to myself about overbearing boys as I shoved an outfit in my bag. I was still kicking myself for being so weak when I stepped outside. Jamie was sitting in the driver's seat of his Jeep while Ever waited by the open rear passenger door. I ignored him and climbed into the back seat, but then he followed me in.

"The front seat's empty. Why are you sitting back here?"

He smiled a boyish smile and scooted closer until our thighs touched before resting his arm on the headrest. I ignored the heated fluttering in my belly and distracted myself by texting Tyra my plans.

"We're going to make a stop before we get on the road," Ever announced.

"Why?"

"Vaughn's coming."

I paused. Was I really about to spend a day alone in a strange city with Ever and his band of arrogant assholes? No. No, I was not. "Then I'm inviting Tyra."

"He's pissed as fuck at her, baby."

Baby?

Not grease monkey, hick, swamp girl, or little troublemaker? Did letting him go down on me really change his perspective of me *that* much?

"I don't care. He was the asshole, and it's *my* birthday."

I was surprised when, rather than argue, he smiled. "Sure, princess."

"Alright…" Ignoring the fluttering in my belly, I glared up at him. "What's up with the pet names? I'm no princess."

From the front seat, Jamie snorted.

"Because despite your backwoods upbringing, you carry yourself as if you were royalty. Always with your nose in the air, expecting your demands to be met."

I racked my brain for a witty or sarcastic response. Something that screamed 'I am a woman and not a cup of jello.' My legs shook under his stare, and I felt gooey inside when he said, "You want Tyra, you'll have Tyra." He dipped his head and whispered, "And later I'll have you."

I didn't respond and spent the short ride nestled in the crook of Ever's arm, pondering his sudden change in attitude. When we reached the gate barring entry to the castle Vaughn lived in, I tried not to gape.

But I did balk at the burly guards wearing perfectly blank expressions and visibly brandishing large guns. "Jamie, I think you made a wrong turn. This is clearly Fort Knox."

Ever squeezed my hip as one of the guards approached the window. Jamie rolled it down, and the guard said, "No visitors."

Before Jamie could respond, Vaughn, already dressed for a

day in the city, appeared around one of the bushes and said, "Let them in."

"Your father said—"

"Then take it up with him." He opened the front passenger door and hopped in. "And please remind *Father* that if he wants to do something about it, he'll actually have to come home for once."

Jamie rolled up the window, and the guard had no choice but to open the gates. The other was already placing a call to who I assumed was Senor Rees.

"So that's your deal," I said when the silence and Vaughn's obvious irritation grew uncomfortable.

He regarded me over his shoulder and lifted a brow.

"You have daddy issues."

Ever squeezed my hip a little harder this time while Vaughn snorted.

"And you don't?"

I shrugged as the car came to a stop. "I never knew my father."

"You're lucky," he spat.

Jamie climbed out, and Ever followed, lending me his hand and keeping hold of mine as we walked through the front doors.

"It's your birthday," Vaughn announced, "so I'll forgive you for being a complete bitch." He pulled me into a hug, and only after nearly crushing me in his arms, I caved and hugged him back. "You can change in the first room on your left," he directed after letting me go.

I took in his appearance: red long-sleeved thermal, blue jeans, and light brown hair slicked back.

"Thanks." I climbed the set of stairs he pointed to and changed into jeans ripped at the knee, plain white long-sleeve, and an olive-green utility jacket. When I made it back downstairs, I found Vaughn in the middle of a heated argument with Tyra.

"Why do you have to misbehave all the time, huh?"

Tyra glowered with her arms crossed. "You're the one who threw a tantrum."

His response was to push her against the front door, and I watched as he held her wrists above her head. "I like your fire, babe, but you need to learn who's in charge."

"This is the twenty-first century. Get over yourself."

His voice deepened when he spoke next. "I'd rather get on top of you." They were kissing hard and heavy a moment later.

"I didn't know you were into exhibitionism," Ever whispered in my ear. He stood on the step above me wearing a black sweater with a gray collar, black jeans, and a solid black Rolex. His hair was perfectly mussed, making him look like trouble and salvation all at once.

"He's bad for her."

He shrugged and pulled me by my elbow into the kitchen. "If she couldn't handle him, he'd have moved on already."

"You better be right."

He pulled two bottles of water from the fridge. "Or what?"

"Or after I'm done kicking his ass, you'll be next."

I took the water he offered just as Jamie ran into the kitchen wearing black jeans, T-shirt, and a thin puffy vest with a silver chain hooked on his jeans.

"You two are so cute that I throw up in my mouth every time I lay eyes on you."

"Jealous?" I quipped even though there was nothing to be jealous of. Ever and I weren't a thing. We were a giant meteor heading straight for Earth with nothing in its path to stop it.

Jamie looked ready to say something, but then he shook his head and began raiding Vaughn's refrigerator. I kept forgetting Ever's relationship status was a touchy subject for him. Maybe because it also meant admitting he already belonged to someone.

Tossing a bag of bagels and cream cheese on the island, Jamie started slathering as Vaughn entered holding hands with Tyra.

"No one said you could eat my food, Buchanan."

"That's because I didn't ask," he said with a mouth full of bagel.

While Vaughn and Jamie traded insults, Tyra rolled her eyes at Ever and pulled me into a hug.

"Loving the tiara, birthday girl!"

"I got that for her," Jamie bragged, abandoning his bickering with Vaughn, who then cuffed him on the back of the head.

"Stop hitting on her," he chewed out.

Unfazed, Jamie winked at me and headed for the door with Vaughn and Tyra on his heels.

I started to follow, but a tug on my belt loop and the sudden wall of flame at my back kept me rooted.

"You better not be blushing," Ever warned.

"Jealous?"

"Murderous," he growled.

"Yeah, well, you should work on that." I felt him staring as I walked away, so I swayed my hips. Jamie hadn't made me blush, but the deep trill of Ever's appreciative groan sure did.

The Statue of Liberty had been our first stop. We then rode to the top of the Empire State Building while Jamie blasted Jay-Z and Alicia Key's 'Empire State of Mind,' frolicked in Central Park, and eventually, stopped for my first taste of authentic New York style pizza.

If anyone ever asked, I'd say it was the best day of my life. Every year, I pretended to forget my birthday so Rosalyn would continue to take her pills.

My friends—well, it was still under review whether I could call the guys my friends—sacrificed their grades and risked their parents' wrath to celebrate me. I wasn't sure if it should, but it felt good.

"How do you like the pizza, princess?"

My stomach did that fluttering thing again as I took another bite. "It's greasy perfection," I said with a mouth full. I eyed the loaded foot-long sub Ever opted to eat instead. "You don't like pizza?"

"You always talk with your mouth full?" He seemed amused rather than disgusted, so I shrugged.

"Told you I'm no princess." I reached up to take off the tiara.

"Leave it."

"Why?" I questioned even as my hand slowly fell to the table. I didn't care about the tiara, and my birthday was just another day, but Ever seemed determined to prove me wrong.

"Because today, the world should be yours."

"And you think this piece of plastic will give me that?"

"Maybe not, but it's a start."

Jamie was busy chatting up some redhead by the door, and Vaughn and Tyra were too into each other across the booth to notice Ever hammering away at my walls. Since arriving, I'd worked to keep a physical and emotional space, and he'd worked even harder to make sure that didn't happen. His hand would find mine whenever we crossed a street or be at my back, steering me through the crowd. Even when he hung back and offered me space, his eyes never left me. As close as he kept me, somehow, I never felt suffocated.

"Why are you being so nice? Why now?"

He leaned back with a sigh. "I told you I'm making up for last night."

"The note you left me this morning was different from the others. You didn't write *once upon a puppet*. Why?"

"It was an apology, Four. I can't force you to forgive me."

"Oh." I can't say why I was disappointed in his response. I guess I was hoping that after touching me the way he did, he'd finally release me from our deal. I needed to know Rosalyn was safe before I went any further with him. "So the notes are your twisted version of Simon Says? *Once upon a puppet* means I don't have a choice?"

"In a way." He glanced across the booth before changing the subject. "What else would you like to do today?"

"Is it possible to experience the entire city in one day?"

"Not really, no."

"Then maybe we should get going. School will be out soon."

Ever didn't argue and paid the tab. On the walk back to the car, Ever dipped inside one of the shops, and Vaughn and Jamie followed, leaving Tyra and me on the sidewalk. Tyra was telling me about some naked cowboy when something slammed into me.

"Sorry," a dark-haired girl mumbled as she sped by with her head down.

I was still staring after her when someone roared, "Louchana!"

A much bigger force stormed by me, and my eyes bucked as I watched the guy grab her by her hoodie. "Give it back," I heard him growl.

"How did you find me?" she hissed. He didn't respond and shoved his hands in her hoodie pockets.

"Um…should we do something?" Tyra questioned.

The girl seemed more annoyed than distressed, making it clear they knew each other. The guy found what he was looking for and headed our way with her hoodie still in his fist, forcing her down the sidewalk. I slipped my hand inside the pocket that held my phone so I could call the police if needed, but it was completely empty.

My phone and wallet were both gone.

Thinking they somehow fell out, I searched the sidewalk. Nothing. When I looked up, the dark-haired girl and the fuming guy now stood in front of us.

"This belongs to you." It wasn't a question, and sure enough, in his hand was my cell and wallet.

She picked my fucking pocket!

"Thanks…how did you know?"

"She does this a lot." He glowered at the dirty girl who looked my age, possibly younger, but I couldn't be sure with the dirt coating her face.

"Big fucking deal," she said with a sneer. "I'm homeless, and I have a better phone, and her wallet only had forty bucks. What kind of rich kids are you?"

"Lou," he warned.

For some reason, my heart pounded as I studied him. Why did he seem so familiar? He had brown hair, blue eyes, wore a distressed brown leather jacket, and a white T-shirt over his broad shoulders and blue jeans over his muscular legs. And he had this aura that promised a thrill if you dared get close.

"Her mom was a hotel maid," Tyra volunteered, "and my dad coaches high school football. What makes you think we're rich?"

"Been trailing you since the Pizzeria. If you're not rich, your boyfriends definitely are." A huge smile graced her face, and I was positive that under all that dirt was a beautiful girl. "Here they come, bestie, and man, do they looked pissed, but you can take them." Her smug smile said she had zero doubt.

Sure enough, the guys stepped from the shop ready to do battle.

"We got a problem?" Vaughn questioned as he and Jamie surrounded them.

Louchana eyed them curiously while her friend stared directly at Ever and greeted him by a name that didn't belong to him.

Who the hell is Danny Boy?

"Harlan," Ever greeted back with a stiff nod of his head. I could tell by the sudden tension that running into this guy wasn't a good thing.

Harlan made a point to look at each of us as if committing our faces to memory. "Aren't you going to introduce me to your friends?"

Ever shifted, blocking me from view when Harlan's gaze lingered. "Why would I do that?"

Harlan didn't answer. Instead, he leaned around Ever and held out his hand. "I didn't catch your name?"

I didn't answer or shake his hand. It felt too much like a trap. He didn't seem bothered by my rejection when he stood to his full height. He was just as tall as Ever, and judging by the lean muscle barely hidden by his clothes, just as powerful.

"You trained her well."

"We're going now." Ever reached behind him and seized my hand. His grip was harsh, but I doubt he noticed, and I didn't complain as he led me away.

"I'll see you soon, Danny Boy!"

I glanced back, but Harlan was already walking in the opposite direction with Louchana at his side.

His head was bent as he listened to something she said, allowing me to see the tattoo peeking from beneath his jacket collar. Suddenly, the familiarity made sense. He had been at the abandoned building in Queens! If this Harlan guy was Exiled, that could only mean one thing.

Ever had just been made.

chapter twenty-two

The Peer

NEEDED TO GET MY SHIT TOGETHER. HOW COULD IT BE THAT IN A city with over eight million people, I run into the one person eager to unmask me? Running into Wren was bad news, and every five seconds, I was looking over my shoulder. Jamie, knowing what running into Exiled could mean, was breaking every traffic law to get us back to Blackwood Keep.

"The way you guys were acting, you'd think that guy was part of the mob," Tyra joked.

If only she knew how close to the truth she really was. When no one responded, she fell quiet. I could tell the encounter was still on her mind when she kept sneaking glances my way. I sighed and forced myself to relax for appearances. This was the last thing I needed. Someone else in my fucking business. Four hadn't spoken since we left the city, and I preferred it that way. She had a great fucking birthday, so I mentally patted myself on the back and considered myself redeemed. After this, I could go back to pretending she didn't exist and that I didn't want seconds.

Jamie got us back to Blackwood Keep in record time. After dropping off Tyra and Vaughn, we made our way home with only music to drown out the tension. I knew Jamie was itching to question me about Wren, but he wouldn't say anything in front of Four. No one knew about our deal, and I was keeping it that way. After hopping out of the Jeep, he shot me a look before disappearing inside the house. I peeked at Four lingering on the other side of the hood and twiddling her fucking fingers.

"You have something on your mind, so speak it."

Her eyebrows rose as her hands curled into fists and dropped to her sides. "I didn't know I needed your permission."

I rested my forearms on the warm hood and met her glare. "It's in the contract."

"Fuck you." She was damn cute when she got all snarly, but letting on how tempting it was to oblige her was out of the question.

"I'm pressed for time."

My double entendre thickened the tension.

Her gaze lost focus.

She sank her teeth into her bottom lip to keep her excitement at bay, and my dick got rock hard.

Careful to hide my need, I twirled my index finger in a gesture to get her talking and fast. Jamie's back seat was only a few feet away.

"Thank you for today." After starting for the house, she muttered, "Prick."

She only made it two steps before I caught her and pushed her against the hood. Her grunt ended with a growl when she felt me close in behind her.

"You're welcome," I whispered in her ear. And then I walked away before I did something idiotic. Jamie lingered in the foyer with a mocking smile.

"Hundred bucks she's pissed but wet as fuck right now."

I felt my lip curling, so I quickly turned my back. "Shut up." Four's pussy wasn't anyone's concern but mine.

"I like her," Jamie rambled on. "I see more of the old you every day, and she's the reason, cousin. I just know it."

"There is no old me." I headed for the stairs with him hot on my heels.

"I beg to differ. My former favorite cousin would have ridden her hard by now."

"What the—she's not a horse." I felt my nostrils flare when I turned on him.

"Give me a fucking break. Of course, she's not a horse. You can't fuck a horse."

I ran my hand down my face and counted to five. "Why are you so interested in my love life?"

"Who said anything about love?" He looked way too pleased about my slip. I knew it was time for me to shut the hell up. "You don't...do you?"

"Don't what?" I knew what he was asking but was hoping he'd just go the fuck away.

"Do you love Four?" he spelled out.

Did I love Four? What an interesting fucking question. Particularly because I hesitated when answering. Four was smart but naïve. Stubborn yet selfless. Fierce yet broken. And she could hold one hell of a grudge. She was pretty without being obvious, yet she made my dick harder than any girl had before. The cherry on top was how she made me feel alive again.

"Why the fuck would I?"

I heard a sound, and Jamie must have too because we both twisted at the same time. Four stood at my door staring back at us. Since her bedroom was closer to the stairs, I knew it wasn't by coincidence that she was standing there. She had come to my room for a reason. When she turned and walked away, my stomach tightened, and a sour taste filled my mouth.

"Fuck," Jamie cursed. "Do you think she heard us?"

"Of course, she did." My response was sarcastic and my tone nonchalant when I felt anything but.

Unconsciously, I ran my hand down my face. This shit between us was starting to resemble a dance. One step forward, and two steps back. I tossed my bag on the floor a little harder than needed, and Jamie wisely took that as his cue to leave quietly.

Fuck it.

And fuck her, too.

chapter twenty-three

The Puppet

M Y BIRTHDAY HAD STARTED WITH A BANG AND ENDED WITH A boom. It was the sound my heart had made after dropping to my stomach. Now it was nothing but shattered pieces. It didn't make sense.

I didn't love Ever, either, but hearing him toss aside the notion so callously hurt more than I would ever admit to anyone. Most especially Ever. He had too much power as it was.

"You're awfully quiet today," Tyra remarked as we walked the hall the next day. "Something happen?"

I avoided her gaze and shrugged. "Everything's back the way it should be."

"That's awfully cryptic." She was still frowning as we entered the crowded cafeteria. Lunch was just another social affair. Hardly anyone ate the food even though it was heaps better than the slop served at a public school. It could almost pass for gourmet. I wasn't surprised given the price tag on tuition. It was obvious the money was being used well.

Today was pizza day, which I couldn't turn down, so Tyra and I grabbed a couple of slices and looked around for a seat. It seemed that everyone felt the same about pizza day because every table except one was full.

"You two going to stand here all day?" Vaughn stood behind us, holding a tray piled high.

"There aren't any seats left."

Vaughn looked around with a frown before sighing when his eyes landed on his usual table. He then balanced his tray on one palm and placed the other on Tyra's spine. "Come on." Gently, he pushed her forward when she didn't budge and glanced at me over his shoulder. "That also means you."

What is it with these guys and being bossy?

When my stomach growled rather loudly, I knew skipping lunch wasn't an option and followed them to the table. Vaughn had seated Tyra next to him, leaving the only available seat next to Barbie.

I sank into the chair with a guilty conscience. All I could do was remember what Ever and I did in Coach Bradley's kitchen and how he belonged to someone else. To Barbie.

The boy in question sat on her other side, deep in conversation with none other than Daniel Kim—the kid whose head I cracked open. The chatter around the table slowly died as I sat. I pretended to be engrossed in my pizza.

After a couple of minutes passed, I figured I'd spend lunch being gawked at until Vaughn barked, "What the fuck is everyone staring at? *Eat.*"

I never thought I'd be grateful to him for anything. When I met his gaze, he winked and returned to his conversation with Tyra. The only one who still seemed to have an eye problem was Daniel Kim. Ever's attention was now focused on Barbie, so his glaring went unnoticed by everyone except me. The animosity in his eyes had me ready to risk the rest of the day on an empty stomach.

"We should do something after school," Tyra suggested and then firmly added, *"Alone,"* when Vaughn started to speak.

He didn't bother hiding his displeasure, which Tyra ignored. I still had my doubts regarding his intentions, but I had to admit his clinginess was kind of adorable. Something told me these feelings he had for Tyra were a first for him. Tyra pretended to hate it, but she wasn't fooling anyone but herself.

"Sure." That earned me a glare from Vaughn.

"I'll text you the details so we can remain undisturbed." She cut her eyes to Vaughn and made a face.

He sucked his teeth and made a point to ignore Tyra by starting a conversation with the guy next to him.

I shook my head at Tyra though I didn't feel *too* sorry for Vaughn. He wasn't even close to being a victim. He was just used to being the one behind the mind games.

Jamie sauntered up to the table with his arm thrown around the neck of a girl I was pretty sure was in my English class. "Why didn't anyone save me a seat?"

"You can have this seat," a pretty brunette offered.

"Don't mind if I do," Jamie flirted.

The brunette started to lift her tray when Jamie smoothly detached himself from the blonde. He helped the brunette from her seat and took her place, but then we were all in for a shock when he seated the brunette firmly in his lap, leaving the blonde he came with standing there looking well...dumb.

"Um...excuse me?" the blonde hissed.

Jamie glanced over his shoulder with a bored expression. "You're excused." He turned his attention back to the table, and the blonde stomped off. I watched as he noticed Barbie and Ever sitting together. Bitterness washed over him until his gaze landed on me, and the twinkle I'd come to dread entered his eye. "What's up, cousin-in-law?" He then winked at me, making it clear his greeting was for me instead of Barbie.

I bristled when everyone, once again, abandoned their private conversations to stare. Snickers moved like a wave around the table but then died abruptly when Ever spoke in a flat tone.

"Your juvenile attempts for attention are beginning to bore me. Maybe you should try another table."

Everyone suddenly looked nervous as they waited to see who he'd kick from the coveted table next. I wanted to see Ever's face, but that required leaning over, making it obvious that I cared.

"Nope," Jamie sassed as he sat back defiantly. "Like you, I like to have my cake and eat it, too." He then buried his face in the brunette's neck, causing her to giggle. If I weren't sitting next to Barbie, I wouldn't have heard her inhale. I could feel her anger as she watched Jamie seduce the girl occupying his lap.

When I met Tyra's wide gaze across the table, she mouthed, "Drama," to me.

I snorted and counted the seconds until lunch was over.

"It must be so hard for you."

I hadn't realized Barbie's words were meant for me until Tyra's gaze shifted from me to her and back again. I met Barbie's blue gaze. "I'm sorry?"

"To want what can't and never will be yours."

"I...I wouldn't know," I lied.

Barbie noticed my hesitation with pursed gloss-coated lips.

"Do you love Four?"

"Why the fuck would I?"

I could still see his perfect lips curling and his cold eyes mocking.

"I guess we have that in common then. I've never wanted what I can't have, either. I guess I have Ever to thank for that." Barbie flashed a fake smile and bumped her shoulder against mine as if we were the best of friends. I'd had enough.

"I'm not going to dignify what you're implying with a response because that would be stooping." I stood up with my lunch tray, drawing Ever's hawk-like focus. "I don't stoop, Barbie. I transcend." I talked myself out of slapping her upside the head with the tray and walked away with more class than anyone at this godforsaken school thought me capable of.

Fuck this school.

Fuck Barbie.

And *fuck* Ever, too.

When school ended, I once again opted to ride with Jamie. The lesser of two evils. He talked my ear off the entire way home though he didn't get much response from me. I was slumped in the passenger seat until Jamie's whistle drew my attention. He parked behind an all too familiar 1975 Honda CB400F Cafe Racer. Gruff had a red one just like it. It wasn't the fastest on the market, but I was in love with the vintage rugged appeal. The fresh yellow and black paint gleamed in the sunlight, and my fingers ached to stroke it.

"Whose bike is that?" Jamie questioned.

I shrugged without taking my eyes from the Racer.

He whistled again. "It's pretty sweet." I could only nod. "Come on." I felt his fingers wrap around my elbow. "Let's see who the owner is."

I wanted to stay with the bike, but I let him pull me inside since I was just as curious as he was.

Inside, we found the kitchen and living room empty as well as the large patio where Thomas and Rosalyn often entertained. "Maybe they're in Unc's office."

I hesitated, so he pulled me the rest of the way. I'd never been in Thomas's office, though I heard him in it a time or two screaming orders over the phone or berating Jamie for something stupid he did.

Jamie knocked on the door. "Unc?"

"Aye, nephew. Don't just stand there. Come in."

He pushed open the door and dragged me inside. I was surprised to find Rosalyn sitting on the leather love seat looking frazzled. No one else waited inside.

"Just who I needed to see," Thomas greeted with his gaze trained on me.

"Whose bike is that outside?" Jamie questioned.

"Apparently, it belongs to Four."

"What? That's not mine." I denied it as if I'd just been caught with a joint.

"A Robert Russell had this delivered for you this morning."

"Gruff sent this?"

Thomas didn't respond, but I didn't need him to. Gruff was so the man! I was already itching to get on the open road. And maybe never come back.

"That was nice of him. I should call and thank him." I made sure to keep my tone level and excitement at bay. But the minute I got away from Thomas and Rosalyn's eyes and ears...all bets were off.

"That won't be necessary, Four." Rosalyn had remained silent until now, and her demeanor told me I wasn't going to like the rest. "We're sending it back."

"Like hell you are."

"You'll choose your words better when you speak to your mother." Thomas's reprimand only added fuel to a burning fire. For a second there, he actually sounded how my father would if I had one.

The words *fuck you* were on the tip of my tongue when the door opened and Ever sauntered inside.

Thomas sighed from behind his desk. "Son, whatever it is will have to wait. I need to speak with Four alone. Jamie, you can leave, too."

Instead of obeying, Jamie leaned against the wall with a grin and his arms crossed while Ever came to stand beside me with his hands in his pocket. "Why are you sending her bike back?"

"This isn't your concern, Ever. Leave," his father bit out.

"She's eighteen now. It's not your right to refuse a gift meant for her."

"She's under my roof—"

"Another fact you failed to realize. She no longer has to be, and she won't be for long if you continue to push her away." He'd directed the last, which sounded like a threat I wasn't bold enough to voice, at Rosalyn.

I felt the ball in my stomach tighten when Rosalyn shot me a look full of accusation.

"She could be in jail right now for street racing—on a stolen motorcycle, I might add. You expect me to give her my blessing to jeopardize her future? I won't put her poor mother through that again."

"Then keep the keys," Ever smoothly suggested. "When her future is no longer your concern, hand them over to her."

Only the sound of Rosalyn's soft sobs filled the room when Thomas sat back in his chair to consider Ever's suggestion. It hadn't dawned on me until now how good Ever was at manipulating people. An image of Ever convincing Thomas and Rosalyn to send me to Europe a year ago popped into my head. Had he beguiled them in this very room just as he was now?

I hadn't realized I was glaring at Ever until he hoisted an eyebrow.

"Focus, Four."

In my peripheral, I noticed Rosalyn's startled reaction. Ever ordering me around was not something I cared for her to witness. With one last scathing glance at Ever, I gave his father my full attention once more.

"I'm sorry. What were you saying?"

He shook his head with a humorless smile. "You're lucky to have found a friend in my son. He can be quite the manipulative prick."

Jamie choked back a laugh while Ever gave no reaction.

"He's proving to be useful." As a small smile tilted my lips, more choking sounded behind me as Jamie's mind no doubt waded in the gutter. "Does this mean I get to keep my bike?"

Thomas sighed and rubbed his smooth chin. I frowned as I struggled to recall if Ever's mom had a cleft chin. "It will be parked in the garage where it will stay until you graduate."

Jamie let out a celebratory whoop and hugged me while Ever stood perfectly still and silent. Rosalyn, visibly upset, rose from her seat and floated from the room. With a nod from Ever, Jamie departed as well with his cousin on his heels.

"Don't worry," Thomas said when we were alone. "She'll come around."

No...she wouldn't. I knew her better than he ever could. "Can I park the bike?"

He hesitated before lifting the key ring from his humungous desk.

"I expect these back."

"Sure." I took the keys and didn't waste time skipping down the stairs and out the front door. Ever and Jamie were nowhere to be found. I shrugged it off and hopped on my very own bike. I couldn't wait to call Gruff and thank him. Suspended in disbelief, I held my breath as I slowly slid the key in the ignition and turned. The vibration of the engine roaring to life chased away my worries and fears.

Mine.

It was all mine.

"You staying out of trouble, girl?"

"No." I snorted and laughed. "Not really."

Gruff grunted, accepting my words as the truth. After spending some time admiring my new bike, I parked it in the garage and returned the keys to Thomas as promised. Now I was lying on my stomach, kicking my feet back and forth as I talked to Gruff.

"I still can't believe you gave me your bike."

"My knee has been giving me trouble. Figured you'd put it to better use than I can. It's got some new parts, which I'm sure you noticed."

I did notice. In fact, I lost my shit. "I wish I could have been there to help."

"Me too, kid."

"Maybe I'll see you this summer?" I couldn't disguise the hope in my voice.

"I'll be here," he answered noncommittally. It was hard to take offense. Gruff was just who he was. "So have you been applying to colleges?"

"A few. Brynwood doesn't really play around," I grumbled, which earned a rare chuckle from Gruff. I had put in a few applications under duress but had no intention of going. The only future I could accept was me professionally racing. College couldn't do squat for me.

I heard a few voices in the background and waited while Gruff responded to them. When he returned to the line, it was to say goodbye. As I reluctantly hung up, I realized I never even got around to telling him that Thomas had confiscated my birthday present. I decided it could wait and started on my homework.

A couple of hours later, Rosalyn came to my room dressed in a killer blue dress and silver strappy heels. Her hair had been French rolled, and diamond teardrop earrings completed her look.

"Thomas and I are meeting friends of his for dinner. Don't wait up."

I had an odd sense of déjà vu as she walked away. I watched her go and stood there long after she'd gone before finally closing my door.

Tyra had texted about seeing a movie, and I had about thirty minutes before she'd be here, so I changed into jeans and my *Days of Thunder* T-shirt before throwing on my utility jacket and heading downstairs to see what I could find for dinner. I wasn't crazy about paying movie theater prices for popcorn and candy.

I heard them whispering, and when I entered the kitchen, Ever and Jamie stopped and stared.

"You know it's a felony to make a girl this uncomfortable."

Jamie's eyes bucked. "You're still expecting us to be gentlemanly?"

"I never expected any such thing." I decided to grab an apple and hoped it would be enough. "What were you two talking about?" I questioned with a mouth full.

"Business que es nachos," Jamie answered with a cringe while Ever chose to stare.

"Let me guess." I giggled. "You got a D in Spanish?"

His eyes hooded at my teasing. "It was pass-fail."

"And your teacher was pretty?"

"Not really," he said with a smirk. "But I am."

Shaking my head, I stole a peek at Ever and felt my tummy clench when I realized he was still watching me. "Why are you staring at me?"

"Because there's nothing else in the room that interests me."

My chewing slowed for a moment as my skin heated, and my panties became damp. "Am I supposed to be flattered?" A knowing light entered his eyes when I shifted, but he said nothing. "I'm going out," I said quickly as I backed away. "Could you tell Charlie?"

"You mean the cook?" Ever mocked.

Mr. Hunt had recently insisted I call him by his first name when he complimented me for not being so uptight. All I'd done was thank him for a great meal. It seemed a shame that gratitude among the elite was a rare occurrence.

"He has a name."

"And now I know it."

I contemplated tossing my half-eaten apple at him when he stood and closed the distance between us.

"If you throw your food at me, you won't be going anywhere but over my knee."

I didn't expect his kiss. It was soft, brief, and almost sweet. A noticeable contrast to the threat that made my heart, and something else just as forbidden to him, to contract.

"Meet me in the garage in five."

"Is that an order?"

"Does it need to be?" he tossed over his shoulder as he exited the kitchen.

I watched him go and hated the sigh that left my lips. I'd forgotten Jamie was still in the room until he spoke. "You should stop pretending you don't want him. He's made it clear he won't reject you."

"*He* kissed *me*."

"And made you want more."

"Screw you." I tossed my apple at him, which he caught and took a huge chunk out of.

"I'm not the one offering," he retorted with a shrug.

Agitated, I folded my arms and stuck out my hip. "Even if he cheated with me, she still wouldn't take you back. Not after everything you've done to hurt her."

It had suddenly become clear that Jamie was practically shoving me into Ever's arms for one selfish reason. Barbie.

"Take *me* back?" he questioned with a tilt of his head. I didn't know what to say, so I stayed quiet. He scoffed and the side of his lips tilted with a mocking half smile. "I suppose he would tell you his side to get into your pants."

"We haven't—"

"Not yet," he interrupted with unchecked arrogance.

"Why are you so sure I'll fuck him?"

"Because he always gets what he wants, and make no mistake, Four, he wants you."

"I—" My denial fled. The truth felt too powerful. "I have to go."

I turned away only for a thought to hit me. "You didn't deny hurting her."

He took a deep breath, and for the first time, he looked ashamed. "Because I have. I *need* to. Nothing else will do."

"Then you deserve to lose her."

I hurried from the kitchen and made my way to the garage. I was in such a hurry that I let the door shut me in. The garage was dark and drafty. I couldn't see a thing, but I felt his presence. Slowly, my eyes adjusted to the dark, and I was able to make out the tall figure.

"You could just flip the light switch next to you," Ever called out. A jingling sound followed.

My fingers quickly fumbled for the switch, and when I found it, light flooded the room. Ever was leaning against the Racer twirling the key ring on his forefinger.

"How did you—"

"I've known the combination to my father's safe since I was ten."

"Why do you have them?"

"I figured you'd want to take your new ride for a test drive."

I narrowed my gaze. "Why would you help me?"

He sighed and ceased twirling the key ring. "I told you we aren't enemies as long as you stay out of my way."

But it couldn't be that simple. Not with Ever. "How do I know you aren't setting me up again?"

"You don't."

Ever was a magnet drawing me close until I stood directly in front of him, hating how feminine he made me feel. "So I should just trust you?"

His nostrils flared. "Your choices have always been yours to make. I didn't put that bottle of Jameson in your hand, and I didn't make you use it as a weapon. Take some fucking responsibility."

"Whatever." I tried to grab the keys, but he jerked them high out of my reach, causing my body to fall into him. My breasts were pressed into his chest, and I held my breath when he lowered his head.

"That doesn't sound like gratitude."

"You're being a jerk."

"And you're being a whiny bitch."

I stretched to make another grab for the keys, which was

a huge mistake. My hips met his, and he kept me there with a hand on my ass when I tried to pull away.

"Give me the keys."

"Say please."

"Never."

"Then I'll take a kiss instead." He smiled, making him even more irresistible.

"You…you h-have a girlfriend," I stuttered.

His playful expression vanished, and he narrowed his eyes. "You seem to only remember that when it's convenient for you." He stared down at me for a moment before his arm came down, and he dropped the keys in my palm. The hand on my ass slid to my hip, and he moved me away. "Be back by ten," he ordered.

I watched him walk away. It didn't feel right letting him leave with a barrier between us, so I blurted the first thing that came to mind. "What if I get caught?"

He paused, and already, I could feel the pain in my chest easing. "They went to the city for dinner and a show," he said without facing me. "You'll be home long before they get back if you do as I say."

"You'd like that, wouldn't you?"

"Very much." He made a quick exit.

Pulling out my cell, I texted Tyra that I'd meet her at the theater.

chapter twenty-four

The Peer

S HE DIDN'T KNOW THAT I'D BEEN FOLLOWING HER SINCE SHE LEFT home. Watching her ride had me wishing I was between her legs instead of that goddamn bike. Stealing the keys from my father had been to satisfy a curiosity. I didn't expect her skill or the thrill of watching her.

I had resigned myself to staying away from Four, but then I came home from school and heard her arguing with my father. My baser instincts had taken over my free will, and I couldn't stop myself from standing up for her. I wanted to beat my chest and roar at our parents and the entire goddamn world that if they fucked with her, they fucked with me. I didn't understand my need to protect her, but I was beginning to realize that I was powerless against it. Even my father was becoming suspicious as I knew he would be, but I couldn't reason with myself to care. I wanted him and everyone else to see that she was mine. Even though she shouldn't be.

Four didn't meet her friend right away. Instead, she took to the deserted back roads. My hands itched to grab hold of her and shake some sense into her each time she took a curve without slowing or accelerated on a straight road. When my speedometer read ninety, and she was still a few car lengths ahead, I promised to get my hands on her ass when I got her back home.

After scaring twenty years off my life, she finally made her way toward town, and I followed her to the theater. Tyra looked amazed as she watched Four park. They said a few words before moving inside, and I watched them disappear as I typed a text.

Ten minutes later, I was walking into the theater with Vaughn. We stopped to load up on popcorn, soda, and candy and made our way into the theater showing the chick flick. Vaughn groaned again when we stood inside the dark room and heard the dialogue. Most of the seats were empty, and after a quick scan, I found our girls sitting in a dark corner on the far side.

Tyra didn't seem all that surprised when she looked up and found us standing over them.

"I knew you'd find me," she grumbled at Vaughn.

"Then why did you bother keeping it a secret?"

Four didn't speak, though our gazes remained locked. Vaughn broke our stare down moments later when he asked her to move down a seat. I was surprised when she obliged. He immediately claimed the seat between Tyra and Four, and I sat next to Four on the end.

"What are you doing here?"

I noticed she didn't have anything to snack on, so I tossed a pack of Twizzlers in her lap. She ignored the candy and repeated her question.

"Thought I'd see a movie."

"And it just so happened to be this movie?"

"Is there a problem, Archer?"

"As a matter of fact, stalking is a very big problem."

"Then why haven't you asked me to leave yet?"

"I don't like to waste my breath."

"So, what would you call this?"

She seemed to think it over before turning in her seat to face the screen. I felt myself fighting a grin when she tore open the bag of Twizzlers a moment later. Vaughn had reclined his and Tyra's seats, and I considered doing the same but decided even that small of a temptation was too risky, so I settled in to watch the movie.

"I can't believe someone actually filmed this crap," I muttered ten minutes into the movie.

She reluctantly met my gaze in the darkened theater. "Why do you say that?"

"Other than the cheesy dialogue?" She nodded, so I asked, "How does someone supposedly smart, successful, and sexy not see that he's a psychopath?"

"Why are you so sure he's crazy?"

"He's trying too hard."

"The movie is called *The Perfect Guy*."

It killed me how naïve she truly was. "There's no such thing."

"The girls at school would disagree. Some would say you're the perfect guy."

"It's a fantasy. None of them know me."

"I heard more than a few know a certain"—her gaze trailed to my lap—"part of you."

"Not likely. I don't have community dick." After Olivia, I'd been particularly selective. Everyone at Brynwood assumed I would only touch a girl if she were hot enough but in truth, I only fucked the ones who were transparent and uncomplicated. And yeah those girls happened to be the ones who were hot, popular and shallow.

Four didn't seem convinced, and I wasn't about to discuss the girls I'd slept with, so I said, "Wanna make it interesting?"

"How so?"

"I bet you he does something fucked up to the cat."

"What?" she snorted as she laughed. "That's oddly specific. You sure you haven't seen this movie?"

"Chick flicks aren't my thing."

"Because you're so macho?" she teased.

Movement behind her caught my eye, and I glanced up just in time to catch Vaughn's hand traveling up Tyra's skirt. They were no longer pretending to watch the movie as they made out in their darkened corner.

"Because I prefer not to spend ninety minutes bleeding from my eyeballs."

"It's not that bad." She giggled, and it felt like a fist had punched its way inside my chest and seized my heart in its grip.

"Do you accept?"

"Depends on what you want."

I pretended to think it over even though I knew exactly what I wanted. "The kiss you weaseled your way out of earlier."

"You have a girlfriend, but I'm the weasel?"

"It's complicated."

"Doesn't matter. Pick something else."

"No."

"Then no bet."

"There's got to be something you want." I was aware that I was borderline begging but couldn't bring myself to care.

"What I want you can't give me."

"What if I offered to release you from our deal?"

Her gaze narrowed on me. "You're *that* sure you'll win?"

I had no fucking clue, but to be honest, I didn't need the deal to control her. Every day, she lost some of her drive for revenge to her determination to resist me. "You in or you out?"

She hesitated for only a split second before saying, "In."

I held out my hand, and she shook it before settling in to finish watching the movie.

Vaughn and Tyra continued to make out.

Sometime later, I heard her soft groan when the cat went missing, and a later scene showed Mr. Perfect with the cat in his home as he watched the heroine through a hidden camera. To fuck with her, I reached into my pocket for my Chapstick.

She peeked at me as I applied my cherry flavored lip balm, so I popped my lips for good measure.

"You're pissing me off." Her gaze was now on the screen again, but she was no longer watching the movie.

"I'm sorry." I offered her the tube. "Would you like some?"

She twisted her lips but didn't respond. When the movie *finally* ended, I led the way out of the theater. Tyra had a hard time meeting our gazes while Vaughn wore a stupid grin. "What's next?" he questioned excitedly as he rubbed his hands together.

Tyra shook her head. "I need to get home. I have a test to study for."

Vaughn narrowed his gaze. "Isn't that in two days?"

"Some of us aren't comfortable cramming," she retorted.

"Whatever." Vaughn trained his gaze on Four. "What about you?"

I pretended not to notice her glance at me before answering. "I have to get the bike home."

"You guys are lame," Vaughn sighed. To Tyra, he said, "Come on. I'll follow you home."

They took off together, leaving Four and me alone on the sidewalk. We slowly walked to the parking lot, and when we reached her bike, she twisted to face me. "I guess I'll see you at home then?"

"I guess so."

With an awkward nod and wave, she hopped on her bike and took off. I stole a peek at her ass just before she turned the corner and groaned. There was no way I wasn't going to follow her.

Hurrying to my car, I almost missed the hooded figure lingering under one of the street lamps. I couldn't see his face, but I knew he was watching me. I felt for the blade in my pocket and took cautious steps toward the stranger. Blackwood Keep was one of the safest places on the eastern seaboard, but instinct told me that I was about to face-off with a predator.

The orange glow grew brighter the closer I came. I searched the shadows behind him just in case he had friends before stepping into the circle of light. When he pushed back his hood, my blood ran cold, and I cursed myself for leaving my Exiled-issued gun at home.

"What the fuck are you doing here, Harlan?" I tightened my grip on my blade just in case he decided to do something stupid.

"I followed you, Danny Boy." He then smiled and said, "You've got a nice set up here. That big fancy house of yours is really impressive."

"Why did you follow me?"

"I never trusted you, but after you saved my life, I figured I might have been wrong about you…but then I saw you in the city, looking like a million bucks, and I realized I'm *never* wrong."

"Whatever you think you know—"

"You and I both know what I know, so let's not insult each other's intelligence. I thought you were hiding something, but I got to say, you're damn good. I never expected to find some rich boy looking for a thrill."

I didn't bother to correct his assumption. My reasons for becoming Exiled were none of his fucking business. "What do you want?"

"Straight to the point. That's the Danny I know. What I want is never to see your fucking face again, pretty boy. If I do, I'll carve it up real nice before letting Fox kill you."

"Does he know?"

When he shook his head, relief flooded me. "Consider us even for saving my life. As long as you stay the fuck away from Exiled, we'll stay even."

He stood to his full height, and I considered killing him, but we both knew I wasn't a murderer. The only blood I would ever spill was Fox's and only if he left me no choice.

"This is goodbye…Ever." He patted my shoulder on his way past, and I felt helpless and enraged as I watched him disappear into the night.

chapter twenty-five

the Puppet

I SLEPT PAST MY ALARM AND DID A MAD DASH FROM MY BED TO THE shower and into my uniform. After the movies, I'd taken the scenic route home. Ever still hadn't made it home when I arrived, so I snuck into his room and left the keys to the Racer on his nightstand. Somehow, while worrying if he'd make it home in time and chewing my fingernails to bits, I'd fallen asleep.

Dressed for school, I grabbed my backpack and rushed downstairs. I was too late for breakfast, but I stopped by the kitchen anyway for one of Mrs. Greene's freshly baked muffins. Judging by the mouth-watering scent my nose was picking up, it was going to be a blueberry morning.

I jumped the last two stairs just as Jamie sauntered from the kitchen with a half-eaten muffin in one hand and two in the other. He grinned when he caught sight of me and stuffed the last of the muffin in his mouth.

"Morning, sleeping beauty," he said with a mouth full of scrumptious blueberry delight.

"Did you save some for the rest of us?"

"I'm a growing boy," he defended.

I started for the kitchen again when his free hand circled my wrist, stopping me in my tracks.

"Heads up. You're riding with me today."

"Is everything okay?" Jamie and Ever usually took turns driving, and on the rare days they drove separate cars, I always chose

Jamie. It was better for everyone that way. Last year, riding alone with Ever had left him with a black eye and me with a threat from him that I should have heeded.

Jamie glanced over his shoulder at the kitchen, and when he regarded me once more, the worry in his eyes caught me off guard. "Here"—he offered up one of his muffins—"take one of mine, and let's get out of here."

"What?" I stared at him as if he'd grown a second head before my very eyes. "You never share food. Why are you being weird?"

He blew air from his lungs and released my wrist to shove his fingers through his hair. "I'm not."

"Then why don't you want me in the kitchen?"

"Ever's not in the best of moods."

"When is he ever?" I didn't wait for a response and pushed past him. I wasn't going to worry myself about which side of the bed Ever woke up on. When I stepped into the kitchen, Ever was rising from his seat at the farthest end of the island with a bowl in his hand. "Hey."

He met my gaze across the room, but there wasn't a flicker of emotion or even vague recognition in his brief glance.

"Hey." The single syllable was frozen over, and I instantly regretted not leaving with Jamie when I had the chance.

"I left the keys in your room last night. Did you—"

"They're back in the safe," he curtly supplied.

"Are you okay?" I questioned while moving closer. I thought I was used to Ever's mood swings, but this felt different.

"I'm fine." He placed his bowl in the sink and met my gaze for the second time. "Jamie told you he's giving you a ride to school?"

That was when I noticed he was still in his pajamas: long plaid bottoms and a white T-shirt.

"He did." I moved closer and realized I might have been a masochist. I now stood in front of him with barely a foot of space between us. "Are you sick?"

"I said I'm fine." He went completely still when I stepped closer until the tip of his sock-covered toes kissed the front of my patent leather ballets. "What are you doing?" he snapped when I peered up at him.

"Checking for signs of distress."

"Archer."

I reeled at his brusqueness. "Is this about the bet?"

"What?"

Before I could talk myself out of it, I rose to the tips of my toes and kissed his cheek. "There. All debts have been settled."

My smile fell when he shoved me away and wiped his skin where my lips had been.

"Keep that shit to yourself, Archer." And then he spat, "I have a girlfriend." Without another word spoken, he stalked from the kitchen, leaving me to wonder if I had any more room in my heart for another scar.

"I think I'm ready," Tyra whispered as our lunch trays were filled.

"Ready for what?"

When she blushed and wouldn't meet my gaze, I got a pretty good idea of what she meant. I took a deep breath to stall for time to figure out how to proceed. Girl talk was still a novelty for me, and now we'd ventured into discussing our sex lives. Neat.

"Are you sure?"

"I'm pretty sure."

"Are you sure *pretty sure* is a good enough sure?"

"Can we stop saying sure?"

"Sure."

We shared a laugh despite my alarm and her uncertainty before the conversation turned serious again.

"I'm ready, and I can't think of anyone better to turn my card in to."

"How about someone who's not a rich playboy?"

Her face fell, telling me my attempt at humor was unappreciated. "You don't know him like I do."

It was hard to argue her point. Hadn't Ever claimed much of the same last night? On the outside, we can only see what people choose to show us. Had Vaughn let Tyra in?

"You're right, I don't, so I should just trust your judgment, huh?"

Her sharp nod was followed with, "Right."

Empty seats were in abundance today. Unfortunately, Tyra insisted we sit at the middle table again. Ever's absence was noticeable when we sat down even though the table was crowded as usual with people standing around hoping to rub elbows with the chosen ones.

Tyra barely touched her food or spoke as she shared frequent, lustful glances with Vaughn. Jamie wasn't around to offer a distraction either, so I kept my nose damn near mashed in my potatoes and ignored the curious glances and obvious snickers.

I wolfed down my food and bolted. The cafeteria door swinging shut behind me cut off the sound of Tyra calling my name. The hallways were mostly empty, but I felt vulnerable left out in the open. I made my way down the hall, hoping to find an empty classroom to duck into until lunch ended.

I was making my way to the second floor when I heard two voices, only one of them familiar.

"I know what you're after."

A feminine snort and then, "I doubt that, but go ahead... shock me."

"You think you're so much better, but your ship is sinking, and you and I both know Captain Prick isn't going to save the day. He's got a shiny new toy, *Barbie*."

"You let me worry about that."

"I could help you."

"Baby steps, Jason. You can't even help yourself."

My fist tightened on the banister, but I forced myself to stay put. Information was much more satisfying than confrontation.

"This is your last chance to join the winning team."

"Why would I betray Ever?"

His sharp smile was pure evil. "Because unlike him, my father will make yours an offer. I have to be a better choice than your old man's golfing buddies, right?"

"You're about neck and neck."

Before Jason could respond, a tall figure brushed past me. Casually, the newcomer rounded the banister and climbed the stairs to the landing. I stifled my groan when I recognized the skin fade and tattoos disappearing under the wave of thick reddish-brown locks. "Interesting place and time for secret meetings."

Jason's scowl deepened, but Barbie's icy composure held as Jamie pushed between them, effectively creating space, before leaning against the wall in a casual pose. The tension was thick enough to choke on as he locked gazes with Jason after a dismissive glance at Barbie.

"What do you want, Buchanan?"

"Nothing in particular. I'm just curious."

"Walk away."

"Funny…I was going to suggest you do the same."

"Careful…I don't see your cousin around."

Jamie's pierced brow quirked. "I guess that means there's no one to stop me from kicking your ass, huh?"

"There's no need for that. We're done here, Jason." Barbie's dismissal and the promise of violence in Jamie's eyes sent Jason scurrying up the stairs and back to whatever hole he had crawled out of.

Once they were alone…well, mostly…their gazes clashed, and in them was unmistakable desire. It made me wonder how they've managed to deny one another.

"I've been looking for you, Bette."

Bette? I mouthed.

"And I've been avoiding you." She attempted to strut away, but with a hand around her waist, he gently guided her until her back was against the wall.

"Stop running from me," he cooed as if attempting to woo her.

When he stepped closer, she held up her hand to ward him off. Effortlessly, his chest pushed against her small hand, forcing her to drop it as he crowded her against the wall.

Strawberry blonde curls bounced and caught the light as she shook her head. "I won't let you do this to me again."

"Do to *you*?" Jamie spat incredulously. "Have you forgotten that you're *fucking my cousin*?"

"You're acting like a child."

I couldn't agree more.

"Did he know you'd always be mine when you gave it up?" A low growl echoed around the empty hall. "I should have been the first and only inside your sweet cunt."

"I've never slept with him!"

A snort that sounded much too casual drowned my gasp of surprise. Was it true or just another lie?

"My cousin gets what he wants," Jamie snarled, "and so do I."

"You don't want me. You just don't like that Ever has me."

"And?"

"What is your problem, James? We had *nothing*. I'm not some toy you can just dust off and play with until you get bored again."

"Then you're remembering it wrong or lying to yourself. Chasing after you was never a dull moment. Playtime with you was always my favorite time of day."

"Yeah, well, we aren't kids anymore."

She pushed past him, and he didn't try to stop her. My surprise quickly turned into panic, however, when I realized Barbie was descending the stairs. Any moment now, she'd notice me and know that I'd been eavesdropping. It was too late to run, so I waited, and not a breath was spilled when her glacial gaze, nearly hidden behind a curtain of thick lashes, met my own.

"Um...hi." I gave a lame wave which she ignored in favor of the point.

"How much did you hear?"

Enough. "Don't know what you mean."

"Leave her alone," Jamie called from above. His hands were shoved inside his slacks, and his jaw was set in hard lines.

She turned her fierce gaze on Jamie but not before I saw the flash of jealousy in them. "She's your problem now?"

"She's none of your business," he bit back.

With a huff, she flounced past me, and we both watched her disappear from sight before speaking.

"What the hell was that?" I hissed up the stairs.

He shrugged and looked away. "You're new here. Tread carefully."

"You shouldn't push up on your cousin's girlfriend. It makes you look like a sleazebag."

With a shake of his head and a scoff, he started up the stairs. I wanted to chase after him, but the bell rang, so I headed to class instead.

The rest of the day passed quickly, and like any other day, I was looking forward to my mechanics class. Dave wasn't as knowledgeable as Gruff, but he had a great sense of humor. I was the first to arrive as usual, but Dave was nowhere to be found. The bay door was open, so I headed that way and found Dave hauling a bag of dog food from his F150. Suddenly, a long whine erupted from a box next to the door, and out popped a black furry head that could easily fit inside my palm and tiny paws that scratched the cardboard.

"Hey, Four. I didn't see you there."

I couldn't take my eyes off the puppy. He fought to free himself from the box, and when he fell back onto the newspaper, I couldn't take it anymore. I lifted him, and he immediately began licking my face to show his gratitude. While he covered me in doggy saliva, I got a better look at him. He had blue eyes and a short, shiny coat of fur.

"I see you got yourself a pup. Don't you think he's too cute for you?"

Dave chuckled, and I wrinkled my nose as I watched him sprinkle some food on the concrete. It scattered everywhere, some of it rolling into the grass. "You expect him to scavenge for food?"

"Huh?" The clueless look on Dave's face made me hug the pup tighter.

"You can't feed him like that. He'll starve."

The pup wiggled in my arms eager to hunt for his food. I set him down and watched as he chased the kibbles around. "So what's his name?"

"Oh, haven't named him. Couldn't find him a home, so he's going to the pound."

"What?"

"I found him on the road outside of town. Almost ran him over."

My heart broke as I imagined such a horrible end for the sweet little pup.

"He didn't have a collar?"

"Nah. He's barely old enough to be off the tit."

My eyebrows raised, and Dave stumbled to apologize, apparently realizing he was talking to one of his students.

"He can't go to the pound. The bigger dogs might beat him up."

"I tried to take him, but the wife wasn't having it." Dave checked his watch and then scooped him up to place him back in the box, much to the pup's displeasure.

My classmates started to arrive, so Dave ushered me inside. For the rest of the day, I couldn't take my mind off the pup that must have lost his mother and siblings. When school ended, and all my classmates were gone, I hurried back outside where the pup was standing on his legs as if he were waiting for me. I lifted him from the sorry excuse for a bed and stared into his blue eyes. "We should go before I come to my senses."

He barked twice, sounding happy.

Convincing Dave to let me take him home had been easier than I thought.

Jay D—named after the champ Joey Dunlop—and I made our way to the parking lot. Jamie had a leggy blonde wrapped around him, but somehow, he noticed me almost immediately.

"What the fuck?" His eyes grew wide when he saw what I carried. "No, no, no."

The blonde turned and wrinkled her nose when she saw I was the one who stole his attention.

"Aw, come on. Don't tell me you don't like dogs."

"How did you even get that thing?"

"His name is Jay D, thank you very much.'

"He's trouble, and you're going to find yourself knee deep in it if you bring it home."

"Let me worry about that."

Jamie surprisingly didn't argue. He shook his head and shot me a look of pity. "Ever's not going to like this, and I'm not helping you explain this to him."

"I don't answer to your cousin."

"Yeah. Okay."

It irritated me when the blonde smirked right along with Jamie. Did the entire school know something I didn't?

"Are you selling tickets?" Jamie joked. "I want a front row seat."

"Ugh. Shut up, and take me home," I ordered as I rounded the front of the Jeep.

"Yes, princess."

"Don't call me that," I snapped a little harder than necessary.

"Because only Ever has that privilege?"

"Because I don't like it."

"If you say so." Jamie dismissed the blonde, and she strutted off in a huff.

I was still shaking my head as we got settled into his Jeep. Surprisingly, Jay D immediately curled in my lap for a nap.

"What?" he questioned while wearing a genuinely puzzled expression.

"You don't have respect for women."

"That's not true." He shot a dazzling grin my way. "I respect you."

I snorted. "I'm not sleeping with you."

"Precisely."

"I don't get it."

"These girls give it up no matter how shitty I treat them. If they don't respect themselves, why should I?"

"You could always take the high road and be a gentleman."

He snorted as he started the car and began the drive home. "You've got a lot to learn about guys, cousin-in-law."

"That's another thing. Stop calling me that. People will talk."

"They're already talking. You're just catching up."

I sat up in my seat and twisted to face him. "What?"

"Everyone thinks you and my cousin are a thing."

"Why would they think that?"

"Property of Ever McNamara is practically tattooed on your forehead, sweetheart."

"Don't call me that, either."

He laughed off my snub while I pouted in his passenger seat. "This is why you and I could never be."

"I agree but indulge me. Why is that?"

"You're too high maintenance."

"What do you call Barbie?"

"A fucking fraud." More quietly he added, "And a plague."

Silence fell, and I found myself feeling sorry for Jamie. He was in love, and he didn't want to be.

"She really got to you, didn't she?"

"What are you talking about?"

"Barbie...you love her."

"And then she fucked my cousin, Four. Your point?"

I was surprised that he hadn't denied being in love with Barbie, but I quickly recovered. "Maybe it's not what you think." Tyra had her doubts and Ever had also implied that their thing wasn't a thing at all.

His hands strangled the steering wheel. "Please, don't tell me you fell for his crap?"

"They don't act like a couple. Have you ever even seen them kiss?"

"Does he kiss *you* in public?"

"*I'm* not his girlfriend." And he shouldn't be kissing me at all. Just this morning, Ever had rejected me, and instead of relief, I felt like he'd ripped my heart out. He didn't belong to me, and this morning made it clear he never would.

"Ever does what he wants, and no one would dare tell him otherwise. Until you."

"*Exactly*. Someone like Ever doesn't keep secrets because he's afraid of the consequences. He keeps them to protect the people he loves."

"So, what are you saying?"

"Why is it when it comes to her, you're so dumb?" I expelled air, questioning why I even cared. "I think he's protecting her from something...or someone."

He was silent for so long, I didn't think he'd respond, but then he said, "From what?"

I shrugged. "Maybe if you weren't such an ass, you would know."

His darkening gaze cut my way. "I never took you for the judgmental type."

"I'm not judging you. I'm saving you. You are the enemy, Jameson Buchanan."

"Hey, hey...I only allow one girl to call me that."

"Let me guess," I laughed, "your mother?"

"Damn straight."

Jay D's nap didn't last very long. I thought I could sneak him up to my room while I figured out how to convince Thomas to let me keep the pup, but that wasn't meant to be. I could hear his happy barks as I searched the cupboards for a water dish. For all of Jamie's talk, he got out of dodge to meet up with one of his many fuck buddies, though he did promise to bring back puppy chow.

"Is that a dog I hear upstairs?"

I peeked over my shoulder and found Mrs. Greene with a basket of laundry tucked under her arm.

"Oh...um."

She sat the basket on the island and moved to the cabinet next to me. A moment later, she handed me a small plastic bowl.

"Thank you."

"I'm sorry I'll miss all the excitement."

I frowned as I moved to the sink and filled the bowl with cool water. "Do you really think Thomas will be mad?"

"I wouldn't worry about Thomas, dear."

What the hell did that mean?

She gave me a warm smile before disappearing upstairs.

After running the water up to my new friend and praying he didn't find anything to chew on in there, I ventured to the master suite for the first time. I figured Rosalyn would be taking one of her afternoon naps. After being a working girl for so long, she had no problem indulging in the advantages of being a kept woman.

I knocked once and pressed my ear to the door, but no answer came. I couldn't hear anything through the thick wood, so I cracked the door and took a cautious peek inside. Light snoring greeted me, and I smiled a secret smile. Rosalyn would die if she knew she snored.

I left her sleeping and went back to my room to get some homework done. An hour later, I threw in the towel. When I wasn't rescuing various items from Jay D's teeth, he was pawing at my ankles to get me to play. Now he whined as he scratched at the door, so I figured it was time for a pee break. Outside, I watched him vigorously sniff the grass searching for the perfect spot to do his business.

"You do know that's imported grass."

I swung around and found Ever standing there in jeans and a gray turtleneck. His hair was perfect, and his golden brown eyes shone brightly. "What's your problem now?"

"Your mutt is shitting on very expensive grass."

"He's not a mutt, and do you mean your father actually paid for this? You know it grows for free, right?"

He didn't respond, so I rolled my eyes, knowing it would piss him off, and turned my back on him. Unfortunately, Jay D chose that moment to notice him and ran his cute butt over to say hello. When Ever pointedly ignored Jay D's attempt at friendship, he began to sniff around him.

"Stop looking at him like that."

"Like what?"

"Like he's beneath you."

"He's a dog," he pointed out.

"And yet he has better manners than you." Jay D then made a liar out of me by chewing on Ever's pant leg for attention. I held my breath when Ever peered down at him, fearing he'd kick him away out of spite.

"Doesn't seem like it to me."

"He's a puppy."

"With no home training."

"I'll teach him." God, why did it feel as if I was explaining myself to him?

"You're under the impression that you're keeping him?"

My hands found my hips as I stared him down. "I don't need your permission."

"No, but you need my father's, and I can already tell based on that shit pile you didn't even notice that it's not happening. Take your mutt back to the pound."

"He didn't come from the pound. He lost his mom," I said while charging him. I made sure to step around the turd Jay D dropped so that I wouldn't make Ever's point. I now stood toe to toe and had to lift my chin to meet his eyes. "And Jay D isn't going anywhere."

"Jay D? What kind of fucking name is Jay D?"

"I named him after Joey Dunlop, my favorite rider, and I don't need your approval."

"What you need is a better name."

"Why are you still standing here?"

"Why are you still talking?"

"I hate you," I said with all the fervor I could muster.

"No, Four. You only wish you did."

"You're mighty full of yourself today." I didn't give him a chance to respond as it was then, through the trees, Jay D spotted Thomas's BMW speeding up the path and decided to run to meet it.

"Jay D! No!"

Thomas didn't slow as I raced to catch my puppy. My heart seemed to pound in tune to Jay D's barks as he ran straight for the BMW's tires.

"Four!"

I heard Ever roar my name, but I had to save Jay D. Just a couple hundred feet from the speeding BMW, he finally stopped with a wagging tail. I scooped him up in my arms, happy that he was okay. It wasn't until I heard Ever scream my name again that I remembered the car racing toward me. Tires squealed when Thomas slammed on the brakes just as Ever's arms found my waist and pulled us out of harm's way.

"Are you out of your mind?" he yelled. His eyes were crazy wild when he turned me around.

"Why are you screaming?"

"You just ran in front of a car for a goddamn dog. Are you *that* stupid?"

"Screw you."

He grabbed my jaw and yanked me into his chest with Jay D the only barrier between us. "I just saved your life. You better have more to say than that."

"Fine. Thanks. Now let me go."

"You're such a fucking brat!"

"And you're a pompous ass!"

"Four?"

Both of us froze when we heard Thomas yell my name.

"Jesus, please say something. Are you okay?" His footsteps were closing in, and Ever was still holding me.

"I want you in my room after dinner."

A shiver worked its way down my spine while heat bloomed between my legs.

"Don't count on that happening."

"Test me, Four Archer, I dare you."

He finally put space between us just as Thomas stepped into view. He looked between Ever and me, his alarm evident. "Is she okay?"

"I'm fine," I answered for myself.

"Why on Earth would you jump out in front of my car like that?"

"Why were you speeding?" Ever questioned his father before I could answer. His indignation was unmistakable. It was even stronger than when he had berated me.

"I have an important meeting in the city, and I left some papers in my office." To me, Thomas said, "Are you sure you're okay, and son, she can speak for herself."

"I told you. I'm fine."

"Good. Now explain what just happened."

"Thomas…" I lifted Jay D up, and he offered a chipper bark. "Meet Jay D."

Thomas's gaze narrowed on my pup.

"What is that?"

"Why does no one seem to recognize a dog around here?"

Thomas's eyebrows rose at my comment, but he chose to ignore it. "Aha…What is it doing here?"

"He needs a home."

"Oh?"

Suddenly, I felt less confident. "I thought maybe I could give him one."

He glanced from me to Ever and back again. "Have you discussed this with your mother?"

I stumbled over my response, completely startled by the fact that he hadn't shot me down right away.

"Not yet." I sounded hopeful.

"Speak to her about it, and then we'll see." He spun around and hurried off.

I jumped up and down and stopped only when Jay D whined.

"I wouldn't celebrate just yet."

"You're still here?" I questioned with a sigh. My back was still turned to him when I felt him press against me, and it took great restraint to keep from leaning back against him.

"You should be glad that I am."

"You're a curse, Ever McNamara." And hadn't Jamie said the same when I accused him of being in love?

I turned and stared into Ever's eyes. The pools of gold were brimming with emotion.

"Then you must be the spell to break me."

He left me standing there and disappeared into the house. I followed behind him with Jay D in my arms, wondering if what he said was true.

"So, Four, tell me how you came into possession of this dog."

We were all at dinner with the exception of Jamie, who had called to say he was tied up. I was afraid to know if he'd meant literally. With that boy, you never knew.

"I didn't possess him. I adopted him."

Thomas's eyebrows rose. "Right. My apologies. How did you come to adopt him?"

"Well, Dave found him—"

"I'm sorry...Dave?"

"My auto mechanics teacher."

"You're taking *auto mechanics*?" Thomas questioned, clearly displeased.

Dave had said when I questioned why he was allotted only a handful of students that for forty grand a year, the parents didn't want their kids wasting time learning a blue-collar trade.

"You call your teacher by his first name?" Rosalyn also questioned at the same time.

"He insisted."

Thomas tensed while Rosalyn looked alarmed.

"That's sort of inappropriate, don't you think, dear?"

"It's not anything like that. He's just laid back."

"He's your teacher. He shouldn't be laid back."

I blew out a breath and tugged on the end of my ponytail. "Can we just get back to discussing Jay D?"

"I just don't think a dog is a good idea. How will you maintain your grades if you're busy training a dog?"

"You let me worry about that."

"It's my job to worry," Rosalyn countered.

Oh yeah? Since when?

The moment we moved in, I hadn't been much more to

her than extra baggage, stowed away and forgotten. "And I'm telling you not to. I can handle the responsibility.".

"Who will clean up after him when he pees and sheds?"

"I'll make sure he does his business outside, and he has a short coat. He won't shed much." I had no idea if that was true but it sounded good.

"And how will you purchase the food or the vet bill if he gets sick? You can't ask Thomas to provide for a dog on top of everything else."

"Then I'll get a job."

"So you'll be working and taking care of a dog? I see the odds of you staying focused on school getting smaller and smaller."

I sat with my mouth agape, wondering where this new Rosalyn had come from. She hadn't been this concerned with me since...well...never.

"I worked back home, and my grades were fine. A dog isn't like having a baby. I can do this."

"I'm just not sure you can."

I felt my lips press tight as my nostrils flared. "You owe this to me."

"I *owe* you?"

"You uprooted me from my home so you could become a trophy for your rich boyfriend, and *then* you shipped me off to another freaking country the moment I embarrassed you. So, yeah ...you owe me."

Silence fell, and when tears welled in Rosalyn's eyes, I looked away. I couldn't let her tears back me down. I met Ever's gaze, but he was his usual detached self.

Thomas cleared his throat and stood from his seat at the head of the table. He walked to the end where Rosalyn sat and began massaging her shoulders as if she'd just been through trauma.

Give me a break.

"It seems we've gotten a bit off track here, so why don't we back up?" I didn't speak, and neither did she. "Four, you may keep Jay D for a trial."

Rosalyn started to protest, but Thomas deepened his massage, calming her.

"And when I say trial, I mean it. You'll feed and care for him yourself. The moment your mother or I feel you can't handle the responsibility, he's gone. Do you understand?" His firmness warned me not to test him, so I nodded.

Even though I'd won, I still lost my appetite, so I excused myself and fled to the solitude of my room.

chapter twenty-six

The Peer

WATCHED FOUR RUN AWAY FROM THE TRAIN WRECK SHE HAD CAUSED and almost gave into the urge to go after her. Partially because her mother's dramatics were grating on my nerves. When she finally settled the fuck down, my father returned to his seat.

"So Mrs. Greene tells me you stayed home from school today."

"You have the housekeeper keeping tabs on me now?"

"She was worried about you," he answered, unbothered by my irritation. "You never get sick."

"I'm better now."

"Good. Now have you considered our last discussion?"

"I'm not getting back on the team."

"I've yet to understand why you quit in the first place."

"I lost interest."

"No one that naturally good just loses interest."

Done with the conversation, I tossed down my linen napkin and stood from the table. I wasn't hungry anyway. "I have homework."

I could feel my father's anger as I left the dining room. Of course, Four hadn't come to my room, so I made my way down the hall. I could hear Eminem's 'The Way I Am' pounding on the other side of her door as I contemplated my next move. Every time I vowed to keep my distance, she pulled me right back in. I pushed inside her room, and my gaze immediately landed on Four sitting cross-legged on the floor playing with her mutt.

"I knew I should have locked my door," she muttered without looking up. I chose to ignore her comment. If she really wanted me to stay away, she would have locked the fucking door. I was almost pissed that she hadn't. One of us needed to have self-control, and I had already proven it wouldn't be me.

"So you like Eminem?"

"I stole Jamie's iPod."

Sure enough, I spotted his iPod hooked up to his speakers on her desk. He had been crying about losing it, and all along she had it. I sunk onto the foot of her bed and rested my forearms on my knees so I could see her face.

"You didn't come to my room."

"I was completely serious when I said I wouldn't."

I wrapped her wavy blonde hair in my fist and tilted her head back before kissing her lips. When I pulled away, I stared into her unfocused eyes. "And I was completely serious when I said you shouldn't test me."

"Actually, you dared me to." She pulled away and sighed. "What do you want?"

"I want you…" I thought about leaving it at that but knew that I couldn't. "…to stop causing trouble."

"You like me tame, and you like me wild, remember?"

I would have kissed her again or something else stupid, but the mutt chose that moment to growl and bark.

"Good boy," Four cooed. She scratched behind his ears when he crawled into her lap.

"What kind of dog is he, anyway?"

"I'm not sure…a Lab, I think."

"That's all? I doubt he was bred pure."

"God, you're pretentious." She looked ready to punch me.

Closing my eyes, I prayed for a little patience. When I opened them, she was still glaring. "Dogs have character traits just like humans. It would make training and caring for him easier if you knew his needs."

"Oh."

"I'm not always an asshole," I teased. Her lips twisted with humor, and I was tempted to kiss her again. "Where did your teacher find him?"

"He only said outside of town."

"The easiest way to find out what he is would be to find out where he came from."

"I don't really care, Ever." She whispered the words so softly that I almost didn't hear them. She also wouldn't look me in the eye, so I lifted her chin.

"Then it doesn't fucking matter."

She finally let me see those pretty brown eyes and the surprise that shown through them. "Why are you being somewhat pleasant after this morning?"

"Somewhat?"

"Think what you want, but you're *always* an asshole."

I paused. It wasn't as if I could deny it. A part of me *needed* her to hate me so that maybe she'd be strong enough to stay away. It was becoming more clear every day that I damn well fucking couldn't. Four was a magnet and I stopped resisting her pull a long time ago. "And you have a thick skull."

"Because I don't want you bossing me around?" She pursed her lips, not knowing how hungry it made me.

"Because you don't listen even when you should."

"Maybe I would if the person giving me orders wasn't you."

"What about your mother?"

"She only cares about falling in love. She should have just aborted me when she had the chance."

Anger burned inside my gut as I practically snatched her from the floor. The mutt fell from her lap and whined his displeasure as I laid his mother on her back and settled between her legs. "Don't say shit like that. It's beneath you." It also bled like a fatal wound to know she thought so little of her life.

"How would you know?"

"Even a blind man can see what you're worth." My answer didn't seem like enough. How did I put into words that the mere thought of her not breathing the same air as me made me a little less desperate for my next breath? Could I even trust her with that kind of power?

She snorted and looked away, baring her neck to me. My lips landed on her warm skin, and her body vibrated beneath me.

"What are you doing?" she gasped.

"I'm enjoying you. You owe me a kiss, anyway."

"You're either bipolar or you have selective memory." She shoved me away and sat up while I leaned back on my elbow. "What's your problem, McNamara?" That was her second time asking me today.

Running my hand through my hair, I decided to tell her the truth. "I was feeling fucked up."

"Obviously," she snarled. "Why?"

"I fucked up, and I blamed you." It wasn't much of an explanation, but it was all I could give her.

"Why would you blame me?"

"The guy we ran into the day we took you to the city was Exiled."

"I know. I recognized him. He was there that day I followed you." Her lips parted as worry entered her eyes. "Do you think he made you?"

"I know he did. He followed us here."

She gasped. "Are you in danger?"

"I can handle myself." I waved her off even though her concern felt damn good. It wasn't me I was afraid for. Wren knowing where I lived meant he could get to Four anytime he wanted.

"That guy seemed like he could, too."

She wasn't wrong, but I wasn't afraid of Wren. He was the least of my worries. Never finding Fox was what kept me up at night but I could understand her fear. Wren Harlan was a force to be reckoned with, and anyone who had his loyalty would be unstoppable.

"He won't be a problem as long as I stay away." She didn't look so sure. I brushed her cheek with my thumb, and she finally relaxed.

"What made you change your mind about me?"

"This is going to sound cliché but seeing you run out in front of my father's car made me think twice about keeping my distance. If you had been hurt or worse, I didn't want the last feeling you felt for me to be hatred."

"We haven't exactly been the best of friends."

"It doesn't make sense to me either, but I've been living without a clue since the day I met you."

She looked as uncomfortable as I felt and quickly changed the subject. "So what are you going to do?"

"Nothing. Harlan and I agreed that if I stayed away from Exiled, he'd keep his mouth shut about who I really am."

"But why does it matter? People from different backgrounds join gangs all the time. Who cares if you were spoon-fed diamonds as a baby?"

"Trust me, Four. It matters but not because of how much my family is worth."

"Then why?"

I shook my head, warning her to drop it. She looked like she wanted to argue for a moment before sighing and dropping her shoulders in defeat. "Do you trust him?" she asked in a small voice.

"For now, I don't have a choice, but if he becomes a problem, he'll be dealt with."

"You don't have to be macho for me."

I gave her my most charming smile. "Then who will I be macho for?"

"How about Barbie? Your girlfriend?" She lifted a brow.

"Bee and I are just friends." Immediately, I clammed up. I

didn't mean to say that, and her reaction told me there was no going back.

"You call her Bee?"

"She hates her name and hates Barbie even more." *Fuck.* It felt like I'd been injected with truth serum because I couldn't shut the fuck up.

"How could she hate being called Barbie when she looks like a doll every single day? That's obviously her own doing, right?"

"There's more to her than what any of them sees."

"You love her." Her voice broke at the end. "Don't you?"

"Of course, I do." I quickly grabbed her before she could pull away. "But I'm not *in* love with her." I stared into her pretty brown eyes while my hand on her chin kept her from looking away. "Am I understood?"

She narrowed her eyes and said, "By friends, did you mean with benefits?"

I could only chuckle at her stubbornness. Jealousy looked damn good on her.

"I mean I've never fucking touched her, and I never will."

"Then why pretend? Doesn't it get old?"

"I told you. It's not my secret to tell. And pretending was never a problem until you."

"And Jamie? He thinks you've betrayed him. How can you be okay with that?"

"I am betraying him. I knew what dating Bee would do to him, and I did it anyway."

"Maybe if you told him—"

"She doesn't want him to know, and if she ever does, she'll tell him herself."

"But why you? Why did she choose you to know her secret instead of the boy she loves?"

"She didn't. It was by accident that I found out, but it was my decision to help her."

I watched the battle over whether to believe me or not wage

within her until she said, "Regardless, you still have a girlfriend. The kissing has to stop."

Like hell it does.

I kept our gazes locked as I pulled out my phone, dialed, and placed the call on speaker. "Bee, I'm with a girl I'd very much like to kiss. Will you tell her it's okay?"

Barbette snorted and said, "It's okay, *Four*."

And because I knew my best friend well, I hung up quickly and took Four's mouth before she could allow more bullshit to spill from her lips. Those sexy, delicious fucking lips.

Mine.

It wasn't long before I was swallowing her moans, my hands full of her slender hips.

"Ever. Wait."

"Hell no. I don't want to wait anymore." I kissed her again only for her to push me away.

"What about what I want?"

I stared down at her. "You don't want me?"

I got my answer when I felt her shiver at the promise of having me. "It's not that simple," she raged. "You keep filling my head with possibilities only to take it back whenever you want!"

"I know, Four."

"Don't do that. Don't sweet-talk me. It won't work this time."

"I could persuade you other ways," I offered.

"That sounds, suspiciously, like you getting your way."

"You want me to spell it out? Fine. I want to go down on you, so tell me you want it, too."

She looked torn as her teeth sunk into her swollen lips. "No sex?"

"No sex," I confirmed. *For now.*

She chewed on her lip before saying, "Fine."

"Uh-uh. Give me the words."

"I—I want it, too."

"See? That wasn't so hard." I crouched at the edge of the

bed and yanked her shorts off. I was eager to get my mouth on her. After her panties joined her shorts on the floor, I drank in the sight of her pussy. I leaned in, but her hand suddenly gripping my hair stopped me from getting my fix.

"I'd like to remind you that I have a mean right hook."

"You threatening me, baby?" I made a mental note to make her come extra hard.

"You better fucking believe it."

I tugged her hips hard, making her fall flat on her back. My tongue flicked her clit, shutting her up.

"Oh, God," she shrieked when I did it again. "What was I thinking? This is bad. We're bad."

I ignored her guilt trip and kept right on eating. Sliding a finger inside her, I groaned at how tightly she gripped me and palmed my dick with my free hand. I didn't want to come in my pants like I was thirteen.

I couldn't get enough of this girl.

I knew she was close to coming when her grip tightened in my hair, and her body jerked.

Fuck yeah.

Her hips lifted from the bed when I got my tongue inside her, so I gripped her thighs to hold her down as she rode the wave. Beyond her cries, I heard the faint sound of footsteps in the hall and then her bedroom door opening.

"Yo, Four! I have the dog fo—"

It was too late to pretend that nothing was happening. I glanced over my shoulder and found Jamie standing in the open doorway. His shock was evident as he stared at me kneeling between Four's thighs.

"Get out!" I barked.

He came to his senses and jerked the door closed but not before I caught the sly grin on his face.

"Oh, God," Four panted. "He saw, didn't he?"

"Yeah, he fucking saw." I stood and crossed the room to lock the door—something I should have done to begin with. When I faced her again, I found one of her pillows shoved between her legs.

"Well, what do we do?"

"Why would we do anything?"

"No one can know we did…things."

I laughed. "So, what do you suggest I do? Kill my cousin?"

"Of course not." I was still laughing thanks to the look on her face. "This isn't funny." I laughed harder. "This is all your fault."

"Making you come as hard as you did? Yeah, I'll take the credit for that."

"You have zero modesty."

"Noted." She looked around the room refusing to meet my gaze. "Something on your mind?"

"I need to get dressed." When she finally looked at me, there was a determination in her eyes. "Can you please leave?"

chapter twenty-seven

The Puppet

"Leave?" He echoed as he lifted his sweater.

My heart raced faster with each inch of skin he unveiled. His muscled abs and chest was truly a sight to behold. I was almost sure the pillow nestled between my thighs was soaked.

"We're finished here."

"I don't think so." His eyes were low and his gaze serene as if he were the one who came hard enough to see stars. "We're just getting started."

"You promised no sex."

"We're not having sex." Ignoring my discarded panties, he scooped my shorts from the floor and tossed them to me.

I quickly pulled them on while he dropped onto my bed. My shorts barely cleared my hips when he pulled me down onto his chest.

"Then what is this? What are we doing?"

"We're finding out why this feels right...and then we'll have sex."

"You're so sure."

"I can still taste you, princess. I'm sure."

I dropped my head on his chest to hide my blush. "Don't blame me when you're disappointed," I mumbled.

He chuckled and palmed my ass. "Deal." The silence that followed lasted so long that I thought he'd fallen asleep. "Tell me something I don't know about you."

I lifted my head to look into his eyes, but there was no trace of humor. "You're serious, aren't you? We're really going to have pillow talk?"

His eyebrows lifted. "We could do other things."

"Talking's good," I quickly answered. I laid my head back on his chest and felt it vibrate beneath me as he chuckled. "I collect helmets, usually the rare and expensive kind."

"How many do you have?"

"Twelve and counting."

"And what makes them rare?"

"Nothing. I just fall in love with the unusual and pay more money than they're worth."

"Why not just have them made?"

I purred and stretched as he stroked the base of my spine.

"I'm not that creative. Besides, some that I've bid on were signed or owned by pros."

"I'm assuming you keep them hidden in the boxes you never bothered to unpack?"

I groaned at the reminder of my weekend task. Not only was I growing sick of living out of my suitcase but it also didn't seem as if Rosalyn and Thomas were breaking it off anytime soon. They've now been dating for two years, so at this point, I was just living in denial. "I'm unpacking this weekend, but I don't mind showing them off now."

His hand paused on my lower back. "Is this a trick to get me to help you unpack?"

"Nonsense. I wouldn't want you to break a nail."

I squealed when he rolled on top of me and settled between my legs. We were bold to carry on this way with Rosalyn and Thomas in the house, but I couldn't bring myself to care when he took my hand and laid it over his erection. "So there's no confusion."

I slid my palm down his erection and up again. "You think this makes you a man?"

"I think it helps." He grinned, and then he was on his feet, pulling me from the bed. I didn't have any of the boxes marked, so it took Ever some lifting—at his insistence.

When we found the box, he took that nifty blade of his and cut through the tape. Ever wielding a blade was almost taboo, and watching him handle it made me crave to let him handle me.

I lifted the first helmet from the box and removed the protective wrapping. It was an open-faced helmet with red and white stripes from ear to ear. As far as looks went, it was pretty plain, but there was a rumor that it had once belonged to Vincent Valentino before his champion days.

"This is Four."

"Four?"

"I named them in the order I got them."

"Inventive," he remarked sarcastically while taking the helmet from my hands to inspect. "I like it." I was caught off guard when he slipped the helmet over my head. "I never thought I'd have a thing for a biker chick."

"You have a thing for me?"

"I think I do." He pulled me close by my helmet straps. "You have a problem with that?"

I couldn't answer him without making a fool of myself, so I did the next best thing and decided to kiss him. Unfortunately, I still managed to fuck up when my helmet crashed into his forehead.

"Damn," he groaned while holding his head. "I guess you do."

"Oh, no." I hid my face with my hands as best I could with the helmet still on. "That went wrong."

"I'll fucking say." He forced my hands from my face and then carefully lifted the helmet from my head. "Now try that again."

"Are you sure? I don't think your head can take much more trauma."

"I played football, remember? I've taken harder hits from guys twice your size."

With that said, I stood on the tips of my toes and pressed my lips against his. When I tried to back off, he growled and backed me into the wall.

"More."

Before I could give in, however, someone knocked on the door. We stared at each other with wide eyes.

"It could be Jamie," I whispered.

Ever's expression was doubtful.

"Four?" Dread filled me when I recognized Rosalyn's voice. "I know you're in there, so open up. We need to talk about dinner."

"Oh, God. What do we do?"

I was actually relieved when he smirked. "Let her in."

"She can't find you in here. She'll freak."

"I'll hide in your bathroom."

"Oh...right. I hadn't thought of that."

He smiled and nudged me toward the door before disappearing inside the en suite. For some reason, I tiptoed around the room and wondered if Ever's heart was pounding as hard as mine. I doubted it. He seemed much too casual about being caught for my liking.

Glancing over my shoulder one last time, I opened the door. "Now's not a good time, Rosalyn. I'm doing homework."

"This won't take long," she said firmly before pushing her way inside. I closed the door, leaned against it, and waited. "How could you talk to me the way you did?"

"I'm sorry," I said, which was partially true. I'd meant what I said, but I hadn't imagined it coming out the way it did. "I shouldn't have told you how I felt in front of them."

"What do you mean how you felt? How could you be so ungrateful?"

"You mean you're still pretending you moved us here for me?"

"You were in trouble, Four."

"It was an isolated incident. You knew no one was after me. You just saw an opportunity and took it." Would she stay if she knew we were living with one of them? There was only one way to find out, but I realized when the words lodged in my throat that my heart would never allow me to betray Ever. Even if he didn't feel the same.

"How could you think so little of me? We moved here because I couldn't chance losing you, too."

"You wouldn't need those pills if I weren't around."

"That's not—that's not true. The pills wouldn't be enough if you weren't around."

"That may be true now, but we both know without them, you'd feel differently. You couldn't even give me a name."

"Four *is* your name."

"It's a goddamn number!"

She clutched her chest. "Do not speak to me this way. What has gotten into you?"

I snuck a quick glance toward the bathroom but didn't respond. When her eyes started glistening, however, the words, "I'm sorry," flew from my lips. I couldn't stand to see Rosalyn cry. I couldn't bear hurting her even when she wrecked me every single fucking day.

"I need your blessing to be happy, Four."

"Since when?"

"Thomas is different than the others."

Except, after my father, her relationships crashed and burned, and good men disappeared in the cloud of smoke because of her issues with trust. She played a convincing victim, though.

There was probably some truth to her claim. Rosalyn wasn't a gold digger. She'd fallen for men without two cents to rub together and even less ambition. Thomas was definitely the wealthiest of all her former beaus, but money wasn't what captivated her. Rosalyn was truly a romantic. She was in love with being in love. Finer things were just a bonus.

I peeked again at the bathroom door.

"If you made an effort to know him, you'd see."

I shuddered. *No...never that.* Thomas was a nice guy but getting attached was a huge mistake. It was already too late to turn back with Ever.

"I want you to be happy, Rosalyn. You have my blessing."

I felt like a coward when she cupped my cheek, and grateful tears fell down her own. I wanted out of Blackwood Keep, and I'd let no one convince me otherwise.

Rosalyn hugged me. These came few and far in between. The sensation was foreign, yet I fought against the urge to hold her as she held me. I won the battle and held myself rigidly in her arms.

Another moment, and she released me. Her gaze traveled over my shoulder, and my heart dropped to my stomach when she said, "He really is a cutie."

"What?" I quickly glanced behind me, and my heart rate slowed when I found Jay D in the middle of a stretch. His mouth expanded as wide as it could before he settled his head on his tiny paw, and his blue eyes drifted shut. "Oh...yeah, he is." I didn't dare look toward the bathroom door before facing Rosalyn. "Well, I should probably get started on this homework if I want to keep him around."

I debated the necessity of my statement when she flinched.

"I'll leave you to it."

The sound of her heels quickly faded, so I shut the door and forced all the air from my lungs. I wasn't sure how much time passed before the bathroom door slowly opened. Ever stood on the threshold, his face a blank canvas.

"Your mom's missing a few marbles."

I didn't respond.

"Four?" He took a step closer.

My stomach tightened, and my next heartbeat came slower

than the last. I watched through blurred vision as thick eyebrows bunched just before his gaze dropped to my chest.

His eyes flashed with anger when they met mine. "Breathe."

The deep-timbered command sounded far away.

"Damn it, Four! I'm going to spank your ass for this."

A ghost of a smile lifted my lips as my body fell and everything went black.

Opening my eyes took some time, but the reward was a beautiful sight. Tanned skin over hard planes with dusky peaks…my gaze traveled from chest to throat until I met Ever's unflinching stare.

"Don't ever do something as remarkably stupid as *that* again."

I tried to sit up, but he tightened his arms and rolled on top of me.

"How many times have you done that?"

I averted my gaze. "It wasn't my first time."

"Make it your last," he bit out.

"It's not a big deal," I said despite my pounding headache. "I did it a lot when I was really young. The day I found out my grandparents died was the last time." The grief and hopelessness had been so overwhelming that I had been willing to do anything to escape if only for a moment.

The anger left his eyes, but the determination was still there.

"Promise me."

"Okay."

Satisfied, he kissed my shoulder a couple more times and then settled beside me while leaning over to stare into my eyes. He actually looked afraid for me.

"You do realize you're worried about a person whose existence is debatable, don't you?"

"A name means nothing. *You* decide who you are, and then you show the rest of the world."

I had trouble meeting his gaze. He was always so sure of his place in the world and I envied that. "What if I can't convince them?"

"Fuck 'em."

"You make it sound so simple."

"If your name bothers you so much, why don't you change it?"

"Rosalyn would stop taking her pills." My life had been reduced to keeping her sane.

He settled on his side, and when I turned to face him, he rested his hand on my hip. "How did you get into racing?"

"Benny West."

Ever's brows bunched. "The NASCAR driver?"

"The very one...he's my father."

"Wow." His dazzling grin made it hard to catch my breath. "Think you can get me an autograph?"

"I've never met him." His smile fell as he winced. "The closest I ever got was watching his races on TV. I knew from the first that racing was what I was meant to do."

"And the bikes?"

I told him all about Gruff, and he barely blinked the entire time I spoke about my life in Cherry.

"Your mother really wanted you to quit because of calluses?"

"Yup, and she would have succeeded if not for Gruff."

"I'd like to meet him one day."

"He won't like you. Your hands are as soft as a newborn baby's ass."

"If I had your hands, I'd have carpet burns on my dick."

I gawked. "Did you just admit to masturbating?"

"You didn't know? I've done it at least twice a day since you moved in."

I slapped his chest and snorted, but when he didn't laugh, I met his gaze. "Really?" I squealed when I saw his serious expression.

"You're sexy without effort, and it drives me crazy."

"Who says I don't try?" He eyed my hair before giving me a pointed look. "You can't help but be a jerk, can you?"

He laughed, and I enjoyed the sound with my pout firmly in place.

"I guess there's only room for one of us to be pretty in this relationship."

His laughter died immediately, and I felt as if I'd swallowed my tongue. "Relationship?"

"Uh...I meant—"

"I don't mind being your boyfriend," he said all too seriously. The need in his honey-rich eyes made me want to be his girlfriend, but that could never happen.

"Sorry, but you're taken, remember? And I don't date within the peerage."

"And I never thought I would want an uncouth grease monkey."

My only answer was a purse of my lips, which caught his attention and lit a fire in his eyes.

"Will it help if I said you were the most sexiest girl I've ever seen?"

"Only if you mean it," I teased.

"I do mean it. You're the most beautiful nuisance."

"Ever?"

"Yeah?"

"It's getting cheesy."

He tucked his bottom lip between his teeth, and he must have pressed down hard because it became red and swollen and begged to be kissed. Reading my mind, he said, "If you want something from me, you only have to ask."

"Is that so?"

"It is."

"And what is it that you think I want from you?"

He leaned in, and I was mortified at the satisfied sigh I released after the soft press of his lips against mine.

"I guess we'll see." He stared down at me with what seemed like hope but also uncertainty. I wasn't sure how much time passed before he spoke again. "Tell me more."

I took a deep breath, and he waited with eagle focus for my exhale. The volatility of his emotions surprised me the most as I told him more about my childhood: anger, pity, sadness. Yet he never spoke a word. Dusk had darkened into night when he finally did.

"Baby?"

"Hmm?" My voice was barely a mumble, and I was pretty sure my eyes were closed.

"You're falling asleep."

"I'm not," I denied with a yawn. "And don't call me baby. Now, where was I?"

His chuckle was the last thing I remembered before I drifted off with his chest as my pillow and his heartbeat my goodnight lullaby.

Sometime during the night, I awoke with a start. The air was much cooler than I remembered. Tentatively, my hand slid to the spot where he had been, and I was surprised and nervous at finding it warm but empty. *Tonight really happened.* My gaze moved around the moonlit room searching for his shadow when I heard his sleepy growl.

"Is that my iPod?"

"What do you want, Jameson?"

I tensed at the sound of Jamie's pissed-off chuckle. "Don't call me Jameson as if you're my father. I'm older than *you*."

"What do you want," Ever repeated slowly.

"Are you done playing with her?"

My teeth gnashed. Jamie spoke as if I was nothing more than a house pet. However, it was the bite in his tone that kept me still and my mouth shut.

"What does it matter to you?"

I'd like to know that, too.

"She's a friend," he said almost shyly. My ire instantly cooled.

"You have a funny way of showing it. You've been using her to get back at me."

"Yeah, well, she grew on me."

Silence fell between them, and I worried they'd hear the added weight in my breathing.

"I'm done playing games," Ever admitted almost reluctantly.

"Does she know that?"

"She will."

"And Barbie?"

"She's all yours…if she can trust you again."

"She was never *not* mine, motherfucker."

I'd heard enough. With a huff, I sat up in bed, drawing their attention from the hall. "If you two are done treating girls like Pokémon cards, I'd like to go to bed." When an eager glint entered Ever's eyes, I added, "Alone." I needed time to think without this newfound charm of his interfering.

"Are you sure about that?"

I was thankful for the covers as anticipation shook my body at his husky tone. I clutched them for dear life when he padded over to the bed.

"I'm sure."

He was still shirtless, and when he stepped into the moonlight, I noticed how his jeans hung on his hips accentuating the twin lines of muscle that disappeared under his waistline. Dropping his tall frame into a crouch, he stared at me for a moment as if mesmerized or simply waiting for me to change my mind.

"This is goodnight then?"

"This is goodnight."

I prided myself for sounding firm when all I felt was the need to wrap myself around him and never let go. He seemed to see right through me though with his secret smile, and when he leaned forward, I found myself meeting him halfway. Our lips met too briefly, so when he pulled away, I chased, earning a chuckle and a lingering kiss.

He stood to his full height and headed for the door toward a wide-eyed Jamie. "I'll see you downstairs for breakfast. Don't make me wait."

"Stop bossing me around."

An amused, "Never," was all he said before the door closed.

Once upon a puppet, she caught a ride from Jameson.

For all his talk about the morning after, he chose to sneak into my room and leave me another one of his fucking notes.

In a huff, I tore up the note and watched it rain onto my bedspread. I showered and dressed quicker than normal before gathering up Jay D for his morning relief. Three times during the night, I awoke to whimpers, trudged outside, and watched with sleepy-eyed glee as my pup pooped on the imported grass.

Worth it.

Downstairs, I was able to confirm my suspicions.

Ever had flown the coop.

He was probably kicking himself for all the promises he made or patting himself on the back for his successful lies.

I felt like a fool.

I managed to form coherent responses through breakfast. Of course, Rosalyn was in bed, and Thomas had long left for the office. After breakfast, I wrapped some of the leftover bacon and stuffed it inside my backpack before following Jamie to his car. He fussed when he noticed me carrying Jay D and threatened to pimp him out if he chewed up his custom leather seats.

I had no idea what I would do with Jay D once I got to school, but I knew leaving him alone to fend for himself was not an option.

chapter twenty-eight

the Puppet

THE DAY WAS A BLUR. I SPENT CLASS TIME DAYDREAMING. IN BETWEEN, I pretended not to look for Ever in the hall, and as usual, I only had Tyra to talk to. I had just finished another secret sweep of the crowd when I heard my name called.

I turned with Tyra at my side as Jamie jogged from the other end of the hall. When he stopped in front of us, he winked at Tyra, who sighed and rolled her eyes. He was determined to flirt with her despite her blowing him off.

"Don't make any plans tonight."

"Why not?"

"I'm hosting a gathering."

"A *gathering?*" Tyra quipped. "Who says shit like that?"

"Of course, you're invited, sunshine."

Tyra snorted at his invitation even though we all knew she'd want to go. Chances were Vaughn would be there.

I was less tempted to attend another Brynwood party.

"Where is it?" I was planning to steer clear of wherever he had planned.

"Our place."

With a groan, I turned to Tyra, but Jamie quickly intervened.

"And you can't use her place as a hideout."

"Why not?"

"Because she'll be there if she doesn't want Vaughn playing hide the eggplant with some social climber."

"Who says he would?"

"*I* know he wouldn't, but she doesn't."

One glance at the guilt on Tyra's face confirmed Jamie's claim.

"Sorry," she whispered meekly.

I laid a comforting hand on her shoulder. Even though it had been Tyra's choice to not make their thing exclusive, it couldn't be easy to fear he might actually take advantage of bachelorhood.

"Don't apologize, T-baby. Personally, I find territorial women stimulating."

"Give it a rest, Buchanan. I'm not interested."

He clutched his heart, feigning hurt. "Then I'm afraid I have to go. The captain of the debate team promised to show me a sweet spot to bury my bone."

"How many more disgusting euphemisms for sex do you have?" I called as he sauntered away.

"I could write a book!" he yelled back.

I shook my head as we headed out the double doors and down the path toward the mechanic's garage. We decided to skip lunch so I could check on Jay D, and Tyra could meet him. Dave agreed to keep an eye on him since the academy only allowed him a single period and a class of five. It was a good thing he owned his own mechanic shop in town. I made a mental note to speak with him about any openings. Jay D was going to need things, and my savings wouldn't hold up forever. I refused to use the McNamara's line of credit, so my only option left was a j-o-b.

As we neared the bay door, the smaller door on the left opened and out stepped...Ever.

He stopped short when he noticed me, and Tyra, quickly sensing the tension, excused herself and disappeared inside.

"What are you doing here?"

He slid his hand into his pocket and slowly looked me over. I did the same, noting the worn jeans, white long-sleeve, and a dark sweatshirt with the hood covering two-toned locks.

He wasn't lord of the manor.

He was Danny Boy.

"You look well rested, sleeping beauty. Have a good night?"

Remembering his comments last night about my appearance, I felt a blush warming my cheeks and neck. I wasn't too bewitched, however, not to notice that he'd ignored my question.

"Don't tell me you're transferring to shop."

Dark gold eyes brightened. "I haven't considered it until now."

"Don't." When he flashed straight white teeth, I added, "I'm serious. This is *my* space. *My* thing. I don't need you distracting me."

He moved until he was standing so close I had to tilt my head back to look him in the eye.

"I'm a distraction?"

Only the very best kind.

I answered with a silent nod.

"Fine."

After he kissed my lips, I discreetly took a look around.

"No one's around."

"Did you forget about Dave?"

"A non-factor."

"How arrogant you are."

He shrugged and tilted my chin up higher so he could kiss me again.

This time, I pulled away. "I don't want you kissing me at school while everyone thinks you and Barbie are an item."

Anger made golden honey burn.

"I don't give a shit what they think. I like kissing you."

"Well, I do if they think I'm a whore!"

"Fuck," he croaked, laughing at my accent. "You're such a hick."

"And stop calling me that! It's offensive."

"Anything else?"

"I'm serious about the kissing."

His groan was a deep rumble I felt in the pit of my stomach. "I always wondered what having a real girlfriend would be like… now I know."

"You've never had a girlfriend?"

"No."

I stared into his eyes, forgetting for the moment that I wasn't his girlfriend and could never be.

"I'll meet you in the parking lot after school."

"Okay."

"And, princess?"

I gritted my teeth but answered anyway. "Yes?"

"No more concessions." He turned and disappeared down the path while anticipation raised the hairs on my skin.

Yeah, we'll see about that.

Inside the garage, Tyra was playing in the corner with a hyper and happy Jay D. Surrounding them was all the necessities and luxuries a puppy could hope to have. *What?* In the corner was the fluffiest puppy bed, a neon green tennis ball, various jelly chew toys, a bone he and Tyra were currently playing tug-of-war with, two bowls, one filled with food, the other with fresh water, and around his neck was a collar that matched the blue in his eyes and a sterling silver tag. I picked him up to inspect the tag. Our names and my cell number was on the back. "Where did all of this come from?"

Dave was busy chatting on his cell phone with a happy grin. He smiled even wider when he noticed me watching him and absently waved from inside his glass office.

With a smirk, Tyra said, "I'll give you one guess."

Turns out I only needed one. "Why would Ever do this?"

"You tell me," she smugly countered.

I studied all the new puppy stuff with a shake of my head. "I don't know this game." I sounded as if I'd already accepted defeat.

"Whatever he's after, he's not fucking around, Four."

I buried my face in Jay D's neck to hide how much her words

both delighted and frightened me. Ten minutes later, Jay D was happily covering me in puppy saliva when Dave finally emerged from his office.

"If it isn't my star pupil."

"Thanks again for keeping an eye on him. Has he given you trouble?"

"Nah. He's a good pup. Thank *you* for taking him in. I would have hated to see him in the pound."

"Did you buy all this stuff?" A part of me was hoping he had so Ever and I could return to our original script.

Bushy eyebrows raised in surprise. "Uh...no, Four. I didn't. I assumed you knew your stepbrother was bringing all this by."

"He's not my stepbrother," I corrected with a flush. Stepsiblings wouldn't do what we did last night. "I mean...our parents aren't married. We just live together." *God, just shut up already.*

"Ah. My mistake." He then checked his watch. "Well, you two should get going. The next period will be starting soon."

With a nod, I relinquished Jay D to his brand-new plush bed.

"Oh, Four," Dave called as we made our way out.

"Yes?"

"Just so you know, the money is appreciated, but I would have done it for free."

"I'm sorry?"

"Your not-stepbrother paid me to dog sit during school hours. You didn't know?"

I was simmering on the inside and just barely keeping my composure. "I'm sorry," I said with an even tone. "I didn't know."

"He was quite generous."

"I'm sure he was," I mumbled. I felt awkward and exposed, wondering if Dave might question Ever's motivation. This was above and beyond. *I'm going to kill him.*

"I can give the money back if it makes you uncomfortable. I tried to refuse it, but that young man was pretty persuasive."

Don't I know it?

Dave clearly didn't want to give the money back. He had been griping about getting the heating at the shop fixed for a month now. Taking money from a student is probably against school policy, but Dave was a good guy. He wouldn't have taken the money if he wasn't desperate.

"I'm sure the money would be better spent getting the heat working in the shop. Your employees will need their hands this winter." This was my chance to ask him about a spot on his team, but Ever throwing his weight around ruined everything. I didn't want to risk Dave feeling obligated to grant any more favors.

"Jesus, don't remind me. I don't think I could listen to their whining much longer." He then patted my shoulder. "Thanks, Four. Now get to class."

A moment later, the warning bell rang, and Tyra and I were rushing off to class.

"Does this skirt make me look obvious?"

I eyed the white butterfly print on the black material, which was high around her waist and flowing around the middle of her thighs. Her cropped cream knit sweater showed a sliver of stomach while her burgundy scarf was wrapped around her neck. Out of the entire ensemble, I admired her brown-laced combat boots. "In what way?"

"That he could have his way with me in one of these bedrooms. This house is amazing, by the way." She cast another awe-filled glance around my room. I would have thanked her, but none of this was actually mine.

"I don't think it matters anymore. You've already decided to sleep with him. By the way, have you told him?"

"Not yet. I'm waiting for the right moment."

"To say you want to get it on? It's not like you're proposing marriage. I think any moment is the right moment."

"Maybe you're right." She then frowned at her image and finger-combed her straightened hair. Every few minutes, she'd manipulate it into a different position. She currently had hair falling over her right eye. Five minutes ago, she'd had it over her left. She was acting as if Vaughn hadn't seen her countless times before.

Jamie's guests had arrived an hour ago, but we were still holed up in my room. I was wary, and Tyra was nervous. At Brynwood Academy, being among the one percent wasn't enough. Her father's working-class status and her own as a scholarship student made her an outcast, and well, Vaughn…he was the crème de la crème.

"Are you ready yet?" I playfully huffed.

"Are you?" she countered with an arched brow.

"No," we answered at the same time.

There was a knock, and then Vaughn's smooth as silk voice drowned out our laughter.

"Come out and play with me, Ty-ty."

"Someone's getting impatient," I teased.

Tyra's shy smile was barely hidden as she glanced at herself in the mirror again and rearranged her hair to frame both sides of her face—the exact way she'd worn it when she arrived.

"It's a bit hot in here, don't you think?" She fanned herself before removing her scarf and tossing it on top of her jacket.

"Not really. I think you're nervous."

She eyed me. "Is that what you're wearing?"

I looked down at my black jeans, gray hoodie, and white chucks.

"Yes." I shoved my gray beanie on my head. I had thought to wear my hair down, but the moment Tyra started gushing, I chickened out and pulled out the hat. I didn't want to attract attention, most especially Ever's. His Highness was the reason I was even second guessing my appearance.

"You're not even going to do anything with your hair?"

"I just did."

"Aye yai yai!"

Another knock came, and just as I began to smile smugly at Tyra, Ever's voice filtered through the door. "Hiding won't do you any good, princess."

Not wanting him to have the satisfaction of knowing I was hiding from him, I quickly snatched open my bedroom door. "I'm sure there are plenty of our classmates eager to entertain you." And by 'classmates' I meant the lusty-eyed girls in their come-fuck-me outfits.

"None as fun as you." He was back to looking expensive and untouchable in his gray V-necked sweater and jeans that probably cost more than a month's wages at Gruff's shop.

"You promised you wouldn't be an asshole."

He leaned in until there was barely a finger-length of space between us. "And I'm keeping that promise or else you'd be over my shoulder right now. No more lip," he rushed to add when I started to speak. "Let's go."

He seized my hand and pulled me toward the stairs. I looked over my shoulder and met Tyra's wide-eyed gaze as she followed closely behind.

Ever led us to the billiard room where I was surprised to find maybe twenty people and all of them guys. Some of them played pool or darts while the rest sat around drinking beer. Among them were Max, Daniel, and Adam: the Franco clone, the mohawk, and the bruiser. Daniel's eyes lingered on me when I entered the room. I probably would have hauled ass if I didn't think Ever would make a scene hauling me back.

"Where are the girls?"

"Jamie invited them, and I sent them home."

A cloud of smoke suddenly engulfed us, and I choked on the heavy stench of weed. My head whipped toward the source and found Drake and Ben standing in an intimate circle of five as they passed a joint around. I dropped Ever's hand and darted across the room.

"Drake!"

He was slow to recognize me, but when he did, he yanked me off my feet and enveloped me in gangly arms. "Goddamn," he whooped as he swung me around before setting me on my feet again. "You know how to keep people in suspense. Did you just get back?"

I couldn't help giggling. His happiness was infectious. "Drake, you saw me at the homecoming game *four days* ago. Leave the weed alone."

"Can't. She was my first love." He was momentarily distracted when Ben offered the joint, but to my surprise, he shook his head and faced me again. "So—"

"Any particular reason you need your arms to hold a conversation?"

I squeezed my eyes closed. Ever getting possessive in front of twenty witnesses wasn't exactly keeping whatever we were doing on the low.

"Believe it or not, this is his good side," Drake mumbled before letting go and stepping back. To Ever, he said, "You made your claim, and I'm a stand-up guy." He threw up his hands in surrender while the guys around us snickered and eyed me knowingly. The more daring ones allowed me to see their newborn interest.

Ever had just made me the hottest girl at school.

"There's no claim. McNamara's overinflated ego is tampering with reality."

"Careful," Ever whispered in my ear. "I promised I wouldn't kiss you at school. I made no promises about showing you that you're mine at home."

I spun around and nearly collided with his chest since he was standing as close as he could get without touching me. "Don't you dare."

"Don't *you* dare."

"This isn't a competition."

"Damn straight because it never was."

"There's a word for guys like you."

"Charming?"

"Swine."

He pushed me against the wall, and after a nervous glance around, I noticed everyone was keeping their gazes purposely averted.

"They won't say anything," he assured.

"How do you know?"

"Because I'll break their bones if they do."

"Something you picked up from Exiled?"

"More or less."

I looked into his eyes, searching for a monster but only found a boy haunted by demons that could probably chew mine up and spit them out.

"I want to be alone with you." His hands cradled my hips as he pulled me close.

"But I just got here."

"Because you hid in your room for an hour."

"Doesn't matter. Tyra's here, and I'm not leaving her alone with a bunch of guys."

"Vaughn has her, and he's not letting anyone get to her. Not even you."

A quick peek over Ever's shoulder showed her sitting in Vaughn's lap as he talked football with a guy lounging on the couch next to them. Just then, our eyes met, and she glanced between Ever and me before smiling sneakily.

Before I could make another excuse, he snuck me out of the room with a tight grip on my hand, then led me down another level and a hall that I didn't even know existed.

"I've never been to this part of the house."

"You've been to the theater room."

We both tensed at the reminder.

After clearing his throat, he added, "The wine cellar and indoor pool are down here, too."

Why anyone would need two pools was beyond me. We stopped in front of a door at the end of the hall, and I watched as Ever pulled from his pocket a single key attached to a strip of black leather.

"What's in there?"

"My workroom."

"I didn't know gangsters needed a workroom." I laughed, but it only gave my discomfort a voice.

He smiled as he shoved the key inside the lock while I prayed he didn't have someone tied up inside. I was slowly falling for this boy, and I secretly dreaded what might ruin it.

I held my breath as he pushed open the door and guided me inside. The dim lighting from the hall seeped inside but was quickly cut off when he shut the door. It became obvious after a few moments spent in the dark that he was up to something.

"I don't know what you've heard, but I don't have night vision."

"Are you afraid?"

My heart rate sped up at his sinister tone. I whirled around but could only make out his shadow lingering by the door.

"A little creeped out."

"Some people are turned on by their fear."

"I'm not one of them. Turn on the light."

For a moment, the only sound was that of my heart beating. Then light swept the room. I frantically searched every inch of the room as Ever's arms slid around my waist. The French doors and large windows were covered by bronze shades, shutting out the moonlight. There was a raised wooden platform spanning the length of the room with a black cloth covering whatever rested on its surface. A smaller table with its white surface slanted downward was positioned against the back wall with a high desk chair pushed under. Two black lamps extended from the shelf over the table, and there was a small bookshelf filled with books and large rolls of paper.

When nothing jumped out at me, I drove my elbow into Ever's gut. His grunt as he dropped his arms and doubled over put a smile on my face. "Asshole."

"When I fantasized about you driving your body into mine, that was not what I had in mind."

My skin flushed at his meaning and the vision of us naked and tangled. "And I thought all you and Jamie had in common was Barbie. Interesting."

His pained expression instantly morphed into a fierce scowl. "Say what?"

He closed in, but I held my ground even when I was forced to tilt my head back. Looking into his eyes was like watching the stars and the dawn collide.

"Jamie came onto you?"

"Not lately."

"I'm going to break his fucking collarbone."

"That's really specific. But before you attack your cousin... again...you should know I only meant the two of you share an unnecessary use of sex euphemisms. Jamie's weren't *all* directed at me."

"Unnecessary?"

"Very."

His gaze sharpened as he inched closer, and I suddenly felt as if I were being hunted. "So I should just come out and say I want you bent over that table with your panties around your ankles and my name on your lips?"

"Now you're just being crude."

Strong hands cupped my hips as if he might do just that. "And you care?"

"Hey, I can be as classy as you."

The lustful gleam in his eyes suddenly faded away. "You were never beneath me, Four. I was a shit to make you believe otherwise."

"Don't worry about it. I'm a tough girl."

"I know you are, princess."

"Stop calling me that," I growled as I gripped his sweater. "I hate the way it makes me feel."

"How does it feel?" His voice was husky now.

I had to swallow the lump in my throat before speaking.

"It tingles."

"Where?"

All over.

I didn't reply, so he added, "Don't make me go searching." His gaze was already scanning my body.

"I've been meaning to thank you," I quickly said to distract him. "For Jay D's stuff. You didn't have to bribe Dave, though. He was willing to help out."

"It was insurance to make sure he continued to be."

"Well, thanks to you, I couldn't ask him about a job."

His eyebrows bunched. "Why not?"

"Because I didn't want him to think the money came with a catch!"

He simply shrugged like it was no big deal. Maybe to an elite with the world at his feet it wasn't. "My dad gave you a credit card."

"That I haven't used once, and I don't intend to."

"Then I'll cover Jay D's expenses."

With a huff, I stepped away from him, putting space between us. Thankfully, he didn't follow. "I don't want your help. He's my responsibility."

The depth of his eyes deepened. "And you're mine."

"We discussed this, and the vote was divided."

"Then hang on tight, little troublemaker. I'm going to make you fall for me."

I closed my eyes to keep from seeing the promise in his own. There was still so much that stood between us. Namely, the secret pact he had with Barbie and the fact that he risked his life for seemingly no reason at all. My eyes popped open and narrowed. "Why did you skip school today?"

His jaw tightened as he stared back at me without shame. "I was searching for a way back into Exiled."

"But I thought you were done with that. Why are you trying to get back in?"

"I'm looking for someone."

"Who?"

I expected him to avoid answering so imagine my surprise when he said, "Nathaniel Fox."

Hiding my surprise, I decided to get as much truth out of him as I could before whatever judgment that told him to keep secrets returned. "Who is he?"

"He's one of Exiled's founders."

I sucked in a breath, fighting for composure, but my voice trembled anyway when I spoke. "How do you know him?"

"I don't."

"Then why do you want to find him?"

"Because he has something that belongs to me."

I could feel my frustration building. "What? What could he possibly have to make you risk your life?"

He shook his head and looked almost as if *he* felt sorry for *me*. "You wouldn't understand if I told you."

"How do you know?"

"I just do," he answered quietly.

"Are you sure you're not just aspiring to be the next Gambino or Capone?"

He barked a genuine laugh despite the sadness radiating from him. "I'm sure."

"So if your dream isn't to be the next American gangster, then what is? Football?"

For a moment, he looked as if he were debating something. "Turn around."

After a brief staring contest, I did as he ordered and faced the table that nearly took up the entire room. He moved to the other side of the room and whipped off the black cloth.

I stared down in wonder at the 3D model covering almost every inch of the table. "Is that the academy?"

"It is."

I gaped until I realized how I must have looked and then I shouted, "Ever, it's incredible! How did you learn to do this?"

"I've been taking courses since the ninth grade, but it all started with popsicle sticks. For my twelfth birthday, my mother bought my first Lego set. It was the Empire State Building. I loved it so much I collected as many Legos as I could. I never liked following the instructions. Sometimes I'd play it by ear or sketch shapes that meant nothing, but I just had to build. They were never anything special, but she treated them like masterpieces."

I couldn't believe it. Ever seemed almost shy as he spoke about his passion. He watched me closely as I gingerly moved around the table scanning every piece. He'd modeled what seemed like every inch of the grounds down to the very last bush. I wanted to touch it, but it seemed like one of those things you admired with your eyes only.

"How long did this take?"

"A few months. There was a bit of trial and error."

"But you were determined as always." I flashed him a smile that fell at his blank stare.

"She would have wanted me to."

He moved over to the slanted table and ran his hand over the surface. "My mom bought me this drafting table when I told her I wanted to be an architect. We even talked about building my first model together."

"What about your dad? Did he help you with this?"

With a sad smile, he picked up the discarded cloth and started arranging it over the model again. "My father was thrilled that I found something to call my own, but he was always too busy running the company."

For a moment, he looked frustrated and angry, but then he blinked, and it was gone. I shouldn't have been surprised. Ever never wore his heart on his sleeve. He kept it locked away in a box that put Pandora's to shame.

"Do you think she'll come back?"

He didn't need to ask who I meant. "No."

I gnawed on my bottom lip as I pondered the right words to say. Anyone else would offer false hope thinking he'd want to hear it. That it would cure his broken heart. Thanks to my history with mothers, I offered him something else instead. "Maybe it's for the best. I bet it's painful to be constantly reminded that you're regretted."

He was silent for so long that I wished I had just kept my mouth closed. I had no right sowing doubt in his mind about a woman I didn't even know. "Why?"

"Why what?"

"Why does your mother regret you, Four?"

Shame cast my eyes to the floor. I should have known he'd see right through me.

"Four?" he pressed when I said nothing.

"If the third time's the charm, the fourth must mean tragedy because I didn't just break Rosalyn's heart—I broke her mind."

He was silent for so long. Whatever he had been expecting me to say I was sure it wasn't that. "You were the tragedy?"

I nodded. "She had three miscarriages before me. Rosalyn couldn't understand that her body didn't reject them simply because she didn't love them enough, so when I was born, she suffered. The guilt, the pain it...it broke her."

"Three miscarriages," Ever echoed. I could practically hear the wheels turning in his head. "Four isn't really a name, is it?" His horrified whisper ate at my soul.

"Not to her."

"But why did it matter if she named you?"

"Without a name, I don't really exist. She thought dehumanizing me would make them finally go away."

"Them?"

"The three she lost...she hears them. When it's really bad, she sees them."

"If this is true, why keep you? She could have given you up."

My stomach turned.

How many times had I wished she had?

"Rosalyn was seventeen when she ran away from home on the back of some biker's hog, and eight years later, she returned knocked up and broken. My father had been the fourth man to impregnate her and the fourth to break her heart. Nana and Pop mistook her depression and delusions for a broken heart and hormones. They were lying to themselves, but if it weren't for them, I wouldn't have survived."

"Do you hate them for it?"

"How can I? They must have fought so fiercely for me. By the time I was born she was a full-blown schizophrenic, and so I lived the first few months of my life nameless. Nana and Pop figured once she was better she'd want to name me herself. They were wrong. I imagine it wasn't an easy battle but they eventually convinced her. Or so they thought."

"Did they know why she choose your name? Did they know what it would do to you?"

I drew in a shaky breath. "They knew...but Rosalyn was a minefield and they were more afraid of setting her off."

Ever swore but didn't say more. We both knew it was a shitty way to grow up

"I once read a pamphlet that said with a strong, loving support system Schizophrenics can lead normal, fulfilling lives." I laughed but it was an empty sound. "I bet whoever wrote it didn't count on Rosalyn looking for it in all the wrong places or how deep her grief welled when they made those promises. Still...she got better."

Ever moved closer, but sensing it was space giving me courage, he kept only enough distance so that he could touch me if he chose. "And then?"

"And then I said my first word, and she relapsed." I didn't need to tell him what I could have said to break her. "It depressed her so much she stopped taking her pills."

I hugged myself to calm my trembling body.

"Rosalyn recovered, but she was even more afraid of me than before." Taking a deep breath, I willed myself not to fall apart. I'd been too young to remember much of the beginning, but life with Rosalyn was like a bad record stuck on repeat. It was easy to fill in the blanks.

"My grandparents forbade me from calling her anything but her name, hoping it would keep her sane. They didn't realize that I was only one of her triggers. A broken heart was the other."

A harsh sound spilled from Ever. "So you she could stay away from but not men?" Ever's anger wasn't a surprise but I fully expected it to be me who disgusted him.

Anyone would sympathize with a mentally ill mother who rejected her daughter. They'd say she couldn't help it. That it wasn't her fault. Who could sympathize with a daughter who resented her mother anyway? Why should they when even I hated myself for how I felt?

"She was a hopeless romantic long before she was a Schizophrenic."

"That's no excuse."

"No, but it's reality, and I've lived with it and so should you."

I had the sudden urge to wrap myself around something strong and never let go. Ever was standing only two feet away and I knew without a doubt he'd be my pillar, my anchor, if I needed. But I also knew that if I gave in, I'd never find the courage to speak of this again.

Seemingly giving in, he sighed and said, "Where are your grandparents?"

"Rosalyn spent the first ten years of my life in and out of the hospital. She'd relapsed countless times when my grandparents finally decided to file for custody."

"So what happened?" Ever questioned when I fell silent for too long. "Where are they?"

I closed my eyes. "They died in a car crash before they could see it through."

Ever sucked in a breath.

"Neither of us took their deaths well, but it wasn't just the sudden loss that made it hard. It was because Rosalyn and I both knew we were now stuck with each other. Without her, I would have been on the streets or lost in foster care, and without me, she would have eventually reached the point of no return."

"You hid each other from a worse fate."

I nodded. "And now that I'm eighteen, I no longer need her." I took a deep breath hoping to feel the freedom I've longed for since I was ten. The feeling never came. "She still needs me, though."

Ever blew out a breath of frustration. "You didn't make her ill, and you didn't put those skeletons in her closet, Four."

I turned away because I couldn't stand to see his pity. "Maybe not, but that doesn't change anything. When your father breaks her heart, it will be *me* she stares at with tears in her eyes until she can barely stand to look at me at all. It will be *me* who feels the shame because *I'll* be the one she regrets. God forbid he knocks her up first."

My back was still turned to him when I felt him close in, stop, and then I heard him sigh.

"My father had a vasectomy."

Whipping around, I found Ever's mask in place. "What?"

"When I was four, my mother had a miscarriage. She had just found out I was going to have a sister."

"What happened?"

"Her doctor called it an incompetent cervix. My birth had been difficult for her, and the doctors warned that conceiving again would be risky, but my mother didn't care, and my father indulged her. They found the best doctors money could buy, but an infection caused my baby sister to die in my mother's womb."

"So he got the vasectomy?"

His Adam's apple bobbed as he nodded. "My father wanted a large family, and my mother was distraught and ashamed. She was determined to try again or find a surrogate."

"Why didn't they try surrogacy?"

"Because my father didn't want another woman carrying his child."

I stared at him feeling both awe and envy. "They loved each other."

"It didn't last."

I could only nod. My living here was evidence of his parents' failed marriage. "I'm sorry your mother left you." Guilt suddenly made it hard to swallow. How many times had I wished Rosalyn would just walk away? I had convinced myself that being abandoned couldn't have hurt worse than being rejected every single day. But then I met Ever.

He cupped the side of my face. "And I'm sorry your mother couldn't leave you." I felt his finger wipe away the tear I hadn't realized I shed. He was gentle and soothing, not at all the touch of a killer. It made me wonder...

"The Exiled are murderers, and you're one of them."

He slowly blinked, probably thrown by the sudden change in subject.

"I haven't killed anyone, princess."

"But if you had to...if you were forced...do you really think you could?"

His hand fell away.

"I guess I'll know soon enough."

"I...I don't want you to do this." I was suddenly desperate, willing to give anything—do anything—to keep him from harm. "Whatever you're looking for can't be worth your life. If you want to be with me, promise me you'll stay away from them."

He went so very still while my heart screamed at me to take it back. "Why would you ask that of me?" His voice was a whisper, his question an accusation.

"Because if you're caught, they'll *kill* you. Who says Wren Harlan will keep his word? I've been on the business end of their mercy, Ever. They won't hesitate."

"I'm not going to pussy out for pussy," he viciously spat.

I stepped away from him, leaving my broken heart at his feet. "Is that all I am to you?" I suddenly felt like scrubbing my skin clean.

"Jesus Christ!" His hand whipped out and fisted my shirt before yanking me into him. I didn't get the chance to shove him away before he was lifting me onto the table ledge. Large hands framed my face so I couldn't look away. "Get this through your thick skull, Archer. You. Are. More."

"Then *you* get this through *your* skull. All I'm asking is that you not get yourself killed. You're not some street thug or ruthless killer. You're Ever McNamara. Lord of the manor. King of the academy."

His eyes narrowed. "So if my family's bank account had fewer zeroes, you'd believe that I'm completely fucking serious? You've known me for two seconds."

"You've done more despicable things than I believed any one person capable, but no, I *don't* believe you have what it takes—because what it takes is your soul!" Breathing hard, I shook my head. "You won't be able to give that up."

He kissed me—hard—and when he finally relented, my lips were swollen. "Stay tuned." He moved to my neck, and a moan fell from my lips as my head fell back. I knew that he was only trying to distract me, and still, I was ready to give him everything.

"I'll tell your father," I whimpered. "I don't care if you expose Rosalyn if it means you're safe."

"Tell him what you wish," he taunted. "I'll deny it, and if he believes you anyway, nothing will change." He continued to trail kisses across my skin. "My father hasn't been much of a parent even before my mother left. He helped me drive her away."

I froze in his arms. "What was her name?"

He lifted his head and stared into my eyes. No mask. Only emotion. "Evelyn. Everyone called her Eve."

"Was she your namesake?"

His smile was small but honest. "No, actually. My parents named me after my father's best friend. His name was Sean Everson Kelly. He died before I was born."

"Wait…Your real name is *Everson*? You have two last names?"

He smiled and pinched my side in retaliation, but it didn't stanch my giggling.

"Should we go upstairs and review your manners?"

That sobered me up quickly, and when I shot him a look to kill, he quickly kissed my lips. "You know you'd love it," he whispered against them.

I hid my reaction knowing he was right. He didn't miss a beat though, and it was almost eerie how well he could read me in such a short amount of time. Picking at invisible lint on his sweater, I debated giving my sudden thoughts a voice. Before Ever, I was never this insecure. Now I couldn't stop feeling and wondering and hoping. Not even for a second. I guess at this point of falling, I had nothing left to lose.

"With our moms' miscarriages and our names, do you think our meeting was more than a coincidence?"

His brows furrowed. "Like destiny?"

"Sure." I was breathless when I wanted to be casual.

"Could be." His hands moved up and down my hips as if he knew I needed to be soothed. "I stopped wanting you gone a long time ago."

He leaned in to kiss me, but I stopped him with two fingers pressed to his lips. "It won't matter where I am if you're dead."

Nostrils flaring, he straightened until he was towering over me. If I didn't already know he'd never hurt me, I'd be scared shitless. "Are you with me or against me, Four? That's all that matters to me right now." His eyes narrowed, and the warning was clear.

"Fuck you, McNamara. I'm with you, all right?"

With a savage growl, he shoved his tongue down my throat and yanked on my hips to get me closer. Pressed against each other like this, there was no chance of hiding what we wanted. The heat alone was telling, and any minute now, we'd be a ball a flame. Slipping my hand up his sweater, I traced every dip and bulge while swallowing his groans. When he finally pulled away, he stared down at me, panting and hungry.

"Promise me you'll outsmart them all."

The animalistic gleam in his eyes sent a chill down my spine. "Goddamn, I want to taste you."

It wasn't an answer, but I blushed anyway. I could almost see why Della Grady thought boys were worth our friendship. "I think you have a fetish."

"For going down on you? Definitely." He took a step back, ready to drop to his knees and make good on his claim, but my hand on his shoulder stopped him.

"What if this time I return the favor?"

His gaze sharpened and focused on my mouth, which was surely red and swollen from his kisses. "Open your mouth." The lust in his eyes was intimidating, but I did what he ordered anyway, and he quickly slipped two of his fingers between my parted lips. "Suck, baby."

I closed my lips tightly over thick fingers and slid them down to the knuckle.

"Watch those fucking teeth. I only want that beautiful mouth."

I used my tongue as a barrier, earning a groan and a look of adoration. Another groan and he pulled his fingers from my mouth.

"Can I taste you?"

"You definitely fucking can, but not right now. I want to enjoy it, and that will take time we don't have right now."

He lifted me from the table, and with one last peck, we ended up back in the billiard room where the guys were engaged in a drunken game of Truth or Dare. Tyra was laughing hysterically as Vaughn attempted to dance alone without music. It was hard to believe someone that hot and talented had two left feet.

"Yo, Four! Truth or dare," Jamie yelled.

Vaughn looked relieved when every drunken gaze in the room turned to me.

"Truth." I had no idea why I was bothering to indulge him. There was always a hundred percent chance Jamie was up to no good.

"Did you and Ever finally bang it out?"

A chorus of whoops and snickers followed. Jamie certainly never disappointed. The lascivious and hopeful stares coming from the guys made it clear they were all waiting for the day when they could have Ever McNamara's seconds. If I weren't so uncomfortable, I'd feel sorry for them.

"Jesus, he's asking for me to kick his ass," Ever whispered from my side.

My lips pursed as I glared at Jamie's smiling face. "I wouldn't be opposed."

A wicked grin spread Ever's lips, and then he was prowling across the room. "Move," he ordered the chick in Jamie's lap.

She must have been what kept Jamie occupied for the hour he'd been missing. The moment she scrambled out of harm's way with a shriek, Ever delivered a mean uppercut, sending Jamie and the chair toppling over. "Everyone out! Party's over."

Ever searched for a movie while Vaughn, Tyra, and Jamie lounged on the huge sectional, sharing booze and popcorn. I was studying the numerous pictures of family and friends on the mantle when I came across one of a young Thomas posing with two other guys who looked to be around the same age. One of them had reddish-brown hair and the same cocky grin as Jamie.

"Jameson?"

He groaned and said, "Why do you have to be such a bitch, Four?"

I snickered and pointed to the guy on Thomas's left. "Is that your dad?"

"Sure is," Jamie said with a huge grin. "He was a handsome devil, wasn't he? I'm hotter."

"The sun never sets in your world, does it?" Tyra questioned Jamie, who only shrugged.

"And who is this?" I pointed to the guy on Thomas's right with dark hair and a deep chin dimple. I stared at his smiling face and couldn't put my finger on why he seemed so familiar. I was positive I'd never met this man before. "Is he also a relative?"

Ever looked up with a frown and said, "No. That's Sean."

"Oh...okay." For some reason, I met Jamie's gaze, but he quickly looked away.

Feeling weird, I sat down and ate some of the popcorn Tyra offered. A few minutes passed, and Vaughn had just shot me his tenth curious glance. "What's your deal, Rees?"

"I'd ask you a question, but I don't want Ever ruining this pretty mug."

That earned a derisive snort from Jamie, who held a bag of frozen peas to his jaw. "He could pound me until I looked like Leatherface, and I'd still be hotter than that sensitive Nancy."

"Ooooh, touchy much?"

Jamie sat up lightning quick. "Whose side are you on, Four? When did you join the land of the pricks?" He scowled at me as if I'd betrayed him.

"You humiliated me! *Again.*"

He waved me off. "I told you that wasn't personal."

"When a boy likes a girl, he tells her so," Tyra schooled with thinly veiled contempt. "He doesn't antagonize his friends and family to show his affection."

Jamie simply blew her a kiss, earning an eye roll from Tyra and a slap upside the head from Vaughn.

"Keep those pass-arounds to yourself," Vaughn growled. He then focused on me. "Anyway, I saw your bike in the garage. It's a beauty."

"So, what's your question?"

"Can you really ride that thing?"

Everyone except Ever, whose back was still turned, leaned forward, eager for the answer.

"Ride it, fix it, race it. It won't win, but I could top the speed without killing myself."

Vaughn gave me half a smile and an approving nod as he slouched in his seat again. "I knew it would take a badass."

My eyebrows rose as I nervously toyed with the end of my ponytail. After the party ended, I'd ditched the beanie while Ever had been preoccupied keeping Jamie off him and shoved my hair back into a ponytail. "To do what?"

"Make this apathetic asshole feel again."

I peeked over at Ever: shoulders tensed, nostrils flared, mouth tight. Yup, he was pissed. "Was he really that bad?"

"I'm in the room," Ever woodenly reminded.

"You'd have had better luck sneezing with your eyes open than getting him to crack a smile."

"Still here," Ever snapped.

I decided to take a page from Vaughn's book and ignored Ever. "He was a dick to me the first time we met and every moment after. I'm not sure how much I helped."

Vaughn began blinking rapidly. "Wow! He actually acknowledged you?" I rolled my eyes when he started slow clapping. "You must have made quite the impression."

"She kneed me in the balls," Ever muttered.

That got a whistle from Vaughn and a grimace from Jamie.

"I'm sure you deserved it," Tyra defended.

"Maybe." He then rented *Warm Bodies* at Tyra's insistence and dimmed the lights. It was a pretty cozy setting that set off the butterflies in my stomach, especially when he sat close enough for our thighs to touch. Vaughn and Tyra were openly snuggling on the other end of the sectional while Jamie nursed a bottle of white rum on the La-Z-Boy.

I stared blankly at the flat screen, too on edge to enjoy the movie with Ever so close. I should have been used to it by now, but each time felt like the first.

"Relax," he whispered while the opening credits rolled. "You're safe here."

Goose bumps rose on my skin, making me doubt his claim. Across the room, I caught Jamie's eye, and even in the dark, I recognized the mischief. *He never learns.*

"Hey, cousin. Truth or dare?"

Ever's attention shifted to his cousin. "Dare me not to stop when I smash you in the face again."

"Nah. I got one better." Jamie took a swig from the bottle, possibly for liquid courage. "I dare you to kiss her."

We all reacted at once. I tensed, Vaughn snorted, Tyra sighed, and Ever…smiled.

"Now you're talking."

I let him pull me onto his lap until I was straddling him, and when I looked into his eyes, I couldn't catch my breath. Ever looked hungry. We reached for each other at the same time. When our lips met, it didn't feel like a show, it felt like fulfilling a need that had consumed us both. He kept right on kissing me as if his next breath didn't matter. As if I were his air, his heartbeat, and the blood flowing in his veins. I could feel him fighting to get closer—to make me see I was all he'd ever need—not revenge or privilege. Me.

Or maybe I was just delusional.

I pulled away and averted my gaze as I removed myself from his lap. Jamie, of course, was the first to speak.

"If I doubted he was serious about you, I don't anymore." His eyes flicked between Ever and me before a sneaky smile split his handsome face. "Four, truth or dare?"

"I already played your game. Pass."

"Fine." His head swiveled to Tyra. "Truth or dare, T-baby?"

"Aren't we here to watch a fucking movie?" Vaughn spat.

"Dare," Tyra answered simultaneously. She stuck her tongue out at a glowering Vaughn before focusing on Jamie.

"Make out with Four."

Tyra shot Jamie a crazed look. "This isn't some sleazy porn."

An overly excited and very wasted Jamie adjusted the recliner and planted booted feet on the ground. "Do the dare, and I'll do whatever the fuck you want."

Tyra crossed her arms, clearly unimpressed. "Vaughn, muzzle your friend."

Her dreamboat no longer looked irritated though as he cut his eyes at her.

"Babe...I wouldn't be opposed to the girl on girl."

She quickly moved from the crook of Vaughn's arm and faced him. "Are you freaking kidding me?"

"Just a peck, and I'll also return the favor of a dare."

With a scoff, she twisted around and gave Ever the kindest smile I'd ever seen her bestow on anyone. "And now we're down to our last shot at chivalry. Ever?"

"It's already two out of three," he said with a shrug. "I don't think my vote counts much." A sly grin then appeared on his face.

"Fuck you, guys." She started crawling across the cushions, and my eyes bucked when she headed straight for me.

"Tyra, what are you doing?" I shrieked. My body tensed as I prepared to flee.

"Relax. It's not like we're going down on each other." She pressed her lips to mine, and in my peripheral, I saw Jamie staggering to occupy Tyra's vacant seat. At the same time, I felt her tongue caress the seam of my lips and her soft hands brush over my shoulders and down my arms. Curious, I timorously kissed her back and found her lips soft and tasting faintly of berries.

A groan and a softly spoken, "Fuck," brought me hurtling

back to reality. Vaughn slapped Jamie upside the head when we pulled away from each other.

"All right! Time to pay up," Tyra dictated as if nothing happened. "Any ideas, Four?"

It took me a bit longer to recover, but the idea of payback sounded damn good. "I'd like to see Vaughn and Ever swap a bit of spit."

"The fuck?" Vaughn exploded. "Why not Jamie? He started the shit!"

"And you went along with it," Tyra argued.

"I'm not making out with a dude," Ever growled.

"You promised anything we wanted," she countered.

"Those idiots did," he spat back. "I didn't promise a damn thing."

"Fine. I have an alternative dare, but only if all three of you swear to do it. I promise it won't involve sword fights or bum fun."

"What is it?" Jamie questioned warily. It was funny how pale he looked since he was the one who started all this.

"You don't get to know that yet. Do we have a deal?"

"Your woman's a fucking cutthroat," Jamie hissed at Vaughn, who didn't bother responding.

Tyra must have had as much trouble as I reading Vaughn's mood because her confidence faltered when she offered him a shy smile.

"Don't worry, T-baby. I'm not the only one whose pants are fitting a little tighter."

A vicious snarl tore from Vaughn's throat, and then he was snatching the bottle from Jamie with one hand and forcing his head back with the other before practically waterboarding him with rum.

The bottle was nearly empty when Ever sighed and barked, "Enough."

I was beginning to wonder why Jamie insisted on provoking

them. It was as if he was eager to take a beating. He never fought back even though I was more than sure he could handle himself.

Vaughn tossed the bottle in a choking Jamie's lap and then glared at Tyra and me. "Deal."

"So, what should we make them do?"

After the movie ended, the guys took off. To run an errand they'd claimed. My guess was they were secretly running scared of what we'd make them do. Tyra and I were now holed up in my room in our PJs while Jay D was nestled in a ball at the foot of my bed.

Tyra applied the last coat of nail polish and beamed at her freshly painted toes with satisfaction. "I thought I'd make Vaughn tattoo my name on his ass."

I barked a laugh, making Jay D's ears perk. When he drifted back to sleep, I said, "Think he'd go for it?"

"Hell no, but I can't wait to see his face when I try to make him."

"Ever already has a tattoo," I blurted. It was hard keeping all these secrets bottled inside. I always figured it was just a matter of time before they came spilling out. Besides…what was the point in having a BFF if you couldn't confide in them?

"Really?" Tyra's whiskey gaze was now fixed on me. "He's much too uptight for a tattoo. What is it, and most importantly, *where* is it?"

I had a hard time swallowing, but when my throat was free of doubt, so were the words. "His gang. It's tattooed on his back."

She slowly blinked. "Come again?"

The deep breath I took was for courage, and the prayer was just in case. I didn't want to betray Ever, but I needed to talk to someone. "Ever is Exiled."

"Ever McNamara?" she echoed. "*Your* Ever?"

My Ever. "Yes," I confirmed breathlessly.

"And by Exiled you mean the murderous, raping, pillaging Exiled?"

"That would be the one. I didn't know you knew about them."

"Shit. Who doesn't?"

"I didn't. Until one of them tried to kill me."

"Jesus, Four!" She scrambled to face me, forgetting about the still wet polish that now stained my bedspread. "Shit! Sorry."

I waved her off and hugged my knees.

"How the hell did you get mixed up with them?"

I gave her the short version. "When I was ten, Gruff took me under his wing. He taught me how to ride and fix bikes, and when his back was turned, I raced the fast ones for cash. I'm the reason Rosalyn and I left Cherry."

"You were one of them?" She looked disturbed by the idea.

"Not a chance," I quickly denied. "I went up against one of them during my last race. It didn't end well when I tried to win. Not surprisingly, the Exiled are sore losers."

"Who's Gruff?"

"My old boss...and the only father I'll ever have," I wistfully replied.

"Is he the one who gave you the bike?"

"Yeah...he's the best." A wave of homesickness hit me, and I thought I'd drown in it until Tyra's next question had me breaking the surface.

"Why would Ever join Exiled?"

"He said their leader has something that belongs to him. He didn't say what."

I watched as Tyra digested the news. She shook her head, mumbled, and then shook her head some more. "How do you know all of this?"

"I followed him into the woods after the first day of school. He keeps a car hidden back there with the clothes he wears whenever he does a job stashed inside." I left out the part about me following him into the city and him holding Rosalyn's fragile mind over my head to keep my mouth shut.

"That's why that Harlan guy called him Danny Boy, isn't it?" I nodded.

"Holy shit! I thought that was weird, but I figured it was some movie reference I didn't get."

I shook my head, wishing it were that simple. "Ever becomes this whole other person, and it seems so real, like he's two different people."

"I wondered why he was dressed like that the day you took me to meet Jay D. He usually looks like he belongs on an Abercrombie ad. I figured he was trying to impress you or something." Tyra flashed me a timid smile that I tried to return and failed. Miserably.

"Ever's going to get himself killed, and no matter what I say or threaten—" My voice broke, but I pushed through it. "I can't talk him out of it, Ty." I felt a tear slip from my eye and quickly wiped it away while cursing this newfound femininity. I liked the old era. Before Ever—excuse me—Everson fucking McNamara. I wasn't this girl who cried over a boy and craved his kisses. I was the girl who could rebuild engines and make grown men cry.

"I have to be honest," Tyra spoke hesitantly. "I don't know what to say."

"You really don't know?" I gaped. "I was kind of hoping you could tell me what to do."

Tyra blinked, and I groaned as I banged my head against the headboard.

"I do know I feel less awkward calling you my best friend now that I know more about you than your name. You're a vault, Four Archer."

I stopped banging my head and kept my gaze firmly cast on the bedspread as I let the guilt wash over me. There was still so much I hadn't told Tyra.

"I wonder what he's looking for," she mused. Just then, Tyra's phone chimed, saving me from answering, and when she checked the message, a smile appeared. I was sure her cheeks would have been red if not for her rich mocha skin.

"Vaughn wishing you sweet dreams?"

"Nope. He sent me a pic of his one-eyed monster."

I was tempted to lean over and confirm that she was joking, but I didn't want to risk it.

There was another chime and then, "Now he's wishing me sweet dreams."

"Is he staying over, too?"

"I wouldn't be surprised." She suddenly looked excited and nervous at once. "I think he knows I'm ready. It's like he sensed it and has been on edge ever since." Her gaze turned pleading. "You've got to help me figure out how to seduce him."

"Why do you need to seduce him?"

"Because I'd like to tell him I want him without making a fool of myself!"

"As long as he wants you, that can't happen, and he's made it more than clear that he does."

She pouted. "I know all of that, but it can't hurt to be sexy, right?"

I sighed and thought about throwing in the towel when an idea popped into my head that had me jumping up from the bed. "I saw something in Jamie's room when I was stealing his iPod that might help us."

"Us?"

Shit. Well, the cat was pretty much out of the bag, so I shrugged. "I may be curious, too."

I made for Jamie's room with Tyra on my heels. Once inside, I headed for his secret stash while Tyra looked around. We kept the lights off so we wouldn't alert Jamie if they returned in the next few minutes.

"I didn't expect Jamie to be so cultural."

"Yeah, he's really embraced his heritage."

"Is that Nicki Minaj?"

I caught Tyra eyeing the poster of the mega rap star crouched with her legs spread, wearing only a sports bra, thong, and sneakers.

"Yup."

I sifted through the stack of DVDs while she checked out Jamie's wall of guitars.

"I didn't know Jamie played."

"I don't know if he does or if he's just a collector."

"You've never heard him play?"

"No. Honestly, I don't know much about him."

"I suppose he's too busy pushing everyone's buttons to talk about himself."

"And whenever I ask, he changes the subject or says something rude or perverted."

"Can you blame him?" Tyra questioned dryly. "The last girl he confided in was probably Barbette Montgomery, and we all know how *that* turned out."

Clutching a stack of discs, I rushed over and felt her forehead. "Did I just hear you defending Jameson Buchanan? I bet Satan is making figure eights right about now because hell has frozen over. I thought you couldn't stand him."

"I don't hate him. I want to muzzle him. He's good people as long as Barbie isn't in the room, on his mind, or the topic of conversation ."

I nodded my agreement. One could always tell when Barbie was in Jamie's head because that was when he was his most insufferable. Unfortunately for everyone, it was most of the time. I finally located the DVD suspiciously without a label and held it up triumphantly. "Got it!"

She frowned at the white disc. "What is it?"

"You'll see." I slid the DVD inside the console and grabbed the remote before plopping down on Jamie's bed and patting the seat next to me. "Make yourself comfortable."

"Any reason we can't watch whatever this is in your room?"

"No TV, remember?"

She was still standing, shifting from one foot to the other. "Well, what if they come back?"

"They probably went to a party or something." My stomach turned whenever I thought of Ever doing something Exiled related, so I chose to lie to myself.

"You don't seem convinced. You look like you're about to hurl your dinner." She finally sat and placed her hand on my back. "Is this about Ever being Exiled?"

"I don't like what knowing I could lose him does to me." It was a foreign and unwelcome feeling. Cherry was home, but even there, I didn't have friends who evoked such emotion. Mickey had been a business associate who needed me more than I needed him, and without my set of skills, he'd have never looked my way. Rosalyn was the weight I carried on my shoulders. She needed pills just to endure me, so whenever I thought about letting her go, the only relief I felt was for her sake. Gruff had many roles in my life: father, boss, mentor, and friend, but not even he had rallied this kind of feeling. What I felt for Ever was raw and intrinsic and…addictive.

Aiming the remote at the TV, I pressed play. Music filled the silence and captured Tyra's attention at the same time some tanned, busty blonde appeared on screen wearing a miniskirt, no panties, acrylic heels, and a pink crop top that read 'Wet.'

"Four…what is this?" Tyra questioned warily.

"Porn."

"How did you even know he had porn?"

"I've never lived with anyone but Rosalyn before. I got curious."

"You mean you snooped?"

"It's not as devious as it sounds. Some good can come from it. I learned who my father is by snooping."

We fell silent as we watched the girl on the screen attempt to seduce the boy next door, however, it was short-lived.

"Did you watch the entire thing?"

"I freaked and shut it off as soon as I realized what it was."

The dialogue was cheesy, and the guy was sporting a boner within a minute of meeting his new neighbor. Three minutes later, she was eagerly deep throating her unsuspecting victim. It seemed impossible how much she could fit in her mouth.

"Ugh, I don't—"

A burst of light cut her off, and frustration shifted into horror. Jamie stood on the threshold of his bedroom with eyebrows raised. "I feel cheated," he drawled.

"What are you doing here?" I questioned as if this weren't his room and his home.

"I never left. Ever asked me to stay behind and make sure you weren't up to no good, and I'm glad he did."

"He had you spy on me?"

"I think his intentions were nobler than that."

What possible reason could Ever have to enlist Jamie as his watchdog?

"Then where were you this entire time?"

He rubbed his head with a groan. "Passed out, I think."

It was then that I noticed he was barely holding himself up.

"Jesus, Jamie. Lie down."

With a sly smile, he answered, "Only if I get the middle." He stumbled inside, and after dropping onto the bed between Tyra and me, he focused lazy eyes on the TV screen. "This is my favorite part."

I don't think any of us breathed the entire time we watched the innocent boy next door stuff his mammoth cock inside the seductress' ass.

Jesus. Would Ever expect that? It seemed impossible, yet the evidence was in high-definition on a fifty-inch screen.

"Yeah...love a cock up a nice ass," Jamie casually reflected while I tried not to panic.

"Jesus, Jamie!" Tyra slammed one of his pillows against the side of his head. "I'll be in your room," she gritted before fleeing the room. Not long after, the slam of my bedroom door echoed down the hall.

"Your friend has a stick up her ass," he said as he lay back with one arm behind his head and the other across his stomach.

Twisting around to face him, I shot him a withering look as I crossed my legs under me. "Or maybe you need to tell Barbie how you feel and give the rest of us a break."

Voice flat and eyes dull, he said, "She knows how I feel."

"I was there yesterday, remember? You treated her like she meant nothing to you."

"As I said…she knows how I feel."

I shook my head with a sad sigh. For some reason, I believed Ever when he said there was nothing real between him and Barbie. Did that make me a fool, or was Jamie just blind and stubborn? "You don't fool me, Jameson."

He groaned, then said, "I told you only my mother calls me Jameson."

"Well, what about *James*? Do I get to call you that?"

His eyes flashed before he averted them. "What?"

"Barbie called you James, and you didn't bitch about it." He didn't respond, so I poked some more. "And you called her Bette."

"You must have heard wrong."

Yeah, right. I know what I heard.

"James and Bette sitting in a tree…" I sang. I was about to get to the part where they started kissing when Jamie shoved me off his bed. I hit the floor with a yelp and burst out laughing despite my aching back. When I sat up, Jamie was on his back again, looking like nothing had happened. "Fine," I huffed as I stood to my feet. "I know when I'm not wanted."

He smirked as he watched the porn still playing on his TV with a sudden disinterest.

I started for the door, but a thought had me turning back. "Despite your differences, you know Ever better than anyone."

His heavy sigh filled the room. "Yeah."

"What are the chances I can change his mind about finding Fox?" I didn't need to question if Jamie knew about Ever being Exiled, but him jackknifing into a sitting position told me Ever hadn't been as forthcoming with him as I thought.

"How do you know about that?"

"I followed him a month ago."

"Does he know?"

I nodded, not caring to go into detail. "He's been blackmailing me."

"Oh, man," Jamie cackled. "You two are made for each other." He shook his head and stared at me with equal parts pity and amusement.

"So do you think I can talk him out of going after Fox?"

"Not a chance in hell," he answered soberly.

I huffed my frustration at Jamie ripping away the last bit of hope I had. "Even if it meant we could never be together?"

Jamie shook his head, the warning in his eyes clear. "Don't give him that ultimatum unless you're prepared to lose."

"I can live without Ever."

"Surviving isn't living, kitten. You'll spend so much time wishing for tomorrow that you forget about everything else."

"Time can't heal a festering wound, Jamie. Wishing Barbie out of your heart won't make the pain go away."

"What is it with you?" he growled. "That *bitch* can take a hike off the nearest cliff for all I care."

I was momentarily startled by his viciousness. Jamie's reactions were never this raw. "You're a fool."

"Yeah, well, it takes a fool to know one," he said with a curled lip. "Don't expect Ever to choose between you and his *mother*. Just because Rosalyn is a piece of shit doesn't mean everyone's mother isn't worth the trouble."

I took a step, ready to kick him, punch him, spit in his face, and scratch his eyes out. "Fuck you."

I didn't stick around, and when I made it back to my room, I took Jay D for a walk to keep Tyra from noticing my tears. I lingered a bit longer than usual in the hope that the chilly October night would freeze my heart. When I made it back to my room, Tyra was softly snoring, so I decided to take a quick shower before bed. I ended up staying under the water long enough for the water to run cold, and by the time I finished brushing my hair, I decided that the asshole Buchanan had been right. So far, Ever had outsmarted me at every turn. That aristocratic son of a bitch would probably just call my bluff and turn cold again. Could I risk that?

Feeling myself crashing after an eventful night, I quickly brushed and flossed. The moment I stepped from the en suite into my bedroom, I knew something was off. The light from the lamp I left on had been extinguished, plunging the room completely into darkness, and a figure far too large to be Tyra's reclined against my headboard. I couldn't see his face, but I didn't need to. I was all too familiar with the breathlessness, the heat, and the throbbing between my legs his mere presence created.

"Where's Tyra?"

"Vaughn got lonely."

"They left?"

"They're down the hall in the guest room."

If Tyra was right about Vaughn knowing she was ready, then she was in for a busy night. Away from her father for the entire night, it was the perfect opportunity. I was suddenly grateful for the dark so Ever couldn't see my blush. "Sleeping soundly?" Sexual clairvoyance or not, I prayed he'd be patient with her.

"I wouldn't know. I'm not with them," he answered dryly.

"He better not force her into anything."

"Vaughn spends half his day turning down pussy. He doesn't need to rape to get laid."

"His arrogance is exactly what concerns me. What if she bruises his ego?"

There was a click, and then a soft glow illuminated his

scowling face and shirtless torso. The air in the room became stifling as his eyes narrowed. "I swear to fuck you better not be speaking from experience."

"What? No!" My face flooded with heat for an entirely different reason now. ·

He held my stare for a moment longer before relaxing against the headboard once again. There was still tension as he kept me locked in his gaze, but at least I could breathe again.

"Vaughn would never hurt her, but I'm sure you already know that or else you would already be down the hall dragging your friend back to safety."

"True, but one can never be too sure," I sassed.

He didn't reply as his eyes fell. I clutched my towel a little tighter, suddenly remembering I was naked underneath. The towel was the plushest I'd ever used but still not nearly enough to help me feel less exposed.

"Truth or dare?"

"Ever..." I had a good feeling where this was headed.

"Truth?" He rose from my bed with hungry eyes and stalked across the room. "Or dare?"

"The game is over."

"I'm not done playing."

"I'm tired," I said with a sigh. "Get out."

I'd just barely kept my voice from shaking, but of course, he noticed. He was now close enough to touch me though he didn't. "Truth or dare, little sister. Unless you're afraid."

Little sister?

I didn't know about this game. In fact, I was so far out of his league it would have been wise to surrender. But I couldn't, and he knew that.

"Truth." I sounded bolder than I felt but...whatever worked.

"Do you only want to fuck me because I'm your big, bad brother?"

I cocked my hip, going for mildly irritated. "Our parents' hooking up doesn't make us siblings, McNamara. Besides, Rosalyn will clean your father out long before anything permanent happens." It was a lie. Rosalyn was no gold digger, but I was hoping an argument would end this game.

"Answer the question," he demanded, not missing a beat.

I pressed my lips tight together. There was no coming back from a scandal like the one he was offering. It had only been minutes ago that I decided not to take the plunge. I preferred my feet planted firmly on the ground.

"Don't do this to me." I shook my head wildly, displaying my desperation.

"I'm not, princess. I'm doing this to *us.*"

"*Why?*" I whimpered while hating myself. Effortlessly, he often made me forget myself. I feared that one day, I'd wake up an entirely different person. Someone who was soft and easy to bend.

"Because I'm tired of the pretense. I've never denied myself, puppet, and I don't intend to start now."

"So what? I'm just supposed to drop my towel and spread my legs for you because it's what you want?"

"Yes."

I shouldn't have been shocked by his gall and arrogance, but even more, I shouldn't have been turned on by it. Thinking of a way to stall him until I could get my head back on straight, I planted a hand on his chest and stood on my tip toes. He instinctively bent until my lips reached his ear. "Then *I* dare *you.*"

Straightening, he stared down at me with a perplexed expression. "Excuse me?"

"I. Dare. You." My hand had trailed from his chest down to the waistband of his jeans where my fingers toyed with the bronze button.

"To?" In his eyes, I could see his determination to own me and the knowledge that I was already his.

"Make me want that, too." I sounded eager and hopeful as if I weren't wishing he'd fail.

"You already do," he accused with narrowed eyes. I could tell he wanted so badly to prove it. The ache between my thighs begged me to let him.

"And yet, I'm saying no."

chapter twenty-nine

the Puppet

I WAS AWAKENED THE NEXT MORNING WHEN TYRA FELL ONTO THE BED with a troubled sigh. "Everything okay?" I questioned while trying to shake the grogginess.

She rolled onto her side so that we were facing each other. "Help me, Four. I had no idea how far I'd fallen."

That woke me up. "Did you—"

"No, but man, did he make me regret it."

My eyebrows rose when she shivered a little.

"I assume that's good?"

"Oh, it's very good," she confirmed with a satisfied nod.

"So what happened?"

"Nothing...and everything."

"How enlightening."

She picked up on my sarcasm and smiled. "He...um...he used his fingers"—she bit her lip as her eyes widened—"and then his mouth, and it was *very* good but then..." A deep frown appeared.

"What?"

"Nothing, and that's exactly where it went wrong. I told him I was ready, and he told me he disagreed."

"Wow." I didn't know what else to say, but Tyra looked like she had plenty, so I waited.

"He said he wouldn't fuck me until he was sure I understood that this couldn't go further than sex." When Tyra burst into tears, I was forced to admit that Ever had been right that night in Coach Bradley's kitchen. It just seemed so odd since Vaughn's behavior this past month was not of someone just looking to get laid. He seemed to genuinely like her. "That asshole said I was his friend, and he didn't want to hurt me."

And what a fine job he was doing.

Tyra wiped at her tears before sinking inside her head. I also retreated inside my head and began to wonder when life stopped being so simple. In Cherry, I went to school, worked at the shop, and made sure Rosalyn kept taking her pills after a break-up. Now I had drama, friends, and boy problems. I admit my life before Blackwood Keep had been lonely, but that was just one emotion. I was now juggling six on a good day.

"I know what we should dare them to do," Tyra announced. Almost twenty minutes had passed since either of us had spoken.

The wicked gleam in her eyes made me grateful I wasn't the guys. "This should be good."

Tyra told me the dare before hopping in the shower. Surprisingly, it wasn't as sinister as they deserved, but it would do. I definitely couldn't wait to see Ever's face when we told them.

A hungover Jamie had been the last to come to breakfast. I caught him sneaking me an apologetic look or two, both of which I ignored. I was used to his cattiness now, which incidentally, was one of the many problems I'd inherited since moving to Blackwood Keep. Moments like last night were when I missed home the most.

Ever pretty much ignored me while Tyra pointedly ignored Vaughn. He seemed genuinely confused as to the reason, and unfortunately for him, even if Tyra would have wanted it, I wasn't feeling charitable enough to enlighten him.

While we ate whatever breakfast we could drum up since Mr. Hunt had the weekends off, Tyra and I delivered the news. Ever and Vaughn would be getting piercings, to each of their horrors, and Jamie, the emotionally unstable ass, would write a letter from the heart and read it to an audience of his choosing before graduation. Since he already had a piercing in his nose and God knows where else—I was pretty sure I glimpsed a nipple ring at some point—Tyra and I decided it wouldn't be much of a challenge for him to get another one.

Before leaving to complete their dare, Ever surprised me by pilfering the keys to my bike. He made sure I saw the promise in his eyes just before he walked out the door with Vaughn and Jamie. I was pretty sure the keys came with a catch, but I'd worry about that later.

It was mid-afternoon when they filed into the garage. Jay D was busy getting into everything while I was teaching Tyra the basic functions as she straddled the bike.

"Looking good, T-baby!" Jamie's grinning face and the new hoop that replaced the stud in his nostril was the first to capture my attention, but when I searched Ever and Vaughn's faces, I found them bare.

"We had a deal. Where's your piercing?" Tyra demanded. She'd hopped from the bike and stood with her hands planted on her hips.

Ever's mask remained intact, but it was Vaughn who gave them away. "You're going to have to search a little lower," he answered with a twinkle in his eye.

A blushing Tyra fell silent, and when I met Ever's gaze again, there was a challenge there. *Not going there.*

"You already had that one," I said to Jamie.

His answering grin only deepened my curiosity.

"Let us in on the gag, will ya?"

"We did your dare," Vaughn said with a shrug, "and unless you're willing to go searching, you're just going to have to take our word for it."

Fuck. Once again, I'd been outfoxed. It was becoming clear that I needed to sharpen my game. I was pretty sure this had been Ever's doing. His silence spoke volumes.

Tyra rolled her eyes, but then a wicked gleam, identical to the one she had this morning, entered them a moment later. "Maybe we should get pierced in secret places, and see how they like it."

I tapped my chin with my forefinger. "What an interesting proposal, Miss Bradley."

"Is that an invitation?" Ever pinned me under his stare as he waited for my answer. I hesitated, wondering why his voice sounded thicker—almost too thick to understand what he'd asked.

"Hardly." It would be far more fun to keep him guessing.

"Be careful playing with fire, Four." He spoke his words with care and when he said—"There's a hundred percent chance you'll get burned"—I understood why. The flash of metal, piercing his swollen tongue, must have made it pretty hard to speak. I felt heat pool in my stomach as he headed for the door with Jamie on his heels. I couldn't believe he'd chosen to pierce his *tongue* of all places. While the addition looked damn sexy on him, I didn't understand his choice. It didn't fit the meticulous elegance I'd grown used to.

Vaughn was a little slower to follow as he walked backward with his arm raised and his finger pointed at Tyra. "Get that pretty little pussy pierced. I don't mind. You just remember that I offered you a treasure hunt. Reciprocity. *Is.* Mandatory." The moment he disappeared inside the house Tyra and I gaped at each other.

"Did he say your…" I gestured to her part in question.

"You don't think he—" She gestured to her part in question. Our eyes bulged at the same time.

"Oh. My. God!" Tyra screeched. "He. Did!"

Tyra announced she was running home to show her face to her overprotective father but not before sharing her painful idea to get a Brazilian wax. She'd reasoned that even though she was out of the running to get her cherry popped, she should still be prepared. I didn't disagree. Vaughn may have turned her down, but any moment now, his desire would overcome him. Of course, she didn't want to do it alone and insisted that as best friends, it was mandatory that we got our pubes ripped from our vaginas together.

"Success is where preparation and opportunity meet."

"Did you just quote Bobby Unser?"

"I figured if you wouldn't listen to me, you'd listen to a role model. I googled it right after I called for a reservation. Smart, huh?"

"A tad unfair, but who's measuring?"

"Lighten *up*, Four. It's totally worth the fifteen minutes of torture. You won't have to shave for like a month."

"I *don't* shave. Well…not *really*."

"Seriously? You have a bush?" She looked as if I'd just admitted to having herpes.

"I trim the hedges. I just don't whack them all down."

"Wow…I have a newfound respect for Ever. Didn't you say he's gone down on you *twice*? I hear some guys are jerks about it."

I shrugged, unsure how to answer. I'd never thought it a big deal, but now that I was feeling self-conscious, I agreed to go. After she left, I took Jay D upstairs, grabbed number six, and was back in the garage before Ever could catch wind of what I was up to. I wasn't sure if he'd actually stop me, but I wasn't willing to chance it, either.

An hour later, I'd convinced myself that nothing topped the high of going a buck on an open road until I flew through the gates of McNamara manor and found Ever waiting at the end of the drive. I kept my bike pointed in his direction and was slower than I should have been to decelerate. Ever didn't flinch when I finally braked a mere foot away. Shame. While I knew he wouldn't shit himself, I was hoping he'd at least break a sweat. I plucked off number six, a yellow and black open-faced helmet bearing the Eye of Providence and the Hamsa, and smoothed my flyaways back—something I never would have cared about before—before meeting his gaze.

"Something the matter?"

He nodded toward the helmet now resting between the handlebars. "I didn't take you for a religious person."

He was still all tongue when he spoke, but somehow, he made it work. Still, I had a hard time hiding my amusement, and of course, he didn't miss a thing as he narrowed his eyes.

"It was Rea Anderson's—three-time Superstock champion— until she was forced into retirement when her leg crapped out."

He didn't seem impressed. "You've been gone a while."

"I didn't think you'd notice."

"If my father checks the mileage, you're fucked."

I smirked as I twirled the keys around my finger. "Don't you mean *we're* fucked?"

"I'm not the one who will care if you lose the bike," he bit back.

His words were a blow to the gut. My chin lifted as I crossed my arms. "Then why did you help me?"

"Silly me. That was before I saw you ride."

My eyes narrowed. "I sure as hell don't remember asking for your opinion, but while we're on the subject, let me fill you in: I know what I'm doing."

"Which is exactly what makes you reckless. You know better."

"What do you know about bikes or riding one, for that matter?" His silence was all the answer I needed. I kicked the stand in place, swung my leg over the bike, and stomped toward him until there was nothing between us. "What I do may seem scary to *you*, but I've been on the back of a bike before I even grew breasts or learned why the space between my legs makes assholes like *you* think you're in charge."

I was breathing fire and seeing red. How dare he criticize when he knew less than shit? Racing was my *life*.

Glittering golden orbs stared down at me, and then he was pushing forward. I had no choice but to retreat or be knocked down. I should have known better than to get so close. When pushed, Ever always pushed back. He kept coming until I was straddling my front tire with nowhere else to go.

"You think being a brat will push me away? I promise, it only makes me want to bend you over those handlebars and show you the reason why I'm in charge." And just like that, I was engulfed by the fire I'd been spitting a moment ago. "Tread carefully." He turned on his heel and, without a second glance, swaggered back inside.

I was still standing in the same spot when Tyra pulled up a moment later. I was on autopilot as I listened to her retelling of Coach Bradley's interrogation while I stored the bike away. Inside the house, we found the guys in the family room. Vaughn and Jamie were playing against each other in some first-shooter game, and Ever pretended to be engrossed in their bloody battle when he took the offered key ring. When our fingers brushed, I felt the spark, and I knew he did too, but he continued to ignore me. Rolling my eyes, I retreated upstairs.

Tyra managed to book a same-day reservation for waxing, so after a quick shower, we were on our way. I wish I could say it hadn't been that bad, but even after marveling over how soft and smooth I was down there, I seriously doubted I'd ever return. Tyra assured me I could get it this way by shaving, although it would require frequent upkeep. On the drive back to McNamara manor, I began to wonder if Ever would like the change. Hypothetically speaking, of course.

chapter thirty

The Puppet

WHEN SUNDAY MORNING CAME, TYRA AND VAUGHN WENT HOME, and that night, Rosalyn and Thomas returned from another business trip disguised as a getaway. Rosalyn loved to be the center of attention, so how she managed to endure Thomas's work ethic was a mystery to me.

I was pouring a glass of milk to go with the cookies Mrs. Greene made when Rosalyn glided into the kitchen.

"Four, how are you?" she inquired as if I were an acquaintance and not her daughter.

"Let's see," I drawled with thinly veiled sarcasm. "I still have a 3.5 GPA, no injuries, diseases, or pregnancies, and I'm close to getting Jay D to roll over." *Oh, and I almost fucked your pretend stepson this weekend.*

"Four, why must you give me a hard time?"

Because you deserve it. "So, how was Maihama?"

The morning after our argument, they'd taken the company's private jet to one of the resorts in Japan. I figured pretending to care about her life was better than arguing about mine.

"It was brisk. Even more so than here. I think I may sit the next one out. I haven't traveled this much since Chet."

I immediately went on alert at the mention of heartbreak number two. He had been the rock star who'd nursed her back from the dead only to get her hooked on drugs.

"What do you say we have some girl time the next time Thomas goes out of town? It's about time, don't you think?"

God, I stopped wanting that years ago. "If you need an alibi, I'm sure your friends at the country club can help." Even though my intention was to brush her off, I sincerely hoped her growing popularity held. Rosalyn had always had trouble maintaining friendships. Usually, her friends would become frustrated, or she'd lose interest.

"Oh, well, I just thought we could have girl talk. You know—hair, makeup, clothes. It's been so long since I've seen you in anything other than greasy overalls I forgot how beautiful you are."

"Rosalyn." Despite my grievances, I felt my cheeks flush.

She giggled and winked. "I've embarrassed you."

"A bit."

"Honestly, dear, you'd be used to being told you're beautiful by now if you would just get over this phase."

And just like that, the bubble I'd been floating in popped. "I'm pretty busy with school and Jay D. Besides, I have no intention of wearing makeup or changing my clothes."

"What about your gorgeous hair? I could show you different ways to wear it now that it's grown back."

"Don't bother," I said as I strolled backward with milk and cookies in hand. "As soon as I find the time, I'll be cutting it off again."

"Don't you dare. I forbid it." Her gaze suddenly shifted behind me. "Oh, hello, Ever."

"Rosalyn."

I peeked over my shoulder in time to see him give her a polite nod. He was standing so close I wondered how I hadn't felt his presence.

"Your father is in his office if you'd like to speak to him."

A curt 'thanks' was all he gave before sliding past me. I watched him pull one of his many bottles of orange Gatorade from the fridge, barely feeling Rosalyn's soft hand on my shoulder as she clicked out of the kitchen in her heels.

"What's the deal with you and those drinks?"

"The deal?" he echoed as he eyed Mrs. Greene's fresh cookies with regret. I guess the swelling still hadn't gone down although he wasn't as hard to understand as he'd been yesterday.

"Other than water, I've never seen you drink much of anything else. Are you addicted or something?"

"No." The air turned stale after that, so I turned to leave. "Hey."

I stopped even though common sense screamed at me to keep walking. "Yeah?"

With a motion for me to follow, he left the kitchen and headed for the stairs in the west wing. We didn't exchange words until we entered his workroom. Standing by the doors in case I needed a quick getaway, I watched him move to the other side of the room to his drafting table. After setting down his drink, he picked up some papers and began studying them. I could see the wheels turning in his head but couldn't tell what he was thinking or what made him seem almost nervous. I could definitely tell the feeling was a novelty for him—because who would ever tell Ever McNamara no? I certainly didn't seem to be able to.

After a few seconds, I lost my patience and cleared my throat. "So, is there a reason you brought me here?"

With papers in hand, he crossed the room until he stood in front of me, and I was surprised when he handed them to me. I hesitated to take them until I noticed the logo at the top.

"What is this?"

"I did as much as I could, but you'll have to prove you don't have a concussion before you can apply for a license. You can take the test online, so I created the account and paid the fee. Your login, password, and membership details for the network are also there. Rosalyn still has her health benefits through the company, so I used that as proof of medical coverage."

My mouth opened and closed for a few seconds. "So is this an apology for insulting me earlier?"

"It's not the Road to Rookies Cup, but it's a way in, right?"

My heart swelled at his hopeful look. The night he insisted on pillow talk, I'd told him all about my dream to race in the Grand Prix and how Rosalyn had denied me my best chance: the Road to Rookies Cup.

"I don't hear any singing, so it's not over just yet." I smiled shyly, causing his own boyish grin to appear.

"You'll just need to fill out the direct deposit and tax forms and provide a copy of your birth certificate before you can complete the application."

"I—I don't have a bank account."

His eyebrows bunched. "Where did you keep the money you earned at the shop and from racing?"

"I worked for Gruff before I was legal, so he paid me cash off the books, and of course, the money I made from racing was dirty." I shrugged while feeling a little embarrassed. The more we learned about each other, the further apart our worlds seemed.

Ever studied me for a long moment before kissing my lips. "No biggie, baby." He was backpedaling across the room before I could register what had happened. I touched my fingers to my lips, feeling them tingle while he booted up his laptop and hopped online.

"What are you doing?" Deciding this wasn't a trap, I moved to stand next to him, only for him to pull me into his lap. He had a banking website pulled up and began the process to open up an account.

"Do you know your driver's license number?"

"People actually memorize that?"

With a chuckle, he grabbed the laptop and said, "Hang on, baby." As soon as I circled my arms around his neck, he stood and headed for the private stairs with me wrapped around him. We got my license from my room before heading to his. After setting up my bank account, we completed the tax form, and I promised

Ever I'd ask Rosalyn for my birth certificate at dinner. I could tell he knew it was a conversation I was not looking forward to having and that if he left it up to me, I'd probably back out.

Jamie had invited us out to go bowling, but we declined and spent the day locked away in Ever's bedroom, talking about everything and nothing at all. At dinner that night, Ever tempted fate by barely taking his eyes off me. I was having a hard enough time figuring out a way to convince Rosalyn to fork over my birth certificate. Since I was eighteen now, she couldn't legally keep me from racing. That left my birth certificate as the only card left she had to play.

"Hey, Rosalyn?"

"Yes, dear?"

My words tumbled out quicker than I intended. "I need my birth certificate to complete an application."

One perfectly arched eyebrow rose. "A college application, I hope."

Not good. Rosalyn was well aware I planned to skip college. I was already bordering ancient for a pro-motocross rider, so wasting another year much less four wasn't an option. I filled my lungs with as much air as I could. When Ever's brows drew together, I remembered to exhale and prepared for the shitstorm. "It's for my motocross license."

I watched her take a sip of her water to disguise the crack in her composure. "We talked about this."

Each time I broached the subject was the same. Rosalyn would say no, and I'd beg until she guilt-tripped me into a corner with tears and accusations. Not this time. "We have, but now that I'm eighteen, the discussion is over. I'm racing."

"Apparently, not without your birth certificate."

The malice in her response didn't go unnoticed. Ever leaned forward as if ready to pounce while Jamie, with his mouth set in an O, leaned back in his chair. Thomas, the last to react, slowly lowered his glass of scotch with a scowl.

"Rose."

She didn't respond as we locked gazes. "Fine. Then I'll petition for a copy."

"You won't do it under this roof."

The icy sensation started at the tip of my fingers and quickly spread until I was mute and immobile. Had she just threatened to kick me out?

It wasn't fear that snuffed my fire. It was the wound she'd carved so mercilessly. For years I'd been her crutch when she was terrified of standing on her own. But then Thomas stepped in and looked beyond what the others couldn't and provided what they wouldn't.

Did Rosalyn no longer believe she needed me? Was she no longer willing to endure me?

"That's not for you to decide," Ever growled. "This isn't *your* home."

"That's enough," Thomas barked at his son. With a gentler tone, he said, "Four isn't going anywhere." His sharp blue gaze moved to my mother dearest. "Rose, you're out of line."

"The only one out of line is my ingrate of a daughter and your boorish son. Why is he even defending her when they barely speak? It's getting to become a habit." She threw a withering look Ever's way.

Ever, cool and uncaring as always, slowly relaxed in his chair. Jamie patted his shoulder, barely biting back a grin.

"Be reasonable, Rose. It's her life, and while we can encourage her to take a safer path, we cannot force her onto it."

I wondered if he'd say the same if he knew about his son's extracurricular activities. Jamie must have shared my thoughts since he now wore a smirk.

"Thomas, you can decide what is best for your son, and I will decide what is best for my daughter." I felt the force of her glare once again and matched it. "You should remember the pain it cost me to give you the life you're so eager to risk. You're ungrateful and unworthy."

She stood from the table and strutted away with Thomas on her heels.

"Damn, that was cold," Jamie muttered. His pensive tone was the straw that broke me. Rosalyn's claim was nothing I hadn't heard before, but this was the first time it had been witnessed by others. Besides, being pitied by two people who were broken themselves must mean I'd sunk to a new low.

Shoving away from the table, I fled.

"Are you going to talk about it, or am I going to have to guess?" Tyra questioned as we cracked open our textbooks.

I had asked Tyra for a ride to school and was gone before Ever or Jamie had a chance to corner me. After dinner, they had come to my room separately, but I let their knocks go unanswered and cried until I fell into a deep sleep. At school, I dropped Jay D off with Dave and headed for the library with Tyra to study for our midterms next week.

"Do you want the detailed version or the summarized?"

"Ugh." She pushed her textbook away and turned to me. "I can't wrap my head around calculus this early anyway. Give me the detailed."

By the time I finished giving her the rundown and had answered her millionth question, the first-period bell was ringing, so we packed up and headed to class.

"I've always been bummed about not having a mother, but after hearing all of that, I think I'm good."

Only after we'd grown close and after very careful prodding did Tyra share that her mom had died giving birth to her. She even admitted that the hardest part was having to settle for knowing her through everyone else's memories.

"They're not all like Rosalyn, or so I hear." A wave of guilt made me want to take the words back. Truth is, no one would have blamed Rosalyn if she had given me up. While she had never been cruel, she kept an emotional distance between us. Not so much that she couldn't reach out when she needed me but far enough that I couldn't threaten her sanity.

Tyra and I went our separate ways, and before heading to first period, I stopped by my locker to stash my books. I planned to spend my first period figuring out how I could get a copy of my birth certificate. Knowing Rosalyn, she'd probably already destroyed the original.

"Why'd you take off this morning?"

I nearly jumped out of my skin, which caused me to drop my textbook. The sound was loud, slowing gaits, lowering voices, and redirecting gazes. As usual, Ever ignored his admirers as he retrieved my textbook from the floor and placed it in my locker. The moment his hand cleared, I locked up and took off for the computer lab. I knew I was being a tad bitchy, but I couldn't stand being pitied right now. The computer lab was empty, so I sat in the first vacant seat. I didn't realize I was being followed until Ever sank into the empty seat next to me.

"Don't you have class?" I questioned as I booted up the computer.

"Don't you?"

I sighed while keeping my gaze locked on the computer screen. "I can't do this right now, Ever."

There was a pause and then, "I just wanted to make sure you were okay."

"No, you wanted to be controlling."

My chair scraped the floor when he jerked it sideways until I was facing him, and if that weren't enough, he grabbed hold of my chin and forced me to look him in the eye. Bastard. "The last thing I'm feeling right now, Four, is in control."

And I believed him. It was right there in his eyes. The last thread unraveling. I pulled my chin from his hand, but I didn't look away. The plea in his eyes had won me over. "I took off because I didn't want to face you, so please don't make me."

The plastic groaned when he gripped the sides of my chair and leaned forward. "You think I give a shit that your mother's a cunt?"

I made a noise that sounded like desperation and despair. "Rosalyn just thinks she's protecting me."

"Enabling her doesn't make you a better daughter. It doesn't make you more worthy of life. It just makes you her prisoner. Last night wasn't her illness talking. It wasn't about love and protection. It was Rosalyn being selfish."

"I don't care if she kicks me out or never speaks to me again. I actually think she'd be better off, but what if I'm wrong? What if I do this, and she goes off her meds? I've always been the one to put her back together, not tear her apart."

"You aren't the reason her head is fucked up. It's no one's fault, but the choices she made were her own. Don't let her stop you from making yours."

"I'm not backing out." I didn't miss how the tension left his body at my assurance. "I just wish racing didn't come with such catastrophic consequences."

He unfolded my fist, and I realized I had been digging into my palm with my fingernails. Ever kissed the abused skin. "Don't fret, princess. We just need a game plan."

"We?"

The late bell rang, but we both ignored it as his hands slid around my hips and cupped my ass. We were close. Close enough to kiss. Close enough to become one. "I know what I want, and nothing's going to stop me from taking it. Can you say the same?"

I leaned in until our foreheads touched, wanting nothing more than to feel his lips pressed against mine. His eyes gleamed, daring me to take what I wanted—racing, Rosalyn or what's right be damned.

But then the door opened.

And the chorus of laughter that followed suddenly stopped.

My back was to the door, but the whispered curse that fell from Ever's lips told me what I needed to know.

We had been caught.

Ever leaned back in his chair as his hardened gaze followed the whispering group heading for the back row. I couldn't hear what they were saying, but the glances and snickers gave me a pretty good idea. This was not good.

"Don't worry about them," Ever dictated. I tore my gaze away from the group, expecting to see his cool demeanor firmly in place. Instead, there was calculation and a burning urge to do damage control.

"You first."

He rose with the grace and authority, resembling a king rising from his throne, and dragged me to my feet. "Let's go."

As if we didn't have an audience, he led me with his hand on the small of my back all the way to my classroom. I was thinking of an excuse to give my teacher when Ever pushed me against the wall and took the kiss we'd been denied.

My heart was racing. Because someone could catch us at any moment and also because he was sending a message with his lips and his hard body pressed almost desperately against mine.

He wasn't backing down.

He needed me.

Maybe as much as I needed him.

My stomach growled when I walked into my Women's History class, and I immediately regretted skipping breakfast. I still had another hour until lunch, but there was no way I was going. Getting through second period without spending it locked in a bathroom stall had been hard enough. Word about my almost-kiss with Ever had spread quickly, and for once, it wasn't just a rumor. There was no mistaking the compromising position we had been caught in.

My phone vibrated just as I took my assigned seat, so I fished it out of my back pocket and flipped open the screen.

MICKEY: In your backyard with ten in the pot and counting. You in?

My palms began to sweat as I read Mickey's message for a second time. There was no pretense of concern or friendship or even small talk despite the fact that I hadn't heard from him in over a year. For Mickey, it was business as usual.

How did you find me?

His reply came instantly.

MICKEY: I'm a resourceful man.

You asked my neighbors?

MICKEY: Yup.

I sighed. If Mickey was able to find me so easy, then it meant if they wanted to, the Exiled could have followed us right to Thomas's doorstep. Rosalyn hadn't exactly been discreet about our upgrade. I didn't bother getting angry at being duped. I knew from the start that moving in with Thomas solely for my protection was a sham. If you leap off a cliff and fall on your ass, it's better to claim being pushed rather than admit to jumping.

I must have taken too long to respond because my phone buzzed with another message from Mickey.

MICKEY: So you in?

My thumb hovered over the keypad. It was stupid to hesitate. I could already feel the rush of racing coursing through my veins. Mickey might have saved my life, but that didn't mean I could trust him. Not when I almost ate a bullet because of him.

The desk next to me creaked, and assuming it was Amanda, Brynwood's very own *Gossip Girl*, I welcomed the distraction and started to speak. That was until I noticed perfectly curled strawberry blonde hair and icy blue eyes staring back at me.

"I think that seat is taken."

"This won't take long." Uninterested in anything Ever's girlfriend-not girlfriend had to say, I refocused on my phone and texted Mickey that I'd think about it.

Stupid.

"You may think that whatever you're doing with Ever means something, but it doesn't."

I let out a dry laugh, not at all surprised by Barbie's chosen topic, and mumbled, "You didn't seem to care the other night."

"Ever can have his fun, but don't get any ideas. He's not going to be with you."

I met her gaze and hated how truly beautiful she was. "You don't even love him."

"He's my friend. I care about him, and he cares about me, which is why I'll be the one to wear his ring, and you'll never be anything more than a thrill."

It was all I could do not to hurl my guts up. I never thought I'd be this girl: claws out and teeth bared over a boy. Especially for one who would always be out of my league. "Keep your satin panties on, Barbie. I have no desire to become the girl he marries and eventually ignores. Maybe I'm just a phase, but you're in for a long life of phases. In a year, it will be some co-ed, and ten years after that, his secretary, until he eventually fucks the nanny. I'm not after your trophy life." I leaned forward with a smile. "So back the fuck off."

I was surprised when, after a few seconds passed, she simply nodded once as if satisfied—or what-the-fuck-ever—then rose from the seat, and moved down the aisle to her own. Amanda appeared moments later looking distressed as she plopped down in a huff. I wasn't expecting her to shoot me an accusing look, which instantly put me on edge.

"Hey," I greeted hesitantly.

She ignored my greeting and hissed, "I thought we were friends, Flower."

"Sorry?" I felt my eyes narrow. We'd always been friendly

but friends? She'd never had much to say to me other than to gossip about other people. Not to mention, she still didn't know my name when we've been sitting next to each other for weeks.

Seeing my defenses up, she suddenly burst out laughing, which was obviously forced. She wasn't the least bit amused and neither was I. "You didn't tell me you and Ever were a thing. It's all over school!"

So that was the reason Barbie bared her claws.

"You shouldn't believe everything you hear." I was surprised at the lack of anger in my tone. I only heard exhaustion and wasn't sure which reaction was worse.

"Everyone saw him at your locker this morning." I started to roll my eyes when she added, "And, apparently, you skipped first period together to get cozy."

"We weren't cozy."

"My sources say they saw him kiss you." Like a coin, with a flip, Amanda's amusement vanished and condemnation returned. "You do know he's with Barbie, right?"

I shook my head—not in answer but in defeat.

Goddamn you, Ever.

Of course, Amanda misread my gesture and gasped even as her eyes brightened with an eagerness to enlighten me with the juicy truth. Fortunately, Mrs. Roberts saved my ass when she walked into class and ordered us to turn to chapter eleven.

Not so fortunately, I was on my own as the open stares and the whispers followed me around for the rest of the day.

chapter thirty-one

The Peer

"T HE ELMER HOLMES BOBST LIBRARY OPENED ITS DOORS IN 1973 and serves as the primary research facility for NYU." I tuned out our guide as I openly watched Four gazing absently at the swaying purple banners. Unlike the rest of our group, she didn't hang on the Ambassador's every word and instead spent much of the hour-long tour daydreaming. Probably of her crossing a finish line at two hundred miles per hour instead of a stage after four grueling years. It wasn't as if attending university was out of her reach. A diploma from Brynwood Academy and a check from my father would open almost any door. All she had to do was want it.

Except I witnessed her sheer determination to race and knew she would never consider anything less. Including a degree from an ivy league. I couldn't help but respect her for being grounded in who she was. Four only changed on her terms and offered no apologies. It was part of what made her so goddamn irresistible. That and her heart shaped ass. One minute, I was pushing her away and swearing her off for good, and the next, I was ready to buy her flowers and serenade her ass.

Fucking hell.

As if sensing my attention, she peeked over her shoulder, and instantly, we locked gazes. The connection was short-lived, but judging by the stiff set of her shoulders, I knew I wasn't as easy to ignore as she wanted me to believe. It would serve her right if I dragged her stubborn ass inside one of these empty study rooms and reminded her why I held her strings. I couldn't get Four out of my head while she went out of her way to avoid me.

It's been eleven days.

Eleven. Goddamn. Days.

I knew the rumors circulating our school were why she'd turned cold. They all wanted to know if I was sneaking in her bed at night. My moment of weakness ended with Four taking all of the heat. It was why I gave her the space she wanted and hoped she'd come to me on her own—before my patience ran out. Clearly, she was more pigheaded than I gave her credit.

Unable to withstand the emotional and physical distance anymore, I maneuvered through the small portion of our senior class until I stood next to her. Discreetly grabbing her elbow, I pulled her to the rear away from prying eyes.

Glancing up at me, she sighed but didn't pull away as we fell further and further behind. "I don't recall hearing your name when the group chaperone did roll call," she grumbled.

"I ditched my group."

"Because you do what you want without consequence?"

We both knew she wasn't talking about me being here.

Placing a hand on her spine, I shoved her into an empty dark corner underneath the stairs just as the last of our group passed through a set of double doors. The guide's droning and the footsteps of our classmates quickly faded. Leaning down until my lips touched her ear, I growled, "Because I couldn't resist your flame, Archer."

"Stalker."

"Brat."

"Prick."

I clutched her hips and yanked her lower half until there was no space left between us. "Mine."

Her body trembled as her forehead rubbed against my own when she shook her head. "Never," she whispered.

Resisting the urge to kiss her, I took a deep breath, exhaled, and said, "I'm sorry for what happened."

"No, you're not."

No, I wasn't. Everyone at school now knew she was mine, and I couldn't find issue with that. I didn't regret it one goddamn bit.

"You calling me on my shit?" I couldn't help grinning.

"Someone's got to."

"Yeah?" Forgetting that at any moment we could be caught, my hand slipped under her skirt and petted her pussy through her damp panties. "Who gets to call you on yours?"

"Ever..." she moaned.

"Good fucking answer."

"That's not what I—"

A throat cleared, interrupting her protest.

I peeked over my shoulder and found who I assumed was a silver-haired NYU professor wearing red-rimmed glasses, pearls, and a disapproving frown.

"If you two would come with me, I'll escort you back to your group."

I heard Four's sharp inhale and knew she feared exposure. No way was this woman not going to report what she saw. It was one thing for our classmates to suspect we were fucking, but a teacher confirming it to our parents was another thing entirely. Thinking quickly, I grabbed Four's hand and made a run for it. We pissed off a few people during our mad dash through the crowded library—namely the guy who spilled his coffee to get out of our way—and drew even more attention. Ignoring a chorus of "Hey!" and "Stop!" we burst through the nearest exit marked Emergency Only and set off a piercing alarm.

"Shit."

After looking around for a place to hide and finding nothing, I started forward so we could cross the street, but the sound of Four's laughter drew me to an abrupt stop. She was still smiling brightly after I turned to face her, and I swallowed hard when I realized that I'd gladly be caught red-handed if it meant I could live in this moment a little while longer.

Still giggling, she said, "That was fun."

"Oh?"

She nodded before chewing on her bottom lip thoughtfully. "And it made me realize something."

"What's that?"

"I'm not the troublemaker," she answered with bright eyes. "You are."

I knew the exact moment she realized her mistake. Her fallen visage mirrored the turmoil raging within me, and I cursed myself for confiding in her at the beach. She hadn't been wrong with her assessment, and even though she'd meant it as a compliment, she also knew why it was anything but.

I now wondered if finding Nathaniel Fox would even make a difference. I was still the same person I was four years ago. I only became good at hiding it.

"Oh, Ever, I didn't mean—"

"It's fine." I cleared my throat to rid my voice of the emotion weighing it down and said, "We should get back."

She didn't argue as I led the way.

Twenty minutes later, we rejoined the group with Mr. Fletcher, Four's pre-calculus teacher and group chaperone, none the wiser. The tour had come to an end, so we were promptly directed back to the buses.

Neither Four nor I had spoken a word in more than half an hour, but still, I stayed close as we waited to board the bus. After that unlikely encounter with Wren on Four's birthday and knowing he could still be watching me, I wasn't leaving her safety up to chance. Stealing a peek at her, my stomach turned at the dejection written on her face, so I decided to say something—anything—to bring back her smile.

"Four—"

Jamie, unfortunately, chose that moment to appear wearing a shit-eating grin. "Did you see Brittany Hall?" he asked me.

"Who is Brittany?" Four inquired with her arms crossed. "Some girl you two are running a game on?"

It was a good thing her back was turned or else she would have caught my smile. I bet she had no idea of the jealousy seeping from her pores.

"No, pretty girl." Jamie tapped the tip of her nose and snickered when I scowled. "Brittany is the residence hall where our mothers met their freshman year. They were roommates."

"Oh." She then whirled around only to stumble back when she found me standing closer than I'd been a moment ago. "You didn't tell me your mother went to school here."

"I was a little distracted, princess." I struggled to hold in my laugh when she glanced at Jamie to see if he'd heard.

Goddamn, she blushes beautifully.

Lucky for her, Jamie had already lost interest when a leggy co-ed with an inviting smile took a seat on a nearby bench.

Entrapping me with her big brown eyes once again, she said, "Did your father also meet your mother here?"

"My father went to school out in Pennsylvania, but he eventually met my mom."

"Yeah, and my pops was a buddy of his pops," Jamie added, seemingly forgetting all about the brunette.

I could tell Four had more to ask, but one of the chaperones herded us onto the bus. She quickly ascended the short steps and sat in the first seat available. The bench had been empty leaving an empty seat next to her, but since I didn't care to talk about my mother anymore today, I kept going.

I could feel her gaze on me as I walked away and heard Jamie say, "Don't take it personally. He's just being a mama's boy."

It took every ounce of control I possessed to not toss Jamie's meddling ass out the window.

Sitting at the back of the bus, I had a perfect view of Four whispering with Jamie. Letting my head fall back, I closed my eyes to mentally prep for the fight still to come.

Since the rumors started, Tyra had been driving Four to and from school. Their little arrangement ended today.

Once upon a puppet, she rode home with the peer and didn't give him any lip.

I didn't have to wait long for her reply.

TROUBLE: Let's just skip to the end when the peer learns he doesn't always get what he wants.

A smile teased my lips just as Vaughn nudged me.

He lifted his chin toward the entrance where Four and Tyra had just emerged. Tyra was busy babying Jay D, and Four was too distracted by that piece-of-shit phone to notice that they were walking into a trap. Brows furrowed as she caught her bottom lip between her teeth—an emotional cue I'd come to recognize and exploit—Four was still staring at her phone when she came within arm's length. Hooking my arm around her waist, I pulled her into me. Her sweet scent tempted me to devour her while her body instinctively molded into my own. Simultaneously, Vaughn played interference by smoothly escorting Tyra to her car and almost got a chunk of his arm taken off by an upset Jay D. It was their own fault no one was around to come to their rescue. The field trip had ended, and the school had long ago closed for the weekend, but the girls naively assumed we'd eventually grow bored waiting and give up.

Four still had her phone flipped open, so I peeked at the message to see who had her so distracted since I never responded, but the screen was so cracked I couldn't make out the message. I made a mental note to take care of that situation and focused on my current one glaring up at me. Letting her see everything I was feeling in return, her shoulders slumped with a sigh.

"I'm not doing this." She shook her head as if that would make me believe her.

"Good. Now get in the car." I pushed away from the hood with her in my arms and walked her to the passenger door.

"Ever—"

"I'm tired of fighting this." I now had her trapped against the door with my hips pressed against hers. "Tell me what I need to do to have you. I'll break bones." I punctuated the vow with a kiss on her neck. "Ruin reputations…" Her body shivered when I trailed lower. "Destroy futures." Her moan felt like a tight, warm grip around my cock. "I just need you to be mine."

"You only have yourself to blame. Don't you dare punish others for what *you* did…for what I let you do."

She suddenly sounded strong and sure—as if she were capable of walking away if I let her—but one glance showed me she was torn between right and wrong. It was too bad that I wasn't.

"Get in the car." My voice sounded rough to my own ears. "I need to get you home."

"Why?"

She sounded breathless with the anticipation I knew was building within her. "You know why."

I kept one hand on the wheel and the other on Four's stocking-clad thigh the entire ride home. I could feel the heat from her pussy on my hand. The desire to slip under her skirt and make her come built with each second.

Just a mile from the house, her moan when my thumb brushed her center shattered my restraint. I was ripping open her stockings, shoving her panties aside, and strumming her clit before I could come to my senses.

"God, Ever."

"I know, baby."

I slid my fingers down, loving the feel of her newly smoothed skin, and teased her opening. I wanted to ask who she'd waxed her pretty little pussy for. For her sake the answer had better be me.

Instead I said, "Lift your leg."

She did as she was told and rested it against the door. Four following orders got my cock hard as fuck every time. Every. Single. Time. She hooked her finger inside her panties to keep them out of my way, and I rewarded her by sliding inside her.

"So damn wet. So damn mine."

I wanted to pull this car over and get my mouth on her, but I knew it wouldn't stop there, and she deserved more than losing her virginity in a fucking car.

Every other second, I was chancing a glance at her. She was so beautiful when she came. I didn't want to miss it. Once I cleared the gates, I threw the car into park and took all she had to give. Her cry when she came was a lyrical masterpiece. After she slumped against the seat, I didn't waste time sucking her juices from my fingers. Hands down, she had the sweetest nectar I'd ever tasted. Her panting was the only sound as I drove us the remaining distance to the house.

I started to speak when a voice in the back seat beat me to it. "Thanks for the free porn. You assholes forgot I was back here, didn't you?"

Four instantly turned red while scowling at me as if I had betrayed her. I'd forgotten Jamie had ridden with me that morning, still hungover from late-night partying. He must have stowed away in the back seat and crashed while I waited around for Four.

"Aargh!" Four shoved her skirt back in place, slammed the door after hopping out, and stomped inside the house.

With a groan, I rested my head against the seat and willed my erection away.

"You're damn lucky, cousin, when you don't deserve her."

"I know."

He clapped my shoulder before stumbling out of the car and disappearing inside the house. The burner phone I used for Exiled business began to ring as I parked the car inside the garage. I debated answering until curiosity won me over. It was better I knew if I had a price on my head.

"This is Danny Boy."

As usual, Shane didn't bother with pleasantries. "We need you for a job tonight."

I tamped down my surprise that he wasn't grilling me about my absence and said, "I'll pass. Find someone else."

"It's not an option, but you knew that already. Normally, we wouldn't use a fucking tenderfoot on the honcho's personal errands, but Harlan's got his hands tied dealing with something more important. You're the next best thing, kid."

I stared into the distance, itching to ask about the job occupying Harlan's focus, but I didn't want to seem too interested. Now that my cover was blown, it was possible this was a trap. Maybe Harlan had never even left Blackwood Keep…

I was ready to decline and spend the night buried inside princess when he added, "The boss man will be personally overseeing this job. Be at the junkyard by midnight, and don't fuck up."

Fuck.

Making Four submit would have to wait.

I was finally getting an audience with Nathaniel Fox, and I knew if I passed up this opportunity, there wouldn't be another.

chapter thirty-two

The Puppet

HAD MY HEAD IN MY TEXTBOOK, BUT MY MIND WAS A MILLION MILES away. I think I was more disturbed by how easily I'd given in than having Jamie witness it all. Ever touched me, and nearly two weeks of resolve just melted away. He'd actually fingered me with one hand while driving home to take my virginity with the other. The promise of him inside of me obliterated common sense, and even now, I had to press my thighs together to lessen the ache. A groan, the first sound I'd made in hours, slipped out. I actually expected him to pursue me, and when he didn't, it only made me feel worse. I needed to get my head in the game for the race tonight, and mourning my loss of dignity was getting in the way of that.

Mickey had texted me this afternoon with the location. I just needed to figure out how to get in and out with no one—especially Ever—the wiser.

I also needed a ride.

I was debating how successful I'd be getting Ever to lift the keys to my bike without answering any questions when the knock on my door came. Knowing it was him on the other side, I hurried to answer. It was time to test my skills in deception.

I opened the door, and rather than striking features, I was greeted by nothing. Stepping into the hall for a thorough look, I found it empty, but when I turned back, I discovered a small white bag hanging from my doorknob by the drawstrings. I retrieved the bag and locked myself in my room before inspecting the bag. With only the gray Apple logo as a clue, I opened the bag and found a white box bearing the same logo and a picture of a phone along with paperwork inside. I dumped the contents on my bed, and when a familiar slip of notepaper fell out, I rolled my eyes to keep from smiling.

Once upon a puppet, she accepted this trinket as the smallest token of the peer's affection.

I picked up the paperwork and found my name listed among Thomas, Ever and Jamie's, along with what was allegedly my new phone number circled in red. A curse exploded from my lips when I noticed the price of the phone. There was no way in hell the phone could possibly be worth that much! Curious now, I threw the top from the box and marveled over the shiny flat surface. It wasn't that I'd never seen an iPhone before, but I certainly never owned one—and never expected to, especially if the amount it sold for was real. I gingerly lifted the phone from the box and tapped at the screen like I'd seen people do, but nothing happened. After a quick inspection, I noticed the flat, round button at the bottom and pressed it. I marveled at how bright and clear the screen was and all the bells and whistles. It took me a while to find the text app, and when I did, I typed in Ever's number and found it already saved under 'Boyfriend.'

Someone was mighty presumptuous.

I quickly sent him a text and got an immediate response:

Is this for real?

BOYFRIEND: All yours, baby.

You didn't have to do this.

BOYFRIEND: Yeah…I did. Ditch the relic.

Rolling my eyes, I bought myself time to think of a response by changing his contact name to something more fitting.

Thank you, I suppose.

PRICK: Leave your door unlocked tonight.

I'm not repaying you with sex.

PRICK: You'll do as I say.

I was ready to tell him how much I wouldn't be doing that when I received another text.

PRICK: And we both know it will be because you want to.
Maybe.

But he didn't have to know that.

And I didn't have to make it easy for him.

A cold shower will be all you have to look forward to tonight.

I became anxious when a response didn't come instantly. I was searching for something else to say when his response, along with a picture, came through.

PRICK: Wanna bet?

When I clicked on the image, my new fancy phone slipped from my grasp onto the bed. With shaking hands, I retrieved it and gaped at the picture of an erection fit for a porn star trapped under gray cotton sweatpants, tanned six-pack, and the deep V trailing below his waistband. I could tell the picture was taken in his room while lying down. I just didn't know how many girls he'd shown it to. Jealousy strung a sharp chord in my chest as I texted my reply.

How old is this pic?

PRICK: Couple mins…why?

The breath I held released in a rush of relief. I wasn't sure I should like what this boy did to me, but I craved more of it. Checking out the picture he'd sent one last time before deleting, I changed his contact name again.

No reason.

EVER, PhD: Jealous?

No.

EVER, PhD: I feel possessive of you, too.

Stop talking.

I waited anxiously for his response. When ten minutes passed and none came, I tossed the phone aside and took Jay D for a walk to clear my head before I had to face him at dinner.

Dinner had started out as just another dull affair until Rosalyn handed over my birth certificate to everyone's surprise—other than Thomas's, of course. I had a strong feeling he played a hand in her change of heart, especially when she visibly held back her displeasure during her silent acquiesce.

It was just an hour until midnight, and since Ever not so surprisingly disappeared before I could ask for the keys, I enlisted Tyra's help. She was excited to see me in action but warned me that lying to Ever wasn't such a smart idea. I simply reminded her that I wasn't just going to roll over whenever Ever commanded. She shrugged, but I could tell she fully expected to remind me how she'd 'told me so' soon enough. I pushed Ever to the back of my mind and got my head in the game.

"So, how much do you get if you win?"

"Thirty percent of the profits."

"That's it?"

"Mickey takes half for himself, and the remaining twenty percent goes to flipping the money of the winning bets."

"So if you win, you'll make a lot of people happy?"

"Pretty much."

"And if you lose?"

I suddenly felt apprehensive about bringing Tyra along. It had been so long since I raced that I'd forgotten the danger in it. Some people were sore losers, and when money was involved, bitterness sometimes turned into rage.

"Maybe you shouldn't stick around. I can bum a ride from Mickey after the race is over."

Her expression quickly became eager. "Are you kidding me? There's no way I'm missing you race. I need to see it for myself."

"It's not safe. Some of Mickey's buyers don't like to lose."

"All the more reason to make sure you have a friendly face in the crowd when you cross the finish line."

I blew out a breath, knowing I was about to give in against my better judgment. "Stick close to Mickey. He's a flirt, but I'm confident you can resist him."

She tapped her chin thoughtfully. "Maybe I should invite Vaughn and let him see for himself that I have options."

"Mickey isn't exactly the boy next door, and Vaughn is much too whipped to care. It will be the brawl of the century."

She cackled and banged her fist against the steering wheel. "You might be right."

I checked my new phone for the thousandth time to ensure my absence hadn't been discovered. It didn't escape Tyra's notice. "Why didn't you invite him? I'm sure he would want to be there with his nose in the air and a hand on your ass to stake his claim."

"Somehow, I don't think he would approve given what happened the last time I raced."

"He won't like you lying about it, either. I wonder which offense will get you spanked?"

"You're relentless."

"I'm also right."

"I should have never told you about him trying to spank me." I could feel myself flushing from the memory.

"Don't worry. You and Ever's kinky secrets are safe with me."

"You do know Vaughn is just as domineering as Ever? Maybe even more so."

"There's no way he'd get me over his knee without a fight."

"Don't be so sure. If I hadn't used my wits, he would have succeeded."

She groaned and sighed. "How did we get here, Four? I can't remember a single moment before Vaughn."

"I don't think I can, either."

We left each other to our thoughts, and an hour later, we drove through gates with a sign that read Hoarders Paradise and discarded junk waiting in piles beyond.

"I'm glad to see you've still got it even though you and I both know you held back," Mickey groused.

I'd just finished a few test runs, committing the course to memory. There was also no way in hell I was going to trust my life on an untried bike. The makeshift course was about a couple of miles long. There were more than a few tight turns and lanes that would barely fit one rider, not to mention the difficulty seeing what was ahead with all the heaping piles of junk to navigate through. The natural terrain wouldn't make winning easy, but it was nothing I couldn't handle. I was actually looking forward to the challenge. Being faster wasn't going to be enough. I'd also have to be the most cunning and daring.

"It's better if my competition believes they have the win in the bag. The assumption will make them sloppy."

He rubbed his hands together and nodded slowly in approval. "Keep it up, snow bunny. I like my women wily. Win this race, and I may have to propose."

"Mickey…"

"Right. Right. No racial slurs. I know your rules." He then flicked his chin to Tyra, who was looking around nervously. "What's up with your friend? She got a man?"

"Seriously? You were *just* hitting on me."

He smiled wide. "What can I say? I like to gamble."

"And the house always wins, Mick. She's very much taken."

He shot me a skeptical look. "Are you just saying that because you secretly have a thing for me?"

"Yeah…no. Her boyfriend's a quarterback with a jealous streak a mile long, so watch where you point those beady little eyes."

He lifted his shirt to show off the gun tucked in his waistband. "I'm not worried."

Suddenly, I was very grateful for not having invited Ever and Vaughn. Mickey may have lost a few screws, but Ever and Vaughn weren't exactly working with a full deck, either.

A whistle pierced the air, and after a quick glance over his shoulder, Mickey turned serious. "Do I need to remind you of my rules?"

"I remember. Is anyone going to try to kill me this time?"

"I hope not, but I've got your back, and I've got a few men out there to ensure sportsmanship at all times."

I breathed a little easier, but I would still keep my eyes open. Mickey couldn't be everywhere at once, and you never knew what evil might slip through the cracks.

chapter thirty-three

The Peer

I WAS CAREFUL TO INHALE ONLY THROUGH MY MOUTH TO AVOID breathing in the horrible stench of the junkyard. The black bandana I had wrapped around the lower half of my face did little to mask the smell. It was a cold night, and the hoodie I wore under my leather bomber warded off most of the chill. I was having a harder time keeping my irritation in check.

Shortly after arriving, I didn't catch more than a glimpse of the man I assumed was Fox before a gun was shoved in my hands and the order to ensure our rider passed the finish line first was given. Shane warned there were men standing guard about a quarter mile apart who wouldn't hesitate to kill me if they spotted me. Taking heed, I made sure to find a blind spot between the last sentry and the finish, but I still hadn't figured out how I would accomplish the task. I was only willing to damn my soul for one man, so spilling the blood of an innocent wasn't an option.

Wary of this all being a trap, I made sure to enlist the help of Eddie and Siko, who were somewhere out there laying low and observing. Vaughn and Jamie had also insisted on having my back tonight, adding to my confidence that I'd live to see another day.

Checking the time, I realized the race would start any minute, and I couldn't help but think of Four. This was her world, and for a moment, I worried if somehow she'd found a way back to it. I debated texting her to assure myself that she was safely tucked into bed and waiting for me with the door unlocked.

The sudden roar of engines in the distance drowned out my thoughts, and I ducked inside one of the rusted school buses that reeked of mold. I didn't want anyone to see me before it was time.

There were only a few hundred feet between me and the finish line, so whatever I did had to be done with stealth.

The sound of the engines grew increasingly louder as they closed in. Since the race was unsanctioned, and they couldn't risk the police being tipped, I would only have one shot. Making sure the other rider didn't cross the finish line was my ticket to getting close to Fox. How far was I willing to go for that chance?

The ground began to shake, so I took that as my cue as I sunk into the shadows behind the partially opened door and waited with a gun in my hand. I figured flashing it would be enough to unnerve the rider. I just had to wait for the right moment.

The lead rider turned onto the straightaway, and I grimaced when I deduced that it wasn't Hannibal, Fox's rider. He wasn't far behind, but the first rider's lead was enough to make me break a sweat. If I failed, Hannibal wouldn't win. The bus had been dumped at the end of the straightaway just where the curve began with the door facing the oncoming. My position was perfect. I just had to ensure my timing was, too.

With the lead only a hundred feet away, I marveled over how small in stature the rider seemed. I was ready to make my presence known when the rider suddenly shifted in preparation for the turn and the moonlight illuminated their unusual headgear.

Recognition delivered a powerful blow to my gut.

I threw myself back into the shadows with a vicious curse just as Four, followed by Hannibal, took the turn. I didn't stop to see if either of them had noticed me and drove my fist into the door of the bus with a roar until my entire arm ached.

I was fantasizing about how I would even the score once I got Four alone when the reminder of Shane's contingency plan if I failed barged through the red haze. Without a thought to how she'd betrayed me, or even a clear plan, I took off into the night to save her ass.

chapter thirty-four

∞

the Puppet

"**O**H, MY GOD! YOU WERE AMAZING!" TYRA SCREECHED AS she clapped and jumped up and down. She was completely oblivious to the nasty looks she was drawing from the crowd while I was all too aware of the hostile scowls from those who lost a lot of money tonight. "Do you think you could teach me how to ride? Maybe I can go pro, too."

"Are you forgetting about medical school?"

"Fuck med school. They can teach me how to save lives, but they can't teach me the ways of the badass."

Mickey approached us with a grin the size of Texas and a fist full of cash. "Yeah, you still got it," was all he said as he handed over the cash. His eyes were warning me to make a hasty getaway as he jerked his head toward the exit.

I didn't need to be told twice. "Time to go," I said to Tyra.

"We aren't going to celebrate?"

"I told you…this isn't that type of scene."

We made it to her car without any hiccups, but my heart didn't stop pounding until we passed through the gates.

"So how much did you win?" she quizzed half a mile down the road. The junkyard was but a speck in the rearview mirror.

I quickly counted out the cash, and my eyes bucked when I reached six grand. It was my biggest take yet.

I was about to answer when she whispered, "What the hell?"

Looking up, I spotted an older model green Accord and navy

Impala blocking the road. A man was standing a few feet from the cars while one sat on the hood, another in the driver's seat with his foot planted on the asphalt, and a fourth man on the furthest side standing in the driver's door.

"Four, what is this?" Tyra's voice shook as she stopped the car twenty feet away.

"A setup."

"What do they want?"

"I'm guessing they want the cash."

"Are we going to give it to them?"

"It looks like we don't have a choice," I mumbled. I'd already spotted the gun the point man held by his side. Forcing confidence in my voice to mask my fear and keep Tyra calm, I said, "Stay in the car. I'll handle this." I stuffed the money under the seat just in case I was wrong and exited the car.

"Do you mind moving your car?" I gingerly approached the thin man of average height with a receding hairline and too-thick beard. The rest of his crew matched his unsavory appearance. "My friend and I are about to break curfew, and I don't want my stepdad calling the cops like he did the last time that happened." I laughed so I'd appear at ease while hoping he'd heed my warning. Underaged girls with parents who cared? Maybe he'd think twice about killing us.

"Hand over the cash, little girl, and we'll let you go home to daddy."

I could feign ignorance, but I was almost sure he'd just kill us both and take the cash anyway. "How do I know you won't kill me anyway? I've seen your faces."

"What exactly are you going to tell the police? You'd be just as knee deep in shit." He lifted his gun, but instead of pointing at me, he aimed at Tyra. My heart lurched when I heard her cry out. "I'm not going to ask you again."

I took careful steps back with my hands out until I reached the car. Tyra was frozen stiff as I retrieved the money from under the seat. I assured her that we'd be okay, but it fell on deaf ears as she stared down the barrel of the gun.

Walking back over, I felt my ire rise at the smug look on his face. "My boyfriend is a vengeful son of a bitch. If you kill us, you'll be looking over your shoulder for the rest of your life."

He smiled, showing off a chipped front tooth.

The moment I offered the money, the sound of racing engines filled the night as headlights set on high beam chased away the remaining darkness and blinded everyone in the vicinity.

Every second that followed happened too quickly for me to recall. Gunfire rang out, and the sound of bodies hitting the ground followed along with screams and curses. I hadn't realized I was huddled in a ball on the ground until I felt myself being lifted in strong arms and carried away. Footsteps pounded the pavement, and then I was tossed into the back seat of a car. The door slammed along with the sound of others, and then only the sound of tires screeching could be heard.

"Four, are you okay?" The voice sounded familiar, but I didn't dare open my eyes. I was afraid of what I might see. "Four! Four!"

My eyes involuntarily popped open, and I found Jamie staring back at me from the front passenger seat. "I-I'm okay." I glanced at the driver. Ever's jaw looked carved from stone as he focused on the road with a tight grip on the steering wheel of the Crown Vic. I was sure he had been the one to rescue me from the gunfire. "Tyra?"

I was almost afraid to know the answer. If anything had happened to her, I would never forgive myself.

"Vaughn is trailing us in her car."

I exhaled, feeling some of the weight lifting from my shoulders. I also noticed the fact that Jamie was doing all the talking rather than Ever. "Thank you," I meekly voiced with my eyes glued to Ever. My nervousness only heightened when he didn't reply.

"I can't believe that was you out there tonight," Jamie said with awe and a shake of his head. Either he was oblivious to the tension surrounding us or ignoring it completely. "You have some serious skill, girl."

"Thanks. I've been riding since I was eleven."

"No shit?" he exclaimed.

I simply nodded before laying my head back against the seat and closing my eyes. Jamie caught the hint and didn't speak again. The silence brought me a small bit of peace.

I woke up on top of a plush bed inside of an even more luxurious hotel suite with no memory of how I'd gotten there. "Lay low until morning to make sure you aren't being followed and, even then, be careful. We'll do the same." I listened as booted footsteps moved across the next room. A door opened, and then the gruff voice spoke again. "Franklin will want to speak with you when you get back."

Back? Where the hell was I?

I quickly sat up as footsteps approached, and a moment later, Ever appeared in the doorway. His mask was in place as his eyes emotionlessly roamed over my body as if searching for something. I did the same and was happy to see he was unharmed.

"Where are we?"

"Hotel." He then turned away, and I stopped breathing when he laid a gun on the dresser.

"Did you kill those men?"

"Does it matter? Would you rather it have been you dead instead of them?"

"No, but you—"

"I didn't kill anyone," he bit out.

"Then who?"

"Thirteen."

"Who is that?"

He turned and met my gaze with some reluctance and asked a question of his own. *"Why?"* The way he stressed the word let me know he wasn't questioning my curiosity. This was something else entirely.

"Why? Why what?"

"Tonight," he slowly pronounced as he stalked across the room, "was my one and only chance to get to Fox." He stopped at the edge of the bed. "I lost that chance by saving you, instead. Why?"

I wrapped my arms around myself, wishing they were his instead. "I—I don't know why."

"Because I love you, Four, and that's the problem." His golden eyes glittered as he stared down at me. "If I didn't, you'd be beaten and broken or dead, but at least then, so would Fox."

"I'm sorry." I should have been elated hearing that he loved me, but all I felt was guilt because clearly loving me had cost him a great deal.

"You're not, but you will be."

Sick of being bullied and threatened, the last shredded thread snapped. "What does he have that is so goddamn important?" I screamed.

"My mother!" he roared.

The room had fallen deathly silent as my shock pushed away the anger. I would have dropped to my feet if I had been standing as I recalled Jamie's harsh words from two weeks ago.

"Don't expect Ever to choose between you and his mother. Just because Rosalyn is a piece of shit doesn't mean everyone's mother isn't worth the trouble."

I'd been too hurt and too distracted to realize I'd had the answer all of this time.

"I...I don't understand."

"I never asked you to," he shot back. "It was *my* fight. My demons."

"I'm sorry." I was starting to sound like a broken record.

"Why are you sorry, Four? This is what you wanted all along, right? To save my soul?" Slowly, he clapped. "Congratulations. You succeeded. Now who will stop me from breaking yours?"

His cruelty made my heart race as tears welled. "Don't."

"Don't what?"

I crawled to the foot of the bed where he stood and tugged him close with my fists in his shirt when he tried to back away. "Don't make me hate you again. Don't become cold again. Just… don't."

"Why should I be the only one to lose something tonight?"

"Then take something from me. Whatever you want. All that you want. Take until it's enough to make it right again."

He didn't respond, so I leaned in to kiss him and was mortified when he dodged my lips and took a step back. My heart sunk into my stomach when he retreated until his back was against the wall.

"Please…" The plea slipped from my lips involuntarily.

"Take off your clothes." The determination I had a moment ago quickly fled. Noticing my hesitation, he said, "Take them off, or I'll rip them off. Your choice."

With shaking hands, I unzipped my leather jacket and removed it from my body. Standing from the bed, my boots and pants followed and then my thermals, until I was left in my green cotton bra and panties.

I imagined this moment before.

He'd run his hands over my body and tell me I was beautiful.

In reality, Ever didn't touch me or utter a goddamn word, but boy, did he look his fill. Hiding my disappointment, I hooked my fingers in my panties to remove them when he finally spoke.

"No."

Pushing from the wall, he crossed the space and cupped my hips with warm hands. They roamed up my side, making me shiver until he reached my bra. His scent calmed me like wildflowers on a summer day or the ocean on a calm night.

"Look at me."

I hadn't realized until that moment that I had been gazing at his T-shirt-clad chest. When I met his gaze, he unhooked my bra and gently slid it down my arms. My panties were next, and when they laid discarded on the floor, he dropped to a crouch.

"Yesterday, when I touched you, I thought I'd go crazy." His voice was soft and filled with awe as he gazed at my bare pussy. "When did you do this?"

"A couple of weeks ago." I was amazed that there was still not a single hair there.

He placed a tender kiss there and then ran a finger through my lips. "So soft."

I almost fell over when he hooked my leg over his shoulder without warning. I shoved my fingers into his hair and held on as he ate me. The friction from the warm metal circling my clit intensified until I was a gasping, crying mess. My legs shook when he released me and stood. I watched as he reached behind him to grip his shirt by the collar and pull it over his head. His body was a sculpted work of art. I wanted to see more of him.

When I reached out to undo his belt, he snapped, "Don't touch me."

My ire quickly returned. "You can touch me, but I can't touch you?"

"Please."

I swallowed. It would be hard, but I could do it.

"I want to see you."

I restrained myself from running a finger down his abs while he looked as if he was having an internal battle. When the fight ended, his only response was to push me until I was flat on my back. He wouldn't look me in the eye. Honey gold darkened as he stared between my legs.

"Show me your pussy."

I did as he demanded.

"Touch yourself."

I did that too and was delighted when he undid his belt and

slid it free. I grew alarmed, however, when he folded it in half. "I'm tempted to use this on you." My hand fell from my clit and dropped onto the bed. "Don't stop," he ordered, but it sounded strangely like a plea. The belt fell from his hand onto the floor, and I resumed pleasuring myself.

He swiftly kicked his jeans aside, leaving him in black boxers.

"Ever, I—" Words were lost as the pleasure built.

"Keep going, princess. I want you wet and ready for me."

He shed his boxers, and for the first time, I saw all of him. A whimper escaped me as I debated if he would even fit. Luckily, he didn't allow time for my fear to build. With a condom in hand, he moved between my legs before ripping open the wrapper with his teeth and sliding the rubber down his swollen cock. He then lowered his body on top of mine. Taking my chin in hand, he held my gaze.

"Whatever I want, right?"

"Yes."

My breath caught when he found my entrance and pushed inside. Deeper and deeper, he buried his length inside of me, but when the pain intensified, I planted my hands on his abs to stop him. Gently, he took my wrists and placed them above my head before plunging the rest of the way inside me.

Head thrown back and body arched, I cried out. I could feel him watching and waiting for the moment when he could move. It wasn't long before the pain ebbed and throbbing between my legs made me hungry for more.

"Fuck me."

He didn't waste time, pulling back and driving into me over and over until I was delirious. The sound of our bodies coming together mingled with animalistic grunts and desperate moans.

Too long had we waited for this.

"You feel like you're mine," he growled in my ear. "Are you mine?"

"I'm yours."

"That can't be true," he taunted. "*My girl would do what she's told.*" Shifting onto his knees, he held me down with his hands on my waist and pounded into me. I was willing to obey his every command as long as he kept giving me his cock. Just as I was ready to tell him so, he sat back on his haunches and lifted me onto his lap. Hands planted on my hips, he slowly lifted me up and down on his length. It took some getting used to, but before long, I could feel the familiar pressure building inside me.

"I'm going to come."

"Come with me, princess."

"I never meant to hurt you," I cried just before shattering in his arms. His release wasn't far behind. The sound of his grunt and the feeling of him jerking inside me had me coming apart for the second time.

He fell back onto the bed, taking me with him. I could hear his heart racing as we fought to catch our breath.

"Ever?"

"Yeah?"

I lifted my head and met his eyes and even though the room was dark I still saw the pain in them. "You can't go back now. What will you do?"

He was silent for so long that I didn't think he'd answer but then he said, "Let her go and hope that she's happy." Feeling guilty, I laid my head on his chest to avoid his gaze and rationalized that I couldn't truly hear his heart shatter.

I wasn't sure how much time had passed lying in the darkness. An hour? Maybe two? He had grown soft inside me, and when I shifted my hips, I could feel his cock stirring.

"Don't. You'll be sore tomorrow."

"I don't mind."

He shook his head. "I don't think I can be gentle."

"Take what's yours." I worked my hips, bringing his cock back to life. "What's always been yours. We can worry about the consequences later."

I had trouble peeling my eyes open hours later and coupled with the ache between my legs, I never wanted to leave this bed. *At least I'm clean.* I felt my skin heat as I recalled the gentle yet thorough way he'd cleaned me after I finally threw in the towel. Of course, I had been the first to do so. We had gone at it with little breaks in between until just before dawn. He almost seemed determined not to waste a single chance to be inside of me.

His side of the bed was empty and cold, so I checked the nightstand for a note and found none. My backpack containing my phone, keys, wallet, and change of clothes was probably still in Tyra's car. With no other options, I decided to take a much-needed hot shower and wait for Ever to return.

My jaw dropped at first glance of my naked body in the mirror. I looked as if I'd been fighting all night rather than making love. He'd left evidence of passion on my neck, breasts, and thighs. My clothes would hide most of them, but the two on my neck wouldn't be as easy to conceal, so I decided to ditch my usual ponytail and wear my hair down. Twenty minutes later, I emerged from the en suite and found Ever sitting on the edge of the bed, looking down at his phone. It wasn't until I inched closer that I realized he was actually fiddling around on *my* phone.

"What are you doing?"

Not realizing I was standing there, his head snapped around in surprise. It made me wonder what on my phone had so successfully captured his focus.

"I brought your bag up," he said rather than answering.

I was too thrown off by his flat tone to make a big deal about it.

"Is everything okay?"

Ignoring my question, he picked up my backpack from the floor and dropped it in front of me. "Get dressed."

"Are you still upset with me or something? I thought after last night—"

"You thought spreading your legs for me would make me forget what you did?"

"But you—"

"I took what you freely offered. You were eager to please, and I needed to relieve some stress. Turns out you're no different than the girls who bat their eyes my way, hoping to get fucked."

I was too shocked by his cold demeanor to lash out the way I should. Last night, he gave as much as he took. I could still hear him uttering those three words. "Ever, I'm sorry for hurting you."

"Doesn't change that you did."

"I see. And when you said you loved me?"

He winced, and if I had blinked, I would have missed it. He then pocketed his phone and retrieved his keys from the nightstand. "We should go. Tyra and Vaughn took off thirty minutes ago, and Jamie's waiting for us downstairs."

When he turned his back and crossed the room, I took a deep breath and called his name. The sound was barely a whisper, but he heard. "If you don't apologize and hold me right now, we're *done*."

I hated how small I sounded.

I should have been stronger. More confident.

Maybe then he wouldn't have walked out the door.

chapter thirty-five

the Puppet

WE RETURNED HOME THAT MORNING, AND I WAS SURPRISED when Thomas greeted us at the door with a threat and a vicious scowl.

"I'll have the entire police force combing the streets the next time you three stay out overnight without my knowledge."

"Sorry, Unc. We lost track of time."

"For nine hours?" Our curfews had been set at ten on school nights and midnight on the weekends, but Thomas was rarely around to enforce his rules, and the house staff kept their heads down. Ever offered nothing when his father looked to him for an explanation. He'd never been the type to offer excuses—or apologize—when he was wrong, so I wasn't surprised by his silence. Neither was Thomas, apparently, when he dismissed him a moment later.

"Four, I'd like to speak with you," Thomas hailed when I started for the stairs. Even though I dared not look at him directly, I was aware of Ever's sudden hesitation to leave. I wasn't the only one to notice Ever lingering. "Did you need something, son?"

Unwillingly, my eyes fell on him and found him watching me with a white-knuckled grip on the banister.

"I got what I needed."

His meaning wasn't lost on me. Looking away before either of them noticed the hurt his words created, I listened to Ever's footsteps fade and to Thomas's sigh.

"If he's giving you trouble, you'll let me know, won't you? I know my son can be cold and aloof…even with me." The concern he displayed was genuine, and I admitted for the first time that Thomas was a good man, but I still couldn't trust him with the truth.

"Thanks, but I can handle your son." I pushed my hair behind my ear, wishing for a do-over of the last twenty-four hours. Then again, if I could alter time, I would go back a year, instead.

Thomas's eyebrows bunched when the movement drew his attention to my neck and the hickeys my hair had been covering. *Shit!* Casually, I pushed my hair back in place only for the nervous chord in my stomach to tighten when he cast a worried glance up the stairs.

"Is there something you want to tell me?"

"Um…nothing comes to mind."

My prayers were answered when he didn't mention the marks his son had left on my body. He then excused himself, leaving whatever he needed to speak with me about a mystery. Was it possible he suspected that Ever or even Jamie had been the one to mark me? After a moment of deliberation, I shrugged it off, deciding that if he had suspected his son or nephew, no way would he keep silent.

Eager to check on Jay D, who had been unexpectedly left alone overnight, I flew up the stairs and burst into my room. The damage I found was about what I expected. An excited Jay D hopped from my bed covered in the feathers and cotton that used to make up my bedding. His food and water bowls had been tipped over, the bottom of the curtains chewed, and in one of the far corners were his droppings.

He whined as he pawed my legs with wagging tongue. "I'm sorry, Jay." I picked him up and scratched behind his ears before taking another look around my room with a wince. "I guess I deserved that, huh?" He barked and licked his answer all over my face.

It took an hour to clear out Jay D's handiwork, and other than the barren bed and the small carpet stain that my mirror did a good job of covering, my room was back to normal. I'd replace my bedding with some of the cash I'd won, and then I'd buy Jay D's forgiveness with a new chew toy or two.

I was clipping Jay D's leash to his collar to take him for a well-deserved walk when I heard a throat clear. Standing in the open doorway was Jamie, accompanied by Ever. Since coming home, they had both showered and changed into fresh clothing. Jamie wore a distressed denim jacket, yellow long-sleeve bearing a white hand flipping the bird, skinny brown joggers that sagged at the crotch, and chocolate leather Timberland boots. Ever's choice of clothing was also casual though far more uptight: forest green sports coat, white cowl-neck sweater with the front tucked into dark blue jeans, and brown leather belt with matching hiking boots.

Jamie took a slow look around my room while Ever pretended I didn't exist.

"You two looking for something?"

With a shrug, Jamie threw a thumb over his shoulder. "Ever here decided to take the scenic route." I didn't miss Ever's jaw clench when Jamie exposed him. "We're heading over to Vaughn's."

His announcement reminded me that I needed to call and check on my friend. Getting a gun pointed at you wasn't easy to bounce back from. A year later, I still had the occasional nightmare.

"Oh, well, have fun."

I stood to my full height and grabbed my not-as-stylish, not-as-expensive windbreaker from my closet. I heard them whispering and told myself I didn't give a shit what they might be saying even though I lingered in my closet longer than necessary. The whispering stopped, and hoping they'd gone, I emerged only to find them still hanging around.

"Got any plans today?" Jamie questioned.

I studied their faces, seeking motive, but neither of them gave anything away.

"None that will get me killed." Sometime between almost dying and my life spared a second time, I decided that my illegal racing days were over. I wasn't surprised that Mickey still did business with the Exiled. Trying to kill me didn't make their money any less green. He owed me nothing, so he offered nothing. I also realized that risking my life and freedom no longer made sense. Now that I was eighteen and didn't need Rosalyn's consent, I could feed my addiction legally, and one day, I *will* have my season in the Grand Prix.

"Well, if you change your mind, just use the bat signal."

"Or don't be fucking stupid," Ever acerbically inserted.

Usually, I'd give as good as I got, but this time, words eluded me. Was it because I'd given him everything only for him to discard it like yesterday's trash? After what I cost him, I wasn't entirely sure I didn't deserve his hatred. That didn't stop me from getting pissed though.

"Don't worry. What I do is no longer your concern. Actually, it never was, but *you* insisted, so the next time you're feeling chivalrous, spare me." Unwilling to spend another moment in his presence, I shoved past them with Jay D and didn't look back.

Hours later, I still wasn't able to shake my anger. I so badly wanted to vent to Tyra when I called to check on her, but I forced my drama with Ever to the back of my mind and focused on consoling my friend. .

"If you don't want to be friends anymore, I totally get it." That was a total lie. I'd be completely broken up over losing a good friend.

"Please," she scoffed. "You'll never find a better wingman than me."

We talked until it was time for her shift. I tried to talk her into calling in sick, but she insisted on using the distraction. She also admitted that Vaughn had excelled at damage control last night and this morning. Whatever that meant.

Sick of twiddling my thumbs, I decided to check my email. Not long after Rosalyn handed over my birth certificate, I took the exam and submitted the application for my license. Now I was just waiting to hear back. I was marveling over the convenience of having my email at my fingertips when I remembered it was Ever who made it possible. Without a second thought, I grabbed the packaging from my desk before heading over to Ever's room with the phone and Jay D trailing. Once inside his room, I carefully arranged the phone inside the box, placed it on his nightstand, and then grabbed the notebook and pencil he used for sketching and writing despotic notes. I flipped through the drawings, begrudgingly admitting his talent until I came to a blank page. I told Ever it was over if he walked out that door, but even then, I held onto hope. Maybe it was time I set myself free.

You were never worthy of my strings.

Sunday came around, and I was more than ready for the weekend to end. I desperately needed the distraction school offered. I was in the family room eating my weight in carbs and sugar for breakfast while watching Marquez, Lorenzo, and Rossi battle for the lead in last Sunday's race when Rosalyn sauntered in holding a royal blue dress in one hand and nude patent leather flats in the other. My eyebrows nearly kissed my hairline when she carefully set the items down and sat beside me.

"How are you, dear?" Those four words had been the most she'd spoken to me since our fight a couple of weeks ago.

"I'm okay."

"I wanted to apologize for how I've acted. I may not think much of your dreams, but they are your dreams." *Gee, thanks.* "Just please promise me you'll be careful?"

"Seeing me race might ease your fears. Not to brag, but I'm pretty good."

She stiffened at my suggestion and offered me one of her practiced smiles. "I think that would be nice."

I was pretty certain she'd never step foot inside a circuit. Rather than voice my doubts, I changed the subject.

"What's all of this?"

"I picked out something for you to wear to dinner tonight."

Since when had dinner gotten so formal?

"You didn't have to do this. I'm fine wearing my normal clothes."

"The Montgomery family has invited us to dinner, and I'd like to make a good impression."

I wondered if the churning in my stomach was from all the junk food I'd eaten or the idea of spending the evening being cordial with Barbie and her parents. "Could I sit this one out? I have a lot of homework," I lied.

"Then you probably shouldn't have spent the last half-hour watching TV, dear."

I sighed and made a mental note to use the cash I won to buy a TV for my room. "What's the occasion for the invite?"

"I have no idea, but I'm sure we'll find out at dinner. Make sure you wear your stockings." Oozing grace, she rose from the couch with a reassuring smile.

Shortly after she disappeared, I raced upstairs to Jamie's room, leaving the frilly dress and shoes behind.

"Jamie!" I called as I pounded on his door with one eye on Ever's. It was a big house and hard to tell when anyone was home, but I knew Jamie rarely rose before noon on the weekend. A few more seconds of knocking and the door finally swung open, revealing a sleepy-eyed Jamie with hair sticking in every direction, wearing nothing but red boxer shorts and a sock on his left foot.

"Yeah?"

I shoved past him and waited for him to shut the door just

in case Ever was home. "Know anything about dinner with the Montgomery's?"

He scratched his defined abs and yawned. "What?"

"We're having dinner with them tonight."

The news seemed to rouse him finally.

"The fuck?" He padded over to his bed and searched around the covers until he found his phone. I watched him sit and dial and text and then stand to pace and dial and text before finally giving up. "Ever's not answering."

He left the room without a word, so I reluctantly followed him and watched from a safe distance as he pounded on Ever's door.

At least I wasn't the only one freaking out.

When Ever didn't answer, he pushed into the room. A few seconds later, he was back in the hall looking perplexed and holding a sheet of paper that I instantly recognized. My heart pounded when he held it up and moved closer for me to see. It was the note I'd left him.

"What exactly happened between you two?"

"How did you know about that?"

"It was sitting on his bed. You may be part boy, but your handwriting is still girly as shit."

Thinking there might be a clue, I ran to my room with Jamie on my heels. I immediately zeroed in on the identical slip of folded paper waiting on my nightstand. For some reason, my hands shook as I opened the note. He'd only bothered to write two words.

I know.

Evening came and Ever never returned home. I opted to ride with Jamie to the Montgomery home, although neither of us spoke during the drive. I just stared out the window while Jamie puffed on a cigarette, something he only did when agitated. Fifteen minutes later, we passed through the gates. The home was smaller than the McNamara mansion but still grander than anything I could imagine for myself. Thomas and Rosalyn had beaten us there by minutes, and I no longer wondered if Ever would even be in attendance when I spotted his car parked out front. Jamie, wearing a red dress shirt, black tie, and slacks, and I in lace and chiffon, approached the front door side by side. He rang the bell, and we glanced at each other as if to say 'this is it.' The door opened moments later, and a man with hair salted at the temples and peppered on top appeared.

"Jameson," the man greeted with his hand out, "good to see you again." It didn't sound the least bit true.

Jamie politely shook his hand but didn't bother with false pleasantries. The disdain the two shared for one another seeped from their pores.

Soon, the older man's gaze slid to me and became assessing as if determining my worth. "Hello, young lady. I don't believe we've met. I'm Elliot Montgomery, Barbette's father."

"Four Archer," I returned.

He didn't bother with a handshake or even a smile before stepping aside and inviting us in, and even then, it seemed reluctant. We followed him into the living room where everyone waited. Rosalyn was chatting with who I assumed was Barbie's mother while Thomas sipped from his drink and stared into the lit fireplace. Unable to resist his pull, I glanced to the side of the room where Ever sat broodingly on a love seat next to Barbie. I couldn't help but notice how complete they looked together.

I felt bile rising as I became flushed. I needed a way out of this.

Of course, Rosalyn chose that moment to notice me. "Four, you look beautiful." Her ill-timed compliment put every set of eyes in the room on me. "Come and meet Melissa, dear."

I couldn't even begin to describe how much I didn't want

that. Jamie placed his hand on my lower back and gently nudged me forward when I would have stayed in place. I couldn't do this. No way, no how.

A few steps and I was standing next to a beaming Rosalyn, who pled with her eyes for me not to embarrass her.

"It's nice to meet you," Melissa primly greeted. "Four, is it?"

"Yes." I then proceeded, ineloquently, to string together a sentence. "Um...thank you...for...um...inviting me to your home."

"We're glad you could come. Your mother was just telling me how dedicated you are to your studies."

I fought to keep my face schooled. I guess Rosalyn had been covering her ass in case I was a no-show.

One of the staff announced that dinner was ready to be served, so we all moved into the dining room. I was glad to end the small talk, though I had a feeling the worst was yet to come. It was hard keeping my eyes off Ever, especially when he did such a great job ignoring me. Elliot sat at the head of the table with Thomas and Ever on his left and right. Melissa dined at the other end with Rosalyn on her right and Jamie on her left, which left me sitting across from Barbie and her sandwiched between Ever and Jamie.

We were served salmon, wild rice, and asparagus. Barbie, as if a little carb would actually kill her, was served only salmon and asparagus. I forced myself to eat even though my appetite was non-existent. Elliot and Thomas discussed portfolios, although Elliot's questions were borderline intrusive, but what did I know? Thomas didn't seem to mind. Rosalyn and Melissa talked about the latest fashions. Jamie remained remarkably silent as dinner progressed. I was also content to poke around my plate in silence, but I found it strange that Ever and Barbette didn't speak and barely looked at each other. Barbie seemed resigned while Ever showed no emotion at all.

"So, Elliot, while I appreciate the invitation, I was curious as to the nature."

Jamie finally lifted his head from his plate, and Melissa clapped excitedly.

"Ah." Elliot nodded good-naturedly. "It seems my daughter and your son have great news to share."

Thomas turned to his son, and I think we all held our breath as we waited to hear the news. Ever, however, only had eyes for me when he broke me for the second time today.

"I asked Barbette to marry me."

chapter thirty-six

The Peer

JAMIE WAS BEATING THE SHIT OUT OF ME, AND I TOOK EACH OF THOSE blows without returning a single one. I deserved them. It took Thomas and Elliot to pull him off me, and by then, I was pretty sure he'd broken my nose. While Thomas kept Jamie restrained, I staggered to my feet and just…walked away. I drove myself to the hospital to get my nose looked at—luckily it wasn't broken—and my lip stitched before driving out to Vaughn's to crash.

"Jamie really fucked you up," Vaughn commented with a shake of his head.

I closed my eyes so I couldn't see the disappointment in his. I knew Vaughn would have tried to talk me out of betraying Jamie any more than I already had, so I'd kept my decision to marry Barbie to myself. Bee's parents had been waiting for me to pop the question since I entered the farce of a relationship four years ago.

"Are you and Bee really going to do this? You don't love each other. Anyone with eyes can see that."

"She doesn't have a choice, and I—"

"You're what?" Vaughn prodded.

I'm self-destructing. "I don't know anymore."

The Montgomerys were broke.

Using Barbette to increase the family's wealth had always been Elliot's plan from the moment her beauty was realized. Now that their ship was sinking, he was hell-bent on selling his daughter to the highest bidder. It didn't matter if the suitor was decrepit or cruel as long as their offer pulled the Montgomerys out of the hole Elliot had dug them into and kept them wealthy. Believing I was firmly in his daughter's snare had been what kept him from selling her to one of his golfing buddies.

Bee, Vaughn, and I had been thick as thieves for as long as I could remember. We had never known another girl who ran as fast, fought as hard, and challenged as fearlessly. She had been just another one of the boys until Jamie blew into town one summer and reminded us all that underneath the red ball cap and baggy clothes was still a girl.

The day she met Jameson Buchanan was the first time we'd ever seen her blush, and Jamie, despite his arrogance, couldn't stay away. They were best friends by the end of the summer. I was there when Bee made Jamie promise to return the next summer. She even cried a little when my uncle drove away and threatened to break my nose if I told anyone.

The doorbell rang, so Vaughn got up and looked out the window. I sat up when he blew out a harsh curse. "Well, you better figure it out...Jamie's here."

I was hoping to get some rest before round two, but it wasn't like my cousin to take the time to cool down. He'd much rather explode.

"I'm going to send him home."

"Nah...let him in." I took a look around the living room elegantly decorated with original paintings, crystal vases, and antiques. Mrs. Rees had spared no expense. "On second thought, how expensive is all this shit?"

"Very."

I stood from the couch built for style rather than comfort and started for the door when Jamie rounded the corner. He looked worse than I did even though I was the one with the fucked-up nose and busted lip. His tie was gone, my blood still stained his knuckles, and his hair looked like he'd been tugging at it.

"Call it off."

"Can't."

"I don't give a shit what you think you're protecting her from. She's not yours to protect."

"She's my friend. That gives me just as much right. You're too worried about if she's spreading her legs for me to ask yourself why she doesn't trust you with the truth."

"There is nothing she could say that would make me understand why she betrayed me."

"If that's true, then you've already lost her." Vaughn's warning didn't seem to penetrate. It only made Jamie more determined to have his way.

"Ever, if you do this, you're dead to me."

"I'm sorry you feel that way."

This time, when he charged me and swung, I ducked, barely missing the blow before delivering one of my own. He managed to counter with a powerful jab before we were pulled apart.

"What the hell is going on," Franklin bellowed as he kept Jamie restrained.

"Just working through some issues, pops."

Franklin grunted with a shake of his head.

Jamie bucked to free himself, so Franklin tightened his hold. "Cool it, kid. I don't know what's got you so fired up, but I won't have you knuckleheads destroying my home. Show some respect."

"Let me go. I'm good," Jamie gruffly asserted.

Franklin gave us both a warning look before releasing him. Vaughn loosened his hold on me when Jamie started for the door, but a chuckling Franklin stopped him with a hand on his shoulder.

"Come with me to my office, son. You look like you could use a drink." He quickly pulled Jamie from the room.

I started to nip that shit in the bud, not trusting Franklin alone with my hotheaded cousin, but Vaughn blocked me from going after them. "Move."

"The last person Jamie will listen to right now is you. Just let him go. He'll be alright."

"He better be." I may be fucking Jamie over, but he was still my cousin, and Franklin was a slimy bastard. Vaughn simply nodded before leaving to get an ice pack. I sank down onto the floor, closed my eyes, and in a moment of weakness, I pictured Four.

My father, all dressed for work, showed up at Vaughn's early the next morning. He ordered me inside his car and threatened to put me out on my ass if I disobeyed. Once inside his car, he interrogated me about Jamie's whereabouts. Apparently, he didn't go home last night.

"Would you like to tell me what's going on between you, Jamie, and that girl?"

"Not really."

"It wasn't a request."

"I asked Barbette to marry me, and Jamie got pissed about it."

"Why would he care about you proposing to your girlfriend?"

I shrugged while staring out the window.

"If you want this to end, don't stonewall me, son."

"He's in love with her."

I waited for the lecture, but he was silent as he drove up the driveway. "Is she pregnant, son?"

My head whipped toward him. "What? No!"

"I had to ask. I certainly don't agree with your choice to marry so young. I think you're making a huge mistake, and while I can't actually stop you, I'll do everything in my power to persuade you. Just don't set any dates before you graduate. Give it some time. Please." When I didn't respond, he sighed and drummed his fingers against the steering wheel. "If you truly love her, Jamie will just have to accept that she chose you, but I don't want you to forget that he's family. Talk to him, and in time, he will forgive you." He cut the engine and chuckled. "To be honest, I'm surprised by all of this for a different reason."

"What reason?"

"I was afraid that it was Four one of you boys were sweet on."

It was all I could do not to show my father how close to the mark he'd come.

"What made you think that?"

"I had my suspicions when she came home marked up after being out all night with the two of you." His eyes sharpened as he stared me down. "Know anything about that?"

I shook my head when I couldn't find my voice.

"Good. I'm not sure I would approve of a scandal like that happening under my roof."

"Did you tell her mom?" Four may not ever speak to me again, but I'd warn her anyway.

"I considered it, but she's eighteen and having a hard enough time adjusting. I'm just glad you're getting along after what happened last year."

"She turned out to be pretty cool." *And my everything.*

"I knew you two would just need to get to know each other." He ruffled my hair like he often did when I was a kid. When I mean mugged him, he chuckled, and I reluctantly gave into a grin. We haven't had a lot of moments like these. "Now get upstairs and get your uniform on. You've missed enough days."

My eyes bucked. I didn't think he knew about that, but I'd obviously underestimated how tight his leash was.

"Don't look so surprised. I may run a multi-billion dollar company, but you're my son. *My only son.* I know you sneak out at night, and I know you skip school. The only reason I haven't tagged your ass is that I was once your age…but don't push it." He nodded his head toward the house—a silent order to get moving, so I did.

Upstairs, I heard Four moving around in her room and Jay D making a ruckus. I wanted to go to her, but what would I say? The way she looked at me last night...there was no coming back from that. I showered and dressed in record time, and when I grabbed my notebook from my nightstand, my gaze fell on the phone. Not giving pride time to catch up, I grabbed the phone and headed to Four's room. Figuring she'd shut the door in my face when she answered, I barged inside only to be disappointed when I found the room empty.

I somberly trudged across the room and placed the phone on the nightstand.

"What are you doing here?"

Glancing over my shoulder, I saw Four standing in her doorway holding Jay D's leash. She must have been taking the mutt for a walk. When I turned to face her, however, I felt kicked in the gut. Her eyes were red and puffy from crying, and the color in her cheeks had utterly drained. Knowing that I did that to her made me hate myself even more.

"You didn't have to give this back. It's yours."

"Thanks," she dryly offered, "but I don't need it."

"Then let me take you to school." I didn't give a shit that I was borderline begging.

"Why would I do that?"

"Because we need to talk. I owe you an apology."

"You don't owe me anything, Ever. You made that very clear." She shouldered her backpack and turned to go. I should have let her.

"Please."

Her head turned ever so slightly, and I thought I might have broken through until she spoke. "Good," she tartly uttered. "I like you begging. Now you can watch me walk away like you did."

I've single-handedly turned my life into shit. The news about the engagement spread through school and the town like wildfire. A week later, I was still putting out fires when it got back to me that Four had also been taking some of the heat. I kept close so she'd have my protection until Tyra took it upon herself to enlighten me.

"Stalking her is only making things worse," she hissed. We had Calculus together, and usually, Tyra sat on the far side of the room, but today, she chose to occupy the seat next to me.

"What do you expect me to do? Someone spray painted an A on her locker this morning."

"You made your bed, now lie in it."

She quickly collected her bag to switch seats, but I grabbed her arm to stop her. "Tyra…help me."

"Why the fuck should I?"

"She doesn't eat or talk, and she barely sleeps."

She looked me up and down. "You look like you could use a nap yourself."

"I sit outside her door and listen to her cry the entire night, so no, I haven't been sleeping."

"What do you expect from her? To be your side piece while you live in marital bliss with Barbie?"

"There's not going to be a wedding. There never was."

"Then why did you propose?"

"To buy Barbie some time."

"For what?"

I shook my head in frustration. "I can't tell you, and I've already told Four what I could."

"Obviously, it wasn't enough. You're helping Barbie because you care about her, but does she care about you? She's willing to let you lose the girl you love. A friend wouldn't let you pay that steep a price. It's not easy to bare your demons to someone you don't know, but Barbie wouldn't be doing it for Four, she'd be doing it for *you*."

"Are you saying Four would be willing to be with me even if it's in secret?"

"That depends...how scary are the skeletons in Barbie's closet?"

For the rest of the day, I considered Tyra's advice before finally deciding that I could never ask that of Barbie. The only reason I even knew what her father planned was that I had been in the wrong place at the wrong time. That night, I sat in front of Four's door for the fifth night in a row and let her soft sobs keep me awake.

It was Halloween, and the last thing I wanted was to party, but when Vaughn texted that it was an "Anything But Clothes" party hosted by some college douchebags and that Tyra was bringing Four, I picked myself up from the floor. It no longer mattered as much that today was the anniversary of the day my mother walked out on her family.

I was pretty trashed already after drinking what seemed like an entire distillery, so I had Vaughn drive me since Jamie had kept true to his word. I was as good as grass to him.

One day, when Barbie was safe from her father, I'd do everything in my power to get my cousin back. Even if it meant getting my ass kicked again.

The party was being held in a cul-de-sac the next town over at a two-story home with a small porch, blue shutters, and not much yard. With all the houses on the block, it wouldn't be long before the police showed up. I was hopping out the car before Vaughn came to a full stop, but he'd caught up with me by the time I made it to the front door.

Some of the costumes were pretty inventive while others had kept it simple. I saw a few cereal boxes and iPod shuffles. One guy had made a jumpsuit using a monopoly board, and the cash. Some of the girls were covered up in trash bags, saran wrap, or duct tape. A few guys, like Vaughn and me, made togas out of bedsheets, but one dickhead only wore a pizza box. I dreaded seeing what Four might or might *not* be wearing. While I could appreciate the view, I wasn't eager to share it.

I spotted Jamie across the room wearing the flag of Scotland around his waist and standing next to him was Four and Tyra. They had gone with the popular choice of caution tape. Tyra had fashioned a two-piece ensemble while Four had thankfully chosen to show less skin and made a dress. Her hair was pulled up into her usual ponytail although higher than normal, showing off her slender shoulders. Even in the dim lighting, her skin glistened, making her tan skin look even more kissable. I already knew she'd smell mouthwatering even though her scent wasn't nearly as titillating as when she first came to Blackwood Keep. When she returned from her stint in Europe, I learned that she'd made the switch to *Dove*. The change had nearly driven me insane enough to demand she'd switch back, but I knew she was more likely to castrate me than please me. As much as I loved her scent, I loved my nine inches more.

Tyra was the first to spot us and sneakily warned Four with a nudge before seductively dancing over to Vaughn. He didn't waste time pulling her into him, and they began a lewd bump and grind on the dance floor. Jamie noticed me approaching and leaned down to whisper something in Four's ear before moving away with a scowl. I watched him go until he disappeared into the kitchen where the drinks were most likely set up.

When I faced Four again, her blank stare punched a hole in my heart. "Hey."

"Move along, McNamara. I've got enough problems."

I should have been discouraged, but I'd rather have her hatred than nothing at all. "Can I talk to you?"

"I think I've had enough of what comes out of your mouth." She moved around me, and I trailed behind her until

Jamie came out of nowhere and stopped me with a hand on my chest.

"Why don't you leave her alone? You've done enough."

"Is it her you're really concerned about, or are you just itching for another fight?"

"Shit. Both." He shoved me back, and I stumbled a little, thanks to the booze I had indulged in before coming here. "You're drunk, aren't you?" The disgust in his voice was a bit hypocritical since he was hardly ever sober.

"Ever, just go home," Four pleaded.

"Come with me, and I will."

"I'm not going to do that."

"Then I'm sticking around. Where you go, I go."

"Stalker," Jamie coughed.

I ignored him and begged Four with my eyes to talk to me.

I saw her surrender long before she realized it herself.

"Okay." She headed for the stairs, and I started to follow, but then Jamie stopped me from leaving with a harsh grip on my shoulder.

"You do her a favor when you screw up so the next time that happens, do us all one and stay away."

I nodded and followed her up the stairs. I had no idea how to make it right, but I'd figure it out. We found an empty room, and the moment the door was shut, I exhaled into the dark.

I watched her move across the room putting as much distance between us as possible. It made me wish for a time machine so that I could go back and stop myself from walking out that door. I had been pissed as fuck knowing I'd never get another shot at bringing my mom home. But when I tried to close the door to my heart, I realized Four still had the key. I also realized she didn't make me save her that night. I chose her because I always would. And my mom wouldn't have had it any other way.

"You insist on making this harder than it has to be."

"If I could tell you why I asked Bee to marry me, I would."

"Your secrets didn't break me, Ever. You did. You're warm one day and cold the next. Just when I believe I'm your everything, you treat me like I'm nothing."

"I thought I could let you be."

"And because you're having second thoughts, I'm supposed to just run into your arms?"

"It's what you want, isn't it?"

"What I want no longer matters. For the first time ever, I'm doing what's best for me."

"If you want me to let you go, you're going to have to prove it's what you really want because I won't ever stop trying."

She suddenly had trouble meeting my gaze. "You'll get bored, Ever. You always do."

My eyes narrowed as I pushed away from the door. "You think I got bored?" Four was the single most fascinating person I'd met in a long time. She was an amalgamation of right and wrong and exactly the girl my mother warned would steal my heart and then dare me to take it back.

"I think you seek me out when you need a thrill and then toss me aside when you're done playing."

"If you truly believed that, you wouldn't be worried about me winning you back."

"I'm not worried because you never had me." I listened to the lie slip through her perfect lips and smiled.

"Oh, baby, you're terrified."

chapter thirty-seven

The Puppet

THE POLICE SHOWED UP BEFORE I COULD DENY HIS CLAIM, SO EVER and I got out of dodge before the police could ask us for ID. Tyra and I had ridden to the party with Jamie who had been happy to have a DD. *"As a rule, I don't let chicks drive my wheels, but Four, you're a one of a kind chick."*

Since he had managed to shed his sobriety within an hour of arriving, I jumped into the driver's seat. Starting the car, I caught sight of Vaughn carrying a giggling Tyra bridal style to his car. The front passenger door was yanked open, and assuming it was Jamie, I flashed a smile only for it to fall when Ever slid his long frame inside the Wrangler.

"Didn't you ride with Vaughn?" I was hoping he'd take the hint and get lost.

Instead, he flashed a wicked grin and got comfortable. The back door opened a moment later, and Jamie dived inside.

"I didn't say you were welcome in my ride," Jamie slurred.

"You gonna make me leave, motherfucker?"

Tired of watching them lock horns, I drove off before either one of them could make good on the challenge.

Jamie reached from the back seat and tossed his phone with the GPS activated into my lap. "There's another party not far from here."

"She's not going to another party," Ever dictated.

I had been ready to call it a night until Ever's highhandedness forced me into another rebellion. When would he learn?

I followed the GPS while Jamie clumsily changed clothes in the back seat. Twenty minutes later, we arrived at a corn maze in the middle of nowhere. There were maybe ten or fifteen cars parked every which way. I sent a text to Tyra.

Where are you?

She immediately responded:

TYRA: The party pooper is taking me home. Talk tomorrow. <3

We jumped out, and Jamie immediately announced that he was going to find the beers before taking off. Music was already blaring, drinks were being passed around, the conversation was flowing, and every once in a while, I'd hear a scream or two followed by raucous laughter. It wasn't until a breeze touched my skin that I realized why this wasn't such a smart idea.

I casually looked around and caught Ever eyeing me.

"You're cold, aren't you?"

"No." Another breeze came making me shiver violently. *Why didn't I bring a change of clothes? Better yet, why couldn't I have given my stupid pride a rest?*

Shaking his head, he stomped around me and yanked open the back of the Wrangler. After digging around, I nearly cried tears of joy when he found a sweatshirt. Bliss was short-lived, however, when he shoved the sweatshirt over my head.

"I can take care of myself," I huffed when my head was free, and the sweatshirt fell halfway down my thighs. It covered more than the tape did and instantly provided me with warmth.

"If you were any good at it, you wouldn't be here."

"No. If you weren't such a dick, I wouldn't be here."

"You thought you'd teach me a lesson by torturing yourself? Smart." His sarcasm—and maybe because he was right—had me turning away and rushing toward the entrance of the maze. I thought for sure he'd follow me, but when I glanced over my shoulder, I realized I was alone.

Shrugging, I rounded the first corner and was almost run down by a redheaded cheerleader fleeing from the clutches of some ass-hole wearing a Freddy Krueger mask. When my heart rate finally slowed, I moved through the maze, though a bit more cautiously. After ten minutes of trying to find the exit, I accepted that I was lost. It was unfortunate that I'd also left my phone in the car. I kept going, knowing eventually, I'd find my way out. I could still hear the party going, but I hadn't run into anyone else, and it seemed the deeper I ventured, the fainter the sounds I clung to became.

Though the maze wasn't entirely swallowed by darkness, I'd long lost the bright lights. I would have turned back if not for the sudden hair-raising sensation of being followed. I stopped and faced the way I came with feet spread and hands planted on my hips.

"Ever, I'm not in the mood for games. Show yourself." I immediately shrank in size when a hulking figure dressed from head to toe in black rubber and polyester stepped from the shadows. "Oh. My mistake…Hey, you wouldn't happen to know where the exit is, would you?"

His silence was like ice-cold fingers tiptoeing down my spine. Maybe I was overreacting but…wouldn't someone who was *not* a psycho respond? I stumbled away when he inched closer, but when he lunged at me, I screamed from my belly and bolted. Up ahead, the path split into two, but I didn't have time to debate which one would lead me to the exit or down a dead end.

My heart pumped in overdrive, and the fist in my stomach clenched tighter as I ran down one path after the next. Were those footsteps I heard pounding after me or only my imagination? I wasn't sure how far I'd gotten when I collided with a hard body. I clawed and kicked until strong hands seized my arms.

"For fuck's sake, Four, what is the matter with you?"

The familiar voice penetrated my fear, and I realized it was Jamie staring down at me like I was possessed. I was so relieved I jumped into his arms and threw my own around his neck. There was no way in hell I was letting go.

"What happened?"

"Some creep in a rubber suit was chasing me."

He exhaled as if relieved. "It was probably just one of those assholes."

I laid my head against his chest and nodded even though I was still shaken up. It had felt so real.

"Why did you run off like that, anyway?" he scolded.

"Ever pissed me off."

"You gotta stop letting him under your skin, lass."

As if it were that easy. "You're one to talk."

His strong chest vibrated when he grunted his agreement.

"Do you know how to get out of here?"

"Not really."

I lifted my head to see if he was joking. He wasn't. "Damn it, Jamie!"

"Calm down, girl. This isn't the Bermuda triangle. We'll find the exit eventually." His eyes passed over me approvingly. "You look good in my shit."

I rolled my eyes heavenward. "Let's go."

"We will, but first, I'd like to give Ever a taste of his own medicine."

I was too startled by his hands suddenly cupping my ass to ask what he'd meant.

"Jamie?"

Soft lips pressed against mine, and I had to admit—he was very good. Maybe that's why, when he sought access, my lips parted just a teeny bit. His tongue had no more than swept inside when he was yanked away, and a furious Ever stood in his place. He was now dressed in light gray joggers and white long-sleeve he'd no doubt pillaged from Jamie.

"What the *fuck* do you think you're doing?"

I was the one pinned under his black look even though Jamie kissed *me*. I would have eventually pushed him away, but a part of me had relished the thought of hurting Ever. Needless to say, I was now regretting the impulse.

I looked to Jamie for assistance and found him nowhere in sight. I let out a dry chuckle when I realized he had used me once again to fuck with his cousin. I turned in the direction Jamie had come but didn't get far when I felt Ever's arms wrap around me from behind.

"I asked you a question," he hummed in my ear.

"And I declined to answer. Now let me go."

Of course, he didn't listen and manhandled me into facing him, instead.

"Why did you kiss him?" He looked physically in pain like I'd gutted him with a knife rather than kissed his cousin.

"He kissed me."

"You kissed him back."

I snorted. "Barely."

"I fucked up, so I'm trying to be patient, but you're pushing it."

"How chivalrous, but I told you I would be done if you walked away. You're just surprised I meant it."

"There's no such thing as done." His hand slid to my neck and held me in place while the other pulled down the zipper. "We're in too deep."

Our teeth clashed when our lips met, but neither of us cared. As long as I lived, I would never forget the feeling of having him this close. I heard the tape wrapped around my body tear, and then the cold air touched my skin. He spun me around until my back was to him and then folded me in half with a hand on my nape. Feeling his cock lined up at my entrance I pushed my hips back.

"Oh, and in case you're getting ideas about Jamie…" He shoved hard until he was fully inside of me. "Don't."

My breath caught as pleasure heightened. He was deep and getting deeper by the second. The screams, laughter, and pounding footsteps kept me on edge, but I felt the familiar rush of adrenaline at the knowledge that, at any moment, we might be caught.

"Someone might see," I whimpered.

That only got me a slap on the ass and pounded even harder. His other hand curled around my hip to toy with my clit.

Yes. It wasn't long before I was coming long and hard.

"Come here," he growled when I grew limp in his arms.

I let him pull me onto my knees where he held me by my throat. I had no clue what he intended until his warm release was already coating my lips. When he finished, he tucked himself inside his sweats before crouching down to meet my shocked gaze. "Remember my cum on your lips the next time you think about kissing your next rebound."

Shame coursed through my body, but I refused to let him win. Holding his stare, I licked him from my lips, surprised to find he tasted a little salty but sweet too.

Chuckling, he kissed my lips and stood before offering a hand. I let him pull me up, and the moment I was on my feet, I reared back and punched him. Now he'd have a black eye to go with that split lip. He was glowering when the shock cleared, but then he was kissing me, and it felt even better than blacking his eye.

"I don't like you kissing other boys," he confessed between kisses.

"Well, that's all you had to say," I snapped.

He kissed me again, but this time, it was soft and lingering, allowing me to toy with his tongue ring.

"You making some sort of fashion statement with that thing?"

A wicked gleam appeared in his eyes. "It's not for fashion."

"So the rumors are true." The intrusion of his nemesis had Ever stiffening.

I quickly pulled out of his arms as Jason, dressed as a pirate, strolled down the path on my right with his hands in his pockets. Of all the parties happening tonight, what were the odds we'd be at the same one? I zipped up the sweatshirt and tried to match Ever's indifference but was finding it hard when he did it so effortlessly.

"I thought you learned by now that it's bad for your health to provoke me," Ever said suspiciously casual.

"Don't mind me, King of Brynwood. I'm just enjoying a late-night stroll." Jason shot me a lascivious smile before disappearing around the bend.

"Do you think he saw us?" My chest hurt from how hard my heart was pounding.

"He would have had a lot more to say if he had." Taking my hand, he led me out of the maze.

Leaning against his car, drinking a beer, Jamie flashed us a knowing smile that wasn't entirely friendly. "Took you guys long enough." He glanced down and focused on a piece of torn tape hanging near my thigh. "Frankly, I wouldn't have guessed this uptight prick was into exhibitionism. Especially when the fucker is getting *married*."

Ever ignored him and held out his hand to me. "Give me the keys."

"Aw," I teased, forgetting Jamie's misery. "Macho man doesn't want to be driven home?" He smirked and fished the keys from my pocket. "How do I know you're sober enough?"

"You didn't leave me much choice. Man can't even be wasted in peace," he grumbled.

"I didn't ask you to follow me."

"Because you knew I would," he smoothly retorted.

"Hey, Four," Jamie interrupted, "didn't you say it was some douchebag in a rubber suit who chased you?"

"Yeah," I answered warily. Ever was now staring a hole in the side of my head. "Why?"

Rather than answer, Jamie pointed at the left side of the maze where Daniel Kim, cloaked in rubber and holding his mask, huddled in a circle with Max Cooper, Adam Turner, and... Jason Portland. Jason handed Daniel a beer, and they clinked the cans together while the others laughed outrageously, no doubt at my expense.

My jaw tightened at their triumph at the same time Ever charged. I stared after him with wide eyes. Surely, he wasn't going to fight them? It was four against one! Not even Ever could beat those odds. A moment later, Jamie handed me his beer, cracked his knuckles with a smile, and hurried after his cousin.

Ever was only a couple of steps away by the time the guys noticed him. The first punch landed in Daniel's gut, and then he immediately rammed his elbow into Jason's face. Adam and Max were already backing down with hands raised, but Jamie didn't seem to care when he delivered a mean two-piece and then an uppercut. I thought it was over until Ever picked up Daniel from the ground and whispered something in his ear. He then pointed a threatening finger at Jason before walking away calmer than he'd been a minute ago.

"You guys need to learn how to walk away from a fight," I scolded when they reached me. "Or better yet, don't start them."

"Someone fucks with you, they fuck with us," Jamie lipped. "Get used to it."

"You didn't have to hit those other guys," I argued after we climbed into the Wrangler. "They clearly didn't want to fight."

"My hearing is impeccable," he boasted. "Trust me, they had it coming."

I let it go but not before noticing how Ever never bothered to defend his actions. *Typical.*

A couple of hours and one long, hot shower later, I was in bed replaying the events from tonight. It seemed that all Ever had to do was snap his fingers, and I was right back under his spell.

Slowly and quietly, my door opened, and he slipped inside. "Am I welcome?"

Sighing, I sat up and pushed my hair behind my ear. "You know the answer to that, but you won't care, will you?"

"I'd go if I knew you meant it." If he was feeling cocky, he was smart enough not to show it.

"You're inside my head now?"

"I don't need to be. What you're feeling is always on the surface. You don't bother to hide—especially from me. I like that." When I didn't respond, he locked the door and then slid into bed with me. "Come here." He began to peel away my nightclothes.

"W—what are you doing?" I sputtered.

"There's too much between us already."

I didn't understand what that meant until he shed his pajama bottoms and wrapped his body around mine. It felt good to have his skin melded with mine. I tried not to focus on the *other* part of him touching me.

"I can't believe I let tonight happen," I whispered as I lay in his arms.

"If not today, then tomorrow. I told you, I'm not giving up."

"Even after you're married?" My tone dripped acid.

He took a deep breath and then released it slowly. "I give you my word it will never come to that."

"Don't make promises you can't keep, McNamara."

He didn't respond, but I let him hold me anyway. It was the only thing keeping my heart from splitting in two.

Tomorrow, I'll be stronger.

When his breathing was almost even, I whispered, "We could have been friends, you know. You didn't have to hate me." And maybe then we wouldn't be lying in bed together with nothing between us but our tattered hearts.

"It wouldn't have mattered, princess. I would have fallen for you anyway."

chapter thirty-eight

the Puppet

THE WHISTLE BLEW, AND THE SOUND OF FEET POUNDING THE PAVEMENT was all that could be heard. Pretty soon, I drowned that out too and concentrated on my breathing. When the final bell rang, everyone headed for the locker rooms.

Just one more lap.

Running didn't fill the void, but it gave me an outlet.

After my third lap, I popped Jamie's earbuds out and held my knees. "I wouldn't do that."

Thinking I had been alone, I swung around with my eyes wide. Behind me stood a gorgeous male with blond hair, green eyes, and a friendly smile. He was only a couple inches taller than I was, but what he lacked in height, he made up for with muscle. His arms bulged when he propped his hands on his hips in that masculine way guys did. *Maybe too much muscle.*

"It's harder to breathe down there."

"I think that's a myth."

"Shit. Really?"

I burst out laughing and was floored when he actually blushed. Ever would never blush. "Sorry, I wasn't laughing at you."

"It's okay. I wouldn't mind embarrassing myself again to see that smile."

Oh. Heat crept up my neck and warmed my cheeks. "So, you're in Coach Lloyd's class?" He was covered in sweat, and the gym uniform was molded to him.

"Yeah, I wanted to talk to you, but you ran away," he teased.

"I wasn't running away!" This time, I didn't laugh alone.

"I felt like a creep following you around the track."

My cheeks stung from smiling so hard. "I think it would have been weirder if you watched me."

His eyebrows rose. "Like those guys?"

My face fell when I followed the direction of his nod. *What the hell?*

Across the field, Ever had his arms braced on the bleacher railing. He was staring dead at me with Jamie wearing a shit-eating grin as he stood at his side. I didn't know if it was just my body cooling down, but suddenly, the November air had a biting chill.

"They're just my ride home. What did you want to talk about?"

"Right. Um...Would you like to grab a bite with me tonight?"

My eyes bulged. Was I actually being asked out on a date? I couldn't keep from glancing across the field.

He's engaged, you moron.

My handsome suitor, whose name I still didn't know, rubbed his nape and said, "I'd understand if there was someone else." I saw the truth in his eyes and couldn't help feeling like a fool.

No more.

"What's your name?" I was a little embarrassed to ask since we shared a class, and he probably knew mine.

"Michael."

I stuck out my hand, which felt lame once I did it. "Michael, it's a date."

With a quiet chuckle, his hand enveloped mine.

"You can't wear that dress without these earrings."

"I'm not wearing those."

"But they'll go perfectly!"

"Put down the gold hoops, Tyra Bradley. It's not going to happen."

"Fine," she grumbled and rummaged through her box full of costume jewelry. Rosalyn had my ears pierced when I was a kid, but I stopped wearing jewelry the day I started dressing myself. "How about a compromise?" She held up simple gold studs.

"No."

"Honestly, Four!"

"Be grateful I put on the dress." I didn't even recognize the girl in the mirror. When I told Tyra about my date, she roped me into shopping and then bullied me into buying a light gray sweater dress and flat black boots that reached my calf. My hair fell in waves around my shoulders, and I'd let Tyra coat my lips in that sticky shit. When she came at me with a little brush covered in black gunk, I had to put my foot down.

"I guess we're done here." She looked me over and started squealing. "He's going to eat his heart out!"

I smiled nervously while forcing myself not to undo all of her hard work. Knowing Tyra, she'd murder me and then cry over my dead body. "I don't think he will since he'll be on the date, too."

That got me an eye roll. "I'm not talking about Michael."

I didn't have to ask who else she could mean. My stomach dipped at the thought of Ever seeing me like this. With my hair glossed and framing my face, and the short dress hugging my body, I looked like the kind of girl who belonged on his arm. "Ever isn't the reason I agreed to this date."

"Fine, but just tell me one thing." I met her gaze and waited. "Does he know?"

By the time I jogged across the field after Michael and I exchanged numbers, Ever had disappeared, and the only explanation Jamie offered was that he caught a ride.

"It wouldn't matter. He's with Barbie, and I'm...exploring my options."

"But are you sure it's over between you two?"

"Hard to be over when we never started." The doorbell rang, so I grabbed my phone and after a moment's hesitation, the little purse a teary-eyed Rosalyn loaned me before heading out for her own date night. As much as I didn't want to be seen with such a feminine thing, I could never deny her. I knew too well how much it hurt.

And if I ever had the courage, I would one day admit that against my will I truly loved Rosalyn.

As I stuffed my wallet, phone, Chapstick, and mace inside, I wondered if the purse was simply her sign of approval or a peace offering. It had been more than a week since she handed over my birth certificate, and since then, we'd gone back to living our separate lives.

"Thanks for looking after Jay D."

"Yeah, sure," Tyra absently replied.

I waved goodbye, but lost in her head, she didn't wave back.

Not wanting to keep Michael waiting, I left her to her thoughts and headed for the stairs. When I reached them, I froze on the landing and gaped at the scene happening below.

Vaughn held Michael against the wall with a hand on his shoulder while Jamie boldly reached into his jacket pocket and pulled out his wallet. *No. Oh, fuck no.*

"ID, credit cards, club cards...*condoms?*" Jamie clicked his tongue and pulled out the foil wrappers. "Won't be needing those, playboy."

I practically leaped down the stairs. "What the *hell* do you think you're doing?"

Michael sagged with relief while Vaughn dropped his arm and said, "Just making sure your *friend* will be the perfect gentleman."

I crossed my arms. "Who asked you to butt in?"

"Sheathe your claws, kitten. You're lucky we're letting you go at all."

I whirled on Jamie. "Excuse me?" What the hell made them think they could stop me?

"You heard me."

"Vaughn, you promised!" Tyra shrieked as she flew down the stairs.

"I said I wouldn't kick his ass." He shrugged while keeping his expression perfectly blank. "I didn't."

I started to apologize to Michael when the source of my current woes appeared at the top of the stairs. Ever was dressed casually in a white long-sleeve and dark jeans. He was obviously heading somewhere, but he didn't move, and the black look he gave Michael sent a chill down my spine.

"Her curfew is at ten," Vaughn supplied. "Have her home by nine, or we go hunting."

I didn't waste time grabbing Michael's hand, but we were kept from leaving by Jamie, who insolently took our clasped hands and separated them. "There's a no touching clause."

I'd had enough.

I marched to the bottom of the stairs, and Ever's gaze swept me as I did. Even through the anger, I could see his desire. "Call off your guard dogs and don't interfere."

He lifted his chin. "Or what?"

With a grace I didn't realize I possessed, I turned on my heel and peeked over my shoulder as I swayed toward my nervous date. "You really want to find out?"

"How's your milkshake?"

"Yummy, thank you. I've never had to eat one with a spoon before, though. They were better off just serving a bowl of ice cream."

He tried his luck, but the shake didn't make it very far up the straw. "You might be right."

"It's a gift." I sighed, making him laugh.

Michael had chosen a pizzeria for our date, and I had to admit, it was going well despite the messy start. Michael and I even had some things in common: Sloppy Joes, *Sons of Anarchy*, and an aversion to country music. But when he claimed NASCAR was boring, I seriously questioned seeing him after tonight.

"So, if you don't mind my asking…"

Please don't bring him up.

"What was that all about earlier?"

I sighed and slumped a little in my seat. Rosalyn, if she could see me now, would just die. Michael had been gracious when I apologized and didn't ask questions. I had hoped it would be left at that. Especially since he now knew Ever and I were more than just house buddies.

"I don't mean to pry," he rushed to add. "I never minded the rumors about you and him because I thought they were just rumors."

My heart sank. Was I being dumped? Already?

"After what I saw tonight, I'm not so sure. I like you a lot, but I don't want to get in the middle of anything."

"There's no beginning, middle, or end. Ever is engaged to Barbie. I'm just the girl who sleeps across the hall."

"So tonight was?" He looked hopeful but wary.

"Ever toying with me for the last time."

Seemingly satisfied, he nodded, and we managed to get through the rest of our meal without either one of us bringing up Ever McNamara.

"Laugh all you want, but if I go down again, I'm taking you with me."

After dinner, Michael took me to the local skating rink. Neither of us was any good, but it was fun to watch each other fall.

"You can try, but I have at least twenty pounds on you."

My jaw dropped as I grabbed the rail. "Either you're selling yourself short, or you're calling me fat."

He roared, and to my delight, fell on his ass when he forgot about balance.

"Serves you right." I reached out a hand, which I realized he took out of politeness because I wasn't really much help.

"I don't think I'm going to sit down for a week." He pulled his phone out and checked the time. "What do you say we get you home?"

I peered at his still lit screen and frowned. "But it's only eight thirty. I can stay out until ten."

"Ah, yeah." He rubbed the back of his neck. "It's just that I have some homework to catch up on before I hit the sack."

I might have believed him if he wasn't staring at the floor.

Chicken shit.

After he drove me home, I let him walk me to the door and even agreed to a second date, but any hope I had of this going anywhere died when he walked away without a goodnight kiss.

I found Tyra, Vaughn, and Jamie in the family room watching *Now You See Me* and tried not to dwell on where the lord of the manor might be.

Tyra was the first to notice me and abandoned her cozy spot under Vaughn's arm, much to his displeasure. "So, how was it?" she prodded.

"I had a good time."

She seemed a little distressed by my answer. "Then why aren't there stars in your eyes?"

I peeked at Vaughn and Jamie who were doing a horrible job of pretending not to listen.

"It was only the first date." *Lame.* By the disappointment in her eyes, Tyra wasn't buying it, either.

"I know why there aren't stars in her eyes," Jamie boasted.

"Oh, yeah?" Tyra whirled around to face him. "Do tell."

He shared a smug look with Vaughn. "What time is it?"

Vaughn made a show of checking the time. "Eight fifty-nine."

"And are you happy with yourselves?" Tyra scolded with her hands on her hips.

"My best friend spent the night sulking. What do you think?"

I found myself glaring at Vaughn, and he glared right back. "So, screw me and what I want?"

"You want Ever," Vaughn gritted. Much softer he said, "And Ever wants you."

"That's what happens when you grow up entitled. You never stop to consider what you even deserve."

Green eyes flashed, but he stayed silent, and I didn't stick around. I said goodnight to Tyra, ignored Vaughn and Jamie, and rushed upstairs to get these damn clothes off and my hair in a ponytail.

Love could blow me.

chapter thirty-nine

The Peer

MY HANDS WERE BRACED ON HER DOOR, BUT I COULDN'T BRING myself to knock. I could hear her moving around and cooing nonsense to her mutt as she removed that sexy fucking dress she wore for him and not me.

When I held her after the corn maze, I was ready to do whatever it took to keep her. But then she warned me not to make promises I couldn't keep, and I remembered the one I made four years ago. I was just a fucking kid, but I never regretted the vow.

Until I was forced to watch a guy notice her and not care that she was mine.

I could have ripped him apart and driven him away. It would have been so easy. The hard part had been letting her go.

I didn't count on Vaughn and Jamie stepping in to remind her that she was mine. The selfish part of me hoped she'd submit and call it off, but my wild girl had other plans.

I rested my forehead on the door.

Always so damn troublesome.

A second later, I stumbled over the threshold. I caught my footing before I could kiss the carpet. Four looked ready for bed in her tiny shorts and T-shirt with her hair swept up in a messy bun.

"What the hell are you doing hugging my door?"

I could feel the heat rising in my cheeks, and when her jaw dropped, I looked away.

"A—are you blushing?"

"No." I peeked at her.

She looked like a fucking puffer fish as she held in her laugh.

"So, what did you need?"

You. "Nothing. You going somewhere?" I questioned and instantly regretted it. Not only did I look like a stalker but I was also starting to sound like one, too. Some inherent part of me that Four had awakened wanted to find the nearest blunt object and drag her to my room. Instead, I watched her sassily stick out her hip and cross her arms over her perky tits. Moisture pooled in my mouth when I remembered how sweet her nipples tasted.

"I was getting into bed when I saw your shadow under the door." I didn't speak, and neither did she. "Well, I'm pretty tired," she hinted when the silence became awkward.

"Goodnight." I forced myself back into the hall and had only taken a couple of steps when she spoke.

"Hey, Ever?" The confidence in her voice was gone, and she was chewing on her lip when I turned around.

Don't touch her.

"Yeah?"

"Should dates end with a goodnight kiss?"

I stopped breathing. Did she not realize what she gave away?

I ate the distance between us and enlightened her. I'd long lost count of how many kisses I've stolen, but what I did know was that I'd never gone this slowly with her. I wanted to savor every second.

Closer.

My hands followed the command and caressed down her sides, cupped her ass, and lifted until she was on the tip of her cute little toes, and every inch of her pressed against me. Needing to mark her everywhere, I kissed down her neck. When she shivered against me, my smirk pressed against her skin. *That fucker will never be what she needs.*

As if reading my thoughts, she pushed me away. I wanted to grab her again, but her tears stopped me.

"Four—" I started, but she cut me off by ripping my heart out and pissing me off all at once.

"How can you touch me like that when you do nothing but hurt me?"

"Because I was so damn angry!" I didn't mean to explode, but once I did, I couldn't stop. "I had just gotten back hope of bringing my mother home when my father decided to start a new family instead. My mother was still his *wife*. He didn't even fight for her."

Rather than the understanding I'd come to expect from Four, she stared back at me in disbelief. "Your mother walked out on him and left him with a son to raise alone. What was there to fight for?"

A muscle inside my jaw ticked. "I guess it doesn't matter now. He's moved on."

I could tell that was the wrong thing to say when she flinched. "We're done here."

Fuck! Every time I get an inch with her, I put my foot in my mouth.

I hooked my finger into her shorts and brought her to me. "I don't blame you, baby. Never you."

She coldly shoved me away again. "But you did, Ever. I spent a year in exile because you wanted your *mommy* back. Am I just supposed to forget that?"

"You don't understand. You were a mirror that I couldn't break. Seeing you so wild and brave and free reminded me who I used to be. It wasn't just your body that tempted me. It was your soul, baby. For the first time, I wanted to be free no matter the consequences, and that scared me. I *had* to send you away."

I saw the ice slowly melting away, and for a moment, I had hope.

"No." She wiped her face, leaving wet streaks. "You didn't." The moment her hand fell away, her gaze hardened. "If you had stopped to know me beyond what you saw, you would have found someone who understood more than anyone what you sacrifice every day."

"I know."

She nodded, accepting my shame. "So what do you expect me to do?"

"Forgive me so we can move on." I was lost, without answers, and left with only what was in my heart for survival. "I want to be with you, Four Archer."

She paused. Shock had made her damn near comatose. Up until now, I had never made my intentions clear. I'd never told her exactly where she stood with me. Instead, I left her hanging from a fucking cliff.

"I *did* forgive you, Ever." The tear that fell down her cheek and the way she cradled her body as if protecting herself from me, completely fucking wrecked me. "But then you hurt me for the last time when you got engaged."

chapter forty

the Puppet

WE WERE STANDING OUTSIDE MY WOMEN'S HISTORY CLASS when Michael popped the question. "So, my parents asked me to invite you over for dinner tomorrow night."

Shaking hands clutched the straps of my backpack. "You don't think it's a little soon?"

It had only been a couple of weeks since our first date, and I wouldn't have dared introduce him to Rosalyn this soon.

After our date, I had considered breaking it off, but our second had gone so much better when Ever and his band of arrogant assholes didn't try to sabotage it. Michael had even been bold enough to kiss me.

Sadly, the ache in my belly for the next one never came. And no matter how many times he's kissed me since, I couldn't shake the suspicion that I was only using him as a distraction.

"My parents are a little old-fashioned."

When Michael had picked me up for our date in a blue BMW, I knew his parents had money. Meeting them would be a huge step toward becoming official. What if they didn't approve of me?

Do I even want this?

"Dinner sounds good." I felt like a coward.

"Cool." Noticing that I didn't share his excitement, he added, "Don't look so worried! My parents are gonna love you."

I wasn't worried. I was drowning. And when you're dying, it isn't worry you feel. It's pure panic.

He kissed me in front of our riveted audience, and among them was Barbie. I could tell by her disgusted look that she'd heard every word. I mentally shrugged off her puzzling reaction. She should have been happy that I was no longer poaching on her territory. It certainly shamed me to know that Barbie had been right after all. She was the one to wear Ever's ring.

Michael took off for his own class oblivious to the attention. When we showed up together for the football game last Thursday, people took notice. The tweets and statuses Tyra showed me were all vague, but I was a smart girl.

She chose him over Ever?

Ever is way hotter!

I know he's engaged, but I'd be his side bitch.

No more wondering if he hit that yet.

So much for being undesirable. Can I have next?

First, they slut-shamed me for wanting Ever, and then they mocked me for moving on. High school was a fickle place.

Class started, but I couldn't focus on the lecture Mrs. Roberts was giving about reproductive rights. Feeling Barbie's gaze, I peeked over my shoulder. I expected a mocking sneer, but she was pale and visibly trembling.

Her swift change of emotion was a real head-scratcher. I debated what to do. The angel on one shoulder urged me to comfort her while the devil on my other kicked up her feet and smiled as we both found solace in knowing that Ever would spend a lifetime dealing with Barbie's erratic moods.

The pressure on my bladder had become unbearable by the time class ended, so I texted Tyra that I'd be late for lunch and hurried to the nearest bathroom.

Two girls were primping in the mirror, but the stalls were empty, so I dived inside the nearest one. I was tugging my skirt back down after relieving myself when I heard, "Get out."

I didn't move, but the sound of rushing footsteps told me

that the two girls at the sink did. Seconds later, I heard the lock on the bathroom door turn.

"I know you're in here, Four."

Okay, this isn't creepy at all.

I stepped out of the stall.

Barbie was leaning against the sink with her arms crossed. Her casual stance wasn't one I expected of Ever's prim and proper princess.

His *real* princess.

The color had returned to her cheeks, and she appeared contemplative as she stared back at me.

"Any particular reason why you're stalking me in public bathrooms?"

Barbie had about four inches on me, but if I needed to, I could take her.

She took a deep breath and shook her head. "I can't believe I'm doing this."

"Doing what?"

"At first, I thought you were just someone he was screwing. There have been girls, but he was always discreet. After Olivia Portland, he had to be. Whatever he had to do to keep the rumors at bay. We couldn't risk tipping my father off." She drew in a ragged breath and started again before I could ask questions like *"Why the hell are you telling me this?"*

"My father's company has been losing money for years. Soon, it will be completely bankrupt, and we'll be out on our asses. My father has always insisted on living above his means, so even if he sold the company, it wouldn't be enough."

The frown I wore only deepened. "What does this have to do with Ever?" *Or me.*

She lifted her nose in the air. "It would embarrass my father if he had to downgrade our lifestyle. Once I turned thirteen, it was impossible for anyone, especially men, not to notice me. He's been priming me since then."

"Priming you?"

"To marry someone who could get him out of debt and fatten his pockets."

The last piece to the puzzle finally slid into place. "So Ever is just your meal ticket? You don't love him even a little?" I found it impossible for any girl to get this close to Ever and not fall.

Unless that girl had already fallen.

She stared at her engagement ring, a pear-shaped diamond that glittered in the light and mocked my broken heart. "He's my best friend," she said as if that explained everything. "The promise of marrying into a family worth billions was enough to keep my father patient."

"Why are you telling me this?"

"Ever became a shell when his mother left. I promised myself that I would never hurt him like she did." She sighed as she toyed with the blinding ring on her finger. "It seems only one of us is good at keeping promises."

"So he's got your back, and you've got his. How do I know you aren't making this up?" In my mind, I knew she couldn't be. Her story was too far-fetched to be anything but real. Men haven't auctioned their daughters off for wealth and power in centuries with the exception of a few straggling cultures.

"Since the day I first saw him with you, I knew it was only a matter of time before he broke his word or told you my secret. Ever could have demanded that I tell you myself. He didn't do any of those things. Instead, he fell apart over losing you." She slipped the ring from her finger, and I was completely stunned when she laid it on the counter. "None of this is real, Four. It never was."

She moved for the door, but I couldn't let her leave. Not without answering one last burning question.

"What happens if your father realizes Ever has no intention of marrying you?"

She stared back at me with sad blue eyes. "He'll sell me to the highest bidder."

My heart was too heavy for sleep and no amount of tossing and turning could change that. After letting Jay D do his business, I decided to make a late-night snack. When I was done, the smell of perfectly toasted bread and melted cheese strangely offered me peace with my decision. If I could perfect grilled cheese, surely I could perfect life.

Right?

I stacked the sandwiches on a plate and grabbed a Gatorade. Upstairs, I bypassed my bedroom. It was one in the morning, but I knew he would be awake. The bags I glimpsed under his eyes earlier today told me he hasn't been sleeping and the weight he lost… let's just say I made more than a few grilled cheese sandwiches.

I was glad the door was unlocked because if I woke up Jamie with my knocking, I'd never hear the end of it about the importance of his beauty sleep and maintaining perfect skin.

Jay D rushed inside ahead of me and immediately began to sniff around. The room was completely dark, but I knew he was awake. When my eyes somewhat adjusted, I could make out Ever sitting in the shadows with his back against the headboard and his elbows on his knees.

"Hi."

The silence stretched.

I held my breath as I waited.

And waited.

And just when I thought I might be too late…

"Hey."

We hadn't spoken since the night of my date—actually, he hadn't talked at all. Thomas asked questions that I couldn't answer, and Jamie had begun to look at me accusingly. It was a wonder he cared at all, but maybe, deep down, he knew there was never anything between Ever and Barbie.

"I made grilled cheese."

"Not hungry."

"With grilled cheese, it's not about hunger. It's about the yummy goodness."

He didn't respond, but I wasn't giving up. I climbed onto the bed and sat cross-legged in front of him. "Let's make a deal. For one grilled cheese, I'll tell you a secret. Two grilled cheese, I'll show you what's in my pocket. Deal?"

I chewed on my lip. The bed shifted when he moved. There was a click, and then a soft glow chased away some of the darkness.

"It better be a good secret," he said with a smirk. "I hate cheese."

"What kind of psychopath doesn't like cheese?" *Way to charm him, Four.*

He picked up a sandwich without responding.

"You don't have to—"

But he was already biting into it. A couple more bites and the sandwich was toast.

"Spill," he growled.

I handed over the Gatorade, and he chugged it while keeping one eye on me.

I took a deep breath.

I could do this.

It was both impossible and not so impossible to believe I hadn't spoken the words before.

Here goes nothing.

"I love you." *Damn, that felt good.* And right and—

Did he just *snort*?

With my heart at his feet, I realized that maybe I *was* too late.

"It's nice to finally hear you say it back, but it's hardly a secret." I was ready to remind him of all the reasons I didn't say it until now, but he spoke first. "I love you too."

But even in the dim light, I could see the wariness in his eyes. I gestured to the second sandwich and grabbed the last one for myself. I needed cheesy courage for what came next. I was still nibbling on my first bite when he finished his.

"Show me." I was beginning to reconsider putting up with his bossiness when he said, "Please."

Oh, all right.

Reaching into my pocket, I pulled out the platinum ring. He froze when I held it out. "This was my father's ring. I want you to have it."

"Why?" he choked out.

"Think of it as your promise to me."

He studied the ring for a moment. "What am I promising?"

"That no matter what…no matter why…you're mine."

Dark honey shone with confusion and then disbelief. "She told you?"

"She told me."

"I have something for you too," Ever said as he lazily ran a hand down the naked curve of my hip. He was the first to speak since our big finish. We had just finished making love, and Jay D, to Ever's displeasure, was soundly sleeping at the foot of his bed.

"If it's more sex, I think I'm good until Christmas," I purred.

He snorted. "Like you'd wait that long. I think you love it more than I do."

"That's because you're better at it."

With an arrogant half smile, he said, "Won't argue with you there."

I felt my lips purse as I glared at him. "What you have for me better be diamonds or else you'll be waiting until New Years to fuck me again."

He smiled fully this time and kissed the curve of my hip before reaching into his nightstand and pulling out a slip of paper. He stared at it for a moment as if unsure before wordlessly handing it over. I wanted to see what had caused his change in mood, but I had trouble breaking free from his intense stare.

"Read it," he ordered.

So I did.

**APPLICATION FOR CHANGE OF NAME OF ADULT
IN THE COURT OF COMMON PLEAS OF COWEN
COUNTY, CT PROBATE DIVISION**
TIMOTHY L. THOMPSON, JUDGE
IN RE: CHANGE OF NAME OF
<u>FOUR ARCHER</u>
TO REQUESTED NAME
<u>DARREN ARCHER</u>

The form went on, but the explosion of emotions didn't allow me to see the rest. Fear and hope currently battled for dominance. "I...I don't understand."

"After you told me about how your name wasn't a name, I thought maybe it was time you changed that. I just wasn't sure this was what you would want."

"Then why now?"

He shrugged, but I could tell he was nervous. "Since you're taking a chance, I thought I'd take one, too."

"I don't know, Ever. Rosalyn—"

"She doesn't have to know," he quickly reassured. "At least, not now."

Sitting up, I stared with longing at the paper and the name written boldly in ink.

Darren.

Not too feminine or exotic. It was perfect.

"You chose this name?"

He suddenly looked shy. "I also brought an extra form just in case you hated it."

"I don't hate it. I couldn't." His shoulders relaxed in relief. "But why Darren?"

Softly, he said, "It was the name my mother chose for my sister."

"Oh, Ever." I turned and rained what must have been a thousand kisses all over his face. "In that case, I'm also honored."

"When you're ready, we'll file the petition together."

"Okay," I simply answered while hiding how much his bossiness turned me on.

"About Bee…" he started as I settled in his arms once again, "are you sure you're okay with this?"

"Okay with it? Hell no." I sighed and snuggled deeper into the crook of his arm. "But if I can put up with Jamie, I can deal with Barbie." After she told me what her father planned to do…I gave her back the ring. She didn't ask questions, and I didn't explain myself. In a few months, Barbie would be eighteen and could get away from her father. Until then, we would have to pull the wool over his eyes. "Just so you know—I have rules."

I swung my leg over his body.

"Oh?"

"No kissing." I pecked his lips. "These belong to me."

He grunted his agreement.

I trailed a finger down his chest. "And I don't want her hands on you." I wrapped my hand around his length, and he hardened instantly. "And because I'm not completely unreasonable, you may hug her *only* when in the company of her father." A thought occurred to me as I stroked him. "Do you suppose we should tell Jamie?"

I was flipped on my back, and then he was hovering over me.

"Let's not talk about Jamie when your hand is on my dick."

I snorted and laughed. "Sorry."

He looked completely in awe as he said, "What to do with you, little troublemaker?"

"I can think of a few things."

His hands dipped between my legs, and I gasped.

"Can you now?"

I was about to respond when his eyes bucked, and he jumped from the bed.

"Ever? What's wrong?"

He wore an alarmingly uncomfortable expression.

Before he could answer, I heard a gurgling noise come from his stomach, and then he was backing away toward the bathroom door.

"What—" And then it dawned on me. "Oh, my God." I cackled. "You really shouldn't have eaten the grilled cheese!"

It was clear now why Ever didn't like cheese as his stomach made more noises. Most guys would have saved themselves the embarrassment, but when Ever looked back at me and shrugged, I knew, for me, he would always do whatever it took.

epilogue

the Puppet

"**B**E SURE TO GET THOSE BOLTS TIGHT BUT NOT TOO TIGHT, boy. You don't want to strip 'em."

Ever nodded and, with hawk-like focus, carefully cranked the wrench. I was trying to keep my drool to a minimum watching him get his hands dirty in oil-stained coveralls. He didn't seem to mind, and with an eager mind, he asked questions that Gruff had been all too happy to answer.

Even though I agreed to be Ever's girlfriend in secret, I still needed to know that I'd made the right call. In no way would it be easy to watch Ever dote on Barbie even if it was just for show. I needed to know that the months of jealousy and doubt to come would be worth it. That *he* was worth it.

Who better to offer me that assurance than the man who'd been a father to me? He was also the one person I could count on to give it to me straight, no chaser.

When I called Gruff to arrange the visit, I only told him that I was homesick and missed him, which was true, but he didn't know my other reason for coming or why I'd brought Ever *and* Jamie. Jamie merely served as an alibi. My trip home on the McNamara's private jet would have seemed suspicious if it had only been Ever and me.

The initial meeting had gone better than expected considering how hospitable Gruff had been to me when we first met.

It became clear who Gruff favored since he tasked Ever with

helping him replace the brake pads and rotors on a client's bike while Jamie was tasked with separating the hundreds of nuts and screws Gruff had accumulated over three decades.

I was sitting with my legs crossed on one of the cluttered worktables when Gruff ambled over, forcing me to focus on something other than Ever.

"Now," Gruff started as he wiped oil from his hands on a rag. "Which of these boys are you sweet on, and please tell me it ain't that punk."

I snickered when Gruff jabbed his thumb in Jamie's direction. "Don't be silly, old man. Boys are icky."

Behind Gruff, Ever's lips lifted into a cocky smirk, making it clear he was ear hustling.

"I'd die a happy man if I actually believed you," Gruff retorted.

I felt myself flush crimson as I stuck my tongue out at my mentor.

"See that," he said while pointing at my face. "You never used to do that." He suddenly looked stern as he eyed me carefully. "Which one?" His tone made it clear he wouldn't let it go until I had an answer.

Even though I came for this very reason, I still hadn't figured out how to tell Gruff that I was finally into a boy.

A very intense, dominating, vengeful, arrogant, manipulative yet loving, and incredibly loyal boy.

Not to mention hot as hell.

And he was all mine.

"I—" The words got stuck in my throat, so I decided this wasn't going to happen right now.

But then Ever stepped forward and crushed my decision right under his size eleven shoe.

"It's me, sir."

Gruff spun around, and I quickly jumped to my feet just in case he decided to hit my boyfriend.

Boyfriend…

Yeah, I wasn't getting used to that anytime soon.

"It's you, huh?" Gruff scratched his ever-graying beard. "And what are your intentions with my girl. You gonna make her an honest woman?"

I groaned. We were barely eighteen and here Gruff was talking of marriage. I wondered what he'd think if he knew Ever was technically engaged. To the love of his cousin's life no less. I suddenly wished I had the foresight to hide Gruff's shotgun before having this conversation. I knew better than to say anything, and Ever certainly did too. The only loose cannon was Jamie, who had abandoned his task to watch our little scene with zero emotion in his gaze.

"Actually, she's perfect the way she is," Ever said, stealing my attention back as he grabbed my hand and pulled me close. Holding my gaze, he added, "But I'm hoping one day she'll make an honest man out of *me*."

While I melted at Ever's promise, Gruff simply grunted. I realized that was all the approval Ever was going to get, but it was good enough for me. Knowing Gruff, the jury would be out until the day Ever kept his word, and even then, Gruff would always have one eye on Ever and one finger on the trigger.

"I've got a twelve-gauge filled with bullets, and one of them has got your name on it, boy."

I snickered. "Do you even remember his name, old man?"

"Of course, I do," Gruff said with a grunt. "It's Boy."

I palmed my face while Gruff left Ever and Jamie in stitches.

"I've got a bullet for that one, too," Gruff went on as he glared Jamie's way. "If he ever makes a move on you."

Jamie's laughter quickly died as his expression turned to shock and wariness.

"And even if he doesn't, something tells me that he isn't green to breaking hearts. Probably deserves a couple of them."

"More like five or ten," Ever instigated.

At Jamie's scathing glare, I nudged Ever, warning him with my eyes to shut the hell up. We both knew how petty Jamie could get when provoked.

A moment later, I was proven right when a devious smile took over Jamie's face. "Did Four and Ever tell you the good news?"

My jaw dropped and Ever's hardened. Fortunately, Gruff missed our reactions as he focused on Jamie.

"What would that be?" Gruff asked.

Ever and I both tensed as we prepared for Jamie to spill the beans about Ever's engagement.

With a casual tone, he said, "My uncle is hosting Thanksgiving dinner this year, and we were *all* hoping you'd come."

"Jamie, that's less than a week away. I'm sure Gruff already has plans," I protested.

My heart plummeted to my stomach when Gruff said, "No, I don't actually. My son will be spending the holiday with his wife's family. I'm free." Silence that became more awkward by the second fell as Gruff waited for me to extend the invitation myself. "Of course, I don't have to come if you don't want me to…"

Oh, God. I knew denying Gruff an invitation would crush him. Ever knew it too—and so did his cunt of a cousin who smugly stood by with his tatted arms crossed.

"No, we'd love it if you came. It would mean so much."

Gruff then regarded Ever, who simply flashed him a convincing smile. "I guess it's settled then. I'm coming to Blackwood Keep."

"You have to be quiet, princess." Ever, with his hand now covering my mouth to silence my cries, drove into me from behind, making the old floorboards creak. "Why'd you have to come in here, huh? You know what the man said. No hanky-panky." He punctuated his teasing with another hard thrust and groaned. "You feel so fucking good, Archer."

It was true I'd gotten myself into my current predicament. I'd snuck into the living room innocently, wanting to spend the night in Ever's arms rather than alone in Gruff's drafty spare room, but that had quickly turned into the expressly forbidden. Jamie had taken the sofa while Ever had made a pallet on the floor just a few feet away. I didn't mind one bit and wormed my way under the blankets without waking him. As I'd started to drift off into a sound sleep, I'd found myself with my face down, ass up, and Ever's talented fingers and tongue bringing me to the most intense orgasm I'd had yet. Now I was lying on my belly with Ever's weight pinning me down as he pounded me without mercy or fear that we'd be caught.

"I only wanted to cuddle," I whimpered.

"No, you wanted to be fucked."

I moaned when he palmed my breast and bit the shell of my ear.

"Didn't you?"

"No."

He suddenly stopped to turn me over and look into my eyes. "No?"

Enjoying his sudden uncertainty, I wrapped my legs around his waist, and with a sly smile, I reached between us and led his cock back to my entrance. "I wanted you to make love to me."

Never looking away, he reentered me slowly, letting me feel every hard inch until I was full. "It won't matter if I take you hard and fast or soft and slow, princess. With us, it will always be making love."

We came together soon after with only our hands clapped over the other's mouths and the sound of Jamie's snores to muffle Ever's grunts and my cries.

"You smell so good," he praised once I was resting safe and satisfied in his arms. He'd just finished cleaning me up after spilling on my skin in the nick of time. The close call seriously made me consider birth control.

I lifted my face from his chest and frowned. "I smell like sex."

His perfect teeth flashed behind his feral smile. "You smell like *me*." He lowered his head, and instinctively, I lifted mine to meet his lips. "Every male within a hundred-mile radius will know that you're mine," he growled against my lips.

I began to squirm as the throbbing intensified and heat pooled between my legs.

"Do you think we could get Patty to bottle that?"

"Don't you dare ask her," I hissed. "You nearly gave her a heart attack with that check you wrote her." I shook my head against his chest. "I still can't believe you asked her to make that soap exclusively for me."

"Why would I want someone else smelling like my woman?"

"We're going to have to discuss this possessiveness of yours."

"No."

"Then at least tell me how you got your hands on that kind of cash? Those were *a lot* of zeroes."

He shrugged as if he wrote ten-thousand-dollar checks every day with a perpetual monthly supply order. "I stole my dad's checkbook before we left."

"So what you're saying is that you *plan* these displays of male dominance in advance?"

"Sleep, baby," he mumbled with his eyes closed. He sounded half asleep himself.

I wanted to close my eyes and join him on the other side, but there was still one worry keeping me away.

"What are we going to do about Gruff coming to Blackwood Keep? The Montgomerys are also having dinner with us."

I replayed in my head what followed Jamie's latest diabolical stunt:

The moment Gruff was out of earshot, Ever was across the room with the front of Jamie's coveralls bawled in his fists. "What the hell is your problem?" Ever growled. "You know why Gruff can't come to Blackwood Keep!"

Jamie didn't even try to free himself as his eyes narrowed. "Let me ask you something, cousin. If I knew Four was in trouble, but I kept you in the dark, what would you do?"

Ever didn't respond, but his backing off said everything. "If I could tell you what's going on with her, I would, Jamie."

Jamie relaxed, too. "I know," he said while actually appearing apologetic. "But that doesn't mean I have to accept it."

"I've got it covered," Ever bit out.

Rather than take his word, Jamie shook his head. "I don't trust anyone but me to protect what is mine. Would you?"

"I'm not sure," Ever answered, drawing me back to the present. His eyes were open once again, and for the first time ever, he seemed worried even though he tried to hide it. He didn't know that his mask no longer worked on me. Freeing my bottom lip from my teeth he kissed me and said, "But whatever happens, I choose us."

I sighed as worry fled, and my eyes closed involuntarily. Slowly, I drifted to sleep, the rhythm of his heart my lullaby. Knowing every beat belonged to me, I whispered, "I choose us, too."

acknowledgments

Mama! I've come to realize that not everyone is blessed to have such an amazing, supportive, and dedicated mother. I don't appreciate you nearly as much as I should. And if I was a bitch to you at any point while writing this book, remember that the apple doesn't fall too far from the tree. You probably deserved it.

No, don't drive up here, Mama! I'm kidding!

Friends and family! As always, I'm going to group you all together because there are so many of you, and I can never remember who I neglected the most. Love you!

Rogena! I know the wait was hard for readers, but I think I tortured you the most with this story. Thank you for putting up with me! I'm a shitty client, and you still continue to take my money. I'm not even sure the money is worth it at this point which means... you're an angel.

Colleen! Thank you for agreeing to work with me. If I came off needy and unorganized, I assure you it's completely true.

Amanda! As always, I never know what I want or even why I want it, but you make it happen. If it weren't for you, my covers and marketing would look like a kindergarten project. I'm also grateful to have a designer who lets me be my sarcastic, needy self without taking offense or filing for a restraining order.

Stacey! Thank you for such beautiful artwork and not dropping me as your client while I got my shit together.

Ivan! My precious, spoiled kitty cat. Thank you for not running away all those days I was so busy writing that I forgot to feed you. I remember those howls of hunger like it was yesterday. Because it was.

Tijan! Girl, if it weren't for you encouraging me and asking for this book every day, I would have trashed it a long time ago. You're my idol and my inspiration. I really hope you enjoyed it, and if not, it's your fault for rushing me.

Just kidding!

Shanora! You're the first person I run to when I need to vent and cry and have someone pull my hair because I'm too lazy to do it. You also give great girl talk and inspire me to be better. Also, I saw you a month ago, so I think we're due for another face-to-face meeting in about eight months. Don't be late.

Reiderville! You're my safe place and the only ones I can count on to laugh at my corny jokes. Thank you for waiting so impatiently. You really pushed me to turn off Netflix every once in a while.

Betas! You came in at the last minute and made this book whole. Thank you for the hard questions and the necessary challenges. Anyone who falls in love with this story has you to thank as well.

If I forgot to acknowledge anyone, just remember...there are too many flavors for you to be salty!

Translation: I love and appreciate you.

contact the author

Follow me on Facebook
www.facebook.com/authorbbreid

Join Reiderville on Facebook
www.facebook.com/groups/reiderville

Follow me on Twitter
www.twitter.com/_BBREID

Follow me on Instagram
www.instagram.com/_bbreid

Subscribe to my newsletter
www.bbreid.com/news

Visit my website
www.bbreid.com

Text REIDER to 474747 for new release alerts
(US only)

about

B.B. REID

B.B. Reid is the author of several novels including the hit enemies-to-lovers, *Fear Me*. She grew up the only daughter and middle child in a small town in North Carolina. After graduating with a Bachelors in Finance, she started her career at an investment research firm while continuing to serve in the National Guard. She currently resides in Charlotte with her moody cat and enjoys collecting Chuck Taylors and binge-eating chocolate.

Printed in Great Britain
by Amazon